FOR DAVID AND ANNA WINCH

THAT SUMMER'S TRANCE

I

BENEDICT AND PRISCILLA OAKSHAW SPENT AT LEAST ONE EVENING
a week at the Kennedy Center. Since the late seventies, when things had
started going really well for them, they had bought yearly subscriptions to
the Washington Opera season, the National Symphony, the Washington Ballet, and a series of twelve theatrical productions at the Eisenhower. These
evenings were the zenith of their social and cultural lives, and, in Ben's
case at least, of some other life which he liked to consider metaphysical
and which gave the appearance of being so, since it included elements of
the transcendental and the ideal as well as the worldly and the frankly festive. In his nature these elements were combined in a nameless passion for
celebration, one that no New Year's party, or homecoming game, or Mardi
Gras, or mass could satisfy. It was certainly not religious—it involved vanity
and display too conspicuously to be mistaken for piety—but it was almost
ecclesiastical in its gravity and like religion expressed itself in the periodic
observance of a rite in a temple of some kind, in this case one furnished
with gigantic crystal chandeliers, acres of pile carpeting, haute cuisine, fine

wines, and an atmosphere of exhilaration, gallantry, and grace. Like most men who have been poor in their youth, he liked elegance, and for him an evening at the Kennedy Center was an occasion of unrivalled elegance, one justified by a concern for culture and solemnized by ritual, its handmaiden. He did not admit this passion, even to himself—his urbanity was too hard-won to admit anything that might resemble bathos—but he felt it and rejoiced in it, mindlessly, like a man steeping himself in the vapors of a steam bath. Nothing gave him such a secret exaltation as to stroll, and be seen strolling, through the vast, high-ceilinged, deeply carpeted Grand Foyer under the glittering chandeliers, past the enormous, oddly leprous looking bust of John F. Kennedy, the champagne booths, the wonderfully civil program vendors whose decorum was almost that of acolytes, feeling himself one of the chosen, one of this fraternity of animated, softly laughing, expensively dressed men and women who, gathered in this convention of light and luxury, gave confirmation of his own and of America's success. In them and in the occasion, not only was this exquisitely confirmed, but all things took on for him a glowing, quietly ecstatic conformation. This was where it all came together, Ben thought. This was the meaning, almost certainly, of life, and certainly of civilization—this hour of tranquil, titillating anticipation, of recognition and reward, this sweet, sacramental thrall of The Performance.

He and Priscilla always reserved a table for dinner at six thirty at the Grande Scene on the third floor, and when they had been escorted to it with priestly gravity, and were seated, and he glanced discreetly about the murmurous, magnificent room, twinkling with crystal, silver, and galaxies of diamonds sprinkled through the dusk, tinkling with sounds of decanted wine and of equally delicious and effervescent gayety, he felt his heart swell with a sense of the divine congruity of things. All this was ordained. It was inherent in the first appearance of shaggy man on the smouldering earth. It was the coming to fruition of years—of centuries, millennia!—of industry, sacrifice, and faith, of unyielding adherence to the creed of aspiration that bound them all together in their hour of consummation and communion. And not only his private life was thus beatified, nor those of his fellow communicants in the Grande Scene, now devoutly dispatching their Tournedos Rossini, but those of the performers, somewhere beneath them in the vast honeycomb of dressing rooms and rehearsal halls, tuning their violins or applying grease paint to their faces. For them, too, this was the apotheosis of their lives. Their years of anonymity, indigence and struggle, of the harrowed preparation of audition scenes or the endless rehearsal of arpeggios in cold water flats in the Village or the Left Bank or Notting Hill Gate, had been brought, like that of Ben and his fellow diners, to epiphany. There were ushers and programs to certify their talent, their perseverance, their right to renown. People would read the chronicles of their adversities and achievements in the program notes, nod gravely, and whisper to their consorts bits of testimony to the reality and verity of this experience, as if from The Lives of The Apostles. The house lights would go down, there would be a moment of silence like that heralding the Transubstantiation in the mass, the great velvet curtain would sweep up, the performers would step forward bathed in an unearthly radiance, there would be a burst of applause from the vast dark auditorium, and All would be Redeemed. All would be redefined and justified and pronounced good: the world, humanity, virtue, capitalism, Christianity. God would be reborn. There was nothing to fear, nothing to regret; grief, uncertainty, dissent were swept away by the tide of beauty and ceremony that swept over them, as obscenities scrawled in the sand are swept away by the sea. Certainly there was no reason to feel shame.

In addition to this bath of beatitude which he enjoyed every Friday evening in the Patron's box, Ben learned things at the Kennedy Center that were useful to him socially and in his business, which was advertising. He had become growingly familiar with the scores of the major classical and romantic symphonies, had learned to identify half a dozen piano and violin concertos, was no longer startled by the advent of the specter in *Le Spectre de la Rose*, and regularly sang in the shower, in an exuberant, errant tenor, arias from Puccini, Verdi, and Rossini. He took pride in the fact that he was able, at parties, to speak of these composers with some confidence and even, on occasion, to offer opinions on Purcell along with a few bars of *Dido and Aeneas*. In the field of drama, his judgments were far less adventurous, effusive, or gratuitous than those he offered on symphony, the ballet, or the opera, and this was because it was an art he understood. He understood it better, in fact, than most of the people in the theatre, including any critics who might have been present and many of the performers themselves. He knew more about the stage than most men living, and the feelings that moved in his breast when he watched a performance of Shaw, or Ibsen, or Shakespeare were complex, too complex for Priscilla to make out in the shadows of their private box when he murmured—as he often did—lines that he knew by heart, or closed his eyes and lowered his head in dismay, or smiled and breathed deeply. He understood the stage with a profound intuitive insight, and had once performed on it with brilliance; some had said with genius.

As a young man, three years before he had abandoned it to found his enormously successful agency, Razullo, Inc., he had attended the Royal Academy of Dramatic Art in London, where he had been a student of great promise. His three years at that institution had been the consummation of a passion that was born in him at the age of eighteen when Miss Florence Replogle, his English teacher in Groveland, Florida, high school, had asked him to read the part of Romeo in a classroom recitation of Shakespeare. Until that moment he had done nothing well in his life, nor had the opportunity ever arisen for him to discover that he could. His entire life, except for the hours he spent in school, had been spent digging sweet potatoes, cleaning chicken coops, and weeding strawberry beds on the ten sun-blasted acres of his father's truck farm in the pine barrens of central Florida. He performed these tasks with a dumb resignation and chronic weariness, since he was physically small and frail. At school, he was no happier or more successful. He had a mysterious inability to organize facts, apply basic principles of physics, or understand numerical relationships that made his attempts to acquire an education a prolonged, desperate farce. He could not hit a curve ball, watch a quadratic equation being written on the board without the nauseating certainty that he would be called upon to solve it, and with the exceptions of Independence Day and the discovery of America he could not remember the date of anything of significance that had ever happened on the earth. His lack of stature and evidently of normal intelligence produced a sense of shame and shyness in him that reduced him to paralysis before his fellow classmates — especially the girls — and persons of any authority whatever, from policemen and teachers to the bus drivers and janitors. A wan, spectral sense of unreality possessed him in the presence of adults of almost any kind with the exception of Miss Replogle and of his pale, sad, careworn mother, whose faint, distracted fondness was all he knew of love. As he grew into adolescence, he sank into his own ignominy; he became shy to the point of invisibility; he might, indeed, have disbelieved in his own existence if it had not been so scathingly certified by his shame and loneliness, by the impatience or dismay of most of his teachers, by the cruel, ironic grins of his classmates, and the tyranny of his dark, despotic father, an illiterate tenant farmer whose relationship to Ben was much like that of a ploughman to a mule.

All that redeemed this melancholy evidence of his presence on the earth was his mother's occasional wracked smile or faltering caress, and some unaccountable but inextinguishable auspice he was able to perceive in the quality of light. Nothing could explain or repress the elation he felt in the blithe play of morning sunbeams on the water of the swamp, in the blaze and pomp of noon, however cruelly it failed him at his chores, or in the grave and tender eulogies of sunset, which seemed to promise and to celebrate something far more profound and enduring than his own misery. He would raise his head sometimes above the dusty vines where he knelt digging and, quite inexplicably, smile into the sky. "All will be well," he read in the concatenations of light among the great white clouds and in the shimmer of moonlight on the water of the lake. "It will come true," he saw inscribed in starlight across the dark vault of the autumn skies, and when he gazed into the woodstove on a winter night, he saw this promise written like a rune in lambent letters, or billowing in the firelight like a volatile, rose-colored painting of some fabulous scene that he would one day behold: he saw ardent lovers holding out their unborn arms to him, or the boiling, molten bullion of a yet unminted treasure that would one day spill between his fingers.

Later, when he entered his senior year of high school, a small part of the promise was redeemed in the joy of sitting every day in room 115 in the presence of Miss Florence Replogle. Miss Replogle had eyes of the palest lavender, like Confederate violets, a color suited perfectly to her ambrosial Tidewater accent, her diaphanous dove-gray gowns, and the soft elegiac quality of her smile which seemed to commemorate some distant, doomed and valorous event in which her role had been to fold bandages and read the Psalms to dying men. Everything about her suggested mercy, for which Ben thirsted, and room 115, over which she presided, became for him a shrine and sanctuary, a haven from the suffering he was subjected to on the football field, in the gymnasium, in Mr. Steinberg's algebra class, and in the sun-baked sweet potato fields. On the wall above her desk she had had inscribed in gold-leaf Gothic letters a quotation from "Tintern Abbey," abridged to fit the size of the space and her own modest discontents:

The Mind that is Within Us, so Impress with Quietness and Beauty and so Feed with Lofty Thoughts, that neither Evil Tongues nor all the Dreary Intercourse of Life can e'er Prevail against Us.

Miss Replogle's own thoughts often seemed on the point of bearing her aloft with them, like a rare and volatile gas. Listening to one of her students recite Mrs. Browning's "How do I Love Thee, Let Me Count the Ways," she would become dangerously unstable, listing ethereally from side to side while she gazed out at the live oak trees that lined the playground, her head rising and falling with the meter like a bright yellow balloon filled with helium and tugging at her earthbound body in a gale of similes. Ben loved everything about her, especially her instability. His own attachment to the earth was so precarious that he could appreciate the feelings of anyone who showed a disposition to depart from it. Every week she assigned a pair of recitation exercises, one for girls and one for boys. These were delivered from a little dais she had had installed at the front of the room, while she stood beside the window, her elbow supported by the palm of one hand, the fingers of the other laid delicately against her cheek, on the very verge of levitation. For girls, her assignments ran to Ella Wheeler Wilcox, Sarah Teasdale, or the love poems of Mrs. Browning; for boys, the theme generally combined the martial and the sacrificial: "The Charge of the Light Brigade," "Gunga Din," or "To Lucasta, On Going to the Wars." Ben's first assignment in her class was a narrative poem of Browning's entitled "An Incident of the French Camp," about a messenger boy who heroically completes his mission of bringing Napoléon the news of the taking of Ratisbon before falling dead at his beloved commander's feet. It concluded with these verses:

Then off there flung in smiling joy,
And held himself erect
By just his horse's mane, a boy:
You hardly could suspect—
(So tight he kept his lips compressed,
Scarce any blood came through),
You looked twice ere you saw his breast
Was all but shot in two.

The chief's eye flashed; but presently
Softened itself, as sheathes
A film the mother-eagle's eye
When her bruised eaglet breathes;

"You're wounded!" "Nay," the soldier's pride
Touched to the quick, he said:
"I'm killed, sire!" And his chief beside,
Smiling the boy fell dead.

Ben didn't like the poem. Even in his barely literate state, he was embarrassed by its vulgarity and dishonesty, but he saw in it an opportunity to express his own depthless adoration for Miss Replogle, and so he read it as a love poem addressed to her. He pretended that she was his commander and he the unfortunate messenger, and the boy's four final words he made an impassioned avowal of his willingness to serve her, suffer mortal wounds, and die for her sake. He never knew what instinct guided him in the performance, but the delight and power he felt in the secret wisdom that governed his voice and set his body at perfect ease before his twenty grinning classmates was that of an epiphany. He knew without hesitation, beyond any doubt or fear of failure, exactly how to speak the words to make them peal with devotion and a desire for self-sacrifice that, he rejoiced to see, reduced Miss Replogle to a state of unprecedented rigidity. The most mysterious and delightful thing about it was that it was so easy; it was, he thought, like that uncanny intelligence that set Travis McCullough's feet flying at the crack of the bat to the exact point in the left center field where the fly ball would end its long high arc in his carelessly uplifted glove. This was what it was like to do something well. He felt a joy that warmed him like a sunrise.

When he had finished, Miss Replogle, clinging to the windowsill, pressed her lips between her teeth and said in a constricted voice, "Thank you, Benedict. Thank you very much, my dear."

The next week she altered her curriculum to include the reading of *Romeo and Juliet*, which Ben was happy to discover was poetry of a very different kind. She asked Ben to take the title role, and Peggy Kaufmann, a dark and winsome girl, the prettiest in the class, to read the part of Juliet. Peggy was a girl whom Ben had long and furtively adored and whom he would not otherwise, in twenty years, have dared to ask the time of day. Yet,

kneeling in front of the little platform on which she stood at the front of
the room, the textbook trembling in his hand, he gazed up at her lustrous olive eyes and murmured with an ardor that poured from his parched
soul as miraculously as the waters of Rehoboth from the desert sands:

I am no pilot, yet wert thou as far
As that vast shore wash'd with the furthest sea,
I would adventure for such merchandise.

After a moment of startled silence Peggy replied to this in a hushed
tremolo so perfectly suited to the lines that many an experienced actress
would have envied it:

Thou knowest the mask of night is on my face,
Else would a maiden blush bepaint my cheek . . .

No one laughed, or stirred, or tittered; and when the scene was finished
a strange disconcerted silence possessed the room, in which Peggy gazed
steadfastly at the floor and Miss Replogle's eyebrows twisted in a stricken
look that might have been mistaken for anguish. When the bell rang,
she asked Ben to stay for a moment. He stood beside her desk, scratching the edge of it with his thumbnail.

"You read that scene very beautifully, Benedict," she said. "Very beautifully indeed. I haven't been so moved in this classroom in years. I want
to thank you for it."

"Thank you, ma'am."

"You know, we do an annual stage production, every spring. I'm thinking about doing *Romeo and Juliet* this year."

"That would be real nice," Ben said.

"I wonder if you'd like to play Romeo?"

"I couldn't ma'am. I have to work after school. I wouldn't be able to
rehearse."

"You have to work?"

"Yes, ma'am. I help my daddy on the farm. He couldn't get along without me."

"Not even for a couple of afternoons a week?"

"No, ma'am. It's a lot of work, and they's not but two of us to do it."

She laced her fingers together, laid her hands in her lap and gazed at them for a moment. "How old are you, Benedict? Eighteen?"

"Yes, ma'am."

"You'll be graduating in the spring, won't you?"

"Yes, ma'am."

"What do you intend to do then? After you graduate? Will you go to college?"

"No, ma'am. I'm not smart enough." He looked up at her and smiled. "Or rich enough."

"You'll go on working on the farm?"

"Yes, ma'am. I reckon so. Until I get called up."

She turned her head and looked out of the window. After a moment she said, "I wish I'd known." Ben shifted his feet and stood waiting. She turned back to him and said, "I wish I'd known about you, Ben."

"Known what, ma'am?"

"That you had a gift of this kind. I feel that I've failed you."

"No, ma'am, you've been real nice to me. I appreciate it." He resumed scratching the edge of her desk with his thumbnail.

"Do you have to go?" she asked.

"Well, right soon, ma'am. I got to catch the school bus."

"I see." She breathed deeply and frowned. "I suppose you'd better go along, then, I want to thank you again for reading so beautifully for us."

"Yes, ma'am. I enjoyed it."

She did not speak to him again about auditioning for the school play, for which, on further thought, she chose *Charley's Aunt* rather than *Romeo and Juliet*. It may have been that, in her mercy, she did not want to instill false hopes in him of a theatrical career. She knew the facts he had laconically imparted to her were true and inexorable: he would work on his father's farm until he was drafted into the army and sent to

Vietnam; it was the destiny of most of his male classmates in the graduating class of 1966. She may have been led to reflect on those destinies
in a personal and poignant way that had not occurred to her before; or
perhaps her thoughts were not sufficiently lofty to render her immune
to The Dreary Intercourse of Life that was taking place in Southeast Asia
at the time; and perhaps those events had tarnished for her the rhetori-
cal splendors of "An Incident of the French Camp." At any rate, she
did not assign any more dramatic recitations for her class, and for the re-
maining six weeks of the semester was unusually pensive and grave. She
gave Ben the only A of his academic career for a final grade. When he
brought her a quart basket of strawberries as a parting gift, she pressed
her lips together, closed her eyes, and after a moment of tremulous silence, gave him her blessing, introduced with the question, "Benedict,
do you know what a prodigy is?"

"No ma'am, I'm not sure," Ben said.

"A prodigy is a person who has the ability to perform in an artistic
field in a way that cannot be explained. He has been given a gift from God.
The kind of gift that made it possible for Mozart to play the piano when he
was three, and to compose symphonies when he was twelve. This kind
of gift cannot be understood, and it is not only a great privilege but a
great responsibility. Whoever has been given it has the duty to cherish
and develop it, and to serve mankind with it. It belongs to the world as well
as to him. He has been chosen by God as a vessel through which to
spread the message of goodness and truth and beauty. That is his mission on the earth. I believe you have such a gift. You have in my opinion
a prodigious talent for acting. I have seen a good deal of acting in my life —
I have seen Maurice Evans and Katherine Cornell — and I say this advis-
edly. Unfortunately, Mr. Evans, at the time I saw him, had a speech
defect which was the result of orthodontal work; but even with this handicap he gave a performance of MacBeth that I shall never forget." She
paused for a moment as if gathering her thoughts, which seemed to be
straying slightly.

"Yes, ma'am," Ben murmured.

"I believe very much in destiny," Miss Replogle went on. "I believe that God has ordained a course of life for each of us that is inexorable." She frowned. "That is not the proper word. Immutable, that is the word I was searching for. Immutable. It cannot be altered or avoided. It is the coming to fruition of the spirit, the soul's inheritance." She lowered her voice and tilted her head at him, looking with a pained intensity into his eyes. "And I believe that somewhere, in one of the great theatres of this world, on some appointed day, you will come into your spiritual inheritance. You will find your destiny. I want you to believe that, Benedict. Can you believe that?"

"Yes, ma'am," Ben said with an assurance that she breathed like nard.

"Oh, I'm so glad to hear you say that." She reached out her hand and laid it on his shoulder. "I don't know what will befall you until that day, but you must promise me to take very good care of yourself."

"Yes, ma'am, I will," he said. No one had ever expressed such concern or regard for him before; he seethed with the innocent desire to reward it.

"And if ever there is anything that I can do to assist you as you journey toward that hour of your destiny, you must not hesitate to let me know. I will consider it a privilege to do so." He nodded speechlessly. She raised her hand from his shoulder and laid it on his hair. "Bless you, dear young companion of my spirit," she said.

.   .   .

If Miss Replogle had apprehensions about his career in Vietnam, Ben did not share them. He didn't really know very much about Vietnam. His family did not subscribe to a newspaper or own a radio. Their interest in world affairs did not extend beyond the fences of their farm, and the only discussion he ever heard at the dinner table was brief, churlish, and infrequent, and concerned rat damage, the price of chicken feed, or the necessity of digging a new privy. His only knowledge of the war came from the occasional impassioned declamations of his teachers and the conversation of his classmates. One of these, a girl named Juanita Splaine, had a brother named Justin who had quit school the year before, joined the Marines, and landed with the Third Division at Da Nang. He had subsequently been wounded, hospitalized, discharged, and sent home with most of his left foot missing. As the war was very new and public sentiment had not yet turned against it, he was regarded as the first war hero from Groveland. A picnic had been given in his honor at Flagler Park, and Ben had seen him leaning on a cane under the live oaks chatting with the mayor, Mr. Grayson, the high school principal, and other dignitaries, his chest covered with medals and campaign ribbons and a somewhat stealthy smile playing about his lips. Ben, who was adept at the interpretation of human facial expression, was a little disconcerted by the smile but he liked the blue and scarlet dress uniform, the medals, the public acclaim, and the fact that two weeks after Justin's return, Baker Bros. Oldsmobile, on Osceola Street, hoisted a plastic banner above their used car lot that read: THANK A WAR HERO — BUY YOUR USED OLDS FROM JUSTIN SPLAINE. He did not consider the Marine Corps as a permanent career, but it was a step toward one. It gave one respectability, employment, the gratitude of one's countrymen, a handsome uniform, food, shelter, money enough to buy beer and cigarettes, and a measure of hero worship on the part of pretty girls that would probably enable him to take a certain number of them to bed. Above all, it offered escape from his father's farm. Life held no other comparable prospects, and it seemed to him like a golden opportunity. It did not occur to him that he might be accepting these amenities in exchange for the realization of his destiny, the joy of fulfilled talent, the hope of ideal love, the fellowship of peers, and the possibility of immortality. He did not for a moment believe that he would suffer the fate of Justin Splaine, that he would be maimed, deranged, demoralized, or that his benefits might include a pious epitaph. "Take the money and run," is the way he would have put it, in the vernacular of his time, and the sentiment would have been understood by the millions of young men before him who, in exchange for their birthright, had taken the king's shilling and a day at Ludlow Fair.

He didn't wait to be drafted. Two weeks after he graduated from high

school he got up in the middle of the night, took a burlap sack from under his cot in which the night before he had put his birth certificate, a
slice of cornbread, a tangerine, a toothbrush, and his copy of *Romeo and
Juliet*, stolen from the school library. He hitchhiked to Orlando, sought out
the Marine Corps recruiting office and enlisted for a four-year hitch of duty,
smiling, as he signed the register, the last smile of his innocence. After
his basic training at Parris Island and two months in the Ea Drang valley,
his smile had changed somewhat. It had grown to resemble that of Justin
Splaine, a wary, ragged grin that matched the stealthy panic in his eyes.
Sent to a Rest and Rehabilitation Center on Cam Ranh Bay after his company had been decimated at Chu Prong, he sat down and wrote a letter
to Miss Replogle. He had done a good bit of combat duty, he explained
to her, and felt that he was qualified to apply to the elite Marine Guard
School in Quantico, Virginia. With the training he would receive there,
he would be better able to serve his country and its inspired leaders, which—
like that of the boy in "An Incident of the French Camp"—was his deep-
est wish. Did she think there was any way she could help him secure
such an appointment? Without embarrassment or inconvenience to herself, of course. He remembered that she had told him not to hesitate to ask,
if there was anything she could do to assist him; otherwise, he would not
be troubling her.

The only thing that might have troubled her in his appeal was its un-
familiar tone of pragmatism and its compelling ingenuity, which her devotion to him did not permit her to recognize. Neither did it permit her
to follow his injunction not to do anything that might embarrass or inconvenience her. She did so, wholeheartedly. Miss Replogle had attended
Florida State University where she'd met the partner of the single indiscretion of her life—an undergraduate escapade at Homecoming week—
who had since become the representative from her Congressional district.
Nothing could have persuaded her to seek favors of the man for herself,
but she did not hesitate to do so in Ben's behalf. The congressman, with
a zeal that expressed the depths of his indebtedness to her, wrote to the

Corps Commander, endorsing Ben's application to the Marine Guard School. The Corps Commander was impressed, and shortly after, Ben was assigned to Quantico where, sustained by a wholly novel power of motivation, he did famously. On his graduation, he was sent to London where he spent the next two years guarding the American Embassy in Grosvenor Square. He took with him the last relic of his youth, the link that bound him indesseverably to his past and to the golden vision of his future that had kept him from despair in the sweet potato fields, the barracks at Parris Island, and the mud and blood of Vietnam: his now-tattered copy of *Romeo and Juliet*.

On the eve of his first twenty-four-hour pass in London, he bought a copy of the *Telegraph* and read the entertainment section in search of suitable amusement on his first free evening in the great city. Many such diversions he knew were unadvertised: the delights of Soho, Bayswater Road, and The Windmill were celebrated among his fellow marines, but Ben had loftier diversions in mind. He read the theatre section with awe, astonished at the number of legitimate theatres offering stage productions: more than he had known existed. Among them he recognized the name of the most legendary, The Old Vic, and the fact that on that very evening it was presenting a production of *Romeo and Juliet* seemed augury, a link in a mystical concatenation of events that was leading inexorably—immutably was the better word—to his destiny.

It was the first professional stage production Ben had ever seen, and one such as neither he nor Miss Replogle had ever dreamed of. He sat transported in a six-shilling seat in the first tier while young gallants swaggered and dueled and jested in the stone streets and palaces of Verona, their sword hilts and medallions and the brocade of their doublets twinkling in the sunlight of the plazas and in moon-drenched fatal gardens where they poured out their pride and passion and infatuation with life in a tide of eloquence and ardor that made Ben clench the arms of his chair and tremble with delight. Here was magic, beauty, grace, gayety, renown, such as he had never known existed. Here was a world of illustrious

companions, splendid artifice, and the magnificent transformation of reality. The warm and nebulous radiance that had called to him and comforted him throughout his boyhood was suddenly condensed into substance
and swept into a stately architecture, like stardust being swept into a constellation in the void. He felt that he was witnessing the birth of the cosmos. It took shape all about him in this vaulted, glittering playhouse, this
stately temple that framed the human tragedy before him like arches of the
firmament, this stage illuminated with the light of galaxies, jeweled with
tears and blood and ringing with laughter and rapier blades and the vows
of lovers, this rapt, transfigured audience of angels, this home of revelations.

Why in the name of God, he wondered, riding back to his barracks in
the tube train, would a man want to become a computer programmer,
an accountant, an insurance salesman? Here was a life of eternal magic
and romance and, for anyone sufficiently gifted and resolute, fame and fortune. Miss Replogle had told him he had the first of those qualities, Vietnam had taught him that he had the other. He sat rocking in the plunging
car, simmering in the flames of consecration, and before he arrived at
his station he was sworn to his profession.

Every weekend for the two years of his tour of duty in London, he
went to the theatre, and on his summer furloughs he went to Stratford and
Edinburgh. He saw Shakespeare, Marlowe, Jonson, Congreve, Chekhov,
Coward, Pinter, Osborne, Schaffer performed by the finest actors in the
world, produced with unmatched excellence and splendor in a theatrical tradition that went back four hundred years to the Globe. At night in
his barracks he read tattered Penguin paperbacks of plays that he bought
for sixpence on the sidewalk stalls of Tottenham Court Road and Church
Street, and spent his evenings and Sunday afternoons browsing through
the print shops and bookstores of Charing Cross Road where, with ago-
nizingly counted-out shillings, he bought eighteenth-century prints of
Covent Garden, the Haymarket, Drury Lane, Sadler's Wells, and Tup-
pence-Colored drawings of Garrick, Forbes-Robertson, Mrs. Siddons, Henry
Irving, Mrs. Woffington. Every other penny of his pay he saved, and

when he was sent back to the States to be discharged in the summer of 1973, this, together with his severance pay, totaled twenty-five hundred dollars. He bought an airplane ticket and within a week was back in London, ensconced in a bed-sitter in Notting Hill Gate.

It was August, within a week of the yearly auditions for the Royal Academy of Dramatic Art. Ben had three years of entitlement to study on the GI Bill of Rights. His chances for admission, he knew, were very limited; there was a yearly quota of only ten non-British applicants accepted. The knowledge only increased his determination. He applied, memorized the required speech of Hotspur's from *Henry V* and, for his Optional, the lines that he had spoken to Peggy Kaufmann in Miss Replogle's class and murmured to the moon through the tattered fronds of palm trees in the Asian jungles: "It is my lady. Oh, it is my love . . ."

He auditioned on a morning in mid-August in a Georgian room that looked out onto fabled Gower Street, facing a rampart of oak tables at which were seated eight people of a smiling severity of countenance seen only in nightmares. For the week of agonized suspense that followed he entertained himself recklessly, saving not even enough money from his capital to buy an airplane ticket back to New York; so far as he was concerned, the only alternative was oblivion. On the seventh day a brown envelope arrived bearing the Royal Crest and the news that he had been accepted and would be required to report on the fifteenth of the following month with a pair of plimsolls, a foil and fencing mask, and a copy of the Oxford edition of the plays of William Shakespeare. He did not know what plimsolls were, but the esoteric sound of them seemed to confirm the fact that he had been admitted into a mystery. It was the first step toward those distant evenings at the Kennedy Center which he had so long and so radiantly foreseen. He did not foresee that he would not be situated on the stage on those occasions, but in a patron's box; and he would not have believed, at the time, that it would not matter to him.

In his three years at RADA he more than justified Miss Replogle's faith in him, and in the impulse that had brought him there. When he graduated, at the age of twenty-five, he had earned a Diploma with Merit, signed by Gielgud, Olivier, and Dame Sybil Thorndyke; the firm respect of his fellow students and instructors; and the promise of an illustrious career. His performances, which were never less than skilful and often quite startlingly beautiful in a way that he himself did not understand, invariably filled the Academy theatre with fellow students and their friends and families, moved to admiration and often to tears by their originality, subtlety, and vitality. This was the more unusual because he had grown only a couple of inches since his adolescence and had a sad, gnarled face and a reedy voice that was the despair of his diction masters. He had, however, that ineffable quality of intensity and dramatic wisdom that make it possible for an actor to hold an audience by his silences, his presence, his imaginative existence on a stage, far more than by imposing appearance or mere technical proficiency. He was also, for the first time in his life, popular and personable. Being engaged in the thing he was born to do, among people who respected his talent, he flowered in confidence and charm, and in a terrible determination never again to be poor, obscure, or scorned, a determination that furnished him with an inexhaustible source of energy. He became a kind of primitive hero, and in the little world of RADA enjoyed an éclat much like that of Whistler, a hundred years before, in the salons of the West End. He was regarded as a noble savage, gifted, aboriginal, passionate, and free. He discovered that while a few admire the profound, all are enchanted by the picturesque, and that by the cultivation of that quality in himself he could endear himself to friends and beguile audiences. He bought a cheap twelve-string guitar and sang Appalachian folk songs at parties in a corncrake voice whose quality of genuine lament more than compensated for the fact that it was frequently off-key. The Florida Cracker accent that he had once sought to disguise he learned was not only admired as colorfully barbaric, but was professionally profitable; it won him the lead in *Cat on a Hot Tin Roof,* which one of his instructors produced especially as a vehicle for him. That there was a market value to the stigma of his youth was something he had not dreamed

of, and there was irony in the discovery that it could be used as advertise-
ment of the talent that enabled him to perform, on the stage of the most
distinguished dramatic academy in the world, the plays of another rustic
upstart whose fellow dramatists had described him scornfully as "a country crow beautified with our feathers." When he learned this, Ben took a
fierce pride in the fact that was very unlike the habitual humility of his
younger days. The taste of humility had grown sour on his tongue, and
to subsist on consolation now seemed to him like living on scraps thrown
underneath the table to a dog. He felt his powers and prospects stirring
within him with a thrilling nascent tumult almost like that of puberty,
and they demanded tribute. If it came in the form of infatuation with
the persona of the artless rural prodigy he had artfully created, he was
not troubled by the fact; he would accept it as his due, as he came to accept every prize of his virtuosity. The business of living, he began to suspect, was very like the art of the actor—a skilful impersonation, cunningly
constructed and sustained, which inspired trust, admiration and belief.
This principle he practiced without apology or shame, but the true and terrible privation of his youth he did not dramatize, or seek to invest with
glamor, or consciously exploit, or willingly remember, or speak of, ever,
to anyone but Priscilla.

He met her in his second term at RADA at a garden party given for American students in London by the U.S. Information Service, at which she was
the official hostess. She was a year older than Ben, very pretty, idealistic,
and intelligent, and she spoke and wore clothes in a manner he had not
known was possible, with an exquisite, unselfconscious grace that made
him quail. He had never met such a woman. There was a modesty, gentleness, and unassailable poise in her manner that astonished and, although
he had forsworn humility, humbled him anew. Only the memory of
Miss Replogle made it possible for him to believe that such virtues survived—or, occasionally, had miraculously evolved—in human nature; but
Priscilla's virtues came clothed in an aura of which Miss Replogle was
innocent: the delicate bouquet that is the product of private schools,

tennis and equitation lessons, country clubs, and Caribbean vacations. It was one that was utterly unknown to Ben, and it dizzied him. When he learned, later, that it was one of the spoils of her father's career in coal mining in the West Virginia hills, he was not dismayed. Although Priscilla had long since dedicated herself to the advancement of the arts and renounced the designer clothes, sports cars, and the handsome annuity that were her patrimony, that part of it remained, ineradicably, enchantingly, like a perfume; and it became for Ben the magical cachet of wealth, a kind of attar distilled from toil and suffering. It was mysterious evidence of the power of money to transform, to enlighten, to transcend its own dark origins. It was an auspice and an inspiration to him. Why, out of the sour broth of his own youth, might such a sparkling liquor not be brewed, one that would intoxicate the world?

The garden party had been given at Winfield House in Regents Park on one of those days of molten light and soft, fragrant air which account for some of the most poignant moments of English life and some of the most memorable lines of its literature. It accounted, as well, for one of the most poignant moments of Ben's life and the most memorable passage of his destiny. Priscilla, who had green eyes, had been wearing a diaphanous, lime-colored gown, a pair of jade-green slippers, and a necklace of celadon porcelain, like drops of seawater about her slender throat. He first saw her wearing this ensemble in her ineffable way, walking toward him down the steps of a stone terrace with a tray of canapés and a gentle, earnest, openhearted smile that struck him dumb. He took a canapé from her and stood with it uneaten in his hand while he gazed at her for a full ten seconds, during which her smile grew in sweetness and charity.

"I wonder if I can guess what you're studying," she said at last, when he had reduced the canapé to a pulp between his fingers. "Shall I try?"

He nodded, and while she studied his face, he thrust out his jaw and frowned with a look of ponderous importance.

"Economics," she said. "You're at the LSE."

He shook his head, raised one eyebrow and smiled stealthily.

"Law!" she cried. "You're at the Inns of Court."

"That's pretty close," he said, "The Royal School of Buccaneering."

She laughed like a nightingale, and for a moment his face was naked of all mimicry.

"You're not a priest?" she said, her voice lowered in sudden discretion or confusion. "I mean a seminarian?"

"No," Ben said. "'These are actions that a man might play, but I have that within which passeth show.'"

"Oh, an actor! You're an actor!"

"Yes. Do you like actors?"

"Yes, I do. I like all artists, more than anyone. Where are you studying? At RADA?"

"Yes," Ben said.

"How wonderful! I know you're enjoying it, and learning. It's supposed to be a marvelous school." She spoke to him for several minutes, with fresh animation, balancing her tray precariously. She wished him great success and congratulated him on his choice of a profession. The arts, she said, were the chief hope for the salvation of mankind. Ben told her that he shared the opinion, and illustrated the belief by quoting a poem of O'Shaughnessy's that began, "We are the music makers, and we are the dreamers of dreams . . ." In his effort to impress her, he made the mistake, unprecedented for him, of reciting it in a borrowed style of eloquence, a kind of chocolate-covered tremolo imperfectly adapted from John Gielgud. She listened politely but evidently with some disappointment; when he finished the poem, she said, "Oh, that's lovely," and although she went on to praise its sentiments, he noted that she had little to say about his manner of reciting them. He saw that he had made a mistake, and, later that night, staring into the darkness above his bed, he resolved bitterly to repair it. This was a woman, he realized, who could not be deceived by the picturesque, the genial, or the facile. If he wanted to win her, it must be with honest currency, not counterfeit; and he had decided, already, that he did. Whatever other rewards life might yield to his skill and initiative, this one must not go unclaimed.

He had been reading *Hamlet,* and as he lay staring into the darkness

a passage from the Prince's advice to the players came into his mind: "O'er-
step not the modesty of nature; for anything so overdone is from the purpose of playing, whose end, both at the first and now, was, and is, to hold,
as t'were, the mirror up to nature. . . . Now, this overdone . . . though it
make the unskilful laugh, cannot but make the judicious grieve; the cen-
sure of which one must in your allowance o'erweigh a whole theatre of others." She was the one judicious soul in the theatre, he decided, for whom
he must play truthfully. He was correct in his assumption, although he did
not pause to consider that for an actor it is the obligation only of an hour,
but for a lover, of a lifetime.

On the following Saturday evening he took her to a performance of
Tamerlane at the National Theatre, and having accompanied her home,
he told her the story of his youth. He was standing just out of the rain
under the lintel of the little house she had rented in Chelsea, his breath
streaming in clouds in the cold damp air while he spoke for an hour and
a quarter, in a voice of scarifying sincerity such as she had never heard from
any actor on any stage, of his boyhood on this father's farm. She listened
with a somber, attentive air, her eyes fixed on the distant rooftops. He
told her he had been born and raised in an unpainted shack, beside a
desolate cypress swamp, an hour's walk through pine barrens and palmetto
scrub to the nearest neighbor. He had hauled buckets of water up a hillside to water strawberry beds, and had knelt and weeded the beds for hours
under the midsummer sun, his brains reeling under a sweat-soaked straw
hat. He had cleaned out chicken coops and sacked manure and dug sweet
potatoes until his hands were raw and his spirit ached with desire for the
luminous plenitude and peace he saw prefigured in the light, for liberation
from the shabby, degrading consolations of getting drunk on cheap wine
and watching silent Western movies projected on a sheet against the wall
of the Edge Mercantile Company on Saturday nights, or making love
on the seat of his father's '47 pickup to a pale, listless slattern who smelled,
always and inexplicably, of lard. From that world of fatback and okra and
shoe soles patched with cardboard, a world whose greatest ambition was

a job at Edge's Lumber and Mercantile Company and a weekend, once a year, in Orlando or Daytona Beach, dressed in a Sears, Roebuck suit and bowed by an excruciating humility that made one mumble deferentially to waiters in Howard Johnson restaurants and choose one's food from the price column with a stealthy fingertip. At eighteen, he had run away with a sack across his shoulder and spent three years in Vietnam killing people as poor and humble as himself for reasons he had never questioned or had satisfactorily explained to him.

It was a harrowing story and Priscilla was the only person in the world who would ever hear it. When he finished it, she lowered her eyes from the rooftops to his sodden shoes and said, "Would you like to come in and get warm?"

A week later, in a pub in Bloomsbury where they had met for lunch, he asked her to marry him.

"Oh, Ben" she said. "How in the world can I marry you? I don't know anything about you."

"What do you mean, you don't know anything about me? I've told you my whole life history."

"Well, I know, but that was just the facts. Just what's *happened* to you." He looked confounded. "I mean, that made me feel very—well—" She laid her fingertips delicately against the wall of their booth. "But you're asking me to *marry* you. How can I possibly marry you? I've never seen you act."

"You've never seen me act?"

"No. You might be a terrible actor. I couldn't marry a man who was a terrible actor. I don't know how anyone could."

"There are lots of terrible actors in the world," he said. "And women marry them all the time. It's what they mostly marry."

"Not me," she said.

He stared at her for a moment, sipped his beer, set it down, and stared at her again. "Well, look," he said. "I'm rehearsing *Richard III* right now. We're doing it on the fourth of next month. Will you come and see it?"

She put out a forefinger and ran it around the rim of her glass. "I don't know if I should," she said.

"Why not?"

"Well, I mean—it might be better if I didn't. Supposed I didn't like it?"

"That's pusillanimous," he said.

"Well, there you are. *You* don't want to marry a pusillanimous *woman* any more than I want to marry a bad actor."

"If she looks like you, I do," he said. "I'll marry her in a minute."

"I don't want to talk about it any more. Let's talk about Richard."

"Why not talk about me?"

"I want to talk about Richard. What's the matter with that man, anyway?"

"Just what he says," Ben said. "He is 'not shaped for sportive tricks.' He has no delight to pass away the time, except to spy his shadow in the sun and descant on his own deformity."

Priscilla closed her eyes and shuddered. "That's terrible," she said.

"Yes, it is." He picked up his mug and held it, staring at her. "Listen, are you coming to see it or not?"

"No," Priscilla said. "I don't think so."

He swung the mug in a circle, watching the froth spin inside the glass. "I think I made a mistake," he said, "telling you that story. But I hope you weren't disappointed."

"Disappointed?"

"In your fling with the farmhand."

"*Oh!*" she said in a stricken murmur. "That's a vile thing to say."

He finished his beer and set down the empty mug. "Well, I've got to get back to rehearsal," he said. "I'll call you sometime. When I make my first million."

He got up and went out of the pub without looking back. When he had gone, Priscilla ordered another glass of cider, drank it slowly, smoked a cigarette, gathered up her purse, car keys and driving gloves (she was the only person Ben had ever known who wore driving gloves), then went out and walked the five blocks to the Royal Academy of Dramatic Art. Inside, a uniformed doorman with a ruddy, very dignified face asked what she wanted.

"I'm looking for the rehearsal of *Richard III*," she said. "I believe Miss Fulkes is directing it. Could you tell where the theatre is?"

"It's down one floor," the doorman said. "But it's a closed rehearsal. The rehearsals are not public."

"Yes, I know," Priscilla said. "But she asked me to drop around. I'm from the Ramsey office."

"Ah. Well, you take the stairs, there, and turn right at the bottom."

"Thank you."

She went down the stairs, turned right, and entered the rear door of the auditorium where she slipped into a seat in the back row. The house lights were out and between her and the stage she could see the heads of many members of the large cast of student actors sitting scattered in the darkness. On the stage, Ben, uncannily and apparently congenitally disfigured by a crooked chest and humped back, was seducing Lady Anne, a slender, fair-haired girl who stood beside the coffin of King Henry VI, the father of her husband, Prince Edward, both of whom Ben had slaughtered on his path to the crown. In his gnarled body a deep, incandescent fire seemed to burn that gave his eyes an eerie luster and animated his twisted fingers with a sinister delicacy, like those of a raccoon washing the blood from its prey. They reached out toward the princess in a kind of anguish, withdrawing quickly when she recoiled from them and crumbling humbly to his breast where the tips of them strayed abjectly over his misshapen ribs.

"He that bereft thee, lady, of thy husband," he said to her in a hoarse, afflicted voice, "did it to help thee to a better husband."

"His better doth not breathe upon the earth," the distraught lady cried.

Ben nodded in denial, his eyes burning. "He lives that loves thee better than he could," he murmured.

"Where is he?" the lady demanded bitterly.

"Here." He spread his hands wide. She spit into his face. Ben closed his eyes and after an awful pause, he opened them, raised his hand to touch the spittle on his cheek and smiled. "Why dost thou spit at me?" he asked in a weird, withered whisper.

"Would it were mortal poison, for thy sake!" the lady hissed.

He cringed slightly from the blow of her contempt, quivering like a crab with a crushed shell, and stared up at her with what might have been hopeless adoration, deathly pain, black humiliation, or unholy pride. A devastated shudder ran through her, like an aspen shedding its leaves in a cold breeze. The strange, appalling seduction went on, growing in its intensity until there was a kind of sickening enchantment about it. Ben writhed and muttered, he clasped his arms about his shoulders and dug his nails into them, he reached out fleetingly to touch the sleeve of her gown, bowed his head and turned aside to brush away the tears that glittered on his cheeks. He offered her his sword and ripped open his shirt, baring his breast to it. He fell clumsily to his knees and begged her, if she would not accept his love, to kill him. When she let the sword fall strengthlessly, he looked up at her and demanded with a hushed and horrifying sincerity, "Take up the sword again, or take up me."

"Arise, dissembler," the lady said in a bewildered whisper. "Though I wish thy death, I will not be thy executioner."

"Then bid me kill myself, and I will do it," he said implacably.

"I would I knew thy heart," she murmured.

"'Tis figured in my tongue."

"I fear me both are false."

"Then never man was true."

Her lips trembled and she dropped her head. "Well, well, put up your sword."

"But shall I live in hope?" he demanded, staring up at her with harrowing insistence.

"All men, I hope, live so."

He stood up, heaving himself to his feet with a quick, crippled lunge, and drew an ornate ring from his finger, holding it out to her.

"Vouchsafe to wear this ring."

After a moment of tremulous hesitation she took it from him and slid it onto her finger, murmuring, "To take is not to give."

Ben took her hand and held it in both his own, gazing down at it like a plucked flower. "Look how my ring encompasseth thy finger," he said. "Even so thy breast encloseth my poor heart. Wear both of them, for both of them are thine."

Priscilla got up and went quickly along the row to the aisle, clutching the backs of seats to steady herself. She felt dizzy and could scarcely see through her tears. She had the strange sensation that the world was whirling, roiling, curdling all around her, changing shape and substance in a vertiginous process of metamorphosis. She was not sure that when she stepped out of the Academy door the stone footpaths of Gower Street would be there to receive her feet. She might step into a walled garden with fountains and rose trellises, or a bottomless abyss. She dropped her gloves in her haste but did not stop to pick them up, afraid of what her hand might touch when it groped for them in the darkness.

·   ·   ·

Six months later they were married in a lovely old stone church just off Grosvenor Square where he often waited for her in the garden on summer afternoons, and where she would meet him after she had finished work and they would sit for an hour before they went back to her house in Chelsea, watching the shadows of the yew trees creep across the stones and the lavender dusk enfolding the slate spire of the steeple. Their entire courtship had that curious pictorial serenity, like a stage tableau bathed in the light of tinted olivettes.

Their wedding reception, in the ballroom of the USIS building in Grosvenor Square, was equally theatrical but less serene, and educational for Ben, who was eager to improve his knowledge of the world. It was paid for by Priscilla's parents who flew over from New York for the occasion and insisted on taking over the task of arranging its details. Priscilla was distressed by its extravagance; she would have preferred to slip away

with a few close friends to the Rising Sun in Gower Street, but she yielded
to Ben's obvious bemusement at the prospect of such unknown opu-
lence. The guest list was made up from among his friends at RADA and
Priscilla's colleagues in the diplomatic corps, mostly minor administra-
tive officials from the USIS. In the course of it, Ben withstood sufficiently
the effects of a great deal of fine French champagne to perceive that
there are two types of people in the world: those who lead the life of the
imagination, and those who patronize and exert authority over them.
The relationship between these two was one that he had not previously
seen illustrated, but it did not take him long to observe that although the
spiritual advantage might be on the side of Art, the temporal, and dispos-
ing, one was heavily in favor of Authority. This was dramatized in the course
of the evening by several incidents, some engaging, some perilously close
to indecorous. Most of his friends were in their late teens or early twenties and had seldom drunk champagne or been presented with such an
outstanding opportunity to demonstrate their gifts, their personal charms,
their capacity to improvise, or their colorful Bohemian ways. It was an
opportunity that some of them could not resist. One girl, with shoulder-
length red hair, took off her shoes and danced a saraband on the buffet
table, dipping her toes into the seafood sauce. Another, her eyes fixed on
an eligible young attaché, challenged anyone present to guess the nature
and location of her tattoo, with the promise that if he were successful he
could escort her home to verify the fact and claim his reward; if he were
not, he would be equally welcome to her consolation. A young man in
leather trousers sang the Song of Solomon to his own highly inflamed
accompaniment on a lute. These gaucheries and drolleries were accepted
in good humor by the diplomatic corps, who were trained in imperturbability,
but not, Ben noted, without a shadow of indulgence, the barest suggestion of condescension and of censoriousness which betrayed a judicial
attitude on their part, the understanding, however subtle, that it was their
canons which took precedence, their sense of propriety that must be satisfied, and that when it came down to the business of awarding prizes or

dispensing grants or issuing injunctions, it was they whose opinions must be courted, and whose judgment would prevail. The authority of Priscilla's parents was even more impressive since it derived from wealth, not office, and did not depend on protocol, and because they were, in the most literal sense, patrons of the arts. Her father, Mr. Wallace, had, he told Ben, endowed a scholarship for young performers at the Juilliard School of Music, a gesture Priscilla had suggested and which his accountant had warmly endorsed as a substantial tax deduction. What interested Ben even more was the fact that he occasionally invested in plays — in this case, profitably, he confessed, offhandedly citing *Oklahoma* and *My Fair Lady*. He had made a good deal of money in the theatre, he implied expansively, and yet the respect accorded him by the diplomatic personnel present was unclouded by any imputation of social or moral inferiority. Evidently the theatre did not impart disreputability if one made money from it, only if one made a contribution of imagination and energy to it inconspicuous enough to go unrewarded.

All in all, it was a profitable evening for Ben. Not only did he learn a good deal about the artist's relationship to society, but he put the knowledge to immediate practical use by reassuring his father-in-law as to his own prospects, intentions, and resources, including his newly discovered palate for fine wines which it occurred to him might be gratifying to so generous a host. Mr. Wallace, who had suffered a considerable shock on learning that his daughter had married a penniless student actor who was five feet six inches tall and talked like Daniel Boone, was hungry for reassurance, and this may have accounted for his discovery that there was something to be said for this odd young man after all. He was talented, by all accounts, he was certainly intelligent, he was apparently ambitious, he respected achievement, he obviously adored Priscilla, and he seemed to have a sense of decorum not shared by all of his profession; when the young lady who had danced the saraband offered to do a North African dance of even greater piquancy, Ben put his father-in-law's evident alarm to rest by saying, "I'll speak to her, sir. I'm afraid she's getting a little out of hand." When he did so, the young lady smilingly emptied a bowl of sour cream onto his head.

After their marriage, Ben and Priscilla stayed in London for another year, Ben to finish his course at RADA and Priscilla to complete her tour of duty with the State Department. It was a good year. London had become the hub of a cultural renaissance in popular music, fashion, and the theatre. Mary Quant still reigned in Carnaby Street, half a dozen British rock groups had succeeded to the mantle of the Beatles, and two generations of post-war prodigies—Osborne, Pinter, Schaffer, Nichols, and the rest—had given new life to the British theatre. There was a sense of fervor and energy abroad that Ben could smell in the wind and in which he rejoiced as a thirsty stag rejoices in the scent of water. He would have liked to stay in London and begin his assault on the stage there, since he enjoyed already the distinction which an auspicious career at RADA generates in the small theatrical world of London. Agents and producers regularly attended RADA performances in the hope of finding fresh talent; it was the pool from which the English theatre had, for generations, drawn its water. Ben's reputation had grown among these people; he had, in fact, been offered a small but interesting part in a West End production, but was unable to accept it because he couldn't get a working permit unless he became a British citizen or married an English girl, courses closed to him by his choice, in marrying Priscilla, of what he thought were greater prospects.

When they went back to the States, the wisdom of that choice dimmed, in perspective. They settled in New York since, for anyone who wanted to be an actor, it was the only possible place to live. Not only were the Broadway shows auditioned for and cast there, but New York agents also handled the casting for repertory companies, summer stock, and dinner theatres across the entire country. Priscilla gave up her job at the USIS and went to work as a reader in a publishing house. They lived in an ancient row house on West Fourth Street in the Village that had been partitioned off into apartments. Theirs was on the second floor, a mouldy, mournful suite of three rooms which after the tidy elegance of Priscilla's house in Chelsea was infinitely depressing. For a month they spiritedly refurbished it with gallons of off-white paint, flowered chintz, a chifferobe, a tropical fish tank and a set of bright-colored Impressionist prints from the Metropolitan. It was from here that Ben set out every morning to make his assault upon the American stage.

It proved to be a grim and barren task. In the world of New York theatre he was no lion, no young Turk, no known prodigy. His name, at parties, did not cause heads to revolve respectfully in his direction, there were no smiles of recognition to greet him in agents' offices, no unsolicited offers of juvenile leads or interesting supporting roles, or of invitations to audition for them. There were stares of indifference, niggardly allotments of fifteen minutes of reading time at "cattle calls," sometimes accompanied by undisguised dismay or amusement at his stature and the quaint quality of his speech, often brutally abbreviated and invariably followed by faintly condescending thanks. It was a bitter period, the worst of his life, worse even than the legendary tribulations of most young actors, because he had already enjoyed a certain amount of celebrity and the almost universal expectations, on the part of his classmates at RADA, of his future prosperity. After six months of it, of making daily rounds, of sitting for hours in inhospitable agents' offices or beside a silent telephone, of mailing portfolios of photographs that they could ill afford to impervious agents and producers, his spirits began to flag. He did not lose hope or believe less in himself, but he had for the first time to take account of the indifference, if not the hostility, of the world to excellence, something he had not expected and could not understand. He understood that he did not have the conventional virtues of the average juvenile or young leading man — he was not tall, good-looking, blandly agreeable or equipped with a resonant baritone — but he had never realized the reluctance of the public to accept poetry and passion in their stead. At this point in his life, his disappointment was with the world more than with himself. There were roles, he continued to believe with absolute conviction, that he could

play as no one else could, that demanded lyricism, irony, melancholy,
wit, the kind of aching sensibility that he was able—now, better than ever!—
to bring to them; only one such, he believed, would be enough to gain him
recognition, to launch his career. But he was not prepared for the infre-
quency with which such roles occur in the popular theatre, or for the
distaste of the world in general for disturbing complexities. He would have
appreciated the observation of Nietzsche, in similar circumstances, that "it
is not enough to possess a talent, one must also have your permission to
possess it, eh, my friends?"

In this time of disappointment and dismay he was supported by Priscilla's
unwavering faith in him as well as by his own imperishable belief in that
distant numinous hour in which all would be redeemed. His strength of
purpose was formidable, and in adversity became almost ferocious. It burned
in him like the nude blue blade that spires in the heart of a flame, and
sometimes, in those unhappy days, it seemed to consume much that was
attractive in his personality. Priscilla was disturbed by his long periods of silence, his growing restlessness and impatience and by the saturnine quality that began to creep into his conversation, his face, his physical gestures,
and the quality of his lovemaking. This became less gentle, less skilfully
protracted, if no less passionate. Something uncouth that had always lurked
below the surface of his manner and that had been successfully suppressed
by prosperity or by the promise of it, often seemed on the point of breaking through that genial, artful exterior and threatening their lives, their
future—even their past, in an uncanny way—with some nameless desecration. For anyone less loving or generous than Priscilla this intimation of
disaster might have been demoralizing, but she was wise enough to know
that frustrated and unhappy men do not make ideal lovers, and she understood as no one else could his fear and loathing of the obscurity from
which he had escaped and whose cloud had reappeared above him like
the shadow of a vulture. She had no doubt that it would disappear in
time, that with the single stroke of fortune that he so richly deserved and
which was inevitable, their trials would be over. He would get his break;

the era of doubt and ambiguity would dissipate. The tiny rupture, the instant of awful vacuity, of discontinuity in the great grave continuum of things, the whiff of vile odor from the void, would be sealed over and eventually forgotten.

Fortunately, this period lasted only eighteen months. At the end of that time Ben landed a job for the coming summer with a stock company at a playhouse in the Maryland countryside outside of Washington, D.C. They did a season of six plays which ran for two weeks each, from the first of June to the first of September. The theatre had living quarters for the company on the second floor, above the auditorium, which meant he would not have the expense of renting a room in Washington, and although the salary was a bare Equity minimum, he would be able to save the greater part of it. The plays were typical stock fare—farces, situation comedies, a mystery, and a revival of Coward's *Private Lives*. In all but one of these, Ben had run-of-the-mill supporting roles of the kind which required only journeyman competence to perform. The exception was his single lead, the part of Danny in Emlyn Wiliams's *Night Must Fall*, which was the seasonal mystery. It was one of the rare leading roles of the kind at which he excelled, in this case a charming, demented murderer who carries the severed head of a former victim about in a Victorian hatbox which he keeps under his bed. This strange young man ingratiates himself with an elderly, credulous widow who hires him as a resident handyman and personal attendant, and who is utterly captivated, and eventually slain, by him. Ben got the role because of its lyrical, ominous intensity which he understood and even at the first reading evoked startlingly, and by virtue of the fact that the character was Welsh, a dialect he had learned to speak impeccably in his phonetics classes.

He went down to Maryland in the second week of May and began rehearsals for the opening production. Priscilla was to come down on weekends, stay with him in his quarters upstairs in the theatre so that she would be able to see all of the productions, and at the end of August they would take a two-week vacation. They were both elated. It was far from the

Broadway opening he had dreamed of, but it was at least gainful employment as a professional actor—his first, and therefore an event of great festivity. They celebrated it with a pair of tenderloin steaks, a bottle of champagne and, afterwards, a night of unshadowed delight that was a reprise of their nights in London, enfolded by a peace as tranquil as the sound of English rain against the windowpanes.

"You're happy, aren't you?" Priscilla whispered, laying her fingertips on his face.

"Yes. Are you?"

"Yes, I feel as if I were back in the little house in Chelsea."

"I'm going to buy that house someday," Ben said.

The season was his first and last, a curious, valedictory triumph for Ben. His minor roles he performed with a brilliance that could be measured by the unease it produced in the leading man as well as by the pleasure it produced in the audience. Such characters are written to formula for commercial drama and generally performed in the same way; with the substitution of a name tag, they could be carried out onto the stage in almost any play and positioned there, like mannequins. Ben brought them engagingly to life, however, with the strange, prismatic light with which he illuminated them, and the elegance of his invention. But the part of Danny he conceived with such a rich and tortured malignancy that a wave of genuine horror swept the auditorium like a cold draft, and when it was over, the audience, mostly middle aged, respectable folk carefully coiffured and clothed by Garfinckel's for a summer evening of harmless entertainment, went away with a feeling that mania was abroad in the world, a feeling that they had not bargained for. Amongst them was a man who thoroughly enjoyed himself, however, an imperturbable, urbane, mildly ironic man who was the owner of an advertising agency and therefore a student of human nature and of the practical uses to which a knowledge of it may be put. He came to a Wednesday night performance on the second week and afterwards appeared backstage to introduce himself, congratulate Ben, and leave his card, with the invitation to call him up and discuss the possibility of appearing in thirty-second television commercials. Ben did so; a complementary income from such a source seemed highly acceptable to him. Ted Oglesby invited him to lunch at the Old Ebbitt Grill in downtown Washington, where he disclosed to Ben that he had been awarded a contract by a local automobile agency anxious to expand its business to the suburbs and improve the image of its service department.

"What we want," he told Ben, "is something fresh, sophisticated, and funny, that will appeal to yuppies in Bethesda and Chevy Chase. People who are tired of having to leave their Lincolns and Cadillacs for three days and pay five hundred dollars for a piece of shoddy maintenance or repair work that will break down again in a week. We want to give them reassurance, a smile, and the sense that in Wilson's Pontiac they're dealing with their own kind of people. Now, to do that, we have to scare them first. The best commercials have a little madness buried in them somewhere."

"Madness?" Ben asked.

"Right. The sense that there's madness in the world, that no one is held to account. That chaos lurks behind the scenes. It's something everyone suspects and responds to. It's something you put over very well the other night."

"You want to scare people into taking their cars to Wilson's Pontiac for repair?"

"You can scare people into anything. Why do you think they buy insurance, or go to church on Sunday?"

"I thought they went to church to pray."

"Sure, they pray there. The way they pray in the middle of hurricanes, and when their sons are off at war."

"I'm not very religious," Ben said, "but I thought the church was a place of reverence."

Oglesby cut a piece of London broil and chewed it delicately. "Reverence," he said, "is the emotion a man feels when he sees someone driving a Jaguar or a Rolls. Or reads about Howard Hughes' latest business coup."

"I don't want to start an argument," Ben said, "but I've always understood it was what you felt when you listened to Mozart, or looked at a painting by Velasquez, or read a poem by Emily Dickinson."

"Or one by Wallace Stevens," Oglesby said. "But he made his living selling life insurance."

Ben considered this. "How are you going to scare these people into patronizing Wilson's Pontiac?" he asked.

"Well, I've been giving it a lot of thought, especially since I saw you play Danny. That guy was born to be a service manager. Everybody's met him. He works in ninety-nine percent of the garages in this country. Have you ever taken your car in for repair?"

"I don't have a car," Ben said.

"Well, let me tell you something, taking a car in for service is a metaphysical experience. It's like a peek into the primal chaos. It brings people to the edge of the abyss."

"You want me to play a service manager."

"That was my first idea. Of course, we could approach it another way, a them-and-us thing. First we have Them: this guy who took his car to his regular mechanic. He's drooling, giggling, plucking at his shirt front. 'Meet Mr. Jones,' we say. 'He takes his car to your garage.' Then we show them a guy who takes his car to our people, Wilson's Pontiac. This guy is smiling, serene, sipping a Tom Collins in a lounge chair. He looks up at the camera, purses his lips, and smiles complacently. 'Now meet Mr. Thompson,' we say. 'He takes his car to Wilson's Pontiac in Bethesda.'"

"And the first guy is Danny," Ben said.

"Right. Danny the way you played him in the last scene, gone really haywire. The seond guy is St. Francis. Peace and harmony have been restored to the universe. God exists. You think you could do both of them?"

"How about if it's the same guy?" Ben said. "A before and after thing. In the first shot, he's nutty. But the second time, he's switched garages. Somebody told him about Wilson's."

"That's not a bad idea." Oglesby raised his eyes and studied the far wall.

"Or how about if we have a third character? A psychiatrist? Jones is cracking up, so he goes to this psychiatrist. He tells the psychiatrist, 'My God, it was awful! As soon as I got it home, the carburetor started hissing, then the muffler fell off, then the pistons blew. I can't stand any more, doctor.' The psychiatrist nods, puts his fingertips together, and says, 'I zeenk you zhood take your car to Veelson's Pontiac.' Then we fade in to the guy on his next visit. He's back at the psychiatrist's office happy as a lark, his troubles are over. 'It was like a miracle,' he says. 'If only I'd known about Wilson's earlier.'"

Oglesby was listening intently. "I think you have a talent for this business," he said. He nodded gravely. "Listen, Ben, we do our videos at Brinks, in Silver Spring. Why don't you come down there on Monday morning, and we'll do some takes? At around nine-thirty."

"I can make that," Ben said.

The commercial was a great success. They did the psychiatrist version Ben had suggested, and it ran for three months on all five local TV outlets and increased the dealer's business by 36 percent. Ben's face and voice became familiar to everyone within a fifty-mile radius of Washington, both in its demented and its beatific phases. "Isn't that the man who does the Wilson Pontiac commercials?" people whispered, when the curtain had gone up and he made his first appearance on the stage. "Oh, it *is*! I knew I'd seen him somewhere." He could have played in stock for twenty years without becoming recognizable to so wide an audience.

Other commercials followed. There was one for a locally brewed beer, one for a department store, and one of enormous success for a chain of fast-food restaurants in which he played a gangster besieged by a SWAT team in a bullet-riddled bank who refuses to surrender until a police captain shouts through a bullhorn, "Hey, Dutch, we got Mammothburgers out here." The gangster is shaken, at last throws down his submachine gun, emerges from the rubble with his hands above his head, and is last seen behind bars, manacled, with a napkin tucked into his collar, blissfully munching a Mammothburger. This one Ben wrote the script for. His fame, and his fee, increased with each of these appearances, which he found growingly hard to fit into his rehearsal schedules at the theatre. By the time Priscilla came down in August, he had saved six thousand dollars.

"We can have a real vacation," he told her. "We can have that honeymoon I promised you. Why don't we fly down to Jamaica for a week?"

"Don't you think we ought to save?" she said. "It might be a long cold winter in New York."

"We'll never be this young again," Ben said. "And if we don't go now, we'll never have it to remember. Sufficient unto next winter is the evil thereof." He thought for a moment. "I played in *The Winter's Tale* at RADA."

"I know you did," she said.

He looked beyond her and recited:

Prosperity's the very bond of love,
Whose fresh complexion and whose heart together
Affliction alters.

"I think you're right," she said. "Let's celebrate our blessings."

In a burst of gay and confident extravagance they bought cruise clothes, flew down to Caneel Bay, ate a great deal of rich, exotic food, got very brown, danced in the tropic moonlight, and made love in the jasmine-scented dark. One afternoon, seated in rattan chairs under a canopy of woven palm leaves, with piña coladas at their elbows and sunlight glittering on the emerald sea in front of them, Ben turned to his wife and saw that she was more beautiful than he had ever realized. He looked at her for several moments in a deep contented silence.

"What's the matter?" she asked, becoming aware of the length of his gaze.

"Nothing. My God, Priss, you're beautiful."

Her blush was visible through her tan. "I'm just the same," she murmured.

"No. Or maybe you are. Maybe it's just that I see things better down here, in this light." He turned his eyes out to the dazzling sea. "This is a beautiful place."

"Yes. I could stay here forever, couldn't you?"

"No, not forever," he said. "But it's certainly nice right now." He picked up his piña colada, sipped at it, and set it down. "Priss, I've been thinking. Why should we go back to New York?"

"You just said you didn't want to stay here forever."

"I don't mean here. I mean why live in New York? Why not live in Washington?"

"There isn't very much theatre there, is there?"

"Sure there is. What about the Kennedy Center? And the Arena, and the National, and the Warner, and a couple of very good small club theatres. And there's stock, and dinner theatre, for the summers. And there are the commercials."

"The commercials?"

"Yes. I've got a real head start there. I'm becoming known in Washington. Advertisers ask for me now."

"But Ben, you don't want to do commercials for the rest of your life."

"I wasn't thinking about just doing commercials. I was thinking about opening my own agency."

"An *advertising* agency?"

"Why not? Right now we need the money, and it's a way to make it. In a few years I could open my own theatre." He looked out at the sea. "You know what I hate, more than anything? I hate working for people. I hate taking wages."

"But Ben, you're an artist. You're not a businessman. You'd go crazy trying to run an advertising agency. Or a theatre, either."

"I don't think so. Priss, the greatest names of the nineteenth century were actor-managers: Kean, Macready, Kemble, Beerbohm Tree, Sir Henry Irving, all of them. And they *got* great because they produced their own shows. They knew what they could do best, and they knew how to do it. They didn't leave it up to a bunch of moneylenders sitting in The City some-where. Why do you think the Vic was so great when Olivier was run-ning it?"

"It was a national theatre. He didn't have to worry about money. He got it from the government."

"Or His Majesty's, under Irving?"

"I don't know," Priscilla said. She shook her head and stared off at the sea. "It's sounds crazy to me. What about your career? You're an *artist*, Ben. Don't you want to *act*?"

"I don't know," Ben said. "I think maybe I only wanted to know that I could do it as well as anybody, and better than most. I'm pretty sure about that now."

For Priscilla it was one of those moments of a married woman's life when she looks into the abyss. Who was this man she was married to? Was he an imposter? Had some succubus crept onto his chest in the middle of the night and sucked the soul out of him? She studied Ben's features for a moment as if in fear that she might not recognize them, but they seemed unaltered. That was the same delicate, rather childish mouth that she had heard describe resolutely, with a fierce, subdued shame, the details of his bitter, blighted boyhood. Those were the grave brown eyes that she had wished to heal of their suffering. But was this the soul of the sensitive, as-piring artist whose spark of the divine fire the world would be deprived of unless she tended it? What had happened to him? What mysterious transformation had taken place in his soul? Had she sought, all her life, the love of a poet, only to discover that she had won an ambitious young en-trepreneur with plans for a commercial tour de force? What does a woman do in such a case? Should she file immediately for divorce, before it was too late? Resign herself to lifelong disillusionment? Take a lover? Renounce him and the world forever by joining some secluded order such as the Carmelites? These questions raged in her while she regarded Ben with troubled eyes. He saw the distress and confusion in her gaze and laid his hand on hers.

"Listen, Priss," he said gently, "don't get upset. There isn't anything to worry about."

"I don't know. You seem so different," she said. He studied her face gravely.

"Look I want you to understand this: I never change. I haven't changed for an instant, ever, and I never will. I just want things to be perfect for us. I want everything that was ever supposed to happen come true. I want us to have everything that was ever promised to us. Both of us."

She did not reply, and although she felt an impulse to remove her hand, she left it there, as if consigned irrevocably to the grasp of his own, which he clenched, almost imperceptibly, as if he had felt her impulse.

"I'm not even sure I'm supposed to be an actor," he went on with a gravity and sincerity that, as always, touched her heart. "I don't have the physical equipment for a star, in the first place. I have to face that fact. I don't want to live on a romantic dream forever. I could gamble away ten or fifteen years of my life waiting for the right part to come along, and it might never come. The kind of parts I can play just don't come along every day — kooks and cranks, funny poignant little guys who get a five-minute cameo in a big film starring William Hurt."

"What about Shakespeare?" she demanded. "What about Richard III, and Hamlet, and Mercutio?"

"How many people make a living playing Shakespeare? Maybe in twenty years I could earn a small reputation and scrape together a living playing character parts and doing commercials on the side. But it wouldn't be much of a contribution to the world, and by that time I'd be worn out, stale, fed up, and a bloody bore — to you and everybody else. A lot of people are born into this world with the soul of a Caruso and a cleft palate, and they spend their lives feeding on their own hearts. I don't want to be one of them. I think I can give a lot more in other ways. If I could run a theatre, produce original manuscripts that I believed in, put together a company of people who had genuine talent, create an appetite for real theatre in the world, and cultivate a taste for it in audiences, wouldn't that be a hell of a lot more impressive kind of contribution?" Priscilla listened, with lowered eyes. "I have this awful dream," Ben said. "I get the damn thing all the time, once a month or more." He picked up his glass, sipped at it, and held it in his lap while he described it to her. "I'm on a train, going somewhere, to some large distant city, for an appointment, some very grand occasion at which I'm going to be honored. But I never get there. The train gets wrecked, or sidetracked somehow, or I get off at a whistle stop to stretch my legs and sit down by a creek and just look at the scenery for a while, and I don't get back on in time. I just stand there and look after it, watching it disappear. It's a terrible dream." There was the same harrowed look in his eyes as when he had told her the story of his youth, and the pathos it stirred in Priscilla's breast seemed to reaffirm her dedication to him. This was, after all, the man she had married, the man whose talent she had been born to serve, whose spirit she was sworn to spare from the destitution that threatened to reclaim it. It was her turn to lay her hand on his and murmur, "Don't be scared, Ben. It's all right. I'm always here."

He turned to look at her with a humble gratitude that was unfeigned. "I'm sure glad of that," he said, and raised his hand to lay it against her cheek. "I don't know what I'd do without you, Priss."

Perhaps, she thought, she had not understood entirely the nature of the flame that burned in this man. That it burned still, undiminished, was all that truly mattered. There was, after all, much truth in what she had said about his prospects in the theatre; eighteen months in New York had acquainted them solemnly with that fact. He was too ambitious and too talented to be satisfied with a lifetime of shabby subsistence on summer stock, dinner theatres, and an occasional character role in a low-budget movie or off-Broadway production, growing crabbed and weary and poisoned by neglect until the flame had died in him entirely. Perhaps it was true that he could make a much more impressive contribution, and could lead a fuller, far happier, more exuberant life if his imagination and energy were used to create opportunity, enthusiasm, activity, the kind of noble furor in the world which is the wake of genius and the

work of art. After all, there were fewer Stanislavskys than there were leading men. She became eloquent in her defense of him, which was natural because she loved him and because she understood, even as she
understood the jeopardy of it, the protean quality of his imagination and
the irrepressibility of his talent. She had made it her mission to serve that
talent, whatever course it took, and she could not falter in that ideal.
This is not the way of prudence, but it is the way of love. It is also the
way of privilege. People who are born to wealth and the indissoluble
sense of security that comes with it are freed forever from that most igno-
minious form of need—the need to adjust their ideals to their circumstances. That was her birthright, as Ben's was the audacity that is born of
privation.

"Wouldn't it take an awful lot of money to start an advertising agency?"
she asked after several minutes, when these thoughts had somewhat softened her alarm.

"Not so much. The main thing is the office."

"The office?"

"Yes. Appearances are important in that kind of a business. You'd have
to have an office that was very chic, very elegant and tasteful, that smelled
of success. Lots of rosewood and crystal, a couple of original Modiglianis
or Dufys, a piece of metal sculpture. It gives a client a sense of security,
the feeling that he's in good hands. The office and furnishings would be
the big expense. It we started out modestly, we could handle the paperwork
ourselves, I think. Of course, we'd have to have a lawyer draw up contracts,
and a smart young graphics artist. And there are lots of them, Priss, they
pour out of the universities by the thousands every year, just hungry for a
place to start. I could write the copy myself, and do most of the visuals. You
know what I even thought?"

"No."

"I thought maybe you could do the secretarial work until we got going. Sort of an executive secretary. Make appointments, entertain clients,
stuff like that. God knows you'd be an adornment to any office. It would

be fun working together, too. Going to the office every day, talking over accounts at dinner." She smiled. "I think with maybe fifty thousand dollars we'd be in business."

"You've been thinking about it quite a lot."

"I've thought about it, yes. That's not a lot of money. In one good year, we'd make it back, and double, if my experience with Oglesby is any indication. You know, I've acquired a lot of know-how just working with him this summer. I've made a lot of contacts. People know my work and like me. I wouldn't be surprised if I could win over some of his accounts. I know Wilson's Pontiac and Ponsonby's would want me to go on doing their stuff. It wouldn't be like walking into a dark alley."

"Well, I suppose Dad would lend it to us," Priscilla said. "I hate to ask him, because I swore I never would; but this is different than just asking for money. I mean, it would be an investment, really. We'd pay it back."

Ben had evidently been waiting for her to make this suggestion. "Absolutely," he said, nodding vigorously. "It would be a business loan, at going interest rates. We could even sell him stock, if it came to that." He grinned at her. "Short of a controlling interest, of course. I think he'd see it for what it is, a sound business investment, not charity." He paused and scowled at the sea. "I don't want charity. That's the last thing I want from this world. All I want is opportunity."

"I know, sweetheart," she said. "Let me think about it, will you? I don't know how he'd take it, quite. And anyway, I really hate to ask him."

She thought about it for two weeks and through many sleepless nights. In spite of the delight she took in Ben's enthusiasm—so different from the saturnine silence that had taken possession of him in New York—she was very troubled. She was somewhat shaken by his casual reference to confiscating his former colleague's clients, for one thing, and by the apparent equanimity with which he proposed to abandon his career as an actor. Most of all, she detested the world of commerce and its sovereignty over human society. She still felt as part of her inherited guilt the coal wars of Harlan County and the hundreds of thousands of acres of ravaged farmland and woodland in the West Virginia hills reduced to simmering toxic pools of cyanide by her father's strip-mining. To borrow any part of the profits of that ruthless despoliation of the earth and exploitation of humanity in order to set up a commercial enterprise of their own seemed to her obscene. The only thing that could redeem it in her eyes was if it led to the establishment of a theatre, a house of art, a fortress for what was finest in the human spirit. There was a beautiful ironic justice in the thought that the profits of men like her father, like the Guggenheims and Nobels of the world, could be used to transform the society that had made their wealth and power possible. Maybe Ben was right; maybe if artists had a greater hand in the management of the world's affairs, it would be a better place. Poets had been kings in Israel; and there was some merit in his example of the actor-managers in the history of the theatre. She did not really fear for Ben's soul. The threat to it was far more from penury than from prodigality. There was a fire of aspiration in him that she had never known in any other man, one that would never yield to the temptations of power, venal pleasures, or profligacy. If he had any disposition toward intemperance, it was of a very different kind. One more prodigious, perhaps, and more intransigent, and one far more provocative to a woman.

Mr. Wallace proved very amenable to the idea of providing them with the funds to start their business. He had taken a liking to Ben at their first meeting, and was pleased to hear that he had not resigned himself to a life of meager subsistence as a supporting player or to the sublevels of a trade that was at best a kind of trumpery or frivolity, a kind of colorful, parasitic growth on the body politic. The young man had ambition, enterprise, and was evidently developing a sound sense of reality to accompany these virtues. Mr. Wallace was delighted to hear it, especially as it provided the prospect of dividends, and of being able to announce, on the golf tee or at the Cosmos Club, that his son-in-law had been awarded an account with Dow Chemical. ("He's Oakshaw's, you know. The agency.") He lent them a hundred thousand dollars, fifty thousand of it in exchange for shares of preferred stock and the balance as a deferred loan at an interest rate of 17 percent.

The business thrived from its outset. As he had predicted, Ben was able to woo two of Oglesby's clients to his newly unfurled standard—the Wilson people and Harry's Uptown Grill. Others followed quickly, a caterer, a chain of dry cleaners, a computer firm, and a pet cemetery. For the first year he wrote all the copy himself, did much of the acting, and limited his medium to television. He got in touch with a friend of his from the Village who had studied film at UCLA and hired him on a contract basis to do the photography. The young man was very good: technically proficient, ingenious, hungry, and with a gift for parody that Ben put to canny account. For the Pontiac dealership they did a Bertolucci-like elegy which began with the graveside service for a defunct 1942 Hudson Terraplane at which Ben, the survivor, wept into a handkerchief while a minister spoke sonorously of vanished beauty, severed bonds of devotion, rusted rocker panels, and the need for faith in a world of transience. Afterwards, Ben was seen, briefly, mourning beside a crepe-draped photograph of the departed Terraplane, biting his lips and searching the heavens for meaning while the voice-over exhortations of the minister reminded him that life must go on. In the next sequence he was seen bravely entering the showrooms of Wilson's Pontiac in Bethesda where he was greeted by an understanding and discreet young man who conducted him gently to a 1975 Ventura and, while Ben examined the airfoil contours, the sun roof, and the texture of the leather upholstery, explained to him that beauty, which perpetually fades, is perpetually reborn, that man's aspiration is eternal, that the carburetor has been replaced by fuel injection as the darkness of the cave by halogen headlights. During this homily a similar transformation was seen to take place in Ben's eyes as he reached out to lay a tremulous hand on the Deep-Glo, five-coat, kiln-baked, Mediterranean blue enamel finish. In the final scene he was seen driving a Tonneau-Top Monza Special around a spectacular scenic curve of the Skyline Drive at sixty miles an hour, the wind blowing his hair, his face uplifted to the heavens wearing a smile of reborn faith Franciscan in its rapture.

The commercials were a great success, and chiefly for the reason that although Ben gently satirized the world of the marketplace and a society that lived by the production and consumption of merchandise, he had no real quarrel with it. He certainly didn't want to antagonize the merchants and manufacturers who paid for his advertisements any more than the middle class consumers to whom they were addressed. Their tone was genial, indulgent, engagingly ironic. They appealed to everyone, predators and prey alike, and were basically in accord with the world of commerce they amiably mocked. Certainly there was nothing revolutionary about them. They did not deplore the greed or cunning or mendacity of that world, or seek to promote insurgency among its victims. From watching one of Ben's good-natured parodies one would never have got the idea that its author lived outside that world in passionate renunciation of it like a Brecht or Moliére, issuing bitter, brilliant indictments of it. On the contrary, one got the impression that he felt himself very comfortably a part of it and very well aware that he earned his livelihood in it, as did his audience, which was, almost, the case. His clever little caricatures were in fact celebrations of the world they benignly ridiculed, and expressions of his resolve to prosper in it.

Everyone prospered in that innocuous travesty of life that he was helping to invent and in which he sometimes, wistfully, almost believed. There were no real victims; its inhabitants were a fraternity of the fortunate, suffering only the whimsical afflictions of prosperity, indulging one another's innocent chicaneries. There was no real grief, or plight, or poverty. There were no remote, desolate pine barrens or sharecropper shacks, or acres of unweeded strawberry beds stretching relentlessly to the horizon. *That* was the world that Ben had renounced, whose reality he denied, and whose misery he sought to expunge the memory of, like the smell of lard that still clung mysteriously to his clothing, although he now bought his suits at Garfinckel's and had them dry-cleaned once a month.

But while he had renounced that world, he was not genuinely or indigenously a part of the new world that he had won admission to by helping to create it, and he would never be; his appearance of being born to

it was a performance, like the role of the rustic rhapsodist he had once
played in London. He was an actor, always; he could skilfully assume its
manners, wear its costumes and, having a gift for dialect, speak with its
accent. (He had perfected a languid Princeton drawl which he used to
hilarious effect in some of his commercials.) By a convoluted process of
naturalization he had earned the right to walk its streets at liberty, to frat-
ernize with its inhabitants, to cast his vote in it, and in the event of armed
conflict would no doubt have defended it, but not with love. He had no
real devotion or allegiance to it. His real allegiance was to the world that
existed in the mists of his imagination and longing, a world whose spires
and minarets he saw sometimes rising into golden sunlight, as in a dream.
Often these were moments of unease or disorientation from which no mortal is immune—such as when he looked out of his office window at the
dismal end of a February day and watched a bag lady shuffling through
piles of dirty slush along the sidewalks, or when Priscilla drove him to Union
Station to take the Amtrak for a business trip to New York and he walked
hurriedly past the hoboes sleeping on the benches, or when, after an occasional indiscretion on such a trip, he saw Priscilla running to meet
him down the station platform with an expression of innocent, loving
welcome on her face that struck him like the blow of a cudgel on his heart,
or when he signed a six-figure contract for a series of network spots with
a national company that made a large part of its profit by manufacturing
napalm or selling pernicious baby food formula to illiterate women in Nige-
ria. For some reason, events of this kind evoked the fabulous city of his
fantasies with an especial purity and poignancy. It arose out of the dregs
of the day's disappointments or disjunctions or infamies like a vision of
Camelot emerging from the mists, many towered, gleaming, undefiled,
bathed in the golden light of legend, a myth not of the past, but of the
future. Heaving back in his leather-upholstered desk chair and closing
his eyes, he could sometimes see it, literally. At the center of that city
there was a great colonnaded theatre encircled by a stone terrace like
that of the Kennedy Center but immeasurably more magnificent, whose

portals trembled with a vast, suspiring sigh of wonder from the vaulted auditorium within which an audience of The Elect sat spellbound before the final scene of The Supreme Performance, witnessing the denouement of all the earth's dark history.

That his dream city never took form on this earth was something Priscilla did not understand. If it was a disappointment to her, she did not complain of it; she was too long reconciled to the dictates of his genius, and she had too many compensations to express any discontent. It is difficult to express discontent with a man who is an attractive and proficient lover, a charming companion, and by the age of thirty-nine owns an advertising agency with a suite of offices occupying two floors of the Farquhar Building on downtown Connecticut Avenue, a thirty-eight-foot sailboat, a six-bedroom mansion in Great Falls Estates, a magnificent summerhouse at Cape Hatteras, and a membership in the Congressional Country Club.

Whether he had ever intended to found the repertory theatre he had spoken of with such zeal when he had needed money to found his business she did not know; she prayed so. Once, briefly, his enthusiasm seemed to have been revived, and he had made a careful investigation of the prospects. He discovered that a municipal theatre of the kind he had envisioned enjoys a very marginal existence at best. It almost invariably operates on a deficit, and depends for its subsistence on grants from the National Endowment for the Arts, The Ford Foundation, or other private or government subsidies. Such subsidies are not granted indiscriminately to fledgling enterprises with little more in the way of credentials than enthusiasm; they are the reward of years of effort, industry, proven excellence, and indomitable dedication to the arts. These virtues Ben was not prepared to demonstrate in some secondary venture; his advertising business absorbed them all. As it grew in size, it grew in complexity of organization, in the number of people it employed, the sophistication of its techniques and marketing procedures, and in the fury of its struggle with competitors. He had to direct and coordinate the work of a research department that included highly trained specialists in psychology, sociology, linguistics,

nonverbal behavior, economics, and political science. He had to insti-
tute and organize polls into the buying habits of lower class, middle class,
and retired consumers classified by education, profession, and ethnic background. He had to be accurately and contemporarily aware of the eating, clothing, recreational, medical, religious, and financial practices of
every category of every geographical area of the country, and to choreo-
graph the activities of a huge body of technical professionals—script writers, artists, musicians, photographers, actors, editors, makeup artists, wardrobe
and property specialists, color-correction technicians, and a $1,000-per-hour
video-editing studio where 35-millimeter film was transferred, complete
with a sound track composed from as many as twenty coordinated voice-
over takes, to one-inch videotape. He did all this with great intelligence
and energy, and by the time he was thirty-five his agency was famous
and flourishing to the extent that it was almost unchallenged anywhere between Connecticut and Madison Avenues. To compromise so much by
the division of his energy and time, or to risk it on anything of such uncertain prospects as a municipal theatre, would have been reckless to the
point of absurdity. He had spent years struggling to escape the shadow of
obscurity; he had no desire to invite it back into his life. Whatever the
nature of the instinct that animated Ben's every deed and gesture, the
last word one would have chosen to describe it was suicidal.

They spoke less and less of their plans, of what they were going to do
"when we have the theatre," of prospective sites for it, of interesting young
playwrights they "ought to get in touch with," of the amount of money it
would take to erect such a building or to convert a standing structure somewhere in the city. Perhaps Ben's valedictory tribute to his forsaken calling
was the name he gave his advertising agency on its incorporation papers:
Razullo. This was the name of a roguish minstrel character from the Com-
media del Arte who is usually pictured clad in a feathered cap, a tattered
doublet and a pair of drooping hose, strumming a lute and striding jauntily into a derisive world. Ben had a logo designed for his company in
this form, and when she saw it, Priscilla knew in her heart that it was his

parting gesture to the comrades of his youth, to the uncertain glory of the London days, to the promise celebrated with gin-and-it at parties in The Rising Sun and with kisses in the Chelsea nights with rain beating on the windows like gusts of ghostly applause from some phantom theatre in the dark. It was a sound that Ben heard still when he woke in the night.

For we are haunted by the future as well as by the past, and the unborn are as implacable as the dead and the deserted, and on their spectral stages love is not given in vain, and no blessing is spurned, and no vow broken with impunity, and desire does not fail.

II

IT WAS IN MAY, WHEN THE PROGRAM SCHEDULE FOR THE COM-
ING season arrived, that Priscilla ordered tickets for *Thoughts of Love*. It
was an English play, being brought over from London with the original British
cast after a two-year run in the West End. One of the members of the company was its author, an actress named Gillian Davenport whose name Priscilla
remembered because she had been a classmate of Ben's at RADA.

"Ben, listen to this," she said at breakfast when she was reading the brochure.
"That new British play is coming over in June. The one that's been a tremendous hit in London. *Thoughts of Love*. Do you know who wrote it?"

"No."

"Gillian Davenport. Wasn't she in your class at RADA?"

"Jill Davenport. Yes, she was."

"She's in it, too. Isn't that amazing?"

"It's astonishing."

"I didn't know she wrote."

"I didn't either. Jill Davenport. Lord, I haven't thought of her in years."

"What does she look like?" Priscilla studied the brochure, frowning with the effort to recall. "Does she have long red hair?"

"I think she did, yes. God knows what she looks like now. That was thirteen years ago."

"Oh my gosh. You know who she is? Isn't she the girl who danced on the buffet table, and then poured sour cream on your head?"

"My God, she did. I'd forgotten all about it. You know, I read about that play somewhere. In *Time*, I think; but I never put the two together."

"Was she a good actress?"

"Yes, she was. A very clever little actress. But I didn't know she could write."

"Well, apparently she can. She got wonderful reviews in London. Listen to this." She read him encomia from the *Guardian*, the *Observer*, and the *Times* while he munched a slice of cinnamon toast. "'. . . a high romantic comedy in the vein of English satire that runs from Congreve to Coward, laced with cyanide and garnished with a sprig of rue.' Oh, we've got to see this, it sounds like great fun."

"Won't we be down at Hatteras?"

"No, we don't go down until the thirtieth, and it opens on the fifteenth. It'll be fun to see Jill again, don't you think?"

"I suppose so. Although I doubt she'll remember me."

"They all remember you, those people, you know that very well. Remember what Derek said, last year?"

Former classmates of Ben's often came through Washington with British stage productions, and they were festive if somewhat ambiguous occasions. A good many of them toured regularly as featured players with the National Repertory company, people whom Ben vaguely remembered stumbling in ill-fitting armor through the cannon smoke of Academy productions of Marlowe and Shakespeare, now grown somewhat stouter and less exuberant, but still undaunted, rescued from oblivion by some of the same gallantry they had exhibited at Agincourt. One or two of them had become stars, like Derek Slater, the young man Priscilla had referred to. He had won the Bancroft Medal in his last year at RADA, and his promise had been confirmed by leading roles at Stratford and the Old Vic and featured parts in several films. The year before, he had appeared at the Kennedy Center as Coriolanus, which he performed brilliantly, and when Ben and Priscilla had gone backstage afterwards, he had recognized Ben instantly. Still covered with cold cream, he had leapt up from his makeup table and embraced Ben with a fervor that was touching testimony to the affection and esteem Ben had enjoyed at RADA. "My God!" he had exclaimed. "Let's *look* at you. Where have you *been*, Ben? We all thought you'd have set Broadway on fire by this time!"

"Ben's got bigger ideas than that," Priscilla had said loyally. "He's going to have his *own* theatre soon. So he's set the world of advertising on fire, first, to get some capital." It was an almost ritual statement she used on these occasions—wistfully, and perhaps in half-belief—and although Ben did not complain, the evident necessity she felt to explain his defection, and perhaps to apologize for it, cast a faint pall of constraint and embarrassment between them that did not dissipate, sometimes, for several days. Any such embarrassment on the visiting players' part was dispelled promptly and thoroughly by the sumptuousness of the after-dinner supper to which they were generally invited at the Carleton, or the buffet that Priscilla served sometimes in the poolside loggia of the Tudor mansion she and Ben had built at Great Falls. "My God, Ben," they would murmur through mouthfuls of poached salmon or caviar, "no wonder you gave up this bloody business. Do you know I had six years of fortnightly rep at Huddersfield before I got this part? Have you ever been to Huddersfield? Shuddersfield, we called it."

When Priscilla announced the possibility of another such reunion, Ben finished his coffee, set down his cup, and said, "Well, I guess you'd better check it. I'd kind of like to see what sort of play she's written. If the *Observer* says that about it, it can't be all bad."

"I'll get in some oysters and a Smithfield ham and we'll have them over afterwards. She deserves a celebration."

"Oh, I wouldn't make a lot of fuss. We'll just drop by and say hello."

"Oh, we've got to do more than that, Ben. She'll be hurt."

"Well, I wouldn't overdo it. Jill can be an awful bore. You remember how she acted at our wedding."

"Oh, I know, but she was just a kid, having a good time. After all, she's an acclaimed new playwright."

"Well, get the tickets and we'll see what we think of it. It could be very embarrassing to go back afterwards if we think it's awful."

Ben had to be in New York on the opening night, so they ordered tickets for the twelfth, the Friday before they went down to Cape Hatteras for their annual vacation, if they weren't going to Europe for the summer. Priscilla usually stayed for a month; Ben spent the first week with her and then returned to Washington, coming down on weekends until she returned. Often they went down later for an occasional weekend in the fall, when the summer crowds had thinned and the weather was cool but still fine. It was a particularly busy year for Ben and they had no plans for Europe, so they booked the entire summer season at the Kennedy.

Ben enjoyed summer performances at the Kennedy Center. He came home early on those Fridays so that they could dine at the Grande Scene and still have time to stroll on the terrace for half an hour before the curtain, sipping champagne and looking out at the river in the summer evening. Priscilla always looked exquisite in a soft summer gown, her dark hair swept back to shield one ear, fastened at the other with a diamond barrette that matched the jewel-framed cameo glittering in the delicate declivity between her collar bones. Walking beside her in a white dinner jacket and a silk turtlenecked shirt, Ben rejoiced in their splendor, although his consciousness of it was so artfully concealed that no one could possibly have guessed he had once spent his Saturday nights at a softball game or a juke joint in Groveland, Florida, dressed in a Sears, Roebuck shirt with faded elbows and a turned collar.

There had never been a balmier summer evening than the one they had chosen on which to see *Thoughts of Love*, and Priscilla had never looked lovelier. Earlier in the day, Ben had signed the contract for a profitable account, and the combination of circumstances produced a mild state of euphoria in him that relieved his reservations about the evening: weather of surpassing clemency, a wife in the bloom of grace and beauty, a freshly cleaned and finely fitting dinner jacket, a contract for a national account in hand, and the prospect of a holiday at their beautiful summerhouse in Cape Hatteras. As they settled themselves into their box seats and the great star-cluster chandelier dimmed in the domed firmament above them, Ben felt that he had never come closer to experiencing the fabulous performance of his reveries.

When the curtain went up and he saw the set, he began to suspect that this impression was the most mistaken of his life. After the exchange of the first five minutes of dialogue between the two people on the stage, the suspicion had darkened into a dire conviction, and by the time the curtain went down on the first act he was aware that, far from being transported to Elysium, he had been lured into some infernal region like that of Sartre's *No Exit*, although considerably less elegant. There was certainly no escaping that grimy, ominously familiar bed-sitter with its cracked ceramic fireplace, its flickering gas-ring and shilling meter, its ruptured coffee-colored armchair and lopsided Victorian wardrobe, or the window in the rear wall from which, Ben knew, there was a desolate vista across the roofs of Golder's Green into the murk of Mile End, a desert of chimney pots and rain-swept slate, or down into the dismal areaway below, a region of dustbins, battered prams and coal bins where, in a quaint tribute to innocence, a child's swing hung by a soot-stained rope from a scrofulous plane tree. Many of these elements would have been recognized by anyone who had spent his youth in students' digs in London and who might have been touched by a bittersweet throe of nostalgia. Ben was not. There were certain features of the room too flagrantly distinctive: a gigantic, ruinous stuffed bear with a ragged, verminous pelt and a pair of agonized, unmatched glass eyes, decaying in a corner, its paws uplifted in what looked like anguished supplication; the magenta-colored silk scarf draped

delicately about its loins; the bust of Shakespeare on the mantel, wearing
a pair of sunglasses and a boater hat with BUTLIN'S HOLIDAY CAMPS inscribed
on the headband; even—a sinister detail which Ben verified through his
binoculars—a large wall calendar for the month of June of the year 1973,
with each of the five squares lettered THURSDAY marked with an excla-
mation point in scarlet marker pen. Only Ben could have recognized these
picturesque details because only he of all the people in the Eisenhower
Theatre had been in that room before, and perhaps only he of all the
people in the world could have recognized the inimitable, capricious, somehow menacing irreverence of the sensibility they illustrated. The only
exception to this was the actress who presently occupied it, and who gave
the mysterious impression of having occupied it continuously ever since
the moment when she had spoken to Ben the very words she was now
addressing to the indolent young man lying on the daybed in a pair of jockey
shorts. The single mercy of the scene was that this young man was portrayed not as an American but as an Englishman, and not as gnomish, dark,
and wry, but as well over six feet tall and possessed of a weight lifter's physique.
Ben did not fail to recognize himself, however, although he had been
rechristened Ian and endowed with the face of an Adonis. It would have
been impossible, since his words, although spoken with a Lancashire accent, were Ben's own. It was he who had conceived them, spoken them,
and could almost have repeated them while he listened in horrified enchantment.

"What will you do with Humbert," the young man asked, "if you get this
job at Brighton?"

"I'll have him shipped down, naturally. He couldn't live without me."

"You think he'll stand the trip? He's getting on."

"Well, he'd rather perish somewhere between here and Brighton in a
baggage car than dwindle away in despair without me. He's not like *some*."

"He's not like *any* I've ever seen. What's happened to his ear?"

"It fell off yesterday when I was brushing him. I've got to sew it back on."

"Simple as that."

"Oh, yes, with Humbert. Because his heart is pure. Physical decay doesn't matter if one's heart is pure."

"He doesn't have a heart. He's full of sawdust. You ought to know that—we spilled a bushel of it into Tottenham Court Road getting him into that van."

The young woman—Nona was the the name with which Jill had rechristened herself—laughed and drew up her legs into the lotus position in the middle of the table where she was sitting, in a pair of pink panties and a bra. "Poor Humbert," she said. "Half his entrails trodden in the mire of Tottenham Court Road. And yet his dignity isn't diminished by a jot. It's suffering that does it."

"Does what?"

"Ennobles. Didn't you know that? That's one of the great truths."

"That's one of the great platitudes."

"Oh? What does it do, then? Suffering?"

"It stains the soul," he said.

"Well, that's something I wouldn't know about, of course. Not having any. Soul, I mean, not suffering. Which is just as well, because I don't suppose you come here in search of a soulmate."

The young man reached for the glass of beer on the floor beside the daybed, raised himself slightly, and sipped at it, lying back prone and setting it in the center of his belly where he held it with both hands.

"*She* has a soul, of course," the girl said.

He did not reply to this. The young woman refilled her glass from the bottle of Watney's on the table and poked at the froth with her fingertip. After a moment she sighed and shook her head. "I'm sorry to be so bloody-minded. I don't mean to be a bore."

"That's all right. You need some food, I expect. I don't suppose you've eaten since I was here last."

"Oh yes, I have. I had a glass of water and a caraway seed on Friday."

"What you need is good rich Gruyére." He reached for a paper bag lying beside the daybed, raised himself to one elbow, and tossed it to her on the table. She caught it, unfolded the top, peered inside and began eagerly exploring with her fingertips.

"You haven't brought Gruyére? Oh, God, you have! And a tin of pâté? And what's this? Apples! A pair of beautiful red pippins. My God, *you've* got a soul, all right. It's a banquet!"

"I forgot the biscuits."

"That's all right. I've got some, from last week. My God, Ian, you do make splendid gestures, you know." She took an apple out of the bag and bit into it ravenously. "Lord, they're wonderful. That's what you're good at. Beaux gestes." He gave her an ironic glance. "It's nothing to belittle. It's what gives life its flavor, you know, like the plums in pudding. Raleigh laying down his cape for Queen Bess. The charge of the Light Brigade. Damon offering up his life for Pythias. Or Abelard contributing a pair of plums for Heloise's sake. Otherwise, what you've got is just a great lump of suet."

"I'm not sure how long the world would keep going if we all made gestures of that kind." He got up from the daybed. "If you've got an opener, I'll open that pâté."

"It's in the drawer there, with the cutlery. And look up in the closet love, for the biscuits. They're just above the sink."

He went to the table and took the tin of pâté which she handed to him, then moved on to the upper portion of the stage set off by a pair of potted palm trees. Nona watched him appreciatively.

"You look jolly good, you know, in briefs. It's a pity there isn't a part where you can lay about in them all through the play. I'll have to write one for you."

"Don't forget to put a beau geste in it."

"No, you shall have your beau geste."

He found the opener and began to open the tin of pâté. "This thing is very dull. I could do better with my teeth."

"It was Mum's. She gave it to me when I came down from Shropshire. God knows how many tins of Spam it's opened. But bloody few of pâté."

The young man finished sawing open the tin and began to search the upper cupboard for the biscuits. He found a box and took it down.

"Where are the plates?"

"Just there, beside the biscuits."

He found them, took one down, examined it, blew the dust off it, and wiped it on the seat of his underwear.

"You're very fastidious, too," the young woman said. "That's another thing about you that I like. It shows good breeding. You'll get on very well with the gentry."

"'Nice manners courtsey to great kings, Kate.'"

"Oh, lord!" she said "'For your favor, sir, why God give thanks, and make no boast of it.'"

He brought the plates, the biscuits and the tin of pâté to the table and set them down, then paused to study her face for a moment, lifted her chin and looked into her eyes. She returned his gaze steadily.

"You know what your real talent is, don't you," she said. She put out her hands and took him by the waist with her fingertips. "I'm not at all sure I can get along without it."

"You can get along without anyone or anything in the world, if you decide to," the young man said. "You're the most self-sufficient woman I've ever met."

"We'll see."

"That's why we get along."

"Why we *got* along."

"Well, we've had a pretty good innings, haven't we? Time to break for tea." He picked up the knife and dipped it into the pâté. "How about a biscuit and pâté?"

"I'll have a slice of Gruyére first, to go with the apple."

"How's the apple?"

"It's divine."

He began to slice the Gruyére thoughtfully. "Do you write plays, then?" he asked.

"No. I used to write novels, though, when I was twelve."

"Did you really? What were they about?"

"Incest, murder, rape, pillage. Things of that kind. Jolly good they were, too."

"It sounds it. Why don't you send them off to a publisher? You'll make a fortune."

"I don't want a fortune."

"No?" He handed her the cheese with a biscuit. "What do you want?"

"I want to tell the truth." He looked at her without expression. "I want to find out what the rewards of truth are, in this world."

"It's just as well you don't want to make a fortune, then, judging by what happened to Socrates, and Galileo, and Jesus Christ."

"Perhaps they didn't know how to play it right. Truth can be used like an ace in a poker hand, you know. If you play it right, you can win the pot."

He put a cracker in his mouth and chewed it for a moment. "I wonder if you'd give me an example of that."

"Well, for example, you find out a certain amount of scientific truth and you make an atom bomb with it. Then you intimidate everyone else in the world, and get your way."

"You win the pot."

"Exactly."

"And suppose they don't give you your way? Suppose they call your hand?"

"Well, then you have to show it, of course. You blow them up."

"I see. And truth prevails."

"That's it. In either case. Of course they'd be much better off if they didn't want to see it."

He cut a slice of cheese for himself and bit into it. "I didn't know you were interested in truth. I think you're in the wrong business, if that's what turns you on."

"I don't know how you reckon that."

"Well, it's a strange sort of world to spend your life in, if you believe in truth. Wigs and makeup and fanciful costumes, cardboard castles, and painted trees, and dry ice for cannon smoke."

She looked at him levelly for a moment. "It's silly to say things you don't believe."

"You don't think I believe that?"

"No. I might, if I hadn't seen you play Richard, or Cyrano. That wasn't make-believe."

"Oh? What was it, then?"

"I would have said you were living. That you'd stopped making believe for a while."

"Well, whatever it was, it lasted for about an hour. Truth lasts a good bit longer, I believe. It's supposed to be eternal."

"And when we were rolling about on the bed there, just now, like a pair of ruddy eels—that lasted about an hour, too. Was that make-believe, I wonder."

"That was bed truth."

"Oh. Something like the stage."

"Yes. Something."

"Not eternal."

"No." There was a stark pause. "You never expected it to be, did you?"

She lowered her eyes, touched one fingertip to the tabletop and said gently, "I don't think one ever expects it, in this world. I think it always comes as sort of a huge surprise."

The young man went back to the daybed, picked up his glass of beer and brought it to the table, pulling out a chair and sitting down to face her where she sat with her legs crossed. After staring at her for a moment, he leaned forward, took her toes in his fingers and began to kiss them, one by one.

"Why are you kissing my toes?" she asked.

"I don't know. I was overcome by a depraved impulse."

"They're the most reliable ones you have, I think. I just wish they lasted a bit longer." She made herself a canapé of pâté and munched it for a moment while he went on kissing her toes. "With her, I suppose, it's eternal?"

The young man considered this for some time, studying the foot he held. "I don't think that's quite fair, you know. After all, I didn't have to come up here today."

"Oh, didn't you?"

"No."

"Why did you come up here, exactly?" He did not answer. "You can't pass up anything that's going, is that it? A last little tumble in the hay, and then you'd kiss me on the cheek — or kiss my toes, perhaps — and say, 'Thanks awfully, Ducks. I'm afraid I've got to run now. I'll be late.'"

"That's pretty bloody savage," he said. "And it's a lie. It was your idea, wasn't it?"

"Was it? I've forgotten whose idea it was, exactly." She cut a slice of apple and began to munch it. "Just what is it you're so afraid you're going to be late for, anyway?"

The young man looked at his watch; then, evidently deciding to treat this faux pas as a deliberate piece of parody, he grinned and said, "My entrance, love. My debut, at the Vic."

"Yes, well if *my* father were a baronet, and *I* rode to hounds on week-ends, and gave house parties at Chatsworth, I don't suppose you'd be in such a bloody hurry."

The young man replaced her foot in its original position, stood up and went to the window where he stuck his hands into the waistband of his jockey shorts and looked out at the London skyline. The young woman looked for a moment at his back, nibbling her apple.

"Well, isn't it true?" she asked.

"It's just as true," he said, "as the fact that if I were humpbacked and had green stuff coming out of my ears, you wouldn't give a damn whether I left or not."

"I don't know," she said. "It might be a change. Girls like a change."

"You don't, evidently."

"I'm not quite ready for a change yet."

"Oh? Just when do you think you'll be ready?"

"That's something one never knows, isn't it? When I am, I'll let you know."

"I don't recall that either of us took out a lease on the other's soul."

"You're always going on about souls. I haven't said anything about your soul. I'm not at all sure you have one, any more than me." She bit into her apple and wiped her fingers on her panties. "I should think this girl would be rather uncomfortable, actually, with a soulless lot like us. What does she know about actors?"

"What is there to know about actors?"

"Well, we may not know who we are, but we know what we're not. And what we're not is real. The only time we're real is when we're imitating other people. You just said so yourself. Pretending to be kings and queens in some make-believe land of pasteboard castles and painted landscapes. What's she going to do, associating with a pack of fairy-tale creatures like us? She'll go out of her pretty little mind." She finished the apple and hurled the core across the room, striking the mirror of the armoire. "Bloody little county poppet, mucking about with actors. Slumming."

The young man turned to look at her. "I don't think we're any different from anyone else," he said. "Most people get penalized for being undignified, that's all. We get paid for it."

"If we're very lucky. If not, we get run out of town."

He grinned at her. "Well, you can't blame them for that," he said. "Swimming naked in the Serpentine at midnight. Peeing in the tulip beds in Hyde Park. Stealing stuffed bears."

She laughed, suddenly transformed into elfin merriment. "Only very *old* stuffed bears! Ones that aren't properly attended to. Ones that need love desperately."

"I think this relationship between you and that bear has gone far enough," he said. "People are beginning to talk."

"Rubbish. It's just healthily erotic. I'm not going to *marry* him, you can be sure of that."

"Not even if he's made a baronet?"

"No bloody fear." She began to cut more cheese. "He's not nearly decayed enough to be made a baronet. I shouldn't marry him in any case. What I don't understand is why you want to get married at all. It's so stupid. I suppose if one is a stockbroker or a butcher or something, it's a good thing to be married, but what's the point of it, in your case? I mean you're not keen on having a garden, or a pigeon loft, or doing woodwork in the basement, or anything of that sort, are you? Perhaps you want children, is that it?"

"Yes. I want to have twelve, and teach them all to tap dance, and get up a music hall act called The Flying Fanshaws and Their Dancing Dozen."

"Oh, I didn't realize that. Why don't you train poodles? They're much more manageable."

"Do you want another Black Velvet?"

"Have we got any?"

"I think we can do another round." He went into the kitchenette, opened the refrigerator, lifted the champagne bottle to judge its level, then poured from it into her empty glass, added stout from the Guinness bottle and handed it to her. She took it and sipped, hunching her shoulders ecstatically.

"God, that stuff is good! It reminds me of the day we went up along the Thames to Maidenhead and drank it all afternoon."

"And you fell out of the punt."

"I was *pushed* out. I shan't forget that. That's one I owe you."

"You were nothing of the sort, you were drunk as a lord. Still, you looked very regal, wrapped up in that tablecloth. Like a maharanee." He grinned at her. "I shall never forget you riding back to London in that bus with that tablecloth wrapped around you and that imperial smile on your face."

"We've had some jolly good fun, you know."

"Yes, I know that." He frowned and gazed at the floor for a moment. "I don't know why you can't leave it at that. No regrets. No hard feelings. And thanks for making the trip a bit pleasanter."

"It sounds like Noël Coward."

"There's a great deal of truth in Noël Coward. He's much maligned. I don't understand why he was never knighted."

"He wasn't properly reverent; that isn't hard to reckon."

"I suppose not." He raised his eyes from the floor and grinned at her. "Which ought to be a lesson to you. You'll never be Dame Nona Candlish if you go on the way you are."

"I know. Don't think I don't lie awake at night and wrestle with the thought." She sipped again from her glass. The young man took the bottles to the window where he had left his glass and replenished it. "*You'll* be knighted, you know," she said.

"Oh, yes. Lord Fanshaw of Liverpool. Bloody likely."

"It's quite true. There'll be an Ian Fanshaw Diction Prize at RADA, and a bust of you in the main hall, with your dates on a brass plaque underneath. I intend to scratch a little legend on it with a penknife: 'He pushed girls out of punts.'" The young man snorted. "You don't think that's properly reverent, I suppose."

"I think it's bloody rubbish."

"Perhaps there'll be an Ian Fanshaw Memorial Theatre, and I shall play in it one day. Now there's a solemn thought."

"Well, I hope you don't wear fishnet tights, as you did for Ariel."

The young woman burst into an odd, raucous howl of laughter, spilling beer into her lap. "Do you remember poor old Sir Roger panting away out there in his box? I could hear him all the way up on the stage, like an espresso machine."

The young man opened the refrigerator door, replaced the bottles, and was about to close the door again when he paused, stared inside with something like horror, and said, "Good God. What's this black, leathery thing in here?"

The young woman turned and looked toward him. "Black leathery thing? I have no idea. What's it look like?"

"It looks rather like a bat."

"A bat?"

"Yes. It's in a bowl. With some sort of vile liquid. Are you marinating a bat?"

"No, don't be stupid. Bring it here, let's have a look at it."

He reached into the fridge, lifted out a bowl, and holding it at arm's length with a look of revulsion, carried it to the table and held it out for her to examine.

"It does look like a bat." She leaned closer and sniffed at it, then withdrew her head quickly, her face convulsed. "Aagh! My God! It's certainly not a bat. Not the ordinary, decent sort, anyway. I've no idea what it is. I haven't looked in there, actually, for months."

"Decades, I should think. What shall we do with it? Would you like a bit, with the pâté?"

"No, don't be disgusting. I think you'd better throw it out the window."

"That's a jolly good idea." He went to the window, set down the bowl, and tugged up at the sash. Looking down into the areaway below, he said, "I see you've got that ruddy swing back up. How'd you manage that?"

"The dustman put it up for me. He's an awfully nice chap."

"You'll fall again, and break your neck."

"No, I shan't. I got some new rope from the ironmonger's. It's perfect now. I tried it yesterday."

"It rained yesterday."

"I know. It was lovely."

"You really are insane, you know. If you don't break your neck, you'll get pneumonia."

"Oh, no. I used to swing in the rain all afternoon sometimes, when I was a child in Shropshire. From the plane tree in the garden."

Leaning out as far as possible, the young man turned the bowl upside down and dumped the nameless black object into the areaway below. After watching for a moment, he cried, "Good Lord! One of those cats has got it."

"No."

"He has! I think he's going to eat it."

The young woman leapt off the table and sped across the room to where he stood beside the window, peering down into the areaway, her hands on the sill. "My God, he is," she said with awe. "What do you think we ought to do?"

"What can we do? He's got half of it down already."

"Oh, Ian, look! He's munching on it. The poor beast, he'll die in agony."

"No, he'll be quite all right. They're used to dining on offal, that sort of cat. They thrive on it." He straightened up and put his arm about her waist. "'An army of invincible canaille.'"

She put her arm about his waist in turn and looked up at him.

"Who said that?"

"I did. It's the only thing I ever wrote."

"Just the one line? That's your entire *oeuvre*?"

"Yes. Its the last line of a story I thought I might write one day. That's all I've done of it so far."

"You've started at the end?"

"Yes. I always feel more comfortable knowing the ends of things."

"What's it to be about, this story of yours?"

"About being poor. About the way certain smells never leave you, if you've been poor, like the smell of greasy clothing. And about the transformation of desire." The young man smiled and then lowered the corners of his mouth in an ironic grin. "I shall never write it, however. Perhaps you'd like to."

She gazed at him with a look of solemn, disarmed, suddenly humbled tenderness. "You're a bloody strange man, you know," she murmured in a moment.

He took her into his arms, looking into her face. Their arms tightened about each other in a sudden gust of desire. "And you're a bloody seductive creature," he said harshly. "You bloody gypsy."

"You'd like a bit more before you leave, wouldn't you?" she said. He did not answer. "You think you've had enough?" He still did not reply. She leaned a little away to look up into his face. "Suppose I do as you say? Let you go with no more fuss at all. Just say no regrets, and thanks for the memory. Would you make a bargain with me?"

"What sort of a bargain?"

"Well, I ought to have something in return, I think. Don't you? I mean there's got to be a fair exchange."

"What do you want in exchange?"

"I want you to promise that you'll come back again. Just once more. That's very little to ask."

"You're out of your mind. I'm going to be married next week."

"Oh, I don't mean before. I mean after."

"After I'm married? You're absolutely insane. You don't honestly think I'd come back here after I'm married?"

"Well, you'd like a bit more right now, wouldn't you? Why not next week? And you don't want me to make a fuss."

"You're bloody outrageous, that's what you are."

"No, I'm just a gypsy, as you say. A beggar at the world's gate. I eat crumbs from underneath the banquet table in the great hall. I live on the leavings of the lords. Haven't you got a scrap to throw me, like the cat?"

The young man looked into her eyes for several moments, then drew her more closely against him. She put her hands behind her and unfastened the strap of her brassiere, letting it fall to the floor. Their arms tightened about each other fiercely as the curtain fell.

When it came down, Ben sat with his face drawn, his hands clamped on the arms of his chair, his armpits dampened by a cold sweat. Occasionally, in the course of the abominable scene, he had glanced at Priscilla, who seemed to be enjoying it thoroughly, her absorbed and innocent smile waxing sometimes into a soft chuckle. Once, she had turned to whisper to him. "I didn't know she was so clever, did you?" and he had murmured, "No, I didn't," shaking his head with a wan smile. A round of spontaneous applause greeted the ending of the first scene, and when the house lights went up there was the sudden happy bustle and swelling of conversation that signifies a successfully beguiled audience. There were smiles all around and people turned to each other with animated whispers.

"I think it's marvelous," Priscilla said. "I don't know whether to laugh or cry. It's really very absorbing, I think. Don't you?"

"I don't know," Ben said. "I thought it was a little tedious in spots, but it's quite amusing." He glanced quickly at his program and read with dismay:

SCENE II
The same one-room flat in Hammersmith.
One month later.

"She's a good actress, too," Priscilla said. "She's got all sorts of vitality."

"Yes." He plunged his hands suddenly into his trouser pocket and felt about feverishly with a great show of consternation.

"What's the matter?" Priscilla said.

"Good Lord. Do you know what I've done?"

"No."

"I've locked the keys into the car."

"Ben, you haven't."

"Yes. It just occurred to me. I'd better go and see."

"What can you do? You'll have to call a locksmith."

"No. I know a trick to get the door open. I'll get a wire clothes hanger from the cloak room and bend it into a hook. You just lift up the lever with it."

"But you'll miss the second scene."

"Oh, it'll only take a few minutes. I'd better do it now, so you won't have to wait around afterwards, if she wants to go out for a drink or something."

"Oh, it's a shame. Do it after the show."

"No, I'll feel a lot easier about it if I do it now." He stood up and went out of the box, through the small anteroom and into the hall, closing the door behind him. He went rapidly down the carpeted stairs to the lobby and then a second flight of four stairs to the Grand Foyer. A bartender in a white jacket was setting up the small portable bar for the intermission trade, lining up bottles of green olives and cocktail onions. Ben bought a

glass of champagne and carried it out to the far end of the terrace, a hundred yards away, set it down on the parapet, glanced down at his watch,
took out a silver case and lighted a cigarette. For twenty-five minutes he
stood smoking and sipping from the champagne glass, looking out at the
blaze of lights from Crystal City on the Virginia shore and watching the
traffic on the river. A large cabin cruiser, its running lights blinking in
the dark, was moving steadily upstream toward Key Bridge and the cluster of the Three Sisters islands in the center of the river. The sight produced
a kind of nebulous analogue in Ben's mind of boats, bodies of water, distant islands, refuge. It seemed to him suddenly that all his life he had
been in flight from something, from some nameless disgrace that had never,
until this moment, overtaken him. It had grinned at him from the sweet
potato vines in Florida, and he had fled to Vietnam. In the bunkers, it
had plucked at his sleeve, and he had fled to the Marine Guard School,
and from that to RADA. The almost certainly dire tidings from his father, enclosed in a tattered, thrice-readdressed envelope, the only one he
had ever received since his flight from Florida, he had never read. He
had dropped the envelope, unopened, into the toilet of their flat in Green-
wich Village and flushed it away, like another bit of the ordure of his youth.
The shame he felt at the destitution of the derelicts in Union Station
and the bag ladies plodding through the February slush he had dismissed
with a handsome annual check to United Way, and the divagations of
his own incoherent nature with a ferocious show of industry, a mansion
in Great Falls, a dinner jacket, and a dream. It seemed that none of these
was proof against the ignominy that all his life had stalked him, stealthily
and shapelessly, like the evening fog stealing up the Potomac.

He smoked another cigarette and finished his champagne, glancing occasionally at his watch. When twenty minutes had elapsed, he went back
down the terrace to the glass portals, reentered the Main Hall, set his
glass on the bar, and went up the carpeted steps into the lobby. The second scene was still in progress. Instead of going up the stairs to his box,
he stepped into the auditorium and stood at the back to watch the last

few minutes of the scene, his arms folded, with a look of fortitude across his chest.

The young man was now dressing himself, preparatory to leaving the flat. He stood at the table buttoning his shirt while the girl lay on the daybed in a scarlet silk Hopi coat, supported on one elbow, watching him.

"You've got a button missing," she said. "I thought you had a wife now." He did not reply. "Can't she sew?" The young man raised his head to stare at her balefully. "I should think she could afford a maid, at any rate."

"I thought there was to be no more fuss," he said. "Wasn't that your part of the bargain?"

"I'm not fussing. I'm just concerned about your welfare."

"Very misbegotten concern," he said. "Do you know how I lost that button? Just now, when you were ripping my shirt off in your ungovernable passion."

"That's a bloody canard. Ungovernable passion? You couldn't wait to get out of it."

The young man stooped, picked up a button from the floor and held it aloft triumphantly in his fingertips. "What's it doing here, then, on the floor? Just where it fell, when you clawed it off."

The young woman got up from the daybed and went across to the window seat which she lifted on its hinges, bending down to scrabble about in its depths with her fingertips.

"What are you looking for?" he asked.

"Needle and thread. I've got it here somewhere."

"Don't be ostentatious," he said. "You've never sewed a stitch in your life."

"Bloody lot you know about it. How do you think my hose get mended? Who was it put Humbert's ear back on?"

"On backwards, I might point out. I don't want you mucking about with my buttons. I don't want them on backwards."

"Since you insist I'm responsible, I'm going to fix it. I intend to repair any damage I may have done you before you leave here."

"I haven't the time, love. That'll take months."

"You haven't the time!" She found the thread and stood up, standing with one hand on her hip to smile at him bitterly. "You haven't the time. Not even for your own lot." She advanced upon him, holding out her hand. "Let's have it."

After a moment of hesitation he put it into her hand. She drew out a chair and sat down in front of him, her hands at working level with his chest. She threaded the needle, held the button to his shirtfront and began to sew it on in a leisurely, surprisingly feminine way, as if she were born to such tasks, while she sang softly a Scottish folk tune:

Can ye sew cushions, and can ye sew sheets?
And can ye sing, "Baloo-loo," when the babe greets?
Money, oh, it's little I hae to gie ye,
And black's the life that I'll lead wi' ye.

The young man laid his hand on her hair. "You have rather a sweet voice, you know," he said. She leaned forward and bit the thread through, then looked up at him. He examined the button. "My God, you *can* sew," he said. "I wouldn't have dreamt it." She stood up and looked into his eyes. "Now you'll take care of Humbert, won't you?" he said. "See that he gets a proper diet, and plenty of exercise?"

"Oh yes, he'll be well taken care of."

He evidently found it difficult to think of anything further to say. He lowered his eyes to the table where his glass sat beside a bottle in which there remained a very small amount of champagne. "Well, there's enough left for a loving cup," he said. He poured the champagne into the glass and handed it to her. She took it, looked into it for a moment, raised and sipped at it, then closed her eyes and said, "Saint Genesius, pray for us."

"Who is Saint Genesius?" he asked.

"The patron saint of actors. Didn't you know that?"

"No. I'm surprised that you did. I didn't know you were up on the saints."

"It's my single piece of ecclesiastical lore."

"You've managed with just the one?"

"Just the one, yes."

"Well, it must be a very effective one. I'll remember it."

"I hope you do."

She handed the glass to him. He raised it, finished the champagne, and set it on the table. She stood waiting. For a moment it seemed that he was about to take her into his arms; then he smiled broadly, turned and went briskly to the door. He opened it, stepped out into the landing, and with his hand on the knob, stood watching her for a moment from the hall. Then the door closed tight to the sill with a final click of the latch. The young woman stood staring at it, motionless, as the curtain fell.

Ben went out of the auditorium to the lobby and up the stairs to his box. Priscilla sat anxiously awaiting him.

"Oh, Ben you *missed* it," she said, holding out her hand to him.

"No, no. I watched some of it downstairs, at the back. I saw a good bit of it."

"Did you really? I was so afraid you'd miss the whole scene. Did you get the keys?"

"Yes, no trouble at all. I did my wire trick. I'd have been fretting about it all through the scene if I hadn't. You want to go down for a drink?"

"Yes, a double, I'm a wreck." She dabbed at her eyes with a handkerchief she held crumpled in her hand. "I've wept a gallon of tears, I think."

"Have you?"

"Yes, God, it was so poignant. Wasn't it?"

"Pretty weepy stuff."

They went down to the lobby and Ben bought them champagne. They carried their glasses out onto the terrace and stood at the parapet. Priscilla seemed lost in thought. "Were you there when she danced with the bear?"

"No, I missed that," Ben said.

"Oh, you *did*? Oh, that's a pity. It was hilarious. It was on roller skates, on that little platform thing. And she did a sort of tango with it, and then jumped up on the table and finished it off with a saraband, like she did at our reception. You remember?"

"Yes, I remember that."

"It's a terribly moving play, I think. I can't imagine what's going to happen in the second act. Do they get together again, do you suppose?"

"Oh, I doubt it. After all, it's a piece of bathos, isn't it? Like a popular ballad. They're all sad and sweet. 'Send in The Clowns.'"

"Oh, it's more than that. Now be fair. It has genuine feeling. I hope you're right, though. I'd just as soon she never saw him again. That awful young man."

"You don't like him?"

"Well, he's clever enough, and very good-looking, but thank God I don't know anyone like him. Imagine falling in love with a man like that."

"You think she's in love with him?"

"Oh, yes, there's no doubt about that. Don't you?"

"Well, I don't think of her as Camille, exactly. Just a rather sweet little soubrette. I don't think she's capable of any grand passions."

"You don't?" She sipped her champagne. "Don't you like her?"

"Not very much," he said. "I don't like anybody in it, except the bear."

Priscilla laughed. "He's lovely, isn't he? It was marvelous when she danced with him. This great, solemn, tattered bear, with his boater hat on. He looks a bit like W. C. Fields. There's a kind of zany, grubby, gritty quality about this play that I love. I suppose comedy is really only possible in a badly fallen world."

"What do you mean by that?" Ben said.

"Well, I mean you've got to have imperfection and disaster to make comedy. Why is a great clown like W. C. Fields funny? Because he makes a kind of parody of dignity, and probity, and virtue. He certainly doesn't have any *real* virtue, and there probably isn't any on earth. But you understand, somehow, through the parody, what it is, real virtue. And that it's only possible in a very wicked world. There can't be any clowns in heaven."

"Or any angels on earth," Ben said.

"Exactly. That's what's sad about it." She sipped champagne and watched the distant twinkling lights of the cruiser which Ben had seen a few minutes before, now disappearing into the darkness upstream. "There was a heresy in the church once; I've forgotten what it was called—the Doctrine of Absolute Depravity, I think. Isn't that an awful name? Anyway, it maintained that because this is a fallen world, you can't believe anything anyone says in it. Because we're all corrupt, we have a corrupt version of the truth. What we call truth is actually falsehood, and what we call falsehood is actually truth. So the only people we can have any faith in at all are the deceivers, the passionate liars of this world. I always think of that, when I go to the theatre."

"And it doesn't spoil the fun?"

"Oh, no, it adds to it."

"Well, whatever Jill has done, she's put you into a very philosophical state of mind."

"Yes, she has."

"Well, we'd better get back and see how she resolves this paradox."

The second act, far from resolving it, was so cunningly convoluted that it seemed to Ben, if anything, more sinister than the first. In the course of it, Nona moved out of her lugubrious lodgings in Hammersmith and on through a succession of living quarters and lovers—six of each—men and habitations alike, fell into eventual ruin as a result of the chaos that seemed to characterize all her romantic and domestic interludes. Only with the last of these men did her relationship survive, apparently because it was platonic rather than connubial and thus immune to her proclivity for havoc, as was their apartment. Far from being ruinous and rancid, it was a pleasant, sunny, old-fashioned flat in Knightsbridge furnished with handsome Victorian pieces, a rococo mantel clock (which ran), and antimacassars pinned to the backs of all the chairs. Her companion, and the owner of this establishment, was a journalist, a kindly, genial man named Clarence, twice her age, who read to her from Trollope in the evenings, or cued her with her lines if she was learning a new part for a play. She had met him in a local pub when she discovered that she had left her purse behind and couldn't pay for her beer. He stood the cost of this and many of her other lapses with a shy and courtly air of privilege, as if he were giving succor to a princess in distress. Freed of the frenzies of romance, she lived with him if not in what could be called permanent and confirmed serenity, at least in a kind of bated quietude, like a novice of uncertain prospects in a convent. Up to this point the only constant in her hectic, makeshift life aside from her profession, which she practiced with unfaltering devotion, was Humbert, the bear, who accompanied her everywhere, through every doomed affair and disintegrating dwelling, himself growing in debility, although in dignity, at every move. In Clarence's flat he enjoyed a distinguised situation in an alcove between a pair of bookcases, his boater hat set jauntily above his decomposing ears, his mismatched eyes twinkling sagaciously, like a shaggy, sanguine saint in a cathedral niche. The household had an air of mutual respect and admiration, untrammeled liberty, and a kind of bemused concern for one another's welfare, an atmosphere very salutary for Nona's career.

Eventually, her dedication to the stage was rewarded; she served an apprenticeship in provincial repertory, began to get occasional featured roles in London, then a season at the National Theatre, then leads in West End productions. She grew in confidence, skill, and recognition. Twelve years after her desertion by Ian she had become a star, while Ian, for whom she had predicted knighthood, came no closer to nobility than the bed of the titled lady for whom he had abandoned her. For years he had lived idly on this lady's bounty until, weary of his indolence and apparently inveterate promiscuity, she had divorced him. This Nona learned from newspaper reports which dwelt merrily and almost constantly upon his escapades. The latest of these had been his attempt to auction off an emerald necklace belonging to his ex-wife which had apparently been missing since his departure from her bed and board. Nona cut these stories out of the newspapers, clipped them together, and kept them in the drawer of her dressing table. The latest of them included a photograph of him at the Asssizes, twenty pounds heavier, his eyes encircled by a pair of baggy rings, his cheeks and spirits beginning to sag perceptibly. She slid it into the frame of her dressing table mirror where it provided an edifying contrast to the glow of beauty and success reflected in the glass while she made up her face.

She had never been lovelier, not even in her first-act nubility, and her success was of a kind that she would never have dared to predict. She had reached the point in her profession where she was able to choose parts she considered suitable from the many scripts submitted to her by playwrights and producers. These roles she performed to acclaim, but never to her entire satisfaction. None of them combined ideally the qualities of her peculiar, scratchy, ardent, somewhat crazed, and resolute nature— which was not unusual, because few such plays are written.

She decided to write one for herself, a play that would be the perfect vehicle for her, one that would give her the opportunity to express fully the range of her odd personality, and her views on life as well.

As she wrote it, she sought the advice and encouragement of Clarence, her guide and comforter in all things who, as it turned out, had as keen a critical faculty for drama as he had for life. He counseled her patiently and shrewdly on its plot, characters, and settings, consoled her when her spirits flagged, scolded her when she was lazy, and nursed the play into being. When she had finished it he brought home a bottle of champagne to celebrate and toast its success.

It was called *Magic*. It described the relationship between an aging, dissolute music hall entertainer and a young woman, named Deirdre, who was his assistant in the shabby, rather faded magic show that toured the length of the British Isles. She was the fourth such assistant he had had, and the fourth to perform in the offstage role of his mistress. Her duties, apart from gracing his bed, were to stand decoratively about in a sequined leotard, carry properties on and off the stage with a pretty flourish, and, in the show's final and supreme illusion, to step into a gilded pasteboard

cabinet and, after the door was closed, to shriek with agony each time
the magician plunged a rapier through it from one side to the other. After three such terrifying sword thrusts, the door was opened and there stepped
out, smiling and intact, not the young lady but the magician himself, complete with opera hat, cape, and voluminous black beard. He bowed to what
appeared to be his twin on the stage, who tossed aside the rapier, whisked
off his silk hat, cape, and false beard, and was revealed to be none other
than Deirdre, radiant, unperforated, and smiling enigmatically. It was a
truly startling illusion, the pièce de résistance of the otherwise common-
place repertoire, and managed to keep the show booked fairly constantly
from Caithness to Land's End. It served to sustain them in the careless,
ragged, vagrant existence they cherished, the strolling players' lot of fish-
and-chips and beer and damp provincial music halls and holidays at Black-
pool. It was obvious that Deirdre asked no more of life than this perilous,
vagabond existence so long as she continued to share the bed of the bearded,
black-eyed, silver-tongued magician by whom she was nightly impaled and
transfigured. It was for her an idyll, one that it seemed would never end,
until, in a Brighton public house on a rainy afternoon, he met a barmaid with bright blue eyes and a buxom figure in whom he saw the suc-
cessor to Deirdre's sequined arts. When he made this known to Deirdre,
she bore the news in silence, with the fortitude of those used to the illusion
and ephemerality of life, those who ply the tinsel trade of minstrelsy. The
unhappy drama ended with Deirdre's final performance of the last act of
the magic show: the sword-and-cabinet illusion, which she was playing for
the last time before surrendering her role, her lover, and her happiness
to the Brighton barmaid. She stepped into the gilded cabinet in her fishnet tights, her spangled bodice and rhinestone diadem, and smiled at
the magician as he closed the door upon her. He stepped back, drew his
rapier, thrust it through the cabinet, and, as a cry of agony rang out, the
curtain fell.

This mesmerizing moment of the never-to-be-completed illusion taking place on the stage of an imaginary music hall in Glasgow was, as

well, the last moment of the play called *Magic* in which it occurred and which was being performed on the stage of the Victoria Theatre in Birmingham in the course of a play called *Thoughts of Love* that was being performed on the stage of the Eisenhower Theatre in Washington, D.C. All three of these entertainments came to an end at the same moment, and when the curtain fell, it cut off all that would ever be known of the destiny of the unhappy music hall performer named Deirdre, who was played by an actress named Nona, who was played by an actress named Jill. It also cut off all that would be known of the history of the treacherous magician, who was played by an actor named Ian, who was played by an actor listed in the Kennedy Center program as Colin Winthrop, but whose true identity only Ben, of all the people witnessing the powerful and unsettling illusion that had been woven before them, was aware of.

Why had Nona given the role of the magician to Ian, the man who had deserted her twelve years before? There was much to suggest that it was her purpose in writing it, although she seemed astonished when he appeared at auditions to try out for the part. Perhaps she truly was. Perhaps she was merely moved by his destitution and by the magnanimity that is one of the graces of success to forgive him, to rescue him from the adversity into which he had fallen. Perhaps she loved him still. Perhaps she loathed him, and planned some nameless vengeance. It would not be known. The devious ingenuity of the play itself forbade it, and its ominous and cryptic final scene seemed almost to taunt the audience with such questions rather than to answer them. Perhaps they were unanswerable.

They were darkly tantalizing, however. Ben could not dismiss them, nor could he dispel the strange impression that the play was still in progress somewhere. When the curtain came down, he had the eerie feeling that the dire illusion within an illusion within an illusion was still proceeding toward its climax in some shabby, spectral music hall where revelation loomed amid the dust and smell of sizing and the glitter of sequins in the gloom.

As they made their way back through the maze of concrete corridors toward the dressing rooms, he made an effort to quell his sense of impend-
ing doom by a fervid, determined exercise of reason. After all, it was
twelve years since he had seen the girl. They had gone their ways, followed
their separate destinies, worked out their lives successfully. She had far
too much to occupy her and to rejoice in to be concerned with him any
longer. She was now a celebrated young actress and playwright, no doubt
with film offers already swarming in, with hosts of new friends and admirers,
a burgeoning career, a busy, productive life in the theatre. What possible
rancor could she harbor in her heart toward him? What absurd desire
for revenge? Their affair had been casual, impulsive and ephemeral, like
so many in the theatre. What possible claim could she have on him now?
It was ridiculous, the sense of imminent disaster that clung to his heart
like a vulture to a lump of carrion.

No sooner had he arrived at this conclusion than he knew it to be
self-deception. The play he had just witnessed could not have been written out of anything like fond nostalgia, or reconciliation, or forgiveness.
There was a hard, dark, inextinguishable pain about it, like that of her eyes
as she had watched him depart for the last time from the door of that awful flat, and her attitude as she had re-lived the moment on the stage was
equally and memorably ominous, a frail, funky Medea from Hammersmith in chalk-white panty hose and a vinyl skirt.

But if there was malevolence in Jill's heart, there was only innocence in
her manner. There was certainly nothing ominous or invidious about
her when she greeted Ben and Priscilla in her dressing room. On the
contrary, she was affectionate, spontaneous and charming, full of what
seemed to be genuine surprise and delight to see them both, as viva-
cious, garrulous and gay as in her bear-kidnapping days; and when she stood
up at her dressing table to greet them, her makeup-soiled smock falling
to cover her momentarily revealed, bone-white, bare, remembered thighs,
a faint throe of desire rang thinly in Ben's heart like the chiming of
a fallen coin. She stood without moving for a moment, her mouth

widening in an astonished O before she held out her arms and came quickly across the cluttered room to embrace them.

"*Ben*," she said, in a voice low with wonder. "*Priscilla.* Oh, how lovely. How absolutely wonderful to see you. And how sweet of you to come back." She kissed them both, on both cheeks, clutching them to her and mumbling tenderly.

"Hello, Jill," Ben said. "It's good to see you. You were wonderful."

"You were," Priscilla said. "And so is the play. We were utterly enchanted."

"Oh, thank you, love. Is it all right? God, I'd rather you two thought so than anyone else in the world. Do you know, I was *hoping* you'd come to see it, but I didn't dare to believe it."

"We wouldn't have missed it for the world," Priscilla said. "Ever since we got the season's program we've been lunging at the bit. And you've certainly repaid it. What a magical evening you've given us."

"God, you don't know how sweet it is to hear that. Here, let me look at you." She held them at arm's length and peered at them with a sort of ravenous affection, smiling like a child on Christmas morning. "My God, you haven't changed a bit, either of you. You look absolute infants. How on earth do you do it? What is it, twelve years?"

"Something like that," Ben said. He smiled quaintly.

"I can't believe it. I simply can't. Do you know, this makes the whole tour worthwhile, seeing you two again. I *heard* you were in Washington, from Derek—I ran into him not long ago, and he said you'd come to see him in *Coriolanus*—and I was keeping my fingers crossed like mad, hoping you'd turn up. And here you are, looking like a pair of ruddy cherubim. I don't think it's fair, at all. And I'm an absolute wreck."

"You're nothing of the sort," Priscilla said. "You're just as lovely as ever. And famous and accomplished, as well. In *two* fields. That's what's not fair."

"Bloody lucky, I've been," Jill said. "Trying to justify my existence, one way or another. I've a long way to go yet, I'm afraid. Come and sit down. I've a bottle of gin, if you don't mind plastic cups." She tugged at Priscilla's sleeve.

"Why don't we let you get dressed?" Priscilla said. "We were wondering if you'd like to come and have a drink with us at the Carleton. Are you tied up?"

"No, not at all. No one knows I'm alive, in this country. I'd love to."

"It's just down the street," Ben said. "They have a piano bar, and serve an after-theatre supper. It's very quiet, and we can have a decent talk."

"It sounds heavenly. I wonder if you'd mind if I brought a friend along? A chap named Tony, from London. We're sort of—traveling—together."

"No, of course not." Priscilla said. "We'll wait for you downstairs in the lobby. There's an exhibition of tapestries in the Hall of the Americas that I'd like to look at. It's just around the corner from the Eisenhower."

"Oh, good. We'll meet you there, then. God, how marvelous! I won't be twenty minutes, honestly. Tony's just gone out to get some tonic, and I've got the goo off already."

They strolled along the gallery of Andean tapestries in the long hall adjacent to the theatre while they waited for Jill and Tony to join them. Priscilla seemed genuinely, and mercifully, absorbed in the huge rectangles of crude, hand-loomed fabrics, reaching out occasionally to trace their designs or feel the texture of the coarse alpaca wool. It gave Ben time to settle his thoughts, to create a mood, a set of attitudes, a tone of voice, a repertoire of facial expressions to assume, almost in the way he had prepared for a performance in his acting days. Only when they had finished their tour of the gallery and sat down on a leather bench to smoke a cigarette did their conversation turn to Jill.

"Is she the same as you remembered her?" Priscilla asked.

"I think so. Of course she's considerably more assured and mature, but physically she's hardly changed at all."

"That's what I thought. Of course I only met her once or twice. Did you ever play opposite her, at RADA?"

"Yes. In *The Duchess of Malfi*. She was the Duchess and I was Bosola."

"I didn't know that."

"It was before I met you."

"Oh." Priscilla opened her evening bag and took out the program, musing over it for a moment. "Who's this Tony person she's bringing along? Was he at RADA?"

"I don't think so. I don't remember any Tony in our form."

"There's no one named Tony in the cast. Do you suppose he's an actor?"

"I don't know. But he looks to me very much like Clarence. Here he comes now."

"My goodness, he does, doesn't he? It's amazing."

He was approaching them down the long gallery beside Jill, who was obviously restraining the length and speed of her stride to accomodate his somewhat ponderous gait—touchingly, it seemed to Ben. The man's resemblance to the actor who had played Clarence grew more remarkable the closer he got to them. He was a plump, round-faced man of fifty or more with shining cheeks and heavy eyebrows and the gravely witty, avuncular air of her stage companion of the evening. The play was autobiographical in more than one respect, Ben guessed. The thought added to his reassurance considerably, as did Tony's manner, which was indulgent and yet indefinably proprietary towards Jill. He sat beside Ben in the Mercedes as they drove to the Carleton, listening to the chatter of Jill and Priscilla in the backseat with a benign, attentive air, like a chaperone at a senior prom. It had rained lightly while they were in the theatre, a spring shower that had barely dampened the pavement and the leaves of the sycamores along Sixteenth Street, and outside the open windows of the car the air smelled of cool wet stone and the freshly rinsed young leaves. The fragrant spring night had a peculiar poignance for Ben. It reminded him of spring nights he and Priscilla had driven to London parties with the pavements glittering like onyx outside the taxi windows and the dark scent of the distant Thames wandering like musk through the Chelsea streets. At many of those parties, Jill had been there amid the boom of rock and the tinkle of glasses and laughter and the shrill scent of gin, slim and sprightly as an otter in her glittering stretch-nylon slacks and plastic jewelry, casting him surly glances through the cigarette smoke. He had not expected to be assaulted by any such wave of nostalgia, and he was discomposed in a way he had not been prepared for. The role he had rehearsed for the evening seemed already obsolete, or inappropriate, or transparently fraudulent.

In the Carleton bar he ordered a double gin and tonic and offered a toast which he heard coming with surprising fervor from his lips: "To the success of this tour. May you have the whole of America at your feet."

"Well, I don't know what to say to *that*," Jill said. "Just the odd sailor would do very well. Or Frank Rich, of course."

"Oh, Rich," Priscilla said, and shuddered. "You don't want him at your feet. I'd rather have an octopus. Or that bear of yours." She laughed suddenly, remembering the creature. "You've got to tell me, Jill. *Where* did you get that bear?"

"I bought him in one of those junk shops in Bayswater Road," Jill said. "Isn't he marvelous? God knows how many centuries he'd been there, mouldering away among the bed warmers and stuffed foxes. Do you know what I paid for him?"

"No."

"Ten pounds six. I'm sure he'd been marked down half a dozen times. Probably they were asking a hundred guineas back around the time of Cromwell, but of course there isn't a lot of demand for a bear of that kind."

"I should think they'd have paid you to get rid of him," Priscilla said. "I've never seen an animal in that condition."

"But of course he's very talented," Jill said. "He adds to the play enormously. It wouldn't be the same without him. I think I'm going to have him listed in the cast when we open in New York: 'The part of Humbert is played by himself,' or something. Don't you think he deserves that, Ben?"

"He certainly does," Ben said. "He'll win a Tony."

"*You'll* win a Tony," Priscilla said. "Honestly, you're marvelous in that part. You nearly broke my heart."

"Oh, Priss, I'll never break your heart," Jill said. "Of course it makes things a bit easier when you write parts for yourself. I could have waited a hundred years and never found one like it. It's why I wrote the ruddy play, of course. No one else would hire me."

"You're very lucky to have so many talents," Priscilla said. "How many people do?"

"Very lucky Tony liked it," Jill said. "That's what did it."

"Are you a critic, Tony?" Ben asked.

"Not really a critic," Tony said. He spread his hands deprecatingly. "I'm what you might call a fervent amateur. I do a weekly piece for the *Observer*."

"He's a *professional* amateur," Jill said. "Much more influential than a critic. He does this marvelous weekly column called Let Us Now Praise Unknown Men, in which he talks about people one's never heard of — painters and poets and composers and the like — and he gets you so jolly excited about them that you can't wait to find out more about them for yourself. So people do. Always very profitably, you can be sure. And you know what his secret is, don't you? It's that he only talks about things that he really cares about, truly. Never a word about what he detests or deplores."

"Unlike our Mr. Rich," Priscilla said.

"Oh, absolutely. Tony's an evangelist, not an autocrat. Although he can be very stern, mind you, in demanding justice for his flock of forlorn geniuses."

"A great deal of value goes overlooked in this world," Tony said, "or dismissed as insignificant because it doesn't gratify esthetic standards — whatever they may be — or court approval or affection. I like to think that I can serve as an agent of justice in the universe by championing it."

"But don't you think we must have esthetic standards?" Priscilla said. "Something by which to measure the truth and beauty of a work of art?"

"They're not words that I use, at all, truth and beauty," Tony said. "One hears them used so often by fools and scoundrels that they've become an embarrassment." He lowered his eyes and adjusted his silverware discreetly with his fingertips. "I respect very much Borges's injunction

that in a story about God, God is the one word that should not appear. I
should like to live in a world in which truth and beauty were never spoken of."

"And in which art flourished," Priscilla said.

"Exactly."

"And justice."

"As you say."

"Shall I tell you what happened, with my play?" Jill said. "I must have
sent it to every producer in London, and they turned it down, to a man.
I couldn't even get an agent to handle it. So I got together a bunch of
out-of-work actors, like me, and we begged and borrowed and pawned
everything we owned, and finally scraped together enough money to
rent a little suburban theatre for a week. The Lyric, in Hammersmith;
you remember it? We thought we'd gamble everything on it catching
on. Not a single critic came to see it. Not the bloody *first*. But Tony came,
and wrote very respectfully about it in his column. And the upshot was
we ran not only a week, but for six months. And then moved into the
West End, under the aegis of Duncan Weldon, if you please. That says
something about his influence."

"It says something about your perseverance, too," Priscilla said.

"There you have it, of course," Tony said. "Without that, there'd have
been no play, and we wouldn't be sitting here now. That's what deserves
to be rewarded."

"Well, I hope it's as well rewarded here as in London," Priscilla said.
"When are you going to New York?"

"The first week in July," Jill said. "We're booked for the Schubert, but
there was a mixup of some kind about the dates, so we've got a two-week
layover here before we go up. It'll give us time to see Washington properly."

"You've never been here before?"

"I've never set foot in the country til last week. Tony has, of course, so
he'll be able to show me round. It looks a beautiful city. I've dreamed of
coming here for years." She turned to Ben and smiled. "Do you remember, Ben, how you'd dreamed of coming to London? As if it were part of

your destiny? Well, that's the way I feel about this trip. As if it were ordained. I think some things are, don't you?"

"I suppose they are," Ben said.

"Do you miss London at all? You always seemed so fond of it."

"Oh, yes, we miss it a lot, don't we, Priss?"

"Yes, we do," Priscilla said. "Especially the little house in Chelsea. I loved that house. Do you remember it?"

"No, I don't think I was ever there," Jill said. "I went down to Dartmouth with a rep company soon after we got out of school."

"Oh, I thought you'd been there," Priscilla said.

"No. I remember your wedding, though, well enough. That's where I first drank bourbon, and iced beer! And developed an instant passion for Lucky Strike cigarettes. It was a large part of my education, your reception."

"Of your corruption, apparently," Priscilla said, laughing.

"Oh, no, I'm incorruptible, aren't I, Tony? He says I can't *be* corrupted."

"It's quite true," Tony said. "I've never met anyone in my life who's put so much effort into the attempt, and failed utterly."

Priscilla laughed again. "You're very lucky. Most of us succeed without half trying."

"You had the best of London, you know," Jill said. "It's changed so dreadfully. It isn't like it was in the old days, when you were there. Do you ever get over anymore, at all?"

"Yes, we were over last year," Priscilla said. And in '84, I think. Was it in '84 they did *Nicholas Nickleby* at the National?"

"Yes. Did you see it?"

"Yes. And went back to see Wendy Moresby. She was wonderful in it."

"And you didn't look me up? Now I call that beastly!"

"We didn't have time to see anyone, actually," Priscilla said. "We were only there for a week."

"Well, you wouldn't have found me, anyway. I was locked up in Brompton Oratory with Tony, writing this play."

"How long did it take you?" Ben asked.

"Two years, just on. Tony brought me tea every two hours, and let me out once a week, only as far as the tobacconists. I should never have finished it otherwise. But look here, that's enough about me. I haven't given you a chance to say a word about yourselves." She turned to Ben and cocked her head at him. "Derek said you'd gone into business or something, Ben. Is that true?"

Ben nodded. "Yes. I have an advertising agency."

"Advertising? I don't believe it. How on earth did you learn about advertising?"

"Well, fortunately, there wasn't a great deal to learn," Ben said. "It's very much like theatre, actually. Commercials are really nothing more than little thirty-second dramas."

"I suppose they are, aren't they? What sort of things do you advertise?"

"Anything," Ben said.

"Anything?"

"Aspirin, automobiles, beer, laxatives. Absolutely anything that people will pay me to sell." He smiled pleasantly at her.

"Do you write them, these commercials?"

"Some of them."

"And act in them, as well?"

"Occasionally. Not as often as I used to. I've got the business end of things to take care of, more and more."

"And are you good at it?"

"Well, I make a decent living. Which I couldn't do in the theatre. There aren't enough parts for small, discontented men."

"But Hamlet was a small, discontented man, surely. At least it was written for Burbage, and he was supposed to have been 'a small, dark man.'"

"But people won't come to see him anymore unless he's played by a large, contented actor."

"I know what you mean. It's an awful bind. Still, I always had the absolute conviction that I'd sit and watch you play that part one day on Broadway or the West End. I think all of us did. Don't you miss it at all?"

"Not terribly," Ben said. "I keep pretty busy."

"I suppose you do, very busy. And of course you provide work for a lot of people, including a lot of actors and writers, like me. It's really people like you who keep society going, at all, isn't it? And after all, show business and advertising have been all mixed up ever since people hawked fish by singing in the street. I suppose those were the first commercials, really. And everyone does them, of course. My God, even Olivier and Gielgud do them, these days. I suppose the more exalted you are, the better you get paid. Perhaps *I'll* be exalted enough to be offered them one day. Do you think you could use me, Ben, if I manage to get canonized?"

"I could probably find something for you," Ben said.

"I could be one of those girls who wriggles in and out of her jeans, like Brooke Shields," Jill said. "I look quite good wriggling out of my jeans. I do, honestly, Ben."

"We'll see," Ben said, smiling uneasily.

"I don't think he believes me," Jill said, turning ruefully to Priscilla.

"I think he'd rather use you in his theatre," Priscilla said. "He's going to start one of his own, you know."

"*Is* he?" Jill said. Her large blue eyes widened and her face fell weakly in astonishment. She asked gently, "*Are* you, Ben? Is that true?"

"I've thought about it," Ben said.

"Soon, do you mean? I mean, have you plans?"

"Well, I haven't gotten around to designing it yet. But it's something I'd like to do, when things are going well, and I have the time."

"Oh." She blinked and brightened, her face regaining its animation. "Well, I think that's a marvelous idea. What sort of theatre? Something like the Royal Court?"

"Something like that. A little repertory theatre that would be self-sustaining, for a few years at least. Til we'd built up an audience."

"And you'd be involved in it yourself? I mean act and direct, and that sort of thing? Not just as an investment? Or a philanthropy."

"I'd like to. It's an idea I've been playing with for years." It seemed suddenly to Ben that this was true: that he had thought about it seriously and constantly for years, that it had been the dream that animated him. He felt a desire to talk about it, to deliver an excited exposition of the idea, as once, sitting in The Rising Sun, he had delivered excited discourse on the plays of Webster and John Ford.

"Not that there's anything wrong with philanthropists, God knows. Anyone who gives *anything* to the arts is a hero in my book, even if it's sixpence. And I don't mind where it comes from, even if it's from dynamite, like Nobel's. I don't mind if they blow up the whole bloody world, as long as we poor players get a few pounds from the proceeds."

"She doesn't mean that," Tony said.

"Don't I just. If we could put on one of our little comedies about it afterwards, it'd be worthwhile. I mean, the entire planet for a *Tartuffe*. I call that a jolly good exchange."

"Of course, the trouble is, the theatre would go up with the rest of it," Priscilla said.

"I know. You can't beat them," Jill said. "Still, we can have a good laugh now and again, can't we?" She picked up her glass, drained it, set it down, wobbled her eyes, shivered and said, *"Anyway."*

"Anyway what?" Ben said.

"When you have your theatre, I'm going to write a play for it, and Priscilla's going to direct it, and Tony's going to write a rhapsodic review about it, and we're all going to be immortalized, forever and ever."

"I'll drink to that," Tony said.

"So will I," Priscilla said.

"So will I," Ben said.

They drank until two, in an atmosphere of growing affection and fraternity, Ben's apprehension being eventually dispelled almost entirely by half a dozen double strength martinis, Jill's unexpected congeniality, and by the flood of fondly narrated anecdotes from their youth, tales of RADA costume balls at Claridge's and summer garden parties at the Chelsea Pensioners' Home on afternoons of forgotten, smouldering Junes on the Thames

Embankment, and a hilarious memoir of an Academy production of *Mourn-ing Becomes Electra* in which Ezra Mannon had been played by an enor-mous Iranian with an impenetrable Parsi accent, his wife by a Greek girl made up to resemble Theda Bara, Lavinia by a nervous ex-secretary from Boston in a badly fitting red wig, and Orin by a young man from Holy-well who gave the impression of having just returned, badly shaken, from a fox hunt. Jill described this catastrophe with a gay and nimble gift of parody that had them doubled over in their chairs.

He had been mistaken about her, Ben decided. She obviously bore him no ill will. Her play was no more than a charming memoir of a romantic interlude, a souvenir of a fervent, infatuated moment of their lives which she had laid away with the act of dramatizing it. Perhaps the writing of it had been a kind of catharsis for her; it had washed her clean of whatever bitterness she may have felt toward him. His reassurance waxed into a hazy, bold euphoria that owed much of its zest to the fact that he was evidently out of danger. What he had feared would be a disaster was turning out to be an experience of very pleasant, sentimental reminiscence that revived in him the sense of exhilaration, potency and daring that he had enjoyed in the course of their affair. He began to feel a glowing amity toward her. They would part with a sense of gratitude toward each other, the sweeter for its secrecy, for what they had once shared, for what they owed each other of their greater depth of feeling, their greater sense of self, their greater wisdom. The evening would serve as a fitting celebration of that largesse.

His feeling of amity did not quite extend to Tony. There was much that Ben liked about the man—his wit, intelligence, and modesty—but he found himself uneasily wondering from time to time just how much Tony knew about his affair with Jill. Everything, almost certainly, if they were as intimate as the situation indicated. This was an unpleasant realization that came to Ben slowly and gave a disagreeable tint of disingenuousness or irony to Tony's measured, amiable observations, his smiling silences, his at-tentive reticence. Somewhere in the course of the evening Ben came to feel a vague, unaccountable resentment of what he considered the man's oddly passionless devotion to Jill. It certainly gave no evidence of being at all erotic in nature—he could not imagine that plump, ruddy, faintly epicene gentleman locked in a feverish embrace with her—and yet it was evidently profound and permanent, a fact that disquieted him. He felt moved faintly to indignation by it, or derision. There was something chastening in the man's attentiveness to Jill, something that seemed to discredit his own previous relationship with her, or his present one with Priscilla, or with anyone. He considered the oddity of the fact that he was no longer cheered by their appearance of affection for each other, as he had been earlier. At the outset of the evening he had accepted it as reassuring evidence that she had found consolation and contentment with someone, contentment that would extinguish any possible desire for retribution on her part. Now it seemed faintly presumptuous or derogatory, and part of its power to disturb him was the fact that it was so far from being conspicuously so. Tony was to all appearances impeccably convivial and tactful, appreciative of Ben's wit, respectful of the memories he shared with Jill, and solicitous of his opinions. He asked once, when Jill and Priscilla had retired to the ladies' room and he and Ben were briefly alone together:

"Do you find her much changed, Ben?"

"Yes. I think she's a lot more mature," Ben said. "She has a lot more poise and understanding. Success has been good for her. She's handled it very well. Not everyone does."

"No, that's true," Tony said. "There's been a great improvement, since the play."

"Was she unhappy—before?"

"She went through rather a bad time, I think, but that's behind her now. She has enormous powers of endurance."

"I don't think you ever really know a person until they've had a certain amount of success. Especially a talented person. Talent without success can have some pretty devastating effects on character."

"It can, yes."

Ben impaled the olive in his drink on the tip of a plastic spear. "Of course she was only twenty or twenty-one when I knew her. Just a child, really. We both were. I don't think either of us knew what we really wanted. I don't suppose anyone does, at that age." He put the olive into his mouth and munched at it. Tony smiled at him. "Do you?"

"Well, I'm not sure I agree with you entirely," Tony said. "I have the impression that she always knew exactly what she wanted. It's getting it, of course, that makes the difference."

"That's it exactly," Ben said. He nodded magnanimously. "And sometimes you don't know what it is until you get it. I never did. I never knew Jill could write, either, and I'm not sure she did. I knew she was a very clever actress, of course, but I never knew she could write, or wanted to. It's amazing how you can know someone quite well and not realize the full extent of their gifts."

"Yes," Tony said. "It's one of life's great tragedies."

"You recognized her talent right away?"

"From the first page of her manuscript," Tony said.

"That's an unusual faculty."

"Oh, I don't think so. For anyone who's been exposed to a certain amount of excellence to be able to recognize it when he sees it doesn't seem to me extraordinary. It seems much more remarkable to me that anyone who's read a certain amount of literature, for example, could read the first page of *A Shropshire Lad,* or *Portrait of the Artist As a Young Man,* and fail to recognize that he was in the presence of genius. Yet they both barely escaped oblivion."

"Why don't more people recognize it, then?"

"There are three possible reasons," Tony said. "Stupidity, dishonesty, or ignorance. Ignorance can be corrected, of course, but the others are incorrigible. A man can be educated, but he cannot be made intelligent, or honest."

"I guess you're right," Ben said.

"Have you tried these shrimp rolls? They're delicious."

"Yes, they're very good."

"We don't get shrimp like this in England. We have these wretched little things called prawns. Very much like maggots."

When the two women returned from the ladies' room, Priscilla announced, "We have hatched a plot."

"A plot?" Ben said.

"Yes. I've decided that Jill and Tony should come down to Hatteras with us. They have this two-week layover after the run here, and the best thing in the world for them would be some sun and sea and some very serious loafing. It'll fortify them for New York."

"That's a very good idea," Ben said. He was not sure of this at all, but he nodded vigorously. "They deserve it."

"I don't know that we deserve it at all," Jill said. "But I must say it sounds a marvelous idea. I love ocean bathing, and we're both of us world-class loafers."

"It's a beautiful spot," Ben said. "You'll love it."

"I'm sure of it. But I'm afraid it's an awful imposition, to come barging in on your holiday."

"That's nonsense," Priscilla said. "It'll make it a hundred times nicer. We have all the room in the world, and it'll just go to waste, otherwise. Make her be sensible, Tony."

"I'm afraid she's far more sensible than I, when it comes to loafing," Tony said. "I'm quite unregenerate when it comes to laying about all day with a drink in my fist."

"It's true," Jill said. "I could hardly drag him away from Biarritz last summer. Of course, all the bare bosoms may have had something to do with it."

"Well, I'm afraid you won't see many bare bosoms at Cape Hatteras," Ben said. "It's not very chic. In fact, it's pretty primitive, as far as resorts go. No nightclubs or anything like that. It's about as far from Biarritz as it's possible to get."

"I told her that," Priscilla said. She turned to Tony. "It's very simple and unspoiled, but that's why we love it. We used to go to Cape Cod in the summers, but it was awful. Provincetown has become just like George-town on a Saturday night, but all day *long*. Hatteras is pure peace. Miles of lonely beach and surf and marshes that stretch out to the sky. There's no place on earth that gives your soul back to you so restored and clean and tranquil. I love it there." She laid her hands on Jill's and Tony's wrists. "And you will too. Both of you. Oh, I'm so happy you're coming with us. It's the nicest thing that's happened in years."

"It really is terribly sweet of you," Jill said. "It sounds like heaven. I can't think of anything I'd rather do."

.   .   .

Ben and Priscilla had spent a great deal of money and a great deal of time and imagination on their beach house, which had come to have a kind of mystical importance to them. It stood on the southern tip of the long sandbar that formed the Cape, two hundred yards from the ocean on a hill of dunes, looking out across a field of golden sand oats to the beaten blue enamel of the sea. It was round, a great wooden rotunda built of bare California redwood, set high on wooden pilings and surrounded by a circular sundeck from which, on the seaward side, you could watch the sun rise over the glinting gray morning ocean and, on the landward side, sit and sip sundowners in the evening and watch it slip down, mo-ment by moment, behind the distant black pines of the swampland hum-mocks, a gigantic scarlet gong that cast a glittering rose patina across the rippled water of the sound. There was a huge Plexiglas skylight in the dome above the central living room through which the midday light poured onto the bright-colored Navajo carpets, the bricks of the beehive mantel and the burnished rosewood and blond leather of the Danish furniture. The living room ran through the entire house, and its sliding glass doors opened, front and back, onto the deck, so that before the sun had reached its zenith the room was flooded from the east with cool morning light and, in the afternoons, with the long, soft light of evening. To right and left, the liv-ing room was enclosed by a suite of rooms forming the northern and

southern arcs of its circumference: a study, a kitchen, a "television room,"
and three bedrooms, each furnished with a private bath, twin beds, and
sliding doors that opened out onto the deck. It was a "palace of light,"
Ben said. He had designed it to admit all the illumination of the universe. At night you could see stars glittering in the black sky above the dome
like a great delicate chandelier, and in fine weather, when the moon
was full, it was possible to dine by the milky light that flooded the room
from overhead with a soft, pale nimbus, like a luminous vapor. From the
sundeck you could see north to where the black-and-white spiraled column of the lighthouse rose above the distant dunes, and south to the
bend of the cape where, offshore, the emerald green water of the Gulf
Stream flowed through the indigo sea as distinctly as a creek through a field
of violets. Underneath, between the high pilings, there was a furnace room,
an air-conditioning unit, a shower stall, and dressing rooms where you could
wash off sand and salt and towel yourself dry before going up the flight of
redwood stairs into the kitchen.

Often they went there in winter for three-day weekends and short holidays. They liked to roam along the beaches in the bright winter light
and come back to an open fire and mugs of Irish coffee. Ben loved the
house, in any weather. His visits to it were almost ceremonial, like his visits to the Kennedy Center, and they furnished him with almost the same
intimation of legendary felicity and peace. He had spared nothing in its
construction; he had hired the most expensive architect in Washington
to translate his conception into blueprints and had enlisted Priscilla's
taste in furnishing its decor, even more urgently and liberally than he
had in the case of the house at Great Falls. It seemed even more important to him, in some respects. Virtually everyone owned a dwelling of some
kind; to own one as magnificent as theirs was of course a statement of
success, but to own a beach house added a bouquet to that statement,
like a Legion d'Honneur rosette in the buttonhole of an expensive suit. Like
such a decoration, it should evoke unspoken valor, service, or vision, something more than mere prosperity. Fastidiousness in its appointments was

almost an incumbency of gentility. It was not enough to own things, Ben
understood; one must appreciate them. They must reflect one's respect
for excellence. To be merely acquisitive was greedy and egregious. It reflected not sensibility, but prodigality. One of the quotations he best remembered was not from Shakespeare or Molière or Marlowe, but an
observation of Aldous Huxley's about Confucius's preoccupation with
propriety: "Only in China has the code of the gentleman assumed the
proportions of a great religion." That was very true, Ben thought. There was
something almost religious about true gentility, something beatific that
made it possible to regard all the drudgery and chicanery involved in worldly
achievement, in making money, struggling with competitors, maneuver-
ing for power, as a kind of novitiate, a period of arduous, menial probation—
like scrubbing floors and digging potatoes in a convent—that one had to
go through to attain grace. All this he had attempted to express in his "palace
of light," his place of repose and restitution and revival.

That he depended on the skill of a hired architect and Priscilla's taste
to consummate this vision was neither unusual nor reproachable, he thought;
no man built his own house, suckled his own children, or mended his own
clothes; nor did Bismarck fire his own cannon, or Schubert perform his
own symphonies. Ben did not quite understand the fallacy of this anal-
ogy, or its relegation of Priscilla to the role of wet nurse, seamstress, foot soldier, or first violinist. Nor did he recognize the promiscuity of inviting
her to select the Navajo carpets and tapestries, the Danish furniture, the
sculpture and paintings, pewterware and crystal and objets d'art that she
had worked into a composition which he could gratefully endorse as an
expression of his own sensibility. It was promiscuous, but it was not entirely
fraudulent, because he understood that Priscilla would have been grieved
if she felt she had misrepresented his nature in the selection of these things.
Because she considered him an artist, she ascribed to him a universal
love of beauty and excellence; she expected him to share her own appreciation of the principles of harmony, proportion, integrity and modesty
in all things. Perhaps he did, or was capable of it; she had taught him

almost to believe it. She had devoted her life to nourishing and serving that capacity in him, and he felt that it was almost his duty to confirm her faith in it. In a mysterious way he had come to adopt her vision of himself. It was the vision of himself that he saw illustrated in the house: the donor, votary, and curator of these graceful, elegant things she had assembled in his name, the gentleman for whom she had created this conservatory of what was best and most beautiful. It was the heritage, the harvest, and the issue of his own gifts. As long as she believed this, Ben believed it. As long as she had faith in him, he had faith in himself.

They drove down on the Saturday morning after the last night of Jill's Washington engagement. It was a drive of four hundred miles, about which Ben had apprehensions. In spite of Jill's apparent congeniality, eight hours was a very long time for four people on even the most intimate of terms to sit in unrelieved proximity inside an automobile. Not much was offered by way of diversion in the scenery, which was of little interest, novelty, or significance, from one mile to the next. There were expanses of flat farmland or forest, acres of geometrically unfolding tobacco fields and mournfully monotonous pine barrens, linked by an endlessly reiterated chain of motels, fast-food restaurants, souvenir shops and gasoline stations, which occasionally condensed into the huddle of commercial buildings of a country town: an electrical appliance shop, a chain grocery, a hardware store, an undertaker's, a John Deere distributorship, surrounded by a cluster of dusty streets and bleak, square brick or clapboard houses. It did little to inspire poetic thoughts or lively conversation, even at the outset, and after an hour or two had exhausted its small claims on their attention. In spite of this, everyone was animated and garrulous, with the exception of Tony who had little to say but was unfailingly alert and smiling. Jill's vivacity seemed dauntless in the face of all banality or whatever irregularity of circumstances; she seemed to have some private source of energy that was independent of environment. Some internal process of conflagration of a sun that radiated heat and light inexhaustibly. It was undeterred even by the Howard Johnson's at which they stopped for a lunch of hamburgers, milkshakes, and glutinous apple pie served in a noisy, frigid vault that was paneled on every side by plastic—above, of imitation coral; below, of imitation marble; to right and left, of imitation walnut. Ben felt unreasonably embarrassed by the place, and by the fact that in the four hundred miles between Washington and Cape Hatteras there was virtually nowhere of any greater distinction to eat. He remembered having driven one summer from London to Stratford, and having stopped, on the way up, at The Bull in Oxford, and, on the way back, at the Lygon Arms in Broadway, lovely, quiet, stone-and-timber inns in four-hundred-year-old villages, where one could sip a glass of wine over a delicate lemon sole and gaze out of mullioned windows at rose gardens and glimmering water meadows. He felt oppressed enough by the comparison to offer an apology.

"If we'd had more time, I would have taken the back roads," he said. "So you could see a little of the real America. But we won't get there until around six, as it is."

"Isn't this the real America?" Jill asked. "It looks like it to me, judging from the films."

It took Ben a moment to realize that there was no malice in the comment; she was either genuinely oblivious or indifferent to her surroundings or had developed the same magnanimity toward all forms of imperfection that she had shown to him. Magnanimity, he decided, in the course of the beguiling account she gave of her last week in Washington, which showed her as far from indifferent to her environment. They had had very little time for sightseeing, she said, because they had to re-block the play entirely, owing to the difference in the stage dimensions between the Eisenhower and the Aldwych, where they had played in London. This had taken almost every afternoon, and with having to rewrite and memorize some of the third-act dialogue (which was ambiguous to the American ear), it had left them only two free afternoons in which to explore the city. From the list of celebrated sights and exhibitions Tony had given her, she had chosen the Lincoln Memorial and the Natural History Museum.

"Because Tony told me they both contained exhibits of the most prodigious living things that ever existed in your country—man or beast. We don't have anything like either of them in England. There were never any dinosaurs, and certainly no statesmen or politicians like Lincoln, at least any of either that left any trace behind. The dinosaurs were marvelous, just as I thought they'd be. Huge, hulking, bellowing, ridiculous things that are really quite exemplary, in a way. I don't think we could have done without them. They existed just long enough to give us a sense of proportion about things, to illustrate the limitations of physical size and strength. I mean, you look at them and you realize that's just about as big as it's possible for a living thing to get before it starts to become ridiculous and ineffective. There's an awful lot to be learned about modesty and propriety from looking at a brontosaurus. *I* learned a lot, anyway, learned that I shouldn't be eating this apple pie, for one thing. I feel much wiser for having seen them. And a great deal wiser, and humbler, from having seen that statue of Abraham Lincoln. I don't like statues, at all, as a rule. They're all much too large, of course—especially the ones of politicians. You feel they're such a monstrous exaggeration; no one could be that big, or justify such a heroic image of himself. But that's the largest statue of a human being I ever saw in my life, and the only one that doesn't seem extravagant. It seems too *small*, somehow, as if no possible image of the man would match his real dimensions. And then, he seemed so oddly un-American to me. I mean, so bloody sad. Such an unbearable look of grief in the man's face. More like a Russian, really, than an American. I mean, you don't often see a melancholy American, do you—a real live one? You're all so full of beans, you people. And here's this great, sad, stone giant sitting there gazing out at the city with that brooding, brokenhearted look of his. It's really quite an eerie thing. I think it'll haunt me forever. You feel as if you can't escape the man's gaze. I still feel him staring at me, wherever I go, and it makes me bloody nervous, I don't mind telling you. When we were walking away, I tossed an empty cigarette pack at a waste basket at the bottom of the steps, and I missed it, of course—I always do, and generally don't give it another thought. But I hadn't taken two steps when I thought, my God, he's looking at me. He saw that. Something else to add to the man's grief. So I went back and picked it up and dropped it in the waste bin, properly. I did, actually. I don't suppose I shall be able to do anything wicked at all now, without feeling that man's gaze on me. Bloody unnerving to think about. I mean, I shan't be able to pop into bed with a chap or have one over the eight without thinking, 'You'll never get away with this. Old Abe's got his eye on you. What do you want to do, break the man's heart?' It's quite uncanny. Something eight years of parochial school couldn't do."

"He's given you a conscience," Tony said.

"I'm afraid he has, you know. And a completely different idea of this country, I must say. Why do you suppose he's been glorified the way he has? Much more than Washington or Jefferson, or the rest of your heroes. He certainly doesn't seem typically American to me. Makes one wonder if he *is*, really. If he's more American than most, I mean. If there's some awful grief at the heart of this country that he's expressed, for everyone. Could that be true?" She looked at Priscilla, who smiled and shook her head gently as if lost for a reply. "Bloody strange experience, altogether. I shouldn't have wanted to see anything else, I don't think, even if we'd had the time. Although Tony's furious because we didn't get to the National Gallery. He says I've got to see the Rudels, and God knows when I'll get back again."

"We have one that you can see," Ben said.

"Oh, you *haven't!*" Jill said. "This man that Tony raves about? The sculptor?"

"Yes. We picked it up at an exhibit he had years ago, before anyone began to collect him. Priss found it at a little show in New York."

"How extraordinary," Tony said.

"Oh, well, I *noticed* it," Priscilla said. "But Ben *bought* it. I took him to see it because I knew he'd love it, and he said we had to have it, the minute he laid eyes on it. I think he loves that little piece of sculpture more than anything else we have."

"How very wise," Tony said.

"Well, it's turned out to be," Ben said. "But I wasn't sure it was, at the time. We paid ten thousand dollars for it, which seemed pretty extravagant at that point in our lives. You know what it's worth today?"

"Ten times that, I should think," Tony said.

"Very nearly," Ben said. "That's what his single pieces are bringing, of that size."

"Of course he had the very good sense to die," Tony said. "Which brings the price up."

"Yes." Ben nodded uneasily. Tony's approval had for some reason become important to him and he would have preferred it unclouded by any shade of irony.

In the case of the beach house, it was not. When he slid back the glass door of the sundeck to allow his guests to enter, Tony advanced into the room, paused to look thoughtfully about, laid a finger on the warm rosewood of the dining table, and turned to Ben with a small, circumspect smile, the smile of a peer congratulating his host on the wine.

"This is quite lovely," he said.

"Thanks. We put quite a bit of work into it, didn't we, Priss?"

"I thought you said it was primitive," Jill said with a little gasp. "My God, it looks like Hampton Court Palace."

"We didn't say the *house*," Priscilla said. "We meant the Cape. The beaches, and town, and everything."

"This is the Rudel," Tony said, advancing toward a piece of metal statuary that stood on top of the piano, a child in a swing with a blown skirt and happily uplifted face.

"Yes."

"Exquisite." He went across to the piano and clasped the figurine gently between his palms, holding them to it for a moment as if enclosing a child's face. Jill came and stood beside him and he handed it to her carefully.

"Oh, my," she said. Her face fell suddenly in a look almost of sorrow.

"Now you see what I was telling you about this man?"

She nodded, set the figurine back on the piano and touched it with her fingertip.

"It's lovely, isn't it?" Priscilla said.

"It's almost enough to console one for everything he's ever lost," Jill said. "I don't know how it's possible to make a thing like that, in the twentieth century. Was the man an idiot savant?"

"He was a great, glowering, untidy creature with a greasy beard," Tony said. "They say he ate raw fish."

"Well, it couldn't be that that did it," Jill said. She turned away with a little laugh, as if embarrassed by her show of feeling. "I used to eat cockles by the quart, but nothing came of it." She wandered across the room, her eyes roving across the paintings, prints, and tapestries, to a sofa upholstered in soft blond leather where she sank down and stared out through the glass doors at the distant, burning sea. "Lord, what a lovely place. I think I'll just cancel the show and stay here all summer. Would you mind?"

"I'd be delighted if you stayed right on that sofa forever," Priscilla said. "You're just what we needed to make the place perfect."

"Do you mean another ornament?"

"I mean a muse."

Esther Padgett, a local spinster who worked as their housekeeper through the summer, came out of the kitchen and stood smiling in the door. She was in her early thirties, a pale young woman with nervously straying eyes and hands whose prettiness and shapeliness seemed to be rapidly deteriorating, like a wax doll left in the sun.

"Welcome back, you-all," she said. "I been expecting you. It's nice to see you-all again."

"Thank you," Priscilla said. "It's nice to see you, Esther. I'd like you to meet Miss Davenport and Mr. Griswold. They're going to be staying with us for the next week." She turned to Jill and Tony. "Jill, Tony, this is Esther Padgett, who keeps this place from falling into ruin, practically singlehanded."

"How do you do," Esther said. "I hope you folks have a nice visit."

"Thank you," Jill said. "I hope we won't be too much trouble."

"No, ma'am, you won't be no trouble."

"How do you do?" Tony said.

"I think you'll find everything how you want it," Esther said. "All what you wrote me to do. I aired the place out good, Mrs. Oakshaw, and changed the linen and brought in some ice. I turned on the air-conditioning this morning, so's it'd be cool. I had the man check it out last week. It's set at seventy-two, is that all right?"

"Yes, it's very comfortable," Priscilla said.

"There's butter in the fridge, and eggs, and bacon. I got everything on the list except marmalade. They don't carry Robertson's no more at the Red and White, so I brought you some beach plum jelly Momma made."

"Oh, that's marvelous!" Priscilla said. "She makes the best jelly in the world. But you shouldn't have done it."

"Oh, she was proud to send it up. Elbert come down this morning and helped me set up the porch furniture. You know one of them chairs has got the webbing tore?"

"Yes, that happened last summer," Priscilla said. "I'll have to get it repaired."

"You want me to take it up to Thurlough's?"

"No, don't bother. We'll take it some time next week. Did you find the Cinzano?"

"Yes, ma'am, it's in the cabinet. Daddy got all the liquor up at Manteo last week. I don't think they had none of that champagne you had on the list, so he got some other kind. I hope it's all right."

"I'm sure it is. Were you able to get the things for dinner?"

"Yes, ma'am, I got everything you wanted. They had some real nice shrimp down at the dock."

"Oh, wonderful. You're an angel, Esther."

"I'm just now polishing up the silverware in the kitchen. I reckon I better get it finished."

"Thank you so much for everything. The house looks beautiful."

"Thank you, ma'am. It's real nice to meet you folks." She smiled shyly and went back into the kitchen.

"Now, I'll tell you what we'd better do," Ben said. "The ladies can have a shower while Tony and I get the bags from the car. Then we'll settle down and have a julep. I'll show you where your room is. Do you like the morning sun, or afternoon?"

"Oh, the morning!" Jill said.

"OK, we'll put you in the east wing, then. Right through here."

He led them across the circular hall that enclosed the central room to one of the bedrooms in the eastern quadrant. It was papered with a fine triple stripe of dark gray on pale burgundy and hung with four original Bonnards and a cluster of Picasso drawings above the applewood bed-head. There was a chalk-white bureau and dressing table with a blood-red lacquer sconce holding aloft a single ivory amaryllis blossom at each side of the mirror.

"God's teeth!" Jill said. "Just like the old digs in Hammersmith. Wouldn't Humbert love this."

When they had bathed and changed their clothes, they sat on the western deck and drank mint juleps in the shimmer of the fading afternoon. It was still and hot, with a luminous, vaporous brilliance everywhere, a feeling of almost timeless tranquillity, like that of childhood. The women had changed into summer dresses and the men into shorts and sports shirts. They sat at a large round table with a tesselated top of tiled mosaic work on which was a silver pitcher, several massive ashtrays of glazed pottery, and their glasses, with fingerprints pressed into the frost. Their conversation, after an initial spasm of vivacity, had grown desultory and languid, qualities it seemed to borrow from the afternoon, whose sights and sounds were idle, extemporary, briefly engrossing, and ephemeral, parts of a huge, pacific pattern of things that seemed not to have altered since the earth began: a gull flying over on a steady, earnest pilgrimage, the glitter of sunlight on a chip of mother-of-pearl in the sand of the yard, a sudden, catastrophic boom of surf from behind the dunes, instantly resumed into the silence, a woman calling to a child somewhere in the distance with faint but startling clarity, inscribing a warning on the stillness like an epitaph: *Young man, didn't I tell you not to go out there, it was too deep?* It was evident that everyone's thoughts were inward, on other times and places, curiously evoked by the indolent, eternal present of the place. Even Jill's usual volubility seemed transposed into memory.

"It's absolutely incredible," she said, staring at the purple crests of the huge, massed clouds beyond the marshes. "A month ago I was in Hampstead celebrating this tour with a crowd of chaps in Jackstraw's Castle, and I'd never even heard of this place. I didn't even know it existed, all this sand and water and silence, and here I am staring at—what's it called?—Pamlico Sound, as if I'd been born here, and Hampstead were a dream. Do you suppose when I go back there I'll dream about this place, the way I've just been thinking about that afternoon in Hampstead?"

"*I* do," Priscilla said. "When I go back to Washington. I think about it all winter. Especially when the pipes freeze, and the roof starts leaking, from the ice."

"And it sort of keeps you going, I suppose? The thought that it's here, unchanged, all this sun and water."

"It certainly helps. When you have people like Emporia Plumbing to deal with. Of course we have our share of problems here, too. What with wind and water damage from the hurricanes."

"Have you actually been through one here?"

"No, but we got the tail end of one, one year, that changed direction all of a sudden and came roaring in to shore. It was awful, driving back. The road was flooded all the way up to Kitty Hawk, and we stalled out twice and had to sit for hours until Ben got the distributor, or whatever it is, dried out."

"Do you think we'll get one this time?"

"Oh, no. They've been talking about a tropical depression on the news for a couple of nights, but it's way off beyond Eleuthera. We might get a little high surf, but that's all. There's nothing to worry about."

"I shouldn't mind," Jill said. "I've never been in a storm. I must say it sounds jolly exciting."

"It's exciting, all right. Until the roof flies off, or the water comes up through the floor. We'll give you anything you like except a hurricane."

"We may give you a squall, if you like," Ben said. "Those are quite exciting."

"They *are*," Priscilla said. "I kind of like squalls. Sometimes the current goes off, and you have to light hurricane lamps and sit and play cards or read. I love that, because Ben reads aloud to me sometimes. He read *Wuthering Heights* in the last squall and it was wonderful. Of course, Emily Brontë should be read with wind howling outside and rain pelting against the windows."

"How lovely," Jill said. "A performance in a holocaust. Like the Windmill. You know that girly place, in Soho? They never closed, during the war. They used to give performances all through the blitz, with bombs banging about and buildings falling down all around. All these girls standing about stark naked and these chaps sitting there ogling them like oysters."

"The Bible says desire shall fail," Tony said. "But I suppose it's the last thing to go."

"That or righteousness," Jill said. "There were church services going on, too, all through the blitz. I think there's something heroic about it, in either case."

Priscilla laughed. "There is something heroic about it, isn't there? The pious and the prurient, both carrying on until the end. I wonder which of them was wisest, or most blessed." She turned to Jill. "Where would you like to be, at the Apocalypse?"

"It'd be the Windmill for me, every time," Jill said. "Provided I still have my figure. Which I think is likely, the way things are going."

"I'm afraid you're right," Priscilla said. "What about you, Tony?"

"I think I'd choose the Turner room, at the Tate Gallery," Tony said.

Priscilla nodded. "That's a very good place to spend one's final moments."

"Where would you like to be?" Jill asked.

"I think I'd like to be in my kitchen, baking bread," Priscilla said after a moment.

"Ah," Tony murmured.

"What about you, Ben?"

"Oh, I don't know," Ben said. He scratched his wrist offhandedly. "In RFK Stadium, I guess. The last quarter of the Redskins-Cowboys game, with the Skins leading, thirty-four to zero."

"Who on earth are the Redskins and the Cowboys?" Jill asked.

"Football teams," Priscilla said.

"He's not serious."

"Oh yes, he is. My God, is he. He actually managed to get season tickets last month, after trying for five years. People would kill for season tickets to the Redskins."

"Would they? Why?" Jill asked.

"Well, they're very, very difficult to get," Priscilla said. "They're almost more important in Washington than an invitation to the White House." She sipped delicately at her drink.

"You mean you've arrived, or something, if you can get them? Have you arrived, Ben?"

"Oh, no," Ben said. He grinned at her.

"I don't believe you about this bloody football game. Why won't you tell us? I want to know where all my friends are going to be when the big bang comes."

"I thought the big bang was the beginning of things," Ben said.

"The beginning and the end. It goes round full circle."

"No, the end is going to be a whimper. Isn't that what Eliot says?"

"Well, he's wrong, as usual. He was constantly mistaking whimsey for wisdom. Or virtuosity for vision. That's what Tony says."

"I don't remember saying that," Tony said. "But it seems quite sound to me."

Jill blew smoke into the air from her cigarette and watched it dissipate in the clear blue air. "I'll bet I know where you'll be. In a theatre. Am I right?"

"I suppose a theatre would be as good a place to be as any," Ben said.

"The Windmill?"

"No, I don't think so. Not the Windmill." He smiled amiably.

"Not even if I'm up there on the stage posing as Venus de Milo or somebody?"

"I probably couldn't get a seat, in that case. You'd be sold out."

"What, the way you manage to get tickets? Rubbish. You can't use that as an excuse. I'll expect to see you in the front row."

"All right, I'll be there," Ben said. "If you promise to sing one of those folk songs of yours."

"One of my folk songs?"

"Yes. That one you used to sing at parties sometimes."

"'The Wild Mountain Thyme'? Do you remember that?"

"Oh, sing it for us," Priscilla said. "I love that song."

"I don't know if I could, just now." Jill said. "I'm pretty well squiffed, you know."

"That didn't use to bother you," Ben said.

"Well, I'll try." She held her glass in her lap and gazed off at the purple peaks of the mountainous clouds beyond the sound, her voice breaking into a clear, sweet soprano:

I will build my love a tower
By yon clear and shining fountain
And upon it I will gather
All the flowers of the mountain.
Will ye go, laddie,
Will ye go?

If my true love will not come,
I will surely find another

To pull wild mountain thyme
All around the purple heather.
Will ye go, laddie,
Will ye go?

"Oh, that's lovely," Priscilla said. "I think I'll be there too, if you'll sing that for us."

"Yes, so shall I," Tony said. "I think we should all be together, somehow. And it's very appropriate for the end of things. A song about lost love."

"I think we need another drink," Ben said. He raised the pitcher of julep.

"Not for me," Priscilla said, covering her glass with her hand. "I've got to go and help Esther with the dinner. We won't eat til midnight if I have any more."

"I'll come and help you," Jill said. "I'm very good at whipping potatoes."

"No, you won't. You're on holiday. Esther and I have a system. You have another drink, and I'll call you when we're ready."

"I think perhaps I'll go and lie down for half an hour, in that case. Is that all right? I don't often get up as early as we did this morning."

When the women had gone in through the glass door Ben held the pitcher aloft and asked, "How about you, Tony?"

"Just a touch, if you've got some there," Tony said. When Ben had re-filled his glass he sipped and said appreciatively, "It's jolly good, this julep. One's always reading about it, in American novels. I see why, now. It's a Southern drink, isn't it?"

"Yes."

"You're Southern, I believe Jill said."

"Yes. I'm from Florida, originally."

"Oh, yes. That's your vacationland, down there, isn't it? Miami and West Palm Beach. All glitz and ermine, I believe."

"That's just the Gold Coast," Ben said. "It's different, inland. Or was, when I was a boy."

"Oh? What's it like there?"

"Orange groves," Ben said. "Truck farms, and cattle. It's farm country."

"Oh, yes. Florida oranges. Is that what you did? Farming?"

"Yes. We did a little of it. What part of England are you from, Tony?"

"A village named Godalming, in Surrey. Do you know it?"

"No, I don't."

"Lovely old place. My father was a master there, at Charter House. What we call a public school, only of course it isn't public, as you know."

"Did you go there?"

"I did, yes. Unfortunately."

"Why do you say that?"

"Well, it's a rather equivocal position, being the son of a master at one's school. The other boys look on you as a sort of enemy spy, and of course the masters are determined to show you no favoritism whatever. As a result, one belongs to neither world, neither the governors nor the governed. One must develop one's own view of things, which doesn't very much please anyone. I suppose it's what decided my profession, really."

"I should think you'd consider that fortunate," Ben said.

"Well, perhaps it is. But it's a very solitary one. Most of one's friends are either long dead or not yet recognized as living." He sipped from his drink. "Occasionally, of course, one is able to help confirm the existence of a genuinely living creature, which makes it all worthwhile."

"How did you meet her?" Ben asked.

"I was up in Glasgow and went round to the Citizens Theatre, where they were doing a thing of Brecht's called *Arturo Ui*. She had just a small part, three or four lines, but she was onstage a good bit, and when she was, she was unmistakably present. One of those actors you can't take your eyes off, no matter what's going on. Well, I went round to see her, after, and asked her out to dinner. One thing led to another, you know, and when she came down to London in the spring, I rang her up. She was getting bits and pieces, walk-ons in theatre clubs, a bit of TV. And she was writing this play. So I asked if I could have a look at it. She had just the first act done, and didn't know quite how to go on with it. I read it and saw that it was very good indeed. We talked about it, and I tossed in a few ideas of my own, for what they were worth. She was barely making enough to pay her rent, and hadn't really the time to work on it. So I asked if she'd like to move in with me and not have the rent to worry about. She said she thought she'd like that, so the next day she showed up at my place, lugging this mouldy great bear up two flights of stairs. As it turned out, we got on quite well."

"A good thing for both of you," Ben said.

"Yes, quite. For the three of us, you might say. Very best thing in the world." He held his glass between his hands and gazed at it for a moment as if considering whether or not to end his story at that point. He decided to do so, apparently, turning to Ben with a delicate, circumspect smile. "It's extraordinary how things work out."

"Yes," Ben said.

"Now, speaking of my profession, I'll tell you what I think I'm going to do, if you don't mind. I think I'll just slip in and finish up my column for next week. I've got to wire it in by Friday."

"Not at all. As Priss says, you're to do just as you like."

"Good. Want to get some of my impressions down while they're still fresh. Do you dress for dinner?"

"Well, Priscilla likes people to wear shoes, but otherwise we're very liberal."

"Oh, good. You don't want to let things slide too far." His smile grew in benignity. "I can't tell you how I'm enjoying this."

"Good," Ben said. "That's what we want to hear."

It grew from dusk to dark while they ate, and stars began to flicker in the dome above the dining table. Ben lit the candles and slid open one of the glass doors to the deck so that the pound and wash of the distant surf added to their conversation the ceaseless, darkling discourse of the sea.

Priscilla had decided to introduce their guests to local cuisine with a Southern shore dinner, which was a great success. It began with a shrimp bisque and went on to an entree of crab cakes with corn pudding, kale and hush puppies and a salad of huge, home-grown beefsteak tomatoes that Esther had brought fresh from the market that morning. Ben served a Maryland wine with the meal, a fine, flint-dry chardonnay from the Boordy vineyards in Westminster.

"I want your candid opinion on this wine," he said as he filled their glasses.

Jill sipped and blinked ecstatically. "Oh my, that's wonderful."

"It is indeed," Tony said. "Dry as a bone, but not bitter. Is it French?"

Ben handed him the bottle which Tony took and held into the candlelight to read the label. "Boordy. Good Lord, it's made in Maryland."

"Only a few miles from where we live," Ben said.

"I'd no idea you made wine like that. I could get addicted to that."

"I could get addicted to the lot," Jill said. "Those crab cakes, my word. Quite different to what we get in England."

"Like the shrimp," Tony said. "Another species of creature entirely."

"Even your sun is different here, do you know that? It's so tired and uncertain in England. Even on the Mediterranean. It's so ruddy savage here, or something. You don't feel as if you want to expose yourself to it lightly."

"That's a very good policy," Priscilla said. "You can get some terrible burns in this sun that take weeks to heal. And they can turn into melanoma years later. Even a single bad burn."

"You'll scare her to death," Ben said.

"Well, she should be warned. She doesn't want to open in New York covered with blisters."

"No fear of that," Jill said. "I've learned to be very careful."

"I've got some number fifteen lotion that I'm going to make you use. It's a total block."

"Total block? Oh, I don't want that. I want at least a tiny bit of burn to remember the place by. Wouldn't nine or ten do?"

"All right. We'll get you some tomorrow, but you've got to promise to use it. I'm not going to have my guests go back looking as if they'd been through the inferno."

"Oh no, just touched by a spark of the divine fire," Jill said. She settled back in her chair with her wine glass in her hand and gazed up at the dome. "That starlight would be almost enough, I think. God, how clear the sky is here. One almost never sees the stars in London. It's odd, to realize that. Something else to add to one's discontent."

"I hope we don't add to your discontent," Priscilla said.

"Well, you mustn't make me too happy, or I'll never write another word. Contentment is the artist's greatest enemy, someone said. Who said that, Tony?"

"No idea," Tony said.

"Well, we'll try to give you something to grumble about," Ben said. "How about having to make your own breakfast? Is that enough in the way of adversity?"

"Quite all right with me, I don't have breakfast. What is the regimen, anyway? I don't want to violate any sacred traditions or anything."

"There are no sacred traditions here except free enterprise. You can do anything you like that you can get away with," Priscilla said. "The only thing we're not accommodating about is breakfast. You can get up anytime you please and have anything to eat you can find in the fridge, provided you make it yourself."

"Just a cup of tea for me," Jill said. "I can't stand food before noon."

"That's all Ben ever has. He gets up about five every morning and goes for a long ramble up the beach to watch the sun rise. But you can sleep til noon if you like."

"No fear," Jill said. "I shall be up at dawn, here. It's not like waking up in Hammersmith."

"We usually take lunch down to the beach," Priscilla said. "And then spend the afternoon just loafing. Swimming or sailing or fishing. We could rent a charter boat if you want to go out and try for a marlin. Or we could go across to Okracoke one day, if the weather's nice. That's an island, about an hour off the tip of the banks by ferry. It's a beautiful trip, and an interesting old place. It used to be Blackbeard's headquarters."

"Blackbeard? Wasn't he a pirate?"

"Yes. A very ferocious one. He terrorized the Spanish Main from here. With the help of the governor, with whom he shared his loot."

"Did you hear that, Tony? A pirate cove."

"I told you we've always been hospitable to free enterprise," Priscilla said. "The original settlers were wreckers. That's how they made their livelihood, I understand."

"Not really? You mean they wrecked boats deliberately?"

"Yes. That's how Nags Head got its name," Priscilla said. "At least according to legend. They used to tie a lantern to a horse's neck and send it out on the banks in bad weather to lure the boats to shore. They would capsize on the Diamond Shoals, out there—" She pointed through the open door to the dark, star-sprinkled sea. "They call it the Graveyard of the Atlantic."

"Murder and pillage," Jill said. "I'd no idea the place was founded on it. You said it was peaceful here."

"It's very peaceful now. We've mellowed quite a bit."

"Have you? No more buccaneering? We've missed all the excitement then."

"We'll find some excitement for you," Ben said. "Have you tried dinghy sailing?"

"No, but I watched them at Cannes last summer, and it looked marvelous. Have you got one?"

"Yes. We'll take it over to the sound one day. It's a good safe place to learn. Very calm and shallow."

"Calm and shallow. That's my sort of thing."

Priscilla rang her silver service bell and Esther came in from the kitchen to collect their plates. She gathered them up quickly and silently with lowered eyes, and Ben saw that her lids were red and swollen. She returned from the kitchen with a hot beach plum pie which she set in front of Priscilla with a serving knife.

"It looks wonderful, Esther," Priscilla said. "Are they plums from last summer?"

"Yes, ma'am. You want coffee, ma'am?"

"Please."

The girl went hastily into the kitchen, her lips pressed together. Ben glanced questioningly at Priscilla. She shook her head gently and began to serve the pie. "This is Esther's specialty. She makes it every year for our first night on the Banks. I think you'll find it's unlike anything you've ever tasted."

"Indeed it is," Jill said, when she had tried a mouthful. "It's divine. Tony, taste it."

"It is," he said. "I don't suppose one dare ask for the recipe."

"It wouldn't do you any good," Priscilla said. "I don't think you have beach plums in England."

"You should export it," Jill said. "It would be far more welcome than hamburgers. Why is it you keep the best of your things at home? You're a canny lot."

"I suppose we don't have enough of them to go around," Priscilla said.

After coffee they left the table and sat in lounge chairs while Ben served liqueur. Priscilla carried her glass to the piano and played the first five of Beethoven's Diabelli Variations. The distant thunder of the surf mingled with the fragile, tranquil music and made a strange fugue of violence and delicacy.

"Oh, that's magical," Jill said. "You played it like an angel, Priss."

"An angel with a broken wrist," Priscilla said. "It's one of the few things I can manage, because it's very simple and romantic. Like me."

"You're nothing of the sort. Either of you."

A horn honked in the driveway below the house and Esther came out of the kitchen. "That's my dad," she said. "I'm going now, Mrs. Oakshaw."

"All right. It was a lovely dinner. Thank you, Esther."

"I'll be over at five o'clock tomorrow evening."

"Are you sure you can manage it?"

"Yes, ma'am," the girl said. She smiled hastily to the guests, as if unwilling to expose her face to their gaze. "Good night to you folks."

"Good night," Tony said. "It was a marvelous meal."

"It was," Jill said. "I've never had such pie in my life."

"Thank you, ma'am." She ducked her head and went quickly into the kitchen. In a moment they heard the slam of a car door from below the house and then a motor diminishing into the distance.

Ben said, "Well, what was all that about?"

Priscilla shook her head regretfully. "Oh, she's having trouble with Elbert. She's in an awful state."

"They breaking up or something?"

"I don't know. Let's not go into it."

"I think they'd both be better off," Ben said. "It's not what you'd call a union made in heaven."

"Well, let's not go into it, Ben. After all, it's her business."

"Well, I hope she gets it straightened out," Ben said. "You've got to keep the cook happy."

Priscilla lowered her eyes and laid her hands in her lap. "She's not just the cook," she said. "She's a friend. And a very sweet person."

"She seems it," Jill said. "What's the problem with this Elbert chap? Doing the dirty on her, is he?"

"I hope not," Priscilla said. She closed the piano and stood up. "Will anyone have some more Drambuie?"

"Not I," Jill said. "I'm ready for bed, myself."

"I'll bet you are. It was a long trip. You must be exhausted." She went to the glass doors and slid them closed. "I hope the surf doesn't keep you awake. It's rather loud tonight."

"No, I love it," Jill said. She got up from the sofa and went across to Priscilla and kissed her on the cheek. "You really are an angel, you know. It's like heaven, this place. You make me feel ashamed."

"Don't be silly. Ashamed of what? It's a delight, having you here. I hope you sleep well."

"*I* shall sleep like a stone," Tony said. "Good night, you chaps. And thanks for everything. It's been a splendid day."

"Good night."

In the bedroom, Priscilla undressed silently.

"What's the matter?" Ben said. "You unhappy about them?"

"No, of course not. They couldn't be more charming. I'm worried about Esther."

"What's the deal with her and Elbert, anyway?" Ben said. "Has he split, or what?"

"I don't know. He's up to something unpleasant. He says he wants to sell his boat and go up to Raleigh to study data processing."

"Data processing?" Ben said. "What gave him that idea?"

"He says that's where the future is. The charter business is running dry, he says, and he wants to get out."

"Well, maybe he's right. There's a hell of a lot of competition, and that boat of his is pretty old. It must cost him a fortune to maintain it. He's probably smart."

"He's not smart, he's cunning," Priscilla said. "Do you know what Esther's been doing?"

"No."

"She's been saving up her money for two years so they could get married. Or thought she was. Everything she's earned working for us she gave to him to put in the bank so he could get the boat repaired in the spring. He said they had to have something solid to start with. Now he says he wants to spend it on this data processing course up in Raleigh."

"Well, it sounds smart to me," Ben said. "He'll probably make a hell of a lot more money. They'll be better off."

"*He* will," Priscilla said. "*They* won't. He's not going to marry her."

"How do you know that?" Ben said.

"He met this girl from Raleigh down here last summer. She was staying at the Bayside Motel, and Elbert started seeing her. Ethel says he was down there almost every night while she was up here working for us."

"She know that for a fact?"

"Yes. People have told her. You can't keep that sort of thing quiet in the village for long."

"Huh," Ben said. He slid open the door to the deck, switched off the lamp and got into bed, lying with the back of his head cupped in his hands while he looked up at the ceiling. "Well, maybe it's just over. Hell, things are over sometimes. People just have to face the fact."

"He won't admit that, though. He lies to her. He won't admit he's been seeing this girl. Or that he wants to go up to Raleigh because she's there. He lets Esther think he's going to marry her."

"Well, maybe he is," Ben said. "Maybe this was just a summer thing he had with this girl. Maybe he's sincere about it."

"He's lying. He doesn't have any right to humiliate her like that," Priscilla said. "It's not decent. People ought to have the courage to tell the truth." Ben did not reply. "You don't really like her, do you?"

"I like her fine, as a cook," Ben said.

"You keep saying she's a cook."

"Well, she is. She's a *great* cook, and that's about it. I mean she's not really terribly thrilling as a person, is she? She doesn't have any imagination or ambition. And she smells like lard."

"Like lard?"

"Well, you know what I mean. She's got that kitcheny smell."

"I never heard you say anything like that before," Priscilla said.

"I've never really given her a lot of thought," Ben said. "Anyway, it's not your problem, is it? You've got plenty to worry about."

"I don't have a thing to worry about," Priscilla said. "That's what's the trouble with me. I never did."

"Never did? Listen, how about when we were in New York, living on cat food, practically. How about getting this place fixed up the way you did? And the house? How about when we were starting the business?" Priscilla pulled the sheet up to her chin and turned over in the bed, staring out into the moonlight on the deck. "Don't get so worked up about it," Ben said. "People's problems are their own. You can't solve them for them. You know that, Priss." He laid his hand on her shoulder and kissed the back of her neck.

"There's so much indecency in the world," Priscilla said. "It makes me sick."

"There's no sense getting so worked up about it. You've got a houseful of guests to worry about right now. Come on, get some sleep."

After several moments she said, "Good night."

"Good night." He touched her shoulder again but she did not turn over to be kissed. He lay beside her looking up at the ceiling until her breathing grew regular and deep. This took an hour or more, and as the moon rose outside, the milky pool of light on the floor withdrew stealthily toward the deck like an embarrassed ghost. Ben could not sleep. When the LED display on the bedside clock read two-fifteen, he got up carefully so as not to awaken Priscilla, put on a silk robe and went out to the kitchen to make a cup of tea. This was not unusual; he often woke at three or four in the morning, made a cup of tea, and carried it out to the deck where he drank it slowly, smoking a cigarette while he looked out at the ocean in the moonlight. It had become an almost nightly ritual, one that gave him a deeply satisfying, proprietary sense of peace. While he drank his tea and smoked his cigarette, he felt in solitary possession of the vast moonlit sea spread out before him, the stretch of bare beach glimmering between it and the house, the pale dunes, and the great black starlit vault of the sky. It was very much like sitting in his box in the Kennedy Center on an opening night watching the resolution of the vast concatenation of things that had begun with time and had awaited this moment to be revealed to the eye of man.

This night he did not have quite that feeling of eminence or distinction. The sea seemed enormously, darkly indifferent to his presence, the expanse of moonlit sand glowed with an eloquence not intended for his eyes, the breakers thundered distantly in a rumbling rhetoric that was not addressed to him, or to any of the privileged, ghostly spectators who sat beside him in the lofty darkness. Their meters pounded in his ears like the chant of pagan hordes from the wild marches beyond a castle wall.

He stood at the deck rail with his robe fluttering lightly in the sea breeze exposing his chest to a cool, intermittent caress that played across his flesh like the tips of blowing tresses. For some reason, a line of Eliot's "Prufrock" came into his mind as if carried there on the night wind like the taste of salt: "'Til human voices wake us, and we drown." He took the pack of cigarettes out of the pocket of his robe, extracted one, lit it from the one he was smoking, and dropped the stub of the first down onto the sand below the deck where it glowed for a moment or two before it went out. While he watched the dying light of the cigarette he heard the soft whisper of footsteps on the planks of the deck and turned to see Jill coming toward him around the curve of the deck. She was wearing a white nylon, calf-length negligee, and the robe, her face, and her bare legs glowed liked alabaster in the moonlight.

"Well," he said quietly. "I didn't expect to find you here. Couldn't you sleep?"

"No. Couldn't you?"

"Oh, I often get up and have a cup of tea out here at night. It's so beautiful."

"It is, yes. Unbelievable." She came to the rail and stood beside him, looking down at the pale, phosphorescent line of foam where the breakers thundered on the sand. "Have you got a cigarette?"

He took out the pack and offered it to her. She plucked one from the pack and mumbled, "Mmm." He took the lighter from his pocket and lit it, shielding the flame from the breeze with his cupped hand while she bowed her head over it. She inhaled deeply, raising her head to blow the smoke into the wind. "Lovely breeze."

"Yes."

"Warm breeze, starlit sea, moonlight. Everything one could ask."

"Very nearly," Ben said.

"Very nearly? What else could you ask for? This marvelous house, an advertising empire to go back to, a beautiful, adoring wife waiting in your bed. I'd say you were jolly lucky, Ben."

"I'd say both of us were."

"I suppose we are, yes."

"Tony seems very nice. I like him."

"Do you? I do too. I needed an older man, I suppose. I never realized that before."

"Yes, you did."

"I must say you and Priss seem to have struck it off very well. I wasn't sure you would, at all."

"She's quite a wonderful woman," Ben said. "I realize that more and more."

"So she seems. I'm not sure you deserve her, you know."

"I'm not sure I deserve any of this," Ben said. "Life is very much a matter of luck, I think. 'Being there,' as Jerzy Kosinski says."

"Oh, it's more than luck. One needs luck, too, of course. But it's more than that."

"I guess it is. Having a talent—a faculty of any kind—is luck, of course. But it's what you do with it that counts."

"Yes. That's what counts."

"You've certainly done the most with yours. You deserve congratulations. You really do, Jill."

"Thank you."

They stood for a moment in silence, listening to the distant tumult of the breakers.

"I often think about some of the really talented people we had at RADA. People I've never heard of since, and I wonder what's become of them."

"Yes, I know.

"Whatever happened to Jackie Queen, for example? God, that girl was so good, and I've never heard a word about her. Do you know what she's doing?"

"Jackie died three years ago, of an overdose," Jill said. "At some wretched hospital out in Mile End."

"My God," Ben said. "That's terrible. She was one of the most talented people I ever knew."

"Yes, she was."

"How do you know that? Did you keep up with her?"

"No, I saw it in the paper, just by chance. I hadn't seen her in years. We were in a little rep in Brixton together in '78 I think it was, and I lost track of her after that. We were supposed to get in touch, when she came back to London, but I never heard from her. I called the number she gave me, but it was disconnected. I don't think she came back, at all. I heard later that she'd gone off to the continent with some Greek businessman or other. At least that's what Norman Tozer told me. Evidently it all went to pot. He left her stranded in Rome or something, and she came tottering back to London a month or two before she died. I don't know all the details." Ben thought about this silently. Jill drew on her cigarette and blew out the smoke.

"Of course she was always a little crazy," Ben said. "She seemed to be just barely keeping it together, even at school. I'm not sure the theatre is the best profession for a girl like that."

"No, it's pretty wild out there," Jill said.

"Well, you seem to have survived it pretty well," Ben said. He turned to smile at her.

"Oh, yes. 'Ambition should be made of sterner stuff.'"

"Yes," Ben said. "And that's the melancholy truth. You know, I'm really delighted, Jill, that we met again like this."

"Yes, I am too."

"Are you really?"

"Yes, absolutely, It's wonderful to know you've done so well. I suppose I'd rather you'd done it in the theatre, but it's the fact that you still . . . have an affection for it . . . that really matters. Do you honestly intend to start one of your own?"

"I'd like to, very much," Ben said. "Or produce plays, or fund a fellowship or something. One thing I've thought of doing is setting up a scholarship for an American student at RADA."

"That would be marvelous," Jill said. She turned to him with a faint, wry smile. "Do you remember when we talked about there being a Benedict Oakshaw Prize at RADA one day?"

"*You* talked about it," Ben said. "I never put any stock in it. There'll much more likely be a Gillian Davenport Prize for playwriting."

"Oh Lord, it sounds like nominating me for canonization. I'm not sure I deserve that."

"I think you do. I don't think you realize what you've done."

"What have I done?"

"You've added a piece of poetry to English literature. You deserve to be beatified, at least." Jill turned away from him, smiling, and leaned with her elbows on the railing. "It's true. And I think I understand how hard it was. To turn an unhappy moment of your life into poetry, out of patience, and talent, and wisdom."

"Oh, Lord, wisdom!" She chuckled softly.

"Yes, wisdom. There's a lot of wisdom in your play. I can appreciate that more than anyone, I think."

"It must have given you quite a turn, watching it."

"I have to admit it made me squirm for a while. I felt pretty uncomfortable, and pretty sad. But then I sat there watching it and I began to realize that it was beautiful. A kind of poem, and I didn't feel uncomfortable any longer. It seemed to grant me amnesty for anything I may have done that was foolish, or vain, or selfish. For anything either of us may have done. Beautiful things do that. They seem to redeem everything, even the pain or sadness that they're made of."

"That was very nicely put," Jill said. "Thank you."

"Don't you feel that way?"

"I suppose they do, if they're beautiful enough. If they're true. But I don't write that well."

"I think you do."

"Oh no, not yet. But perhaps I will."

"I feel pretty sure of it," Ben said. "And I'd like to be a part of it. I mean that. It would be a privilege to help put it on the stage. It might well be the greatest contribution I could ever make to the theatre."

She turned to look at him as if searching his face for irony.

"Is this what they call being patronized?"

"No, it's certainly not that." He smiled solemnly.

"Perhaps it's one of your beaux gestes."

"No, not one of my beaux gestes." He laughed in a lightly chastened way.

She leaned against the railing facing him, the wind blowing her gown lightly, exposing the slender thighs that he remembered, with sudden excruciating clarity, having once stroked with his fingertips.

"I thought perhaps you'd changed," she said. "But you're still the same, in many ways."

"What ways?"

"You still sleep in the buff, I see." She smiled rakishly.

"I see you do too." He felt the words catch in mid-sentence with a quick glottal gulp, as if he had been struck across the throat. He tried to dispel the strange impression this must have made with a smile. "I suppose we're both incorrigible, in some ways. And I'm not sure I regret that. It's a mistake to exchange charm entirely for wisdom."

"That sounds *very* wise."

"Not wise enough to cost me all my charm, I hope."

"Oh, Lord, no. You? You don't have to worry about that."

He thought for a moment about the double implication of this. "I suppose I should say thanks for that, but I'm not sure." He laughed again.

"Take it as you like."

He stood looking at her for a moment, feeling his smile writhe and fade convulsively, like the features of a watercolor portrait exposed to the rain. This process of watery expunction seemed to penetrate his flesh and bones and to involve his brain and muscles. A mindless, liquefying impulse poured through him to take her in his arms and kiss her.

"Well, I guess I'd better get to bed, if we're to be up at dawn," he said rather harshly.

"All right. I'll just stay a minute longer. Have you got another cigarette?"

"Yes." He took out the pack and offered it to her. She plucked one out and dropped it into the pocket of her robe. "You'll need the lighter." He handed it to her and she put it into her pocket with the cigarette.

"Thank you."

"I'll see you in the morning," he said. "Good night."

"Good night, love."

The word stung him like a splash of dulcet acid. It had an invincibly possessive sound that seemed to dissolve the twelve years that lay between their last meeting and this moment. She might have been bidding him good-bye from the door of her flat in Hammersmith after one of their Tuesday afternoon trysts. He took his cup from the railing and went in through the glass door to the living room. When he slid it closed behind him he saw that she had turned to face the sea, her short gown blowing like a Greek chiton in the wind.

·   ·   ·

In the morning the wind had dropped and when he got up at five o'clock it was close and still, with a colorless, pearl-bright light on the sea and the feel of a hot day coming. He did not stop to make a cup of tea before he went for his morning walk along the beach. Jill was not yet awake— or not yet abroad, at any rate—and he was afraid that she would appear while he was making the tea and ask to join him.

He sat out north toward the lighthouse, watching the light intensify into a soft, mercurial blaze on the horizon where the sun was rising. He walked on the hard sand through the shallow cold glissade of water that slid down the beach in a thin, swift-running pane. It splashed his legs and sprayed his thighs with a volley of cold drops that made him cringe. When he had walked two miles he sat down on a huge, bleached timber that lay half-buried in the sand and watched the sun rise above the sea. It came up through a cloud bank that burst into milky incandescence, spilling a silver light across the water. The sight of the daybreak calmed the turmoil that had kept him awake most of the latter part of the night. He looked back down the beach toward the house to assure himself that Jill had not followed in his wake. He would have to avoid any further têtes-à-tête with her, he decided categorically. He could not subject himself again to any such demented impulse as the one that had seized him last night on the deck. He still felt shaken by the recklessness of his own feelings. What in the name of God was the matter with him? Was he so incredibly promiscuous, or infirm of purpose, or faithless, or fatuous that he could be tempted by the girl, after having scarcely given her a thought for twelve years? Did she have some inextinguishable allure for him that had lain smouldering in his breast all that time like an ember? Why had he very nearly allowed himself to risk his marriage, his small claim to dignity, the whole of his present extremely pleasant existence on such an insane impulse? It was unbelievable, grotesque. It was ludicrous, in fact. That was by far the best way to regard it: a ludicrous moment of aberration, inexplicable and of no real significance, like the urge to hurl a rock through the window of a deserted factory, or weeping at the sight of Celia Johnson's face in an old movie. Such moments passed, one went on for another twelve years, or twenty, or a lifetime, without ever remembering them again.

Of course there had been very little risk at all, in fact. There was almost no chance that Priscilla would have come out onto the deck at that moment; and as for Jill, he was sure that her discretion was impeccable. She was obviously just as anxious to preserve her relationship with Tony as he was to preserve his marriage, and he had no doubt that she had grown in sagacity just as she had grown in experience and beauty. Which she had: she was even more beautiful than she had been as a girl. There was something womanly and grave and resolute about her that added depth and substance to her wit and vitality. And then, of course, she was successful; that made a difference, with anyone.

The sun broke free of its enclosing cloud, and in the sudden dazzling light of morning, the day's first shadows were born, little ragged remnants of the night that lay behind every stick of driftwood, every seashell or pebble or carcass of a crab. He walked back to the house watching his own stride beside him on the sand, lengthened into matinal nobility.

When he got back to the house everyone was up and there was a cheerful morning stir in the kitchen where Tony was cooking scrambled eggs and delivering a polemic on the arts.

"Consider that in preparing these scrambled eggs," he said, "I am functioning as an artist. Which is quite true. You may have heard it said that everything really enjoyable in life is either illegal, immoral, or fattening. A complaint which Aristotle overlooked in forming his conception of the arts. He insisted that they should be leached of all impurities, as today we leach our food of everything that appeals to the sensual appetite — oils, animal fats, salt, sugar, cholesterol, and so on — and that they should be fortified with moral precepts, as today we fortify virtually everything we eat, from milk to breakfast cereal, with vitamins, vegetable fibre, and activated ergosterol, whatever that may be. He worried that the citizens of Athens, in witnessing the excesses common to Greek drama — adultery, incest, the serving up of roasted children at the dinner table — were subjecting themselves to unnecessary and debilitating suffering and horror and, what was even more alarming, that they might develop a taste for these excesses, so that eventually — as proved to be the case among the Romans — they might revel in the spectacle of young men being devoured by lions or chopping off one another's arms and legs. It was his prescription that such horrors were excusable only if they had a moral purpose, only if they edified their witnesses sufficiently to produce in them a suitable aversion to such practices. The enjoyment of anything brutal, vulgar, unduly voluptuous or salacious for its own sake was degenerate, and productive of nothing but decadence. This is the view which is still prevalent in the West among such critics as your Mr. Trilling and our Mr. Leavis. Now, fortunately for you, I am preparing these eggs according to the precepts of the gourmet, not the critic. Suppose, however, that I should prepare them according to Aristotle's prescription. That I should use no salt whatever — " He swept the salt shaker over the pan lavishly. "No debilitating spices, such as pepper." He peppered the eggs vigorously. "No butter." He cut a generous chunk of butter from the stick set on the countertop

and flipped it into the frying pan. "No such debasing seasonings as garlic." He added a delicate sprinkle of garlic powder to the mixture. "No parsley. No fine ground Parmesan. And furthermore, that I should remove
the yolks before cooking them, and serve them up with unleavened toast
and warm barley-water, which is quite free of caffeine. How many takers
should I have?"

"What about Marmite?" Jill said. "You can't make decent eggs without Marmite."

"I'm afraid we don't have any," Priscilla said. "We keep a very classical
cupboard."

Tony raised his eyebrows lugubriously and went on stirring the eggs with
a wooden spoon. "The point is," he said, "that the gourmet is limited by no
Aristotelian demands or expectations. He asks only delight. He understands
that art is quite indifferent to moral imperatives or critical injunctions.
He accepts its prodigality, which is that of any genuine vision of perfection.
Sometimes it edifies or nourishes, and sometimes, I daresay, it damages the
digestion. Some few feeble souls it may corrupt. But this does nothing to
discredit its supreme and inimitable function, which is to make life toler-
able to many of us who would otherwise die of boredom, or disgust, or horrors which are far from fanciful. It is savory, exciting, full of 'nimble, fiery,
and delectable shapes,' as Shakespeare puts it so well. And therefore,
dangerous." He shook a sprinkling of parsley leaves into the pan. "Which
is no doubt why Plato banned poetry from his Republic. Politicians are not
noted for their hospitality to art. It is inimical to their own makeshift pretensions to perfection."

"Well, you can't wonder, really," Jill said. "When you've got people
like Sappho and Anacreon turning out the sort of stuff they wrote, it's apt
to make any politician nervous." She was applying suntan lotion to her bare
legs which projected from beneath a scarlet Hopi coat. "Of course if
he'd been really thorough about it, he'd have got rid of the lunatics and
lovers, too. Shakespeare also said, 'The lunatic, the lover, and the poet
are of imagination all compact.'"

"I think both our prime minister and your president would approve of that," Tony said. "Just think how safe and tidy our streets would be then. Nothing but businessmen in sight."

"I'm surprised you're not an artist yourself," Ben said. "You have such an understanding and appreciation of it."

Tony lifted his hand emptily. "I have no talent, old boy. I'm only a voyeur, an amateur. My only joy is to behold it, and, very rarely, to watch a genuine work of it being brought to perfection. Which is the second greatest privilege of this world." He raised the wooden spoon from his panful of scrambled eggs and tasted them delicately. "About these eggs, however, there is no need to apologize. They're quite perfect." He dipped out another spoonful and offered it to Priscilla. She nibbled thoughtfully, swallowed, and nodded.

"Absolutely perfect. There's no doubt about it. They're straight from heaven."

"Let's have a taste," Jill said. Priscilla passed the spoon to her. She tasted the eggs and scowled. "Well, you come from a different part of heaven than I do. They've got no Marmite in them. You can't have eggs without Marmite. And they're not cooked nearly enough. They're practically raw."

"You don't come from heaven at all," Tony said. "You come from other regions entirely, where you're used to having things scorched, no doubt."

"I don't suppose you mean Hammersmith."

"Quite possibly."

Ben brought his tea to the table and sat down beside Priscilla, putting his arm around her shoulders.

"How was your walk?" she asked.

"Great. It's a beautiful morning. I could have walked forever."

"Did you hear the weather report?"

"No, what's it say?"

"They say that storm's still hanging around. It's stalled off Bermuda."

"We thought we'd take a lunch down to the beach and just loaf this morning," Priscilla said. "Soak up some sun and salt water and let everyone get rehabilitated."

"Is that all right?" Jill asked. "We're feeling very idle." She put the cap back on the lotion bottle and rubbed her hands vigorously along her thighs.

"Anything is all right," Ben said. "This is not a Platonic paradise. Not even poetry is forbidden."

"I'm very glad to hear it," Tony said. He brought his pan of eggs to the table. "Anyone for ambrosia?"

"Not I," Jill said. "They're bloody awful."

"I don't eat before noon," Ben said. "I'll have another cup of tea in a minute."

"I'll have some," Priscilla said. "I say they're heavenly."

They sat in silence while Tony and Priscilla ate their eggs, nodding to each other and murmuring rapturously. Jill crossed her legs, picked up her teacup and stared out through the glass doors at the sea. "It seems to me we've already got Plato's paradise," she said. "War, and chauvinism, and sexism, and slavery. Got it to a T. They should all be very happy, really, the bloody Platonists. I prefer old Omar's version, since poetry's to be allowed." Staring at the sea, she murmured:

A book of verses underneath a bough,
A loaf of bread, a jug of wine, and thou,
Beside me, singing in the wilderness.
Ah, wilderness were paradise enow.

"Not with me singing beside you, I'm afraid," Tony said. "I can't get through 'Three Blind Mice' in one key." He looked at her in a gently afflicted way, like a man suffering a twinge of arthritis while he spoke. She laughed and leaned across the table to take his hand.

"Never mind, love," she said. "We can bring the gramophone."

When the others had finished their breakfast and gone in to shower and shave and change into their swimming suits, Ben prepared the picnic lunch. This was his province, on which Priscilla never intruded. It was for him a ritual, a luxurious rite which he performed devoutly and with quiet passion, in the way that men of leisure polished the hardware of their yachts or cultivated orchids. For the eighteen years of his youth he had lived on a relentless diet of fatback, okra, and boiled potatoes, and for him expensive and exotic foods had come to have an almost sacramental significance. It gave him a feeling of exquisite tranquillity to make elaborate lunches, slowly and methodically, with a fastidious attention to detail, garnishing a deviled egg with parsley, studding a sauce with capers, setting a floral wreath of sliced tomatoes around a bowl of seafood salad. When he suffered a temporary spell of anxiety or fatigue from a particularly complex or ferocious business deal or was depressed by the sight of a derelict huddled on a grating above a metro station on a winter evening, it calmed him to go into the Sutton Place Gourmet, an expensive catering establishment in Bethesda, and roam along the aisles studying the wine labels, imported cheeses, Huntley and Palmer's biscuits, exotic blends of tea or tins of plum pudding from Fortnum and Mason's, Icelandic brisling, Perugina chocolates. The scents, the delicate wickerware containers, the foreign labels, the discreet, soft-spoken clerks, even the tabernacle-like architecture of the place was soothing, mystical, a sort of gastronomic equivalent of a tour through an art gallery or the Grand Foyer. Often, before they went down to Hatteras, he spent an entire afternoon shopping for a supply of delicacies with which to delight Priscilla and their guests. It was not that he was a gourmand or a glutton; he was very conscious of his weight, never over-ate, and many of these epicurean delights he did not himself particularly enjoy; it was simply that they were sumptuous, emblems of taste and luxury, like his Bonnards and Pollocks, and it restored and reassured him to contemplate them and know that he could afford almost any of the chef d'oeuvres that caught his eye.

He made a lunch of slivers of cold salmon laid geometrically on a nest of shad roe and watercress, a wheel of Brie and a Roquefort in a beguiling willow box, English water biscuits, French *gaufrettes*, a thermos of cold vichyssoise, and a salad of squid, endive, feta, and Greek olives. He packed the food into a large wicker hamper and worked three bottles of chardonnay into cracked ice in the cooler. When it was ready he called them in from the deck and they descended onto the beach in a caravan, with the hamper, the cooler, a pair of beach umbrellas, aluminum lounge chairs, a folding metal table, and a beach bag stuffed with towels, blankets, Kleenex and sun lotion.

They set up the umbrellas, the tables and the folding chairs, and spent the morning splashing in the surf, sunbathing, and retreating occasionally into the shadow of their canopy, all but Tony, who took up his position there from the start, in a pair of flaming plaid Bermuda shorts and a hooded jacket that Jill had bought him in Washington and which he never took off, even when he made his single venture down into the surf. He waded into the water to his knees, lumbering back hastily before the first oncoming wave, and retreated into the shadow of the umbrella where he sat down and covered his feet, which projected out into the sunlight, with a towel. "I can't afford to get exposed," he said. "I get very pink, like a roast suckling pig, and awaken unpleasant instincts in everyone." Ben lay in a folding chaise lounge and watched Jill and Priscilla tumbling through the breakers like a pair of dolphins, leaping up and staggering about with drenched hair and beautiful glittering bodies when they capsized in the sand, shrieking with delight.

"Nereids," Tony said.

"Yes. They're lovely creatures."

"To know such women would justify a lifetime of misfortune. Indeed, it justifies the eons of oblivion before they ever appeared on this earth, or after they are gone. To think one might never have been born." He said this with such quiet fervor that Ben turned to look at him.

"You are a true connoisseur," he said.

"I like to think so. I consider it my reward for not having been a barrister, and my penance for not having been a poet."

They watched the two women stagger up the sand and collapse into their beach chairs where they began to towel themselves dry, panting and exhilarated.

"You were very impressive," Ben said.

"Oh, God, it's lovely!" Jill said. "It's like splashing about in champagne. One never wants to stop."

"I had to," Priscilla said. "I'm exhausted. I thought you said you weren't an athlete. My God!"

"I'm not, at all. It's pure euphoria."

"How about some cold salmon and white wine?" Ben said.

"You can have my immortal soul for some," Priscilla said.

"I haven't got a soul," Jill said. "But anything else you fancy is yours."

Ben tossed a linen cloth across the table with a flourish, and while the women put on cabana coats and combed their hair he set chilled glasses from the cooler in front of them, opened a bottle of the cold chardonnay and filled their glasses with the misty, sparkling wine. They sipped their bowls of vichyssoise and nibbled slices of cool salmon, Brie, biscuits spread with Roquefort, little savory slivers of squid and spears of endive sprinkled with fresh, sweet olive oil. The air all around their circle of shadow pulsed with light while they sipped cold wine and fell into a sated, glowing torpor, stretching out their legs and gazing at the sea.

"Jolly difficult life, this," Jill said.

"All tears and travail," Tony said.

"It is, you know. Makes one wonder if it's worth it."

"Are you sure you've had enough?" Priscilla said. "There's lots more of everything."

"Good Lord. You're joking."

"Ben puts together a very good picnic lunch, I have to admit it," Priscilla said. "It's something to cherish in a man."

"He does indeed," Jill said. "I never knew a man who did it better."

"The picnic is an art form," Ben said hastily. "Or should be. You have to give yourself into it."

"I quite agree," Tony said. "It is the last ceremony in which the Dionysian impulse is preserved, and often startlingly manifested, to the considerable embarrassment of all concerned. That is what Manet attempted to convey in his famous painting on the subject. There is little wonder that it was rejected by the hanging committee of the Salon in 1863, or that when it was exhibited shortly after, in the Salon des Refusés, it caused a scandal in the sad hearts of the nineteenth-century French businessmen, two of whom seem to be enjoying themselves thoroughly in the painting. But did you know that the ladies in the scene were painted au naturel, in every sense of the word? Antonin Proust, who was a great friend of the artist, tells us that Manet stumbled on the scene in a forest by the Seine near Argenteuil, where they were bathing naked. He remarked at the time, 'It seems I must do a nude. All right, I'll do one for them. They'll slay me for it, but let them say what they like.' And slay him they very nearly did."

"Is that true?" Jill asked. "How utterly delicious."

"Oh, yes." He looked at her fondly for a moment. "Manet understood women, and their relation to society, as no other artist of his time. Or of any time, I think. In the whole history of painting, there is only one woman whom I absolutely adore, and that is his Olympia. Let me tell you what Valéry wrote of her. I happen to remember his remarks verbatim because they are dear to me: 'Olympia shocks, evokes a holy terror, imposes herself on us, and triumphs. She is a scandal, and yet an idol; a force, and the personification in public of the shameful secrets of society.' These are the words of a poet, you should remember; not a critic."

"I think we should drink to them," Ben said. He opened another bottle of wine.

"You're feeling very festive," Priscilla said.

"We can't let these people go back without understanding the American position thoroughly." He was feeling a little drunk.

"Well, I'm going to put off that knowledge for a while," Jill said. "Or I shall be too drunk to profit by it. I'm going to walk up to the lighthouse." She stood up and looked at Tony, who had pulled his hood down over his eyes, lain back in his lounge chair, and apparently retired. She nudged him with her toe. "I said I'm going to walk up to the lighthouse."

"Oh, yes? Well, I'm sure you want to be alone," he said.

"Well, I don't *mind* being, of course."

"Good. Let me know when you get back."

"I will. Shall I kick you in the crotch?"

"That won't be necessary. Just a tap on the elbow."

She turned and strode away, sand spraying from her feet.

"Is she angry?" Priscilla asked.

"Oh, no. She just has spells of volatility," Tony said. "Nothing to worry about. When she comes back she'll be right as a trivet."

This proved to be true. She was back in half an hour, galloping gleefully through the sand with a clenched fist held triumphantly aloft.

"Look what I've found!" she cried, falling onto her knees in front of them. She held out a smooth chalky disc decorated with five little perforations like the spokes of a star.

"A sand dollar!" Priscilla said. "It's a perfect one."

"Isn't it lovely? I'm going to put it on a chain."

"You don't often find one that isn't broken, or that's such a perfect shape," Ben said. "It'll make a beautiful pendant."

"Won't it? Look, Tony."

"Extraordinary," Tony said. "I've seen them in the shops, but I've never known anyone to actually find one. I'm sure it's a portent of good luck. You must keep it as an amulet."

"I shall. And you can buy me a chain for it, for my birthday. I think platinum would be nice."

"Oh, just the thing," Tony said. "I'm glad you suggested it."

She put it in her pocket and pressed it to her side, grinning. "I've found a bit of treasure in your pirate's cove. And I've got all hot and thirsty from my expedition. I suppose you've drunk all the wine, you lot of sots."

"I'm afraid so," Ben said. "But there's more at the house. Why don't we go up?"

They spent the end of the afternoon on the eastern side of the sun-deck which was now in shadow, watching the sea darken to violet and the long swells sweeping in, low and glittering like glass, with an ancient, soothing, eternal regularity. Far to the north the lighthouse sharpened in the low light.

"Is it very old?" Tony asked.

"About a hundred years. It's the tallest lighthouse in America. When it was built it was a mile inland, but now the water's right at the base of it. They've had to build a seawall to keep it from tumbling down."

"Do you mean the land's been eaten away that much, in just a hundred years?"

"Yes. We lose a foot or two of it every year. Every time we come down, the beach is narrower."

"Good Lord, I don't suppose there's any danger to the house?"

"Oh, it'll come down, eventually. But not in our time, I hope. Unless we get a really bad storm."

"Housman wrote a poem about that," Tony said. "Do you know Housman? He came from Shropshire, Jill's part of the world."

"Say it for us," Priscilla said.

"Shall I? It's rather grim, I'm afraid. Still." He stared out at the sea and quoted in a sonorous, rhythmic way, as if keeping time with the ceaseless thunder of the breakers:

Smooth between sea and land
Is laid the yellow sand,
And here through summer days
The seed of Adam plays.

Here the child comes to found
His unremaining mound,
And the grown lad to score
Two names upon the shore.

Here, on the level sand,
Between the sea and land,
What shall I build or write
Against the fall of night?

Tell me of runes to grave
That hold the bursting wave,
Or bastions to design
For longer date than mine.

Shall it be Troy or Rome
I fence against the foam,
Or my own name to stay
When I depart for aye?

Nothing: too near at hand,
Planing the figured sand,
Effacing clean and fast
Cities not built to last
And charms devised in vain,
Pours the confounding main.

Priscilla shivered. "It is grim," she said. "I think all poems about the sea are pretty melancholy."

"Oh, no," Tony said. "That one of Swinburne's is very comforting. And the Masefield ones are quite pleasant. There are some very nice poems about the sea. Jill, why don't you tell us that one you say now and again? About the figurehead?"

"I hope it isn't as melancholy as the Housman one," Priscilla said.

"No, not at all," Tony said. "It's rather a religious poem, really." Jill looked into her wine glass. After a moment Ben said, "Well, are we going to hear it?"

She gazed at him for a moment. "Yes, all right. It's a sort of mono-logue, spoken by a figurehead. This carved, bare-breasted figure of a woman that a seaman has taken down from the prow of his ship, after he's stopped sailing, and set up in his garden." She raised her head and gazed out at a bank of purple cloud above the sea, speaking with a kind of decorous modesty, as if reciting a creed:

I was not meant to stand in a sea-edged garden,
Yearning across the wet brown sand for the rumor of ships,
Breasting the dusty surf of the upland daisies,
Sick for the cry of the gulls and the salt on my lips.

Ours was the way of the reef and the thundering billow.
Ours was the way of the wind and the perilous way of the fog.
If hearts must be stouter than yours for the keeping of sea-faith,
Shall a sea-woman follow you home like a wife or a dog?

You who have piled white towers of thunder above us,
You who have trysted afar in golden and fabulous lands,
Shall I watch you feeding the doves in a landsman's dooryard?
Sweeping a landsman's hearth with a seaman's hands?

What will you have to say to your inland woman?
Will you speak to her of the wild and shining roads of our sea?
Safe in the candle-light, as the drowned are safe,
Will you speak of the bitter, bright peril you followed with me?

I shall go back again to the sea and his mercy.
I shall go back to the winds and the measureless skies.
I who have sailed on the tide of his fathomless bounty
Shall die in his gales, and his grace, as a sea woman dies.

"Oh, how lovely," Priscilla murmured. She sat silently, gazing at the sea with a look almost of woe.

"Who wrote that?" Ben asked.

"I've no idea. I learnt it when I was a kid. I don't suppose it's very great poetry, but it gave me the chills."

"It does me, too," Priscilla said.

Esther came through the living room to the glass door and slid it open. "Mrs. Oakshaw, you better have a look at this rack of lamb," she said. "I think it's just about ready."

"All right, Esther. Thank you."

"And, ma'am."

"Yes?"

"I wanted to ask Mr. Oakshaw if he thought he could drive me home tonight. Elbert was going to come get me, but he got held up some way."

"Can you, Ben?"

"Yes," Ben said shortly. "I'd be very glad to." It annoyed him vastly that she almost never addressed him directly but always through Priscilla, as a sort of intermediary, a procedure that seemed to imply fear, distrust, or total lack of confidence in their ability to communicate.

"I hate to bother you, sir, when you got company and all, but Daddy's up to Salvo."

"That's all right. I'll be happy to."

They did not talk very much at dinner. Jill's recitation seemed to have cast a spell over them, and their conversation was subdued and random, furnished with most of its vitality by Tony's occasional congratulations on the rack of lamb, the artichokes, and the Nesselrode pie. As she poured their coffee, Priscilla said, "That poem you said makes me want to take a voyage. I think we ought to go over to Ocracoke tomorrow."

"Marvelous," Jill said. "I'd love to see the pirate's lair."

"We'll have to get up pretty early if you want to take the morning ferry," Ben said. "It leaves at nine."

"That's all right with me," Jill said. "We'll go to bed early and have a good night's sleep. I don't know about you chaps, but I don't think I can stay awake another hour, anyway. I'm worn out from all that tumbling about."

"So am I," Priscilla said. "It always takes me a day or two to get in stride when we come down here."

"I'm done in from eating," Tony said. "My jaws will ache for a solid month, I think."

"How do you feel, Ben?" Priscilla asked.

"Fine with me. We'll just have a drop of Drambuie, and then it's off to Blackbeard's in the morning."

"Let's have a pirate song!" Jill said, restored to sudden vivacity by the prospect. She raised her liqueur glass and chanted in a husky, false baritone: "Fifteen men on a dead man's chest!"

The others joined in the refrain, thumping their fists on the table:

Yo, ho, ho, and a bottle of rum!
Drink and the devil had done for the rest.
Yo, ho, ho, and a bottle of rum!
A wench, and a tune, and a toast to the Pope!
Yo, ho, ho, and a bottle of rum!
And a last jolly jig at the end of a rope.
Yo, ho, ho, and a bottle of rum!

"Now then," she said, as they sprawled laughing at the table, "we're in a proper frame of mind. That's a bit more like it!"

The drive in to Hatteras Village with Esther took only fifteen minutes but it was one Ben always dreaded. Keeping a conversation alive with her was an ordeal at the best of times, and in her present state of gloom it took a heroic effort on his part. The effort was preferable, however, to the silence into which they both sank like stones the minute he stopped making comments about the weather, the state of the road, the Firemen's Fish Fry scheduled for the coming Friday, the beach erosion, or the

number of out-of-state licenses in the village that summer. It was a silence so profound and solitary that it seemed to mock and threaten the
whole elaborate pretense of human intercourse, of civilization itself, like
a black hole sucking inexorably at the desperately glittering constellations of the stars.

"The fish fry is next Friday, right?"

"Yes, sir."

"It was a great one, last year. I'll bet I ate a bushel of bluefish."

"It's always right good."

"The blues been running yet, this year?"

"No, they won't run till August."

"Oh, that's right. August." After a moment he added, "I guess it was something else I had. Maybe flounder."

"Yes, sir, more likely."

"How's your mother been, Esther?"

"She's right well, thank you."

"She was having some trouble, wasn't she? With her eyes?"

"Yes, sir. Cataracks."

"Oh, yes. Cataracts. Well, that's not too serious any more, you know.
They have this new laser operation."

"Is that so?"

"They remove them with light beams. Don't use a knife at all."

"They do?"

"Yes. People can get up and go home just a couple of hours afterwards."

"I didn't know that."

"Yes. Amazing, isn't it?"

"Yes it is."

There was a silence of ominously growing depth.

"Well, I guess you're glad you don't have to cook for us tomorrow."

"I'd just as soon cook as sit home."

"You ought to get up to Avon and take in the movie." She did not
reply. "What's playing up there this week?"

"I don't know. Some show or other."

He pulled with infinite relief into the driveway of her house. "Looks like you've been doing some painting," he said, peering at the house in the headlights.

"Daddy started on the porch, yeah."

"It looks nice."

"I don't know why he picked blue."

"It'll look nice when it's all done. Well, good night, Esther."

"Goodnight, Mr. Oakshaw."

"We'll see you on Tuesday, then."

"Yes, sir."

God help us, he thought, driving back along the dark road with the surf booming behind the dunes, what is the matter with women like that? So goddamned lovesick and gloomy all the time they make you want to kick them. He felt full of a sudden mindless rage at her petty misery and self-preoccupation. Jesus Christ, I'll bet it's what drove Blackbeard to sea. Some woman yelling at him, "Love me, love me, love me," all day long. It's enough to make a pirate out of any man.

Everyone was in bed when he got back to the house. He went into the den, switched on the television and watched a late-night rerun of *Jeopardy*, a quiz show that he was "hooked on," Priscilla said, and which he played with a skill that astonished her. It soothed him like a tour of the National Gallery or the Sutton Place Gourmet. He took a fierce delight in competing with the panel of contestants, and almost always defeated them. He had a prodigious store of general information which he had acquired over the last ten years in an effort to educate himself which had become chronic and compulsive. He had become addicted to learning as he was addicted to gourmet food and works of art, and for the same reason. The fact that he had never been to college clung to him, he felt, as conspicuously as a cheap, mended suit or the smell of lard from his mother's cooking. That his passion for statistics, data, terminology of the most abstruse kind was abject or abnormal he refused to consider; it was, he told himself, the natural interest of a civilized man in the phenomena

of the world around him, although he could not fail to recognize as extravagant the satisfaction it gave him to be able to supply, in the course
of a dinner-table conversation about Central America, the fact that Nicaragua
had a long history of American intervention beginning in 1856, when
the Tennessee adventurer, William Walker, invited to assist the liberals
in the civil war of 1855, made himself president of the country and was
routed only through the joint efforts of the five Central American republics
and the Accessory Transit Company of Cornelius Vanderbilt. There was
an intoxicating prestige in the possession of such facts, and in the ability
to dispense them dramatically on social and professional occasions. Until he was thirty years old he had not known the geographical locations, lan-
guages, or capital cities of any ten countries of the world; this and his equal
ignorance of almost any topic unrelated to acting or the theatre had been
a severe and mortifying handicap in the early days of his career in advertising. The people he hired were highly trained specialists in sociology, psychology, art, demographics, history, politics, a score of subjects, common
and arcane, and he often felt at a humiliating loss in the most elemental
discussion with them of any of these topics. To be so often left writhing
in embarrassed silence before people whose salaries he paid was not only
a professional disability but a personal disgrace, and he had resolved fiercely
to correct it. He began to subscribe to journals and periodicals devoted
to scholarly, often esoteric subjects: the *Antiquarian*, the *Lancet*, the *Nu-
mismatist*, the *American Architect*, the *Turkoman Review*. He bought an
edition of the *Encyclopedia Britannica* and began to read at the rate of
something like ten pages a night, from the first entry to the last (Abd-Al-
Malik to Zworykin), with frequent excursions into intermediate entries
when current events or particular occasions recommended it. He discovered that his memory for facts which in his days at Groveland High School
had languished like a sleeping hound, awoke, ravenous, and was as re-
luctant to part with a piece of information as a bulldog with a bone. He
could produce bits of exotica years after he had read them, with a fidelity
that was astounding and that earned him a growing reputation as an

intellectual. He accumulated the facts of history, science, art and politics in the same way that he accumulated objets d'art, to assuage a sense of poverty and ignominy that seemed to be incurable.

Eventually, as in the case of the art works with which he decorated his existence, he found that he could relieve his sense of destitution by convincing those around him of his prosperity—intellectual as well as material. If his friends and associates, and especially if Priscilla, believed him to be a thoughtful, learned man, it served to ease his own dark misgivings. He began, in a vague, eager, credulous way, to believe it himself, although he was stealthily aware that it was not wisdom he sought, but the name of wisdom. True wisdom, he mournfully suspected, was like Priscilla's gentility: it would have forbidden anyone who possessed it to advertise the fact.

But it was comforting to be regarded by his fellow men as sensitive, wise, and prosperous. In some paradoxical way it confirmed his own abiding suspicion that he was a poor and ignorant man sustained only by a set of illusions, and yet allowed him to honor those illusions, by which he managed to create an identity. All earthly illusions, he realized, were only poor, poetic imitations of some sublime act of artifice, inspired pretensions and inventions which deserved the same respect he felt for an imaginative performance at the Kennedy Center. All men indulged in them; and his own, after all, were innocent enough. They did no one any harm; they were not vicious deceptions of the kind by which politicians thrived and confidence men or counterfeiters gained illicit fortunes. He practiced them only for the purpose of maintaining his self-respect, and perhaps his belief in his existence, which was forgivable, if not heroic. He began to take a candid pride in his role as a rural prodigy at RADA, as a Marine sergeant, an advertising tycoon, an esthete, and a lover. By the time he was thirty-eight he collected facts obsessively, as a kind of impassioned hobby, in the way that other men collected stamps or butterflies or first editions, and enjoyed reciting them in public in the way that other men enjoyed exhibiting their albums or incunabula. Every time he won a game of *Jeopardy* or beguiled a group of friends with some piece of arresting lore, he felt better, stronger, quieter in mind, more kindly, more indulgent of people less gifted or successful than he. It had the effect on him that winning a set of tennis or a round of golf had on some of his friends. They bought drinks afterwards in the clubhouse, and were full of the smiling magnanimity of men enjoying the assurance that they are a match for anyone.

In front of him on the screen, the host, a dapper young man named Alex Trebek, was announcing the category of Final Jeopardy, the game's last round, on which contestants were allowed to bet all or any part of their winnings. "The category is Religion," he said, "and this is the answer." On the screen behind him were lighted the words: HIS NAME IN SANSKRIT MEANS "THE ENLIGHTENED ONE." "You must write down the question to which that is the correct answer," Trebek said. "I'll give you a few minutes to think about it while we hear these important messages. Remember, you can bet all or any part of your winnings."

"I'll bet this house," Ben said aloud. He poured himself a glass of scotch and lit a cigarette while the announcer intoned commercial messages, and pictures of bedroom furniture and luggage flashed across the screen. The contestants seemed uncertain; they frowned, bit their lips, stared into space. "Now, let's see what you have written," Trebek said after this interlude. Two of the contestants had written nothing; their screens were blank. The third had written, "The Prophet." All had wagered large sums of money.

"Who was Gautama Buddha?" Ben said. He sipped his scotch, sprawled indolently in his chair.

"Well, I'm afraid we all did pretty poorly on that one," Trebek said. "The correct question is, 'Who was Gautama Buddha?'" Ben switched off the television and finished his scotch. He did not feel his customary glow of triumph. His victory seemed embarrassingly unimportant. He got up, switched off the light in the den and went out across the living room to the bedroom, pausing to look up through the dome at the pale, astral glow of the Milky

Way. In the bedroom he undressed in the dark and got into bed beside Priscilla, who stirred and murmured, "Everything all right?"

"Yeah, fine. Go to sleep."

He lay looking across her shoulder through the glass door at the pale dunes beyond the house. Above them stars glittered in the black sky in their fragile, delicate equilibrium, balanced in each other's gravities like snowflakes held aloft by a child's breath.

.   .   .

In the morning it was clear and bright, the air washed clean by a midnight shower and cool as liniment on the skin. They sat in the Mercedes at the toll booth waiting for the ferry to arrive, with the doors open and a breeze blowing through the car. In front of them the water of the strait was blue in the channels and green above the shallow sandy bottom, with the low islands and sandbars of the sound lying sharp in the morning light. They had an almost artificially dramatic look of dimension, as if seen through stereoscopic lenses. To their left, the strait was bordered by a long white line of foam where the rollers coming in from the Atlantic broke on the distant shoals. There were gulls wheeling and circling above the ferry landing, sometimes falling out of the sky in a disastrous-looking sprawl to the surface of the water where they righted themselves with a flurry of wings, snatched at a chunk of bread someone had thrown to them, and soared aloft, imperturbable and tireless in their voracity. There were little yellow butterflies flittering above the bluets in the grass beside the road and a clean smell of brine blowing in from the open water.

Jill got out of the car and chased the butterflies, running barefooted in the grass and shrieking like a child while she snatched at the little fluttering yellow rags of color in the air. When she caught one she held it caged for a moment in her cupped hands, then drew it to her mouth and kissed it, too ardently, apparently, because when she flung it free it fluttered down weakly to the ground and clung to a grass blade where it waved its wings in an afflicted way. She wiped her palm against the front of her T-shirt and shuddered. When she came back to the car there was a tiny smear of yellow dust, like pollen, across her breast and on her lips.

"Hold still a minute," Priscilla said, taking a Kleenex out of her shoulder bag. She dabbed at Jill's cheek and then the corner of her mouth. "Angel dust."

"Blood of my victims," Jill said.

In front of them they saw the ferry bearing for the landing far out on the water and everyone cheered. As it came closer they saw that it was a rugged, battered old iron-hulled boat with a faint look of hauteur, like an ancient plow-horse, and the name CLARABELLE painted in faded pink letters on its wheelhouse. It slid into its slip and the landing ramp was lowered to the deck with a chattering of winches and a grinding of metal plates. They drove aboard and parked on the starboard side of the fo'c'sle at the prow, and then got out and went up the metal companionway to the passenger cabin above the engine house. There were rows of benches and a Shipmate stove and a glass-paned door into the wheelhouse where the captain sat on a swivel stool in front of a binnacle and a huge, brass-bound, eight-spoked wheel and grinned at them. He was a man of sixty with a white beard and a face that seemed to be made out of boot leather. His faded pea jacket hung on his shoulders like a tarpaulin over a cast-iron triphammer.

"You'd better keep me away from that man," Jill said, "or I'm apt to do something very foolish."

"You'd better come outside," Ben said. "You'll keep cooler."

They went out and stood on the open quarter-deck beside the cabin and looked down, watching the deckhands chock the wheels of the automobiles and latch the chain across the stern, and then the landing ramp went up and the boat began to shudder with the vibration of the huge twin diesel engines, and the space of open water between the stern and the slip widened and roiled with the churning of the screw, and in a minute or two they were out on the open water of the sound with the wind blowing fresh into their faces and the low islands beginning to wheel slowly to starboard as they turned into the channel.

"Oh, God, it's wonderful!" Jill said. "Is there anything as exciting as a ship? Even a clunky old ferry like this!"

"She's a fine, salty old vessel," Tony said. "And safe as houses, I should think, with that old dog at the wheel."

"You can be sure of that," Priscilla said. "They take these boats across in every kind of weather. They know every sandbar on the Banks."

All around them the water sparkled in the sunlight like shattered crystal and above the sound the sky was a depthless, pure, translucent blue that spread out endlessly on every side and upward beyond the reach of the eyes or the imagination, almost eerie in its silent, teeming vastness. The salt-white spits of sand that slid by distantly and the green mangrove thickets of the low islets in the sound were carved and polished by the light to a scarifying brilliance and exactitude, like cameos cut in turquoise, and an unearthly cleanliness enclosed everything, like the landscape of a dream. It was a dream that did not seem to have a dreamer; everyone was rendered almost senseless by the scene as if they were not mortal observers of it, but had been absorbed into it and become a part of the sky and water at which they stared without sight or speech, their senses barely sustained by the steady throbbing of the diesels and the churning of the wake, which furnished the fragile, solitary evidence of mankind abroad in that immensity. After a while Jill said, "Nothing seems to matter when you get out on the water, does it? Winning or losing, law, love, anger. Even the past, or future. You feel a kind of inhuman, timeless peace. I think that's what it must feel like to die."

"I feel cold," Priscilla said. "I'm going back to the cabin and have a cup of tea. Anybody else?"

"I want to go down to the prow," Jill said. "What about you chaps?"

"I'm game, for a bit," Tony said.

"OK," Ben said. "We'll be up in a minute, Priss."

They went down the companionway which was now wet with spray and

worked their way up between the parked cars to the prow. They had to cling
to the gunwale and lean into the wind that blew across the bow and sent
their hair flying and their collars snapping against their throats. The boat
was smacking regularly into the whitecaps on the open water, and sometimes the spume of a smashed wave blew up into their faces in a cold,
salty spray that stung their eyes and set their lips tingling. Jill clenched
the gunwale with her hands and lifted her face into the wind, howling with
delight, her hair streaming like kelp and her blouse soaked with spray.
She had nothing on underneath the blouse and her small breasts and
the scarlet cusps of her nipples showed as clearly through the wet nylon
as if she had been naked. She seemed to have emerged out of the poem
she had recited at the dinner table like its heroine breasting a cloud of
spume.

"You'd better get back up to the cabin," Ben said. "You'll catch pneumonia."

"Rubbish. I used to swing for hours in the rain."

She clung to the gunwale staring out across the windy blue reaches of
the sound until a heavy sheet of spray broke across the prow and drenched
her face and hair.

"Well, that's it for me," Tony said. "I'm going up, or I shall be soaked
through."

"Me too," Ben said. "Hot tea for me."

"You're a pair of lubbers," Jill said.

"Don't be a clod," Tony said. "You'll catch a chill."

"I'll be up in a minute. I've got to have my fill of this."

The men went lurching back between the parked autos and up the companionway to the cabin which was now filled with passengers peering
out through the foam-flecked windows. They worked their way up the aisle
between the benches to where Priscilla sat, holding their fingertips pressed
to the cabin roof to steady themselves.

"Off watch," Tony said. "And ready for a ration of tea." He rubbed his
hands together and shivered.

"You're soaked," Priscilla said.

"You think so? You should see Jill."

"Why doesn't she come up?"

"Because she's dotty. Got sea-fever or something."

Priscilla had packed the tote bag with a thermos jug of hot tea, a nest of Styrofoam cups, two bottles of mixed daiquiris, a box of Kleenex, and a box of Band-Aids, for emergencies. She put Styrofoam cups into their hands and poured hot tea into them from the jug.

"Ah, that's better," Tony said, sipping deeply. "Marvelous, this trip, you know. I shan't forget it."

"We've got a perfect day for it."

"Oh, absolutely. Sends the blood into spots it hasn't been in for years."

They sat sipping their hot tea looking out through the windows as the bars and low, green hummocks of the strait slid by, rimmed with narrow white beaches where herons stood poised in dire immobility in the emerald water. After a few minutes they saw Jill coming up the companionway from the deck. Her wet hair was plastered to her skull and she looked startlingly nude from the waist up in her drenched blouse. There was a profound and silent attention in the cabin when she opened the door and came back along the aisle, reaching up to press her fingertips against the cabin roof. Some faces became very grave, others were vacantly averted, some stealthily observant, and those of a pair of adolescent boys convulsively exuberant. She sat down between Priscilla and a lady of about sixty-five in a coral-colored suit who edged away from her and pressed her lips together.

"God's teeth, what a thrill!" Jill said. "Almost like losing one's virginity." She massaged her wet hair briskly with her fingertips.

"Would you like some tea?" Priscilla asked.

"Haven't got a noggin of rum, have you?"

"We've got some daiquiri," Priscilla said. "But it's ice cold. Don't you want something hot?"

"No, no, I'll have the grog. Honestly, Priss, you should have come down.

It was glorious. Oh, Lord, that's good." She took another gulp of her daiquiri and peered out of the window. "Where are we now, anyway? Have we far to go?"

"Another forty minutes or so," Ben said. "We're at about mid-passage. I think we're following a different route this time. The channel must have shoaled up over the winter."

"We're in a channel, are we?"

"Yes. It's very shallow in here, and you're apt to go aground otherwise. They have to keep it dredged because it shoals up constantly. You see those buoys?"

"Where? Oh yes, those green things. Are those the channel markers?"

"That's it. If you had a chart you could see it quite clearly."

"Has he got one in there? That marvelous captain of ours?"

"I hope so," Ben said.

"I think I'll ask him. Will he mind?"

"I think he'll be delighted," Ben said.

"Oh, good. I'll just go and see." She got up, carrying her cup of daiquiri, and went up to the wheelhouse door, rapping with her knuckles on the glass pane. Inside, the captain turned and studied her with a growingly happy smile. Jill opened the door and said, "Would you mind if I just came in and peeked around for a moment? I've never been inside a wheelhouse."

"No indeed, lady," the captain said. "You come right on in."

She went inside the wheelhouse and closed the door behind her. The captain beckoned to her with two large brown fingers and she went across and stood beside him at the wheel, bending down to peer into the compass while he tapped the face of it and spoke to her, evidently explaining its mysteries. She stood listening, fascinated, nodding and sipping her daiquiri with a rapt look. When she offered her cup to him he shook his head and laughed, holding up his hand to decline the offer. She questioned him about something, and he pointed to the chart table on the starboard side of the wheelhouse. Jill went across and stood in front of it, peering down at the chart spread out on its surface, then traced a line across it with her fingertip. The captain nodded, smiling. She drank the last of her daiquiri, crumpled up the cup and dropped it into a wastebasket underneath the chart table. The captain beckoned to her. She went back and stood beside him and he invited her to take the wheel. She clutched a spoke with one hand, turning to grin at him. He took her other hand and folded the fingers of it around the opposing spoke, then sat back on his stool and folded his arms, watching her and grinning with approval.

"Well," Tony said. "It looks as if we're at her mercy, doesn't it?"

"Looks like it," Ben said.

They watched while she steered the ferry for several minutes. The captain sat admiringly, unfolding his arms occasionally and leaning forward to touch the wheel with his fingertips to adjust the course. She clutched the spokes fiercely, peering out at the channel markers with her tongue between her teeth. Inside the passenger cabin there was a growing murmur of indignation and alarm. The lady in the coral-colored suit turned her head and stared bitterly at Priscilla. Priscilla smiled at her pleasantly.

"Would you like a daiquiri?" she asked. The lady dropped her jaw open with a snap of her tongue.

"It's a bit heavy on the rum," Tony said. "But you can get it down." The lady got up and went quickly down the aisle toward the stern, seating herself in the farthest empty seat from them and staring at them savagely down the length of the cabin.

"Doesn't like rum, I guess," Ben said.

"No, well you can't blame her," Tony said. "You don't get the good stuff any more. Not since the trouble with Cuba."

Inside the wheelhouse Jill relinquished the helm to the captain and kissed him on the cheek. When she came out, flinging the door triumphantly open, she cried, "Did you see? I've been steering the ruddy boat!"

"Indeed we did," Tony said. "You were magnificent."

"You were," Priscilla said. "You looked born to the helm."

"A very smooth passage," Ben said. "You got us through the reefs beautifully."

"Didn't I just! I'm to be his first mate, and we're going to plunder the Outer Banks."

"Ah, well, you'll need a noggin of rum in that case," Ben said.

"I won't say no to that."

They sat and finished the first of the three bottles, and by the time they docked at Ocracoke they were feeling very merry. Ben drove the car off the ferry and parked it facing the harbor. They got out and walked back through the sand streets of the old village between the nineteenth-century cottages, singing "Cape Cod Girls" in several keys and swinging their shoes by the laces.

"These aren't the original houses, surely," Tony said.

"Some of them. From the early nineteenth century. The lighthouse here wasn't built until 1823, so you can see it's an old village, by our standards. It used to be quite a lively place in Blackbeard's time. He sold his loot here, and people would come across from the mainland to buy it, under the protection of the governor, who got a handsome share of the proceeds."

"Some of it he's supposed to have buried back here in the swamp," Priscilla said. "So if you want to do some digging, you might just be lucky."

"I'm for a bit of tiffin, myself," Jill said. "I'm famished."

"So am I. There's cafe on the harbor where we can get steamed crabs. It isn't far."

They wound their way along the sand road under the shade of the live oaks to the harbor and came out into the bright sunlight of the waterfront where they sat down at a table in front of a clapboard inn with a red tin roof and a sign above the door that read BLACKBEARD'S DEN. The harbor water was dazzling in the light, and through the inlet they could see the distant indigo of the open sea and the surf breaking far out on the shoals. The western arm of the harbor sank into marshland, where an abandoned dory lay bottom up among the reeds, the paint of its hull blistered and flaking and barnacles clinging to its keel like faded dry rosettes. There were many fine, ocean-going yachts in the harbor slips, blazing white in the sun, and a pair of sixty-foot trimarans just in from the Caribbean, their paint gone dull and the lines of their rigging faded to oyster-gray. There was a wonderful salty fetor from the marsh and a constant glitter and tinkle from the steel shrouds of the rigging. They sat with their shoulders baking sweetly in the sun while they ate steamed crabs and fried clams and drank cold daiquiri from the bottle which Priscilla kept underneath the table. It was hot and lazy and measurelessly pleasant, a kind of eternal present, without past or future. No other place in the world seemed to exist, and Ben felt as if they had been sitting there forever, cracking crab claws with wooden mallets and picking meat from them with their wet fingers and washing it down with cold daiquiri and smiling when their eyes met, like fellow miscreants in some endless, ecstatic truancy.

When they had finished eating the waiter came and wrapped up the scarlet shards of crabshell in the paper tablecloth and carried it away. They sat and sipped the last of the daiquiri and stared out at the blue of the harbor water and the wind-wracked cedars on the dunes writhing stilly against the hard blue sky.

"When was he here, anyway, this Blackbeard chap?" Tony asked.

"At the beginning of the eighteenth century," Ben said. "The Royal Navy cornered him and shot him dead in 1718."

"Oh? I thought it was earlier."

"He was a latecomer. These waters are very old in villainy. The Spaniards came first, of course, a couple of centuries before Blackbeard, and carried on in much the same way, only it was the Indians they killed and pillaged, not their own kind. Then Sir Francis Drake arrived and tried to drive the Spaniards out. He sacked Cartagena and San Domingo and St. Augustine, and landed here in 1585. Did you know this was the site of the first British settlement in America?"

"I thought it was at Plymouth," Jill said.

"No, that was much later, in 1620." Ben pointed across the harbor to the sound they had crossed. "Right up there behind our place, between the Banks and the mainland, is Roanoke Island. A couple of sea captains named

Amidas and Barlowe landed there in 1584 and claimed this continent for Sir Walter Raleigh under the patent he held from Queen Elizabeth. They explored for a couple of months and then went back to England with some tobacco and potatoes and a couple of Indians named Manteo and Wanchese. The next year Sir Richard Grenville brought over a hundred and eight settlers under the leadership of a man named Ralph Lane, and then went back to England for supplies. The settlers he left didn't last through the year. They didn't know anything about surviving in the wilderness, and when Drake stopped by here to see how they were getting along, after he burned St. Augustine, they asked him for passage back to England, so he took them. Two weeks after they left, Grenville arrived with fresh supplies and found they'd gone. He left fifteen men to hold the English claim and sailed back. The next year, in 1587, a man named John White came back with a hundred and twenty new settlers. He'd been one of the original Lane colonists, and he was a very interesting guy, an artist. When you get back to London go to the British Museum and you'll see seventy-five drawings he made of the Indians, the first drawings of the native people of this country ever made. When he got back here the fifteen men that Grenville had left behind had disappeared. White got his new people settled and then went back to England for more gunpowder and biscuits. He didn't get back here until 1590, and when he did his new colony had vanished too. The only sign of it was the word *Croatan* carved on a tree, and the word *Cro* on another. Nobody has ever discovered what happened to those people. They were just swallowed up by the wilderness."

"You mean literally?" Tony asked. "They were eaten?"

"No," Ben said. "The mainland Indians weren't cannibals. The cannibals were out there, on the Caribbean islands. That's where the word comes from. It's a corruption of *Caribel,* the people of the Mar Caribe. Maybe the Croatan settlers were just absorbed into the Indian culture, the way a lot of the frontiersmen were, later. Or maybe they were killed."

"Serve them right, if they were," Jill said.

"If they were, they were pretty thoroughly avenged," Ben said. "After 1840 you couldn't find an Indian anywhere on the Atlantic coast. We passed something called The Removal Act in 1830, which made it legal to drive the few of them that were left out west of the Mississippi. Of course, pretty soon they were in the way there, too. In 1871, we decided not even to make treaties with them any more. The idea that they were separate nations and had the right to negotiate with the United States was considered an absurdity. Their claims were dismissed and their affairs turned over to the government. We let them keep little plots of their land here and there to live on—desert and swampland that nobody else wanted—and all the rest of it was opened up to white homesteaders. In 1890, at Wounded Knee, the Seventh Cavalry shot down more than two hundred of them—men, women, and children who had strayed off their allotments—and that was just about the end of the Indians in this country." He felt flushed with the usual self-satisfaction he enjoyed at producing an impressive parade of facts.

"You know rather a lot of history," Jill said. "Does that mean you won't be condemned to repeat it?"

"I don't know," Ben said. "Is it supposed to?"

"That's what Santayana said. Of course he didn't think anyone would ever know enough of it to save himself."

"Little wonder," Tony said. "No one wants to know his own history. Most people won't listen to it."

"Well, I've heard enough of it for one day," Priscilla said. "It makes me shudder. Why don't we talk about something else?" She sounded a little drunk.

"You read Santayana?" Ben said to Jill.

"Quite a lot, yes."

"I've never read him. What do you recommend?"

"There's a poem of his called 'As in the Midst of Battle' that you might enjoy."

"I'll look it up," Ben said.

Far out beyond the inlet a flight of skimmers sped over the surface of the sea, as straight and swift as a volley of arrows. Jill watched them disappear beyond the high dunes of the Cape.

"What happened to Wanchese and Manteo when they got them back to England?" she asked.

"They got baptised," Ben said. "That's all I know about them. I'd like to think they wound up owning the Bank of England, but I doubt it."

"I'd like to think they sowed their seed all over London, like handfuls of maize," Jill said. "I wouldn't mind having a bit of Red Indian blood in my veins."

"Why don't we drink a toast to them?" Priscilla said. She brought the bottle out from underneath the table and tilted it over her glass, but it was empty. She shook it briskly and wrung the neck of it with her fingers.

"Well, it's the thought that counts," Tony said.

"Maybe we'd better sail back for fresh supplies," Ben said.

"I think we'd better," Priscilla said. She turned her wrist and glanced at her wrist watch. "We're apt to miss the ferry if we don't." The bottle slipped out of her fingers and shattered on the stone floor of the cafe, scattering splinters of glass among the tables. "Oh, dear. We'll get thrown out in a minute."

"I don't want to go," Jill said, staring out at the harbor. "You chaps go along. I'll stay here and hold our claim."

"No, no," Tony said. "You might be eaten, or assimilated, or something of the sort. We don't want that."

"Not me. I'm unassimilable and indigestible."

"All right, you stay here and represent the Empire," Ben said. "We'll think about you."

"It's not the bloody Empire I'm representing," Jill said. "I'm a great-great-great-great granddaughter of Manteo, come back to claim her own."

"Well, I hope you've got a good lawyer," Ben said. "You'll need him."

"No, I shan't. I've brought an army with me. We're invincible."

"What army is that?"

"'The army of unalterable law.'"

"You won't reclaim Paradise with poetry," Tony said. "The role of poetry in this world is to lament a Paradise Lost."

"Mr. John Milksop's kind of poetry, perhaps. Not mine. 'Stand and wait,' indeed. Tell that to the Blacks in South Africa." She turned to Ben. "Or to your chaps, when they decided they'd had enough of good King George." She held her glass aloft. "'Malt does more than Milton can, to justify God's ways to man.'" She tilted the glass to her lips, found that it was empty, and peered into it unhappily. "Of course the trouble is there's only so much malt in the world."

"We've got plenty of it at the house," Ben said.

"In that case, I'll come along. I don't want to make a disturbance."

On the ferry she fell asleep between Tony and Ben, shifting her head alternately from the shoulder of one to the other and mumbling peevishly when they changed their positions and disturbed her. The rest of them were drowsy, heavy-eyed and stupefied with the food and drink and salt air, and had very little to say. They sat staring out of the windows as the ferry wound its steady, throbbing course through the blue-green water between the sandbars and islets of the sound.

When they got back to the house it was three o'clock, the middle of a very hot, still, brilliant afternoon, and there was a sense of being enclosed in a vast crystalline dome, like a bell jar. They sat in chaises longues on the sundeck looking out at the shining sea while Priscilla went to make a fresh supply of daiquiris in the kitchen.

"We've got to keep our spirits up," she said. "The natives are beginning to look decidedly unfriendly. Especially that waiter, when I dropped the bottle." There was a mildly drunken frivolity about her that disconcerted Ben. He had never seen her even slightly drunk in the middle of the day before and he realized for the first time that her dignity was something he had come to depend on unconsciously, almost as an element of his universe, like sunlight or oxygen. The thought that it might be exhaustible, or fallible, gave him a faint, odd sense of alarm, something he had not felt since his days of near-destitution in New York.

"I'll get the drinks," he said. "You sit down."

"No, I'm going to change, anyway. I'm perfectly capable."

After she'd been gone for fifteen minutes she came back to the glass door with a paper rose behind her ear, wearing a gold-colored dashiki and carrying a tray on which was an ice bucket with a bottle of champagne, glasses, and a bowl of herring in sour cream. She kicked at the door and Ben got up quickly to open it.

"My God, let me take that. Why didn't you yell?"

"I don't yell until I'm desperate," she said. She carried the tray resolutely to the tile-topped table and set it down. "We're all out of rum. It's champagne or nothing now. Emergency rations."

"Nothing but hardships," Tony said. "We'll never make it through the winter."

"Well, if we make it through the afternoon, we'll pick up fresh supplies when we go in for dinner. There's a liquor store in Manteo."

Ben unwound the wire from the champagne cork and eased it from the bottle with his thumbs. "Here's a broadside for the natives," he said. "This ought to keep them at their distance." He aimed the bottle out across the railing and the cork blew out with a very loud pop and sailed fifteen feet into the air. Everyone cheered. The champagne foamed over his wrist and fingers as he poured a glass and handed it to Jill. "Brimstone and cannon smoke," he said.

"Is that a colonial specialty?"

"Oh, yes. We founded a new world on it." He poured a glass for Priscilla, then one for Tony and one for himself, and held his glass aloft. "Here's to the Revolution!"

"Hear, hear," Tony said.

"And the Jolly Roger," Jill said. "May the sun never set upon her."

"I say, that's coming it a bit strong," Tony said. "I suppose the old rogue in the wheelhouse was filling you with seditious thoughts."

"He didn't look like a rogue to me," Priscilla said. "He looked like Santa Claus."

"Yes, and he had very much the same ideas," Jill said. "At least as the one who used to work in Marks and Spencer."

"Marks and Spencer? The department store?"

"Yes. I used to work there at Christmastime, as lots of unemployed actors did. It was all that kept us going through the holidays. One of them was always hired to be Father Christmas, and one year after I'd been to the Christmas party on the top floor and was feeling a bit squiffed, I thought I'd stop by, for a lark. There were only a couple of kids in the queue, so I waited with them, and when it was my turn I went up and climbed onto his lap. It didn't faze him a bit, you know. He put his arm right round my waist and said, 'Well, you're a very pretty little girl, aren't you? What would you like for Christmas?' 'I'd like a mink coat,' I said. 'Oh, yes,' he said. 'And have you been a good girl?' 'Yes, very good indeed,' I said. 'Ah, well then,' he said. 'I'm afraid you won't get one.'"

Priscilla laughed helplessly, holding her glass aloft and splashing champagne onto her robe. She brushed it off with her hand and said, "Oh, dear. What an awful man. Destroying a girl's illusions like that."

"He didn't destroy my illusions at all. Father Christmas and pirates have always been mixed up in my mind since I was a kid. I suppose it was from watching Peter Pan on the Christmas pantomimes. It's put on every year, you know, and Mum and Dad always took me round to see it in the holidays. It didn't seem like Christmas without Captain Hook and his band of jolly cutthroats. God, I used to love that play. It's what made me want to go on the stage, really. I think the happiest I've ever been was when I got a bit part in it, just after I got out of RADA. Do you know what I played? The front end of the dog, Nana. You know, the great shaggy Newfoundland that looks after the children. That was my debut in the theatre, as the front end of a dog."

"Were you good in it?" Priscilla asked.

"Was I not. I was a sensation. The chap who played the rear end was

an absolute beast, and used to pinch my bottom all through the performance. As soon as I got on the stage I'd feel this vicious nip on the bum
that would send me charging into furniture and yelping like a bona fide
hound. They said I gave a very spirited performance."

"Well, we know what to do, if you start feeling comatose," Ben said.

"So you do. I'm feeling a bit comatose right now, as a matter of fact.
Have we got time for a swim before dinner?"

"Oh, plenty," Priscilla said. "We made reservations for six thirty, but
we won't even need them on a weekday."

"I think I'll have one, then. What about you lot?"

"Not me," Tony said. "I'm going to sit here and quietly decay. But I'll
cheer you on."

"Come along, Priss. It'll freshen you up."

"Oh, I don't think I can. I'd sink like a stone. I'm going to finish my drink
and then lie down for an hour. Ben, you go with her. She shouldn't go
in the water by herself. It's dangerous."

"OK," Ben said. "I could use a dip myself."

"Don't forget the tanning lotion," Priscilla said.

"No, I shan't. I think you're awful clods for not coming."

Ben slid the door closed and said, "I'll see you on the beach."

"Right."

He went into the bedroom and changed into a pair of swimming trunks,
tossing his trousers onto the boudoir chair. Ordinarily, he laid them carefully across the back of it so that they would not get wrinkled. He had
put on his beach robe and had one hand on the doorknob before he became aware of this departure from his usual fastidiousness, and it struck
him suddenly that there was something of unbecoming haste about the
look of them lying crumpled in the chair. He went back and picked
them up, holding the cuffs against his chest with his chin while he ran
his fingers down the length of the legs to match their creases. When he had
laid them across the chair back in his usual way, however, there was
something unpleasantly spurious looking about their precision that dis-

turbed him even more. He stared at the trousers for a moment and then thought, fuck it, and went out through the living room, into the kitchen and down the stairs to the shower stall. In the dressing room beside it there was a linen closet with a stack of fresh towels. He plucked one out, slung it around his neck, hung his robe on a clothes hook, and went out between the pilings to the beach.

Down at the edge of the water Jill was tiptoeing daintily through the running sheet of backwash that slid down the sand from the last exploded wave. It rippled around her ankles and splashed the backs of her legs, and she turned and came mincing up the sand toward him, hugging herself and shivering.

"Cripes! It's cold!" She shuddered.

"Do you good," Ben said. "Get the blood running."

"Get it congealed, more likely."

He tossed his towel beside hers on the sand and walked down to where she stood, bending to scoop up water in his cupped hands and splash his face with it. "Ah, that's good," he said. "This'll wake you up." He bent down to scoop up another handful and tossed it at her. She shrieked and fled, her feet splashing through the foam. He chased her along the edge of the water while she screamed, "No, don't, Ben, honestly! No, that's beastly, *honestly!*" When he caught up with her he took her by the shoulders and marched her down to the surf ahead of him. She struggled frantically, howling with indignation. They tripped and fell, neck deep in the icy surf, and a wave broke over their heads. They came up gasping, their hair streaming over their faces, shocked breathless by the cold. She clawed the hair away from her eyes, her mouth open in horrified dismay.

"Oh, my God, what a *monster* you are!" she cried. "What an absolute *cad*. I never dreamt!"

"You'll learn to love me for it," Ben said. "It builds character."

"I despise you, utterly and forever. I shall live to see you dead."

They heard Tony and Priscilla laughing and cheering on the deck. Priscilla got up from her chair and came to the railing where she cupped her hands to her mouth and shouted, "Don't stand for it. Put sand in his pants. He hates that."

"That's just what I shall do," Jill said. She snatched up a handful of sand and before Ben could elude her, had yanked open the waist of his trunks and flung the sand into them.

"Now that's awful!" Ben said. "That's a terrible thing to do."

"Oh, yes, you're a fine one. I hope it gives you blisters."

They heard Priscilla clapping and cheering on the deck. Tony shouted, "Don't let down the side, old boy. I've got a quid on you."

"I think we'd better have a truce," Jill said. "Or one of us will regret it."

"OK," Ben said. "We'll have a civilized contest." He pointed to the line of surf fifty yards out where the rollers from the open sea broke on the off-shore shoals. "I'll race you to the breakers out there."

"The breakers? Good god, we'll drown. It must be miles over our head."

"No, it's very shallow out there. There's a sandbar. Come on, I'll show you." He dove into an oncoming wave and struck out for the bar in an easy, powerful breast stroke, feeling his body rise and fall on the surge of the swells. He had learned to swim on the lakes and beaches of southern Florida, and he was a very good swimmer and a passionate one. Nothing had ever diminished the exaltation he had felt as a boy at Daytona Beach when for the first time he had swum out into the open sea. It was a magical and purifying experience for him. You swept down into a long glassy trough as the wave passed under you, and then rose swiftly and smoothly on the breast of the next as it lifted you higher and higher like a soaring hawk until from the crest of it you could see as far as the horizon, as if from the peak of a glittering green mountain, and you hung there in a moment of breathless buoyancy and then swept down again, shouting silently with delight. It seemed to him the cleanest and most thrilling thing that it was possible to do on the earth, and it was a large part of the reason that he came here every summer.

Between the beach and the surf of the shoals there was a deep trench where the water was blue and very cold, and then the bottom shelved up slowly to the sandbar, growing greener and warmer as it rose into the light, and as you approached the bar you could hear the growing thunder of the surf and feel the change in the water, and when you let your feet down there was always a feeling of surprise and achievement to find that you could touch the sandy bottom with your toes and stand up, knee-deep, in the lovely, mild, warm, emerald-colored water. You felt as if you had swum the ocean and come up onto the shore of some small island that you had dreamed of since you were a boy and that had waited there for you. "Bali Hai," he thought, when his feet touched the bottom. It was Ben's favorite song. He loved it with a secret, hopeless passion, far truer than the one he felt for "Nessun Dorma," which, shamelessly, he spoke of as his favorite.

When he got to the sandbar he stood up and looked back to where Jill was splashing through the water toward him in a churning, dogged freestyle, not very graceful or efficient, but steady and determined. When she reached the bar she stood up, panting and raking the hair from her eyes with her fingertips, tugged up her bikini pants and leaned over, resting her hands on her knees.

"Hey, you made it," Ben said.

"Did you think I wouldn't? I suppose you expected me to sink out there."

"No, I knew you'd make it. It's another character-building exercise."

"You're bloody concerned about my character, aren't you? I should think you had enough to worry about with your own."

He raised his hands and waved to Priscilla and Tony who were standing at the railing watching them. They waved back, and then Priscilla picked up the tray from the table and went to the glass door. Tony slid it open for her and when she had gone inside he went back and sat down in his chair.

"This is a great place," Ben said. "I come out here and sit and think for an hour or more sometimes. It's a great place to think."

"This is where you think up ways to make people buy things?"

"No, this is where I get away from all that. It's a place for long thoughts."

"Oh, long thoughts. You mean God, and mortality, that sort of thing? You have many of that sort?"

"Once in a while." He sat down in the shallow water and leaned back, resting his hands flat on the rippled sand. The water came only to his waist, and rose and fell mildly, tugging his body back and forth gently on the sand. Jill sat down beside him and they stared up into the blue of the sky. "It isn't really land or sea," he said. "But somewhere in between. You feel sort of disembodied."

"I hope the sharks feel that way about us," she said. "I don't suppose there are any out here?"

"Once in a while you see one, but it's a long time since they attacked anyone on this beach. They do down south further. Piranhas, too."

"Quite a lot of people get eaten in this part of the world, don't they?"

"I don't think you need to worry about it."

She leaned back farther, resting on her elbows, and turned her face up to the sky, closing her eyes and basking in the sun. Ben looked down at her slick, chestnut-colored hair that shone like apple skin and her tangled lashes and the sunlit glisten of her wet pale cheeks and eyelids. He felt the rhythm of his breath become quick and uneven and his heartbeat alter hectically. She opened her eyes and looked up at him.

"What's the matter?" she said.

He stared into her eyes without smiling and said in a kind of stricken mutter, "Jesus Christ, I'm wild for you."

"Now then. You're not having very long thoughts now, are you?"

She closed her eyes again and lay with the water welling up to her shoulders and then receding to her elbows rhythmically, laving her arms like polished ivory. A wave lapped gently over her chin and she raised her hand and wiped her lips with the tips of her fingers.

"You're awfully goddamned fucking beautiful," Ben said in a harsh whisper.

"'Fucking' beautiful?"

"Yes."

"I don't know how you expect a girl to feel about a
kind."

Ben breathed deeply and laid his hand flat on the mound o

"We're not all that far from shore, you know," Jill said with
ing her eyes.

"And I suppose Tony's pretty jealous."

"I suppose so. Why don't you ask him?"

"He'd say something like, 'Well, yes I am, actually, you know.'" He mim-
icked Tony's languid Charter House drawl almost perfectly.

Jill chuckled. "You do that very well. You were always very good at
imitating people."

He pressed his hand down hard on her pubis. "Who do you think I'm
imitating now?"

"A chap I used to know at school."

Ben sat up and folded his legs, reaching down to dig a handful of sand
from the bottom and let it trickle out of his fingers. In the water it washed
apart in a cloud of white silt. He plucked up another handful of sand
and repeated the process carefully. Jill sat up and clasped her knees, turning her head to look at him. She watched solemnly while he spilled another handful of sand into the water.

"Let me ask you something," Ben said.

"Yes? What?"

"Did you think I might act in that play of yours, the way the character
does? Is that why you wrote it?"

She laughed. "Is that what you've been thinking? Good Lord, no. I knew
you'd finished with the theatre, years ago. Derek told me you were up to
your ears in advertising copy."

"What was it, just a sort of fantasy?"

"Yes, I suppose. A sort of wish-fulfillment thing. The sort of thing you
work off in a dream, or play, or novel, as the Brontë girls did. My little
Wuthering Heights. Anyway, it seemed a good idea for a play."

"Did you want me to see it? You weren't by any chance writing it for
me?"

"No, I never dreamed you'd come to see a play of mine. I thought you considered yourself well quit of me. I didn't think I'd ever see you again in my life, honestly."

He drew up his legs and clasped his knees, sitting in her position, and turned his head to look at her. "Did you feel as if you were making your peace with the world, something like that?"

"Oh, well, peace is something one never really finds, isn't it?" She looked up at the house and then back at him. "Do you think we ought to go back?"

"Well, as I see it, we have two alternatives," Ben said. "We can go back and eat lobster, or we can stay here forever."

"I'm for lobster."

"OK."

They stood up and waded back into the lagoon until the water had reached their waists and then shoved off and swam back to the beach, leisurely and steadily, feeling their bodies rise and heave shoreward with the surge of the swells behind them. The waves built up into breakers as they neared the shore, and the final one lifted them on its crest and flung them up onto the sand. They scrambled to their feet and ran up through the streaming backwash to their towels.

"Lovely swim," Jill said, panting while she bent her head and tossed her hair in the towel. "I feel ten years younger. God, what I'd give to have a place like this."

"You'll have one," Ben said. "Just keep up the good work."

"Not me. I'm like a day lily. I bloom for an afternoon and then I'm done."

"Hey, you've barely begun," Ben said.

"Well, I'll write one more, perhaps, before the sun sets."

"Listen, you're going to conquer the world, lady." He draped his towel around his shoulders and waved to Tony, who waved back from his lounge chair on the deck.

"You've made it back, then," Tony called. "How's the water?"

"Lovely," Jill said. As they plodded up through the soft sand toward the house she raised her head and called to him, "You should have come, you know. It was a real adventure."

"I enjoy things vicariously," he said. "A good deal less strenuous."

They went in between the pilings to the shower room and hung their towels on the hooks above the bench. Ben reached into the shower stall and turned the faucets, holding his hand into the spray of water until it had grown warm.

"You going to rinse off?" he said.

"Is it hot?"

"Yep."

She held out her hand to test the temperature. "Oh, good. That's lovely." She tossed her towel onto the bench and stepped into the stall, pressing her hand against the wall to steady herself while she lifted her legs to rinse the sand from her feet and ankles. Ben stood and watched her with a taste of copper in his mouth, standing very still. When she had rinsed her feet she plucked open the waist of her bikini pants and peered inside them.

"Lord, it's all down inside. It gets everywhere."

"Well, take them off and do it right," Ben said. The words rasped in his throat like sandpaper.

"All right. As long as you don't mind."

She tugged down the pink bikini pants and stepped out of them, hobbling slightly on one foot to keep her balance. When she was out of them she tossed them onto the tile floor and stepped back under the spray, turning her face up into it with her eyes closed. The water splashed on her head and shoulders and streamed down her narrow naked hips and over her tight white belly and the sparkling wet red tangle of her pubic hair and down her thighs and legs as if she were wrapped in a sheet of rippling plastic. Ben felt his heart thump like the blows of a fist inside his chest as he watched her reach behind her to untie the strap of her bra and drop it onto the floor beside her pants, her face still turned up blindly into the spray. He undid the waist cord of his trunks and peeled them off, bending down to yank his feet out of them with a clumsy, fierce impatience. He slung them across the room against the wall and stepped into the shower stall beside her, taking the back of her skull in his hands like a melon and kissing her whole head, from the hinges of her jaws to her temples, moving his mouth about her face in a blind, ceaseless, famished way, like a baby searching for the nipple of its mother's breast. She went absolutely limp and her arms fell to her sides like a rag doll's. He picked her up and carried her out of the stall as if he were carrying a drowned woman out of the sea and laid her down on the bench in the dressing room, tugging it away from the wall with his foot. She opened her mouth, and breathed in quick, soft, soundless gasps, lying with her eyes closed while he spread her legs apart and straddled the bench in front of her. She shuddered when he plunged into her and then lay with her hips rebounding strengthlessly while he clutched her shoulders and lunged in and out of her with a ferocity that slid the bench inch by inch across the floor, its feet squeaking slightly on the tiles. When it was over he sat back, panting, then slumped forward with his hands resting on her shoulders, staring down at her until his breathing had eased. She lay with her eyes closed, gasping softly through her open mouth. After a moment he reached down and yanked a strand of her wet hair.

"Hey. You OK?"

She shook her head weakly and then opened her eyes and stared at him.

"Oh, crikey," she said faintly.

"You OK?"

"Yes. It's just that I didn't quite remember what that felt like." They stared at each other, their panting gradually subsiding.

"Well," she said at last. "You must have been in a flipping bad way." Ben did not reply. "What do you think we'd better do now?"

"I guess we'd better get dressed," Ben said. He stood up, swinging his leg over the bench, and reached down to take her hands and pull her up beside him. She stood for a moment with her head hanging, the tips of her fingers resting in his hands. He felt suddenly very awkward and conscious of his nakedness and could not decide quite what to do: whether to embrace her, kiss her, lay his hand against her face, stroke her hair, or whether any such a tender gesture would seem obligatory and condescending on his part. Before he could decide she pulled her fingertips free and turned to pick up her towel from the bench. He picked up his own and they dried themselves silently, bending to rub their legs and thighs with what seemed to him like extravagant care. When she had finished she held the towel to her breasts and reached up to take down her cabana robe from the hook. Ben held it for her while she slid her arms into it and then took down his own. He was suddenly aware of the sound of water still splashing in the shower stall. She watched without speaking while he put on his robe, pushed up his sleeve and went across to the stall, reaching in to turn off the faucets. When the splashing of the water stopped it seemed suddenly very still in the room. The two pieces of her bikini lay in a puddle on the tiles looking very sodden and shabby. He picked them up and wrung them out.

"You want to put this on?" he asked, holding them out to her.

"No, I'll just shove them in my pocket."

He stepped out of the stall and handed them to her. "Don't you think you'd better put it on?"

"No, it doesn't matter." She shoved the damp lumps of cloth into the pocket of her robe and picked up her towel, dropping it over her head and beginning to massage her hair with it. Ben went across the room to where his trunks lay on the floor beside the wall and picked them up.

"Well, I think I'll put mine on," he said. He wrung them out and stepped into them.

"Checks up on you, does she?" Jill said from under the towel.

"No, she doesn't check up on me. I'm just careless sometimes."

"Are you? Often?"

"It doesn't happen often," he said. He tugged the wet trunks up over his thighs and buttocks underneath his robe and picked up his towel from the bench. "You ready?"

"Yes. Quite ready."

She followed him up the stairs into the kitchen and across the living room to the glass door of the deck.

"Ah, there you are," Tony said when they stepped outside. "Feeling better?"

"Much better," Ben said. "It was great."

"Yes, it looked it. Though I must say you look a bit peaked, both of you. I hope you haven't overdone it." He smiled at them amiably.

"Is there a bit more of the bubbly?" Jill asked.

"Enough for a glass, I think."

Ben lifted the bottle from the bucket and measured it against the light. "Yes, there's a glass here," he said. "I can get another bottle if you like."

"No. I just want a sip." He poured a glass for her.

"Tony?"

"No, no, I've had plenty. More than my share."

"One never gets his share of it," Jill said. She drank standing, looking out to sea.

"No, that's true enough. What were you sitting on, out there? A sand bar?"

"Yes, it's like a reef," Ben said. "It makes a perfect swim, out there and back."

"For you chaps, perhaps. I don't think I could make it."

Jill went to the railing and leaned on it, raising her glass to her mouth.

"Priss lying down?" Ben asked.

"Yes. Feeling a bit logy, she said. Nothing serious."

"She usually takes a nap in the middle of the day."

"Best thing in the world for one. Gets the battery recharged. You ought to have one, Jill."

"I think I will," Jill said. She finished the champagne and carried the glass to the table where she set it down.

"That's it," Tony said. "Forty winks and you'll be right as rain."

"Are you coming in?"

"I'll just stay out here a bit longer. It's cooler now."

"Wake me when you come in."

"Yes, right."

She went across to the door and slid it open. Before she went in she said, "I shall remember that swim, Ben."

"Good," Ben said. "We'll do it again."

He finished his drink standing and set down his glass. "Well, I think I'll have a shower and change. You mind if I leave you on your own for half an hour?"

"No, no, it's lovely out here," Tony said. He looked up and smiled. "I've got a letter to write. I'll be quite all right."

Ben went into the house and across the living room to the bedroom, opening and closing the door carefully so as not to waken Priscilla who was lying with a sheet over her, breathing evenly. She was turned toward the deck and her shoulders were bare above the sheet. The venetian blind was closed and it was dark in the room. Ben went to the dresser, slid open the top drawer carefully and took out a white silk shirt. Priscilla stirred and mumbled, "Good swim?"

"Great," Ben said. "I wake you up?"

"No, I was just dozing. What time is it?"

He looked at his watch. "A quarter past five."

"Oh, Lord, I'd better get up."

He laid the shirt on the dresser and went over and sat down on the edge of the bed, laying his hand on her hip. "You get a nap?"

"Mm, lovely. I need a rub."

He put his hand under the sheet and rubbed her back gently from the nape of her neck to her buttocks, feeling the long, naked tendril of her spine ripple under his palm. While he rubbed her back he stared at the glass door striped horizontally in fine bright lines between the slits of the louvers. Once, in the summer of 1967, he had stood in a doorway on Tho Du street in Saigon and bargained with a weasel-faced man in a plastic raincoat for the services of a girl wearing lipstick, eye makeup and a poinciana blossom in her hair who was certainly not more than fifteen years old and who wore the fixed, mirthless smile of a china doll. They had agreed on a price of six hundred piasters for the entire night, which Ben had spent with the girl on a straw mat on a barge on the riverfront while the man, whoever he was, sat outside the door of the bamboo hut and for a large part of the time blew very softly on a wooden flute. There was

an oil lamp burning in the hut which for an extra fifty piasters Ben had persuaded her to leave alight so that he could see the brown buds of her breasts
and her absolutely hairless, cinnamon-colored body. In the light of the
oil lamp he had been bitterly aware that her expression did not change
no matter what he did to her.

Staring at the sun-striped blind in the silent bedroom while he stroked
Priscilla's back, he remembered with awful clarity the hollowness, fragility
of personality, and sense of dispossession he had felt while he sat caress-
ing the apple-skin firmness of the child's body with his fingertips and stared
at the dawn light slicing through the straw blind of the bamboo hut. An
orgasm of a certain kind was a devastating experience. It shocked you
like an explosion in the entrails, blew the guts out of you as he had seen
the contents of a bedroom blown out into the street by the concussion of
an artillery shell: bedclothes, mattresses, bloody trousers, letters, photographs,
lying on the pavement outside a shattered window along with the corpses
of its inhabitants, sometimes not even a calendar left hanging on the
walls to preserve a record of the life they had housed, the encircled dates
of special events and family rituals, birthdays, weddings, holidays, and reunions that had been celebrated there. He felt as he had felt then, like a
set of empty walls, with all his furniture, paintings, acquisitions, his appointment books and ID cards, all the vestiges of his existence scattered
outside in the street. He did not understand the turbulence of this reaction
to a simple act of fornication. Evidently there had to be an element of
depravity about it, an association of some kind with violence, brutality, pain,
long deprivation or despair to produce that catastrophic feeling of evis-
ceration, as if you had been hanged, drawn and quartered. None of his
occasional infidelities in the course of business trips to New York or the
West Coast were of anything like that order. They were casual, fortu-
itous, and entered into in a spirit of good-natured cooperation by everyone concerned, with a certain mild anticipation not much more feverish
than that with which you looked forward to a glass of Cointreau after
dinner, and concluded with no more agitation or regret than that with

which you set down your liqueur glass. They were in fact a tradition of his profession, and he never lost control of the situation or failed to behave with the discretion, care, and equanimity which were a part of the tradition. It was true that he sometimes felt a throe of remorse when he got back to Washington and first saw Priscilla again, but never, after any of them, had he felt anything that resembled being disembowelled.

"You OK?" Priscilla said, turning her head to look up at him.

"Yeah, fine."

"You're awfully quiet."

"I'm just a little bushed. I'll be OK after I have a bath and something to eat."

This was true, he knew. After a time you invariably felt better. After a certain number of hot baths, good meals, successful business ventures, acquisitions that brought with them the aura of piety, initiative, and honor, and after a certain period of adjustment to the traditions of the world of advertising, commerce, and corporation law, you felt better. Not everyone did, of course, but most. He knew of some who had fled to the forests of Washington State and Oregon, or who slept on subway gratings or the benches in Union Station, or who beat their wives or drank themselves to death, and of one, a huge, red-headed boy from Abilene with a gold tooth and a merry smile, who had asphyxiated himself with a hose connected to the tailpipe while sitting in his automobile on the edge of a cliff overlooking the Chesapeake with a copy of Roethke's poetry open in his lap. This was a boy who had been in Ben's platoon at Da Nang and who had turned up in Washington in the summer of 1983 and asked for a job. He had three years toward an English degree at the University of Arkansas, so Ben gave him a job writing copy, at which he did very well for several months, although stoned a good deal of the time. After several months Ben assigned him to a contract with a company that manufactured, among other things, a powdered baby food formula, the chief markets for which were Third World countries where it was sold to illiterate women who had neither the proper instructions nor facilities for sterilizing bottles, nipples, or the water with which they mixed the formula, with the result that their babies began dying in even larger numbers than usual from diarrhea, enteritis, dysentery and other afflictions of the poor. Ben's friend did not learn of this until he had been writing copy for the manufacturer for several months, at which time it was reported widely in the press. Shortly after, he quit his job—abandoned it was probably the better term, since he simply failed to show up one morning and Ben never heard from him again until the police telephoned him several weeks later to notify him of his friend's death and to ask if Ben had any information that might throw light on their investigation. Ben had a good deal of such information, including the fact that his friend was in love with a Vietnamese woman by whom he had had an illegitimate daughter, both of whom he had been trying unsuccessfully for years to get into the States, but he did not divulge this information to the police, or to Priscilla. He gave them the address of his friend's parents in Abilene and he himself called the parents to offer his condolences, tell them all he knew of the circumstances of their son's death—omitting the detail about the baby food formula—and inform them that if they wished, it might be possible for their son to be buried in the Arlington National Cemetery. He said that since he lived in Washington he would be glad to assist in any way that he could with the arrangements. They wanted very much for this to be done, and flew to Washington for the funeral. Ben met them at the airport, brought them home with him to Great Falls where they spent the night, and in the morning drove them to Arlington. It was a cold wet day in February, and he, Priscilla, and the young man's parents walked for half a mile in the rain behind the caisson carrying the coffin to the excavated gravesite where they stood among the almost endless rows of white crosses while the flag was removed, folded into a triangle and delivered to the young man's mother. The coffin was lowered into the ground and an honor guard of three marines fired a two-gun salute.

After that Ben did not think any more about his friend or about Vietnam. He was through with the war. When the memorial was built in

Washington he did not go to visit it, and had not visited it since. He did not share the desire of many Nam veterans to stand and search the black marble for the names of their dead comrades. The war was over. It was a period of pain and guilt and deprivation that he had no desire to memorialize. He threw away the uniform that he had kept for years in a closet in the basement, his Silver Star, his campaign ribbons, the pair of mummified ears of a Viet Cong soldier that he had kept wrapped in gauze and sealed up in a plastic freezer bag; and all the photographs of himself in the service, he tore into small pieces and flushed down the toilet, as he had once flushed down the toilet the only letter he had ever received from his father. He was through with pain, guilt, and deprivation forever. He wanted the history of his life to begin with meeting Priscilla on the steps of the Hutton Mansion in Regents Park on a summer afternoon. But evidently, he thought, as he sat stroking her back in the quiet bedroom, there were earlier episodes in it that would not be renounced.

"Thanks, darling," Priscilla said. "That was wonderful. You better have your shower now. I'm going to get dressed."

.   .   .

He had been afraid the dinner might be a somewhat strained or embarrassingly taciturn event, and decided to prepare for it. While he was showering and dressing he went over in his mind a group of topics, anecdotes, amusing stories, bits of encyclopedic lore that he could use to lighten the atmosphere if it threatened to become oppressive. He had a considerable store of miscellanea, roughly classified by subject, which he sometimes introduced into a flagging conversation to enliven it. For some reason his memory wasn't working as well as usual, however, and he had difficulty thinking of many that were suitable. Almost all that suggested themselves to him seemed to have vaguely ominous connotations of some kind—death, infidelity, disaster—that were not very conducive to festivity. He managed to think of two—an anecdote about Blackstone the Magician and another about one of Shelley's escapades at Eton—that seemed fairly harmless and amusing, and he rehearsed them while he dressed for dinner.

He felt a need to appear at his best, and dressed carefully in the white silk shirt, a pair of massive jet-and-gold cufflinks, a Liberty tie of dark blue and scarlet paisley, and a tailor-made suit of black Italian silk. When he went out into the living room Priscilla said, "My goodness, don't you look elegant."

"Indeed you do," Tony said. "Put me to shame in these rags." He was wearing an open-necked shirt with a gray ascot. "I thought we weren't to dress for dinner."

"We're not," Ben said. "I'm sorry, I wasn't thinking."

"Have you something to celebrate?" Jill said.

"No, I was just daydreaming. I'll go put a sport shirt on."

"Oh, don't bother," Priscilla said. "We really ought to get moving. You look wonderful."

"Quite wonderful," Jill said.

The restaurant was on the western side of the Banks, at the very edge of the sound, and on a fine summer evening its long picture windows opened onto a scene of splendor that put the most livid postcards in the shops to shame. The mountains of clouds that hung above the long, dark-green line of the island hummocks were softly tattered at their upper edges, rising into the light in flaming crimson flares and darkening through rose to deep, plum-purple bases, like cliffs of anthracite with burning forests at their heights. They were huge and solemn as slowly drifting continents, brooding over the scarlet, dappled water and the silent, darkling marshes. High up in the blue, ragged luminous wisps blazed like mercury, and along the shore the blades of mallow and sawgrass lay inscribed upon the crimson water like the black brush strokes of an occult calligraphy. Ben had asked for a table beside the window, and when they were seated and had turned to look out at the majestic panorama of the sunset sound they sat in humbled silence. "God's teeth," Jill murmured after a moment. "How absolutely beautiful. It's unbelievable."

"It is," Tony said. "Quite beyond description."

Ben rejoiced at his choice of restaurants; there were some on the east side of the Banks that were more expensive and served better food but none with a view that could inspire the awe produced by a sunset on the sound. It was very hard to harbor feelings of animosity or anxiety or woe, he thought, confronted with a spectacle like that. All of the passion and foolishness and vanity of the day seemed like a fading fume in the sublimely finite pageant of the earth. Jill seemed to feel the same; her silence was a reverential one, not the bitter, brooding taciturnity that he had feared. She was roused out of it by the arrival of their drinks, and after she had disposed very rapidly of a five-to-one martini she launched into a set of garrulous, faintly ironic monologues that seemed much more likely to become embarrassing than an uncongenial silence would have been. She squinted her eyes and peered at Ben across the table as if dazzled by the light.

"It really is a smashing suit," she said. "Do you mind my asking if you had it made?"

"I did, yes," Ben said.

"You get them made, do you? I ask because it's the one thing I don't think I shall ever get used to, knowing I can have things made for me or buy anything I want in the shops. I don't care at all about most of the things people are supposed to go bonkers about when they get a bit of money—yachts, jewels, limousines, that sort of thing—but I've got this absolute passion for clothes that I can't seem to control. And yet I feel a fool in them when I've bought them. Can't stop buying all these useless bloody clothes that I never wear. If I go into Harrod's or Fortnum's or somewhere, I've got to have Tony along to steady me or I'm apt to go hog wild. Come out with carloads of mink, sables, evening gowns, anything at all that strikes my fancy. I suppose when you've shopped all your life at Woolworth's or Marks and Spencer for ten-shilling blouses you're apt to do that sort of thing. Did you find it very difficult to adjust to?"

"I don't think so," Ben said. "I don't really remember."

"Ah, well, that's a sign you're safely on the other side. I don't think I shall ever be. I still feel like a shoplifter when I go into one of those places and start fingering the designer gowns. I know very well the security people are watching every move I make. You can't fool those chaps. They can sense it, if you feel poor in your heart. And of course you know they know it, and it makes you feel all the shabbier. I suppose by the time I get over the feeling I shall be stone broke again."

The waiter arrived and set a plate in front of her on which was a sword-fish steak garnished with parsley and a quarter slice of lemon.

"Oh, lovely. Thank you." She picked up the lemon, bit into it, shud-dered, put it down, wiped her fingertips on the tablecloth and frowned at Ben across the table. "I must say you wear clothes wonderfully, Ben. But of course you always did. I don't suppose there's a sillier costume in the world than those petticoat breeches and silk weskits men wore in the Restora-tion, with bows and lace all over them, but you managed to look smash-ing in them. I used to look out at you from the wings and think, how on earth does he do it? He looks as if he'd been born to wear those things. And it was the same with Marlowe, or Shakespeare. You look better in a dou-blet and hose than anyone I ever saw. I always looked like a fishwife or a tavern wench, no matter what I had on."

"That isn't true," Ben said. "You looked very beautiful indeed as the Duchess of Malfi."

"Do you think so? Well, perhaps I wasn't too bad in that one. But then, it's different on the stage, isn't it? I mean I don't have a lot of trou-ble with pearls and farthingales and pomanders if I'm meant to be a duchess. They go with the painted flats and paper palaces and stage lighting. But it's different if you're walking down Picadilly in broad daylight. You feel like an impostor. I do, at any rate."

"Well, you don't have any reason to," Priscilla said. "No one wears clothes better than you. You were born to the purple."

"Well, it's very nice of you to say, but it isn't true, at all. Born to the blue, that's what I was—the blue collar. Or the white nylon, or some-thing of the sort. That's the worst of it: no matter what I pay for things, I still feel a fool in them. I had this gown made last spring for the Arts Ball, do you remember, Tony? Half an acre of watered silk. It cost me a hundred guineas, and when I got it on I felt like a maid who'd filched it out of her mistress's closet. I'd have done just as well if I'd gone round to the Salvation Army instead of Regent Street, for all the impression it made. I don't think one ever gets over being poor, and I'm not sure one ought to. I mean if you try and put on the Ritz, you can feel the fraudulence of it, and I think others do, as well. They know it isn't true. It's a bloody affliction."

Tony patted her hand gently. "It's an auspice," he said. "You're the kind of person whose clothes have absolutely nothing to do with their identity, to the confusion of the world at large which puts much more faith in millinery than in merit. Let me tell you a story about Beethoven, who was perhaps the worst-dressed man in the history of the planet. It was said that he never cut or combed his hair, seldom had his clothes washed or mended, and often went for days without bathing. His housekeeping was equally scandalous. He never married, of course, and could not keep servants. His rooms were a dreadful mess and there was never anything to eat in the place. An altogether enchanting man, personally. Well, when he was working on his last piano concerto he was staying at Baden, not far from a town called Wiener Neustadt. A man named Blasius Höfel, a professor of fine arts in the town, was at the local tavern one evening with some of his colleagues, including the commissioner of police, when a constable appeared and said to the commissioner, 'We've arrested some chap who won't give us any peace, at all. He keeps yelling that he's Beethoven, but I'm dead sure he's a tramp. He's got no hat, he's wearing this ragged old coat, and he has nothing on him by which he can be identified.' Well, the commissioner was in the midst of a congenial evening, considered it a trifling matter, and told the constable to keep the man locked up until morning, when he would come round and attend to it. At eleven o'clock that night, after he'd gone to bed, the commissioner was awakened by a policeman with the news that the prisoner was becoming more and more obstreperous. He was now insisting that the musical director of Wiener Neustadt, a man by the name of Herzog, be called to identify him. The commissioner was getting a bit concerned by this time, so he got dressed, went out and woke up Herzog, and the two of them went round to the jail. The moment he saw the prisoner, Herzog exclaimed, 'My God, it's Beethoven!' Herzog took him home, gave him the best room in the house, and the next day the mayor of the town arrived at the house, full of abject apologies. Herzog gave Beethoven some respectable clothes and the mayor sent him back to Baden in the state coach.

"What had happened was that Beethoven had got up early in the morning, gone out for a walk, lost his way, and continued walking the whole of the day, lost in thought about his concerto. Finally, late in the evening, he was seen peering into the windows of village houses, evidently on the point of asking for food or directions. The inhabitants were terrified by his disheveled appearance and called the police, who arrested him. When he protested that he was Beethoven, the policeman replied, 'Oh yes, of course! You're a tramp, that's what you are. Beethoven doesn't look like that.'"

"Was it that he was just careless," Jill asked after a moment. "Or was he poor, as well? Truly poor?"

"Oh, yes. Very truly. He was in debt most of his life, always in financial trouble, and often in dire want, down to a single pair of shoes sometimes, a single ragged jacket, and not a whole shirt to his name, quite literally. For many of his last years he lived in a wretched hovel in the meanest district of Vienna, so wretched that when Rossini went to see him in the spring of 1822, he was nearly heartbroken at the destitution in which he found the great man. He tells us that going down the ramshackle staircase of the house, he wept. On that same evening he went to a gala dinner given by Prince Metternich and, still completely upset by his visit, he spoke to the brilliant assemblage of Beethoven's plight. He was bitterly astonished by the indifference of the court and the aristocracy to the privation of the great man he had just left. He simply couldn't understand such conduct toward 'the greatest genius of the epoch,' as he called Beethoven, who needed so little and was abandoned to such misery. His outrage was so great that thirty-eight years later he described the scene to Wagner with unabated indignation. He had been moved, he told Wagner, 'to express my feelings stoutly and without any discretion at all.' He demanded reasons why these wealthy, privileged people failed to go to Beethoven's assistance, and pointed out how simple it would have been for them to draw up a very small subscription that would have assured the composer of an income large enough to put him beyond need for the rest of his life. This proposal, he told Wagner, failed to win the support of a single person in the company, which included the greatest names in Viennese society. The supreme irony of the evening was that it ended in a concert, at which was played one of Beethoven's most recent trios, a masterpiece that was listened to, Rossini said, with an air of almost religious transport."

There was a considerable silence after Tony finished the story, during which Priscilla let her fork sink to the table and stared at it for a moment.

"Did he ever get the subscription raised for him?" she asked.

"He tried. He wanted greatly to get together sufficient funds to buy Beethoven a place to live. But even when he had added what he himself could afford, the final sum was far from adequate. Eventually he had to abandon the project."

"But how could it be that he was so poor?" Priscilla asked. "His music was greatly admired in his own time. Surely there were proceeds from his concerts, royalties from his publishers."

"Oh, he had a few good years, and an occasional benefit concert made him briefly prosperous. But the main course of his life was a tale of relentless poverty; sometimes, of course, due to his own intransigence. His problems and quarrels with entrepreneurs and publishers were legendary. Some of them were scoundrels and cheated him outright. Others he had to haggle with in fury and despair. Even when the conditions of a contract were favorable according to the practices of the day, they were far from handsome, in our terms. Consider that Schott and Sons—who prided themselves on doing business in a very grand and generous style—paid him sixteen hundred silver florins, about ten thousand dollars in today's figures, for the *Missa*, the Ninth Symphony, and one of the last quartets, combined—the work of almost five years."

"Good God," Priscilla said.

"Didn't he ever work on commission?" Ben asked.

"He did, at times; as did every other composer of his day. But only if the terms involved no compromise of his art. As a chap named Kyd found out, to his great discomfort. He was an Englishman, this Kyd, a major general whose health had broken down and who'd come to Vienna for treatment. He was a great musical enthusiast, and while in Vienna—in 1816, I think it was—he approached Beethoven on behalf of the London Philharmonic Society and asked him to write a symphony for that organization in the manner of the First and Second Symphonies. Regardless of the cost, he assured the composer. He guaranteed a performance by the London Philharmonic and even offered to bring Beethoven to London for the occasion. He asked, however, that the work be 'shorter, simpler, and more easy of comprehension' than the earlier symphonies. Beethoven was furious at the suggestion. He considered it an insult, and expressed his profound displeasure with a nation that could demonstrate so low an opinion of an artist and of art. The next day, when walking in Vienna with Simrock, the Bonn publisher, he saw Kyd in the street. He stopped suddenly, pointed to the man and cried out, 'There's the man I threw downstairs yesterday!'"

"Good for him," Jill said. "I think I shall try that. The next time that bloody producer of mine asks me to rewrite a scene so people can understand it better, I'll just toss him down the stairs." She grimaced bitterly. "And you know where that'll get me."

"Evidently it didn't concern Beethoven," Tony said. "He was willing to stand the cost. A cost which he knew very well." He sipped from his glass, set it down, and turned the stem between his fingers. "The greatest regret he ever expressed about his poverty he put into these words, which I have found worth remembering: 'A man's spirit, the active, creative spirit, must not be tied down to the wretched necessities of life. I have been compelled to set bounds to the duty which I imposed on myself, which is to work by means of my art for human beings in distress.'"

Priscilla was visibly unsettled. She picked up a scallop with the tip of her fork, looked at it for a moment, and set it back down on her plate.

"I hope I haven't upset you with these tales," Tony said.

"It's just that I love his music so very much. I think the Diabelli Variations is one of the most exquisite things we have in this world. When I play it, even as badly as I do, I feel as close to heaven as it's possible for a silly woman like me to get. When I think—" She opened her mouth and exhaled gently.

"Yes, I know," Tony said.

Ben thought about introducing one of his own anecdotes into the conversation at this point, for relief, but they seemed to have been reduced to insignificance by Tony's. In the atmosphere produced by his account of the great composer's sufferings they would have sounded frivolous, he thought, even callous.

Relief appeared very unexpectedly in the person of a vivid, rail-thin, black-haired woman across the restaurant who was waving to them from the table where she sat with a large, faintly embarrassed-looking man in a seersucker suit and a pink necktie. They were the Bishops, neighbors of Ben and Priscilla in Great Falls and fellow property owners at Cape Hatteras. Linda was an amateur actress and wrote drama reviews for the *Bethesda Bugle*, a community newspaper that was distributed free outside of supermarkets. Although she was not a person in whose company he would ordinarily have expected to find refuge, he didn't really dislike her or Chuck— he didn't think he had the right to, since they were after all the people he had chosen to live among—but they were not the kind of people who sent the blood coursing through your veins. None of his friends did, he recognized with rue. He felt the kind of comfortable stupefaction in their presence that he felt in the dining room of the Congressional Country Club, of which the Bishops were also members. You knew they were all of roughly equal incomes, political opinions, golf scores, stock portfolios, and attitudes towards welfare, abortion, national health insurance, the Pledge of Allegiance, and other issues of the times. Some of them had special interests such as bird-watching, Persian carpets, pets, or Arabian horses, but nothing that smacked of any greater heresy than Rosicrucianism or the poetry of Khalil Gibran. A few had somewhat more picturesque penchants — one of the board members was a regular patron of Escorts Unlimited, a service that provided recreation of a very exotic kind indeed — but these displays of imagination and adventurousness were not of a philosophical order, and caused little real concern among their colleagues; at most they produced mischievous but benign allusions in the boardroom. Genuine intellectual energy or individuality that expressed itself in disquieting ideas, dissent, opinions or propositions about life lively enough to produce general discomfort or alarm was considered tasteless, querulous, and, if habitual and unrepented, punishable by ostracism. No one was willing to forego the rewards of that society by being branded an ingrate. For the most part they confined their distinctions to a preference for squash racquets to golf, Ischia to Puerto Vallarta, or Claire Dratch to Lillie Rubinstein. Linda's claim to eminence was her passion for the stage, which Ben sometimes suspected of being fraudulent but about which he realized he had forfeited the right to feel indignation or amusement. One of the articles of protocol among his friends was that you accepted each other's affectations and effusions with a mutual benignity that granted everyone immunity from embarrassment or challenge and gave everyone the opportunity to indulge in some beguiling diversion of his own. No matter how artless or excited their pretensions, or how conspicuous his own, he knew he could expect mercy from them.

"There's Linda Bishop," he said. "Over there, waving to us." He waved back, smiling genially.

"Where?" Priscilla said. "Oh, I see." She raised her hand and waggled her fingers, courteously but not over-encouragingly, a gesture whose restraint was lost on Linda. She was staring at them with a look of avid interest, like a horse that smells oats. She said something to her husband, laid down her napkin and stood up, pushing back her chair.

"Here she comes," Ben said.

She swept across the restaurant in a swift, predatory glide, like a hawk swooping down on a nest of mice. When she reached their table she bent and pressed her cheek to Priscilla's.

"Priss!" she cried. "How marvelous! I've been trying to call you all week. When did you get down?"

"Just on Saturday," Priscilla said.

"Well, that's why I couldn't get you. Hi, Ben."

Ben stood up and allowed himself to be kissed on the cheek. "Hello, Linda. Good to see you. How've you been?"

"Just wonderful. But we've missed you two. It's *months* since we've seen you. Why don't you give us a call once in a while?"

"I don't know," Ben said. "We never seem to have the time for fun. Linda, I'd like you to meet a couple of old friends of mine from London. This is Linda Bishop, and these two are Jill Davenport and Tony Griswold."

"How do you do?" Tony said. He stood up, smiling genially.

"Hello," Jill said.

Linda stared at them with a steady, stealthy smile, as if she saw into their souls. "I *know* who they are," she said in a tone of quiet homage. "I *saw* these two wonderful people only last week, on the stage of the Eisenhower. It was one of the most inspiring evenings of my life."

"You didn't see me, I'm afraid," Tony said.

"You mean to say you're not Clarence?"

"Afraid not. Nothing to do with it. Only a bystander."

"Well, isn't that amazing." She lowered her eyes to Jill. "*You* were certainly in it. You were everywhere in it."

"I was, yes," Jill said. "Can't plead not guilty."

"And you *wrote* that beautiful, haunting play."

"Oh, did you think it was? It's very nice of you to say that. I'm glad you enjoyed it."

"It wasn't exactly what I'd call enjoyment," Linda said. "It was more like devastation." She closed her eyes and shook her head weakly. "I was shattered by it."

"Oh, I hope not," Jill said. "Don't like to go about shattering people. You're all right now, are you?"

"I don't know if I'll ever be the same again," Linda said. "I mean that, quite honestly." She turned to Ben with a look of vast reproach. "Why didn't you tell us you knew this woman? *Why?* What have we done that you should keep this from us?"

"Well, I guess there wasn't any reason to mention it," Ben said. "Didn't know you'd be interested."

"*Interested?* I'd walk across burning desert sand, *barefoot,* to meet this woman." She turned to Jill again. "I'm an actress, too," she said. "Not one like you, but enough of one to understand your achievement. I wish I had the time to tell you how I feel about it. How long are you down for?"

"Just til Saturday, I think."

"Saturday. Oh, damn. What have you got planned, til then?"

"Oh, I don't know. Priss, what have we got planned?"

"Well, let's see," Priscilla said. "Wednesday night there's the play—"

"The play?" Tony said.

"*The Lost Colony,* that I told you about."

"Oh, yes, yes. The play," Tony said.

"And Thursday there's the Morrisons."

"Listen, what about tomorrow night?" Linda said. "Could you come to us for dinner tomorrow? I've just got to sit down and talk to this young lady before she leaves, or I'll mourn for the rest of my life."

"Oh, not tomorrow, I'm afraid," Priscilla said. "I've been planning my jambalaya dinner for tomorrow night, and Esther gave up a date to help me with it." She frowned and then said quickly, "Why don't you and Chuck come over and have some with us?"

"Oh, Priss, how could I refuse! Your jambalaya and a chance to talk to this fascinating woman! These fascinating *people*! That's an irresistible combination. Are you sure it won't be too much for you?"

"Not at all," Priscilla said. "Just another couple of plates on the table. We'd love to have you."

"Well, have us you will, believe me! What time shall we come?"

"Oh, you know, drinks. We'll eat around eight."

"That sounds divine." She kissed them both again and leaned down to press Jill's hand which lay on the table. "We'll see you all tomorrow. I'll be counting the minutes. Good-bye, you lovely people."

"Good-bye" Tony said. Jill smiled at her. Ben waved to Chuck who beamed and nodded from his table.

"I didn't know quite what to do," Priscilla said. "I painted myself into a corner. I hope you don't mind."

"Not at all," Jill said. "She seems quite nice. Is she a good actress?"

"I think so," Priscilla said. "I don't think Ben does, but he's too gallant to say so. She acts and directs for a little community theatre in Potomac. They do some very good things. We saw her in *Streetcar* last summer and I thought she had some very moving moments."

"Lovely play, that," Jill said. "Williams was a marvelous playwright. Your absolute best, in my opinion. Wasn't it awful how he died?"

"How did he die?" Priscilla asked.

"Choked to death on a bottle cap, in a hotel room, all by himself. He was taking pills of some kind, I believe, and tugged the top off with his teeth. These bloody bottles today. You can't get the lids off without a bulldozer."

"Oh, God," Priscilla said. "Why does everything conspire to rob these people of their dignity? You'd think it was the very least they deserved."

"Oh, I don't think he lost any dignity," Jill said. "Not by my reckoning. Suffered a great deal more indignity in his life than in his death, from what I understand. I shouldn't be surprised if he was glad to go, whatever the circumstances."

"Oh, that's *awful*," Priscilla said. "You don't mean that, Jill."

"I don't know," Jill said. "There are times one feels one's had enough,
I think. Anyone, almost. Especially that poor man. All the bloody indignity
he had to put up with."

"You don't feel that way, do you? I don't believe it."

"Oh, I have, now and again. For a moment or two, I suppose. Hasn't
everyone?"

"Well, that's all behind you now," Priscilla said. She reached across
the table and laid her hand on Jill's. "You'll never have to feel that way
again."

"Oh? How do you reckon that?"

"You're a success now. That's all behind you."

"Oh, is it? I had the feeling the worst was yet to come." She laughed
lightly, seeing Priscilla's frown. "You're not to mind me. Talking a lot of rot."

"Well, I do mind. It makes me worry to hear you talk like that."

Jill gazed at her across the table, her face falling into seriousness. She
disengaged her hand from Priscilla's and picked up her wine glass, turning
her head to look out of the window. "You're not to worry about me," she
said. "I'm a rubbishy lot. Quite truly."

"Oh, for heaven's sake," Priscilla said.

"I say, just look at that water now. Like a great bowl of rubies. And
those clouds, my word. Bit difficult to grumble about things when one's
got a world like that to live in." She stared for a moment at the scarlet
water and the rose-edged, towering clouds. "Although I can't say I like
the look of that heron over there. Got something very unpleasant on his
mind, that chap. I wouldn't wonder if there was a frog out there who'll have
a good deal to grumble about in a moment."

"You're incorrigible!" Priscilla said. She laughed and threw a little piece
of bread across the table at Jill.

"It'll be dark in twenty minutes," Ben said. "And then the stars come out
so suddenly it looks as if someone had pricked holes in the sky."

"Let's watch for the first one," Priscilla said. "And then we must all make
a wish. Ben, why don't you pour us some more Drambuie?"

Ben filled their glasses with the thick dark liqueur and they sat and sipped it silently, watching the sky darken from rose to lavender to slate gray. The line of the far shore lost its definition as it sank into the obscurity that swarmed over it as gently as sleep. The sky and water and the soft billows of the clouds were gradually extinguished and gathered into a vast, lustrous darkness, like a sable sea. When they had watched for a few minutes a single faint scintilla of light began to flicker in the black sky above the marshes like a camp fire on a mountain top.

"There it is!" Priscilla cried.

"There it is!" Jill said at the same moment. She laid her hand on Tony's shoulder. "Do you see it, Tony? Just there." She pointed through the window.

"Oh, yes. So it is."

"You see it, Ben?"

"Yes."

"Now we must all make a wish," Priscilla said. She closed her eyes and chanted:

Star light, star bright,
First star I see tonight.
I wish I may, I wish I might
Have the wish I wish tonight.

Ben closed his eyes and tried very hard to think of something to wish for, but his mind went numb. He thought, I wish—but beyond the word there was only a moiling void in which his mind writhed in futility, as if he were trying to remember a name, the title of a book, the face of some-one he had known as a child, or a long-forgotten tune. I can't remember what I want, he thought.

Priscilla opened her eyes and said, "Did everyone wish?"

"I did," Tony said. "A very extravagant one."

"Ben?" He nodded. "Jill?"

"Yes."

"You mustn't tell what it is, or it won't come true."

"No fear," Jill said.

"It isn't really a star," Ben said. "It's Venus. It rises very early this time of month, and it's called the Evening Star, but it's really a planet."

"Well, so much the better," Priscilla said. "It's the perfect one for us to wish on. The Star of Love."

They finished the bottle of Drambuie, became very tipsy and silly. Jill folded and knotted her napkin into a rabbit which sang, 'What Are We Going to Do with Uncle Arthur?' Tony did a disappearing trick with a quarter wrapped up in his handkerchief. Ben challenged anyone to solve the problem of getting a goose, a sack of grain, and a fox from one side of a river to the other without losing anything. No one could solve it, and he found that he had drunk so much Drambuie that he couldn't remember the solution himself. Before the Bishops left the restaurant, Linda brought Chuck to the table and introduced him. He stood nodding and mumbling amiably with the look of a large, gentle, trained animal, like a seal dressed in a seersucker suit and performing uneasily but with a certain pride.

"I liked that man," Jill said. "I do like shy people. My dad was shy. So shy that when he got hit by a lorry and I went to see him in hospital, he said, 'Hello, love. I'm awfully sorry about this.'"

"What a sweet man," Priscilla said.

"He was, you know. I had the idea when I was a kid that God would be just like my dad, if ever I got to meet Him. Not some stern old creature sitting there scowling at you with His fingertips pressed together while you recited all your sins. I thought when I got to heaven, He'd open the door very happily and shyly as if He'd been waiting up all hours for me, the way my dad used to do when I got home from a date, and say something like, 'Come in, love. My, it's good to see you. Would you like a cup of tea?' And then we'd sit in the kitchen and have a cup of tea, and He'd say, 'I'm awfully sorry about your dad having to die, but I don't know quite what to do about it. You see, if no one did, it'd be so crowded down there soon you wouldn't have room to stand up.' That's the sort of thing my dad would say." She looked at Priscilla. "Do you love your dad?"

"I don't know if I could say that I love him," Priscilla said. "I suppose I'm grateful to him, for all he's given me."

"Oh, that's different, I think. Do you love your father, Ben?"

"Not very much," Ben said.

"Oh, that's a pity." She lowered her eyes to the tablecloth and touched a fork with her fingertip. "And you haven't any children, have you?"

"No," Ben said.

"That's a pity," Jill said. "You might have made a very good father, I think." She raised her eyes and gazed at him for a moment without smiling. "I mean, you're very good at games, and riddles, and that sort of thing. And picnics. Children like that. Might bring out the very best in you."

"We want very much to have some," Priscilla said in a soft, disconcerted murmur. "Perhaps we'll adopt, one day."

"Oh," Jill said. "Will you? Well, I do hope it turns out very well for you. Sometimes it does, of course." She raised her glass in which a few drops of Drambuie still sparkled. "Here's to a very happy family life for you, with scores of lovely moppets tugging at your skirts."

"Now don't be cynical," Priscilla said.

"Not cynical at all. Quite the contrary. Just feeling a bit maudlin, that's all. I've no idea why."

"Perhaps you're a bit tired," Tony said. He laid his hand on her wrist. "Might be just as well if we got you home."

"That's a good idea," Priscilla said. "It's been a long day. I think we could all use some sleep."

When they left the restaurant the sky was very clear and black and glittering with stars. Jill put her head out of the window of the car and stared up at the sky, her hair blowing in the wind. Ben drove with one hand on the wheel, reaching across the seat to lay his other on Priscilla's thigh. She covered his hand with her own but when he turned to her, expecting to see her smiling in the darkness, he was chagrined to see that she was sunken in some thought with whose gravity no appeal of his own could contend.

He had expected to feel entirely his old self in the morning, and was disconcerted to find that he did not. He had slept badly and he woke up
suddenly with a sense of alarm as if he had been wakened by a gunshot
or the sound of an automobile collision. He put on a pair of shorts and a
light jacket, went out to the kitchen and made himself a cup of tea which
he drank hurriedly, standing at the table. He still had a sense of instability, of delicacy of personality, as if he were a fine vase made of very thin glass
which would shatter if set down carelessly. He left his tea unfinished—
he didn't want to meet Jill—went down the kitchen steps to the beach
and ran for an hour on the sand. The sea was very rough. There were huge,
steel-gray breakers thundering on the shore and whitecaps as far out as
he could see on the water. Usually he jogged in the morning, but he wanted
to tire himself physically, so he ran fast until he was exhausted and collapsed onto his knees on the sand. After he had sat panting for several
minutes he felt better. He got up, brushed the sand from his legs and walked
back to the house breathing deeply.

Jill and Tony were still asleep and Priscilla was standing at the counter
in the kitchen waiting for a pair of frozen waffles to pop out of the toaster.

"How was the walk?" she asked.

"I didn't walk. I ran. Five miles, anyway." He patted his midsection.
"A pound a mile."

"Don't be complacent," she said. "I'm just about to eat waffles."

"How come everybody's sleeping so late?"

"Too much Drambuie after dinner, I guess."

"Decadence," Ben said. "It's supposed to make life more agreeable,
not bring it to a halt."

"My God, aren't you being pontifical. You've gotten too much oxygen
or something. You're hyperventilated."

"I'm going to have a shower and then go in the study for an hour or
so. I've got some telephoning to do."

"Well, if you sing, make it something very quiet, will you?"

"I was thinking about the 'Triumphal March,' from *Aida*," Ben said.

"Oh, get out of here."

He took a hot shower, humming in a muted, militant baritone, finished with a needle-point cold spray that made his teeth chatter, toweled himself vigorously, put on a pair of slacks and a sports shirt and came out to make a cup of tea to carry to the den. Jill was sitting at the table with Priscilla, dipping a Danish pastry into her tea and nibbling at it like a squirrel.

"Well, you look a new penny this morning," she said. "You off to conquer the world?"

"Just about to," Ben said. "I'm going to have to absent myself from felicity awhile. I've got some telephoning to do."

"How long will that take?" Priscilla asked.

"About an hour. Are you going down to the beach? I'll meet you down there if you are."

"Depends on what Tony wants to do. Jill and I may go down if he sleeps late."

"You want to be careful if you go in," Ben said. "There's a very high surf running. Rougher than hell."

"It must be that storm," Priscilla said. "They said it was off the coast, last night."

"Are we going to have a storm?" Jill said.

"Oh, no. But it gets the water stirred up for miles around. For days, sometimes."

Ben stirred sugar into his tea and carried it across to the study door. "I won't be long," he said. "I've got to talk to Mark about the SureSet account."

"Take your time. We might run in to the village. Jill wants to pick up some postcards."

He went into the study and sat down in his swivel chair, setting the teacup on the desk in front of him. He had had the study redecorated in the fall and it still smelled of the new red leather upholstery of the chair, the small divan against the wall, and the fresh dark green binding of the books in the teak shelves that lined both ends of the room. He felt a great sense of reassurance on entering the office. He tilted back the swivel

chair and sat with his fingers laced behind his head, gazing with a sense
of restored serenity at the leather spines of his books, the bust of Mozart,
the ebony-framed Certificate of Merit from the National Association of
Broadcasters that hung beside the print of Delacroix's Hamlet on the
teak wall paneling. Gradually a sense of reorientation, almost of the rein-
tegration of his personality into its old shape took place in him, something like the gathering together of iron filings into an ordained pattern
by the action of a magnet. The feeling was considerably stronger than
the pleasant sense of comfort and mild sovereignty that he usually enjoyed in the atmosphere of his study, almost strong enough to be called devout. This was his milieu, he thought. This was who he was, this was his
proper setting, this elegant, impeccably appointed stage of the great world.

His attaché case lay on the desk. He opened it and lifted out a folder
marked SURESET PRELIMS which he laid on the desk and opened. While
he sipped his tea he studied an early version of a storyboard for a fifteen-
second commercial for hair spray. In the left column were five consecu-
tive rough ink sketches of the action, opposed to, in the right margin, sound
effects, voice-over, and action instructions, concluding with a sketch of the
product, a can of SureSet Hair Spray, held in the actor's hand with the
label toward the camera, and the notations:

ACTION: Depresses button with forefinger.
SFX: Hiss of escaping spray.
VO: Goes on fast. Holds all day.

Ben picked up the telephone and dialed his office in Washington. After a moment a woman's voice with a very false English "county" accent
said, "Razullo, Incorporated."

"Hello, Margo. This is Ben."

"Oh, good morning, Mr. Oakshaw. How nice to hear you. Are you
having a good time?"

"Wonderful. The weather's perfect. Wish you were here."

"I wish I were too."

"Listen, put me on to Mark, will you?"

"Yes, sir. Have a great holiday, sir. We miss you."

"Thanks, Margo."

In a moment Mark said, "Hi, Ben. How's it going? Having fun?"

"Quite a bit," Ben said. "How are things up there?"

"Not too bad," Mark said. "We signed up Carrigher to do production on the SureSet. He came in with the lowest bid. Did you get a look at Carol's storyboard?"

"I've just been looking at it," Ben said. "Who did the art work? Jenny Lasker?"

"That's right. You like it?"

"I like the action flow all right, but she's got the guy in an undershirt. What is this, anyway? Men haven't worn undershirts for years."

"That's what I told her."

"You had to tell her? Christ, if anybody in the world ought to know that, it's Jenny."

Mark chuckled. "You want it changed, huh?"

"Hell, yes. We want the guy bare-chested. And with one of those Wrap-A-Rong things on. Not shorts. Make sure the research people don't send any of these storyboards to that survey group until they're changed."

"OK, Ben. I was pretty sure that's what you'd want. I held them up."

"Good. Did you do those auditions yesterday?"

"Six of them. Three takes each. We have another six coming in today. They'll be ready to look at when you get back."

"You get Turk Meadows in that group yesterday?"

"Sure did. He came over very well. There's one other guy I think you'll like, too. We haven't used him before. A guy named Halliday the Brooks Agency sent over."

"Has he got hair on his chest? We want a guy with hair. Not too much, though. Not an ape-man, you know."

"He's got hair. A very pretty little patch of it. Very good physique. He looks a lot like William Hurt."

"Not too sensitive, is he?"

"No. Big, but bright. A rugby player."

"What color's his chest hair? Blond?"

"Sort of brown, but not real dark. We can make it blond."

"How about his eyes? They blue?"

"Blue as a mountain lake. He's been doing a lot of still stuff for Marshall Field. Bathing suits and stuff like that. I think you'll like him."

"He sounds pretty good," Ben said.

There was a tap on the study door. Ben held his hand over the mouthpiece and said, "Come in." Jill peeked around the corner of the door and said, "Priss said to tell you we're going to the village. She's getting dressed. Sorry to bother you."

"No bother," Ben said. "Come on in. I'll be through in a minute. There are some books over there that might interest you. One of them is the Shakespeare and Company edition of *Ulysses*."

"Whillikers," Jill said. She knelt on the divan in front of the bookcase and peered at the titles of the leather-bound volumes above her head.

Ben put the phone back to his ear and said, "OK, now what about this ecology survey? Has Carl finished that poll?"

"Yes. He did twenty-five half-hour interviews with middle-class guys twenty to twenty-five who use hair spray rather than pomade or liquid, or bear grease or anything else. Only four of them expressed any concern at all about the ozone layer. Most of them never heard of it. Evidently, guys that use hair spray don't care whether their children die of cancer."

"That wouldn't be hard to predict," Ben said. "I think we ought to emphasize the idea of its convenience and novelty. 'All new, pump-action can for more control, better placement.' It's a waste of time talking about the benefits to the environment."

"You don't think we ought to have somebody do a couple of scripts with just a line in them about it? Something like, 'Kind to your hair, kind to your world.' We don't want to lose the eggheads."

"Eggheads don't use hair spray," Ben said.

Mark laughed loudly. "I guess you're right."

"And listen, tell Gladys I want to sit down with her on Monday morning, that's the twenty-fourth, and go over the schedule. It seems to me we can do a lot more with it. What have we got? Five sports events every weekend until October. What about Monday night football? What about Wimbledon? Christ, that's all day long in finals week. What kind of rating does that have? Six to eight? At five shots a day, that's thirty to forty points. I can see maybe sixty thousand dollars a day right there."

"It's a very big contract," Mark said. "It's going to take a lot of work. I was in there with her for an hour yesterday. We'll have some pretty solid schedule figures by the time you get back. I'll set that up with her for nine o'clock Monday morning. The twenty-fourth, right?"

"Right. I want you in there too, and the Castle people."

"They'll be there," Mark said. "Farnsworth called me yesterday and we went over it a good bit. He's very anxious to get the Kemper Open."

"It's a good idea," Ben said. "It's getting more exposure every year."

"OK," Mark said. "Auditions today. Short list for you by Monday. No undershirts. No shorts. No ecology. Blond chest hair. New storyboards to survey group. Communications workup. Gladys, me, and Farnsworth on Monday morning at nine. Right."

"You know, I'm a little worried about Carrigher, Mark. He can get pretty flaky. You've got to sit right there in the studio and direct the hell out of him."

"I know that, but I like working with him. The guy is good. You let me worry about it, Ben, OK? There's not a better cameraman in Washington. *Or* New York."

"Well, we'll have to learn to live with him, I guess. Send me the new storyboard by Federal Express. I'll call you Friday."

"Right. Have a good time, Ben. How's the water?"

"Just like gin. Swimming in gin."

"I could use some of that."

"I'll bring you a bottle of it," Ben said. "That's the best I can do."

Mark laughed. "OK. Take it easy."

Ben hung up the phone and looked across the room at Jill, who was sitting on the leather divan with the copy of *Ulysses* on her lap, leafing through it carefully with her fingertips. She looked up at him with a very delicate smile. "Well, that was quite impressive. I've never known a captain of industry before."

"We have our moments," Ben said.

"It's all wonderfully arcane, isn't it? What was all that about points?"

"You really want to know?"

"Oh, yes."

"One rating point is equal to eight hundred eighty-six thousand households, which is one percent of eighty-eight point six million households in the country. Which equals about two million two hundred ninety-nine thousand individuals. So if you've got a ten-point program you've got about twenty-three million people watching this young man in the bathroom."

"God in heaven. What does that cost the advertiser?"

"About twenty thousand dollars, every time he sprays his hair."

"And what does it cost to produce?"

"Maybe half a million dollars."

"For fifteen seconds? You can't be serious."

"Very serious," Ben said. "This is serious business. Do you know what the American economy amounts to, in round figures?"

"I haven't the faintest idea."

"About four point five trillion dollars. Do you know how much of that is accounted for by consumer spending?"

"No."

"Three trillion dollars. Almost exactly two-thirds of it. And what keeps it going is advertising. It's the chief impetus of the American economy. The average citizen in this country is exposed to three thousand commercial messages a day, in one form or another—newspapers, magazines, television, radio. The typical American spends a year and a half of his life watching television commercials alone. In one hour of prime-time television viewing he's exposed to more than fifty advertising messages. That's after spending an ordinary working day in which he's been bombarded by ads on the outside of buses, inside of buses, on billboards, in amusement parks, ballparks, subway trains, taxicabs, movie lead-ins, theatre programs, airports, railway stations, waiting rooms, even public lavatories. There is one hundred billion dollars a year spent on advertising in this country. And without it, two-thirds of our economy would wither up and die."

"God's teeth," Jill said. She looked down at the book in her lap. "And this man lived in poverty all his life, like Beethoven."

"They chose to," Ben said. "They were both pretty quirky guys, from all accounts. Joyce exiled himself from his own country. He called Ireland, 'the old sow who eats her young.' He was very proud, vain, and ambitious."

"And the rest of us are not." She closed the book and laid her hand on the cover. "Of course, there is a certain . . . grandeur . . . about it. You're quite a powerful man, aren't you? I don't think I really understood that."

"It's a pretty exciting world," Ben said. "A lot of people don't realize that. When one of these things comes out, it's very much like opening night. You can't wait to read the reviews, and if they're good you not only make a great deal of money, you may have changed the living habits of the nation. Maybe of the world. It's not too different from the theatre."

"Oh, I don't think my play will change the living habits of the world," Jill said.

"You can't tell," Ben said. He smiled at her in a way that he realized instantly was patronizing and that he instantly regretted. "Here and there a sensitive observer may be moved. Like me."

"Oh, really? And has it changed your living habits?"

Ben lowered his eyes. She stood up and put the book back on the shelf and then wandered along the wall, pausing in front of the framed award.

"What did you get this for?" she asked.

"A thirty-second ad for Julius Mandel suits. I think you would have liked it."

"Why?"

"It had Shakespeare in it. It opened up on this guy costumed and made up like the Droeshout portrait: doublet, lace collar, everything. He wiggles his finger at the camera and says, 'Costly thy habit as thy purse can buy, but not expressed in fancy. Rich, not gaudy. For the apparel oft proclaims the man.' Then the voice-over says, 'You get the message? Maybe the language is a little old-fashioned, like the suit; but the advice is still sound. If Shakespeare were alive today, he'd say it like this—' Then we get a quick dissolve on the guy: identical position, identical face, only now he's totally twentieth century: blow-dried hair, shirt and tie, and a Julius Mandel suit. This time he says, 'Make sure you buy the best clothes you can afford, but make sure they're in perfect taste, not flashy or far-out. Your clothes tell people who you are.' Then this gorgeous chick steps into the picture, slides her arm into his, and says, 'They sure do!' The voice-over says, 'Oh, yes, there's one thing Shakespeare would have added if he were alive today.' The Shakespeare character raises his finger and says, 'And make sure the label says Julius Mandel.' He takes a reading on the chick who's attached herself to him, then turns back to the camera and says, 'Yea, verily!' And winks."

"Oh, God," Jill said. "You didn't do that. You didn't use Shakespeare to sell haberdashery."

"Shakespeare wrote pretty good copy," Ben said. "It's one of the most successful commercials we ever made. It brought sales up twenty-three percent and won an Ad Emmy for the year."

"Are you *allowed* to do that? Use Shakespeare?"

"Sure. It's in the public domain. You can do anything you like with it. We used Prokofiev's *Romeo and Juliet* for background music."

Jill shook her head, her face crinkled in a pained grin, like someone smiling through a toothache. "Have you tried the Bible?" she said. "You might use St. Paul for hustling booze: 'Take a little wine for thy stomach's sake.'"

"By God, I never thought of that," Ben said. "If he were alive today, he'd say, 'Make sure it's Gallo Brothers.'" He grinned at her. "You know, I could use you."

"Well, of course, wine's very easy to sell. How about a book of verses and a loaf of bread? You think you could sell poetry, in this kind of a world?"

"If anybody could, you could," Ben said.

"Will you let me know, if you need someone?"

"You're the first person I'll think of. Of course we don't get a lot of contracts for poetry." He picked up the folder from his desk and put it back in his briefcase.

"No, I don't suppose you do. Still, it's nice to know you'd think of me."

He snapped shut the briefcase and laid his hands flat on it. "Well, what do you want to do today?"

"I don't know. What are the choices?"

"How about sailing? There's a nice breeze out there this morning."

"It sounds smashing. I've never been sailing. Do you think I'll manage?"

"There's nothing to it," Ben said. "You'll be handling the tiller in no time. After all, you steered us through the shoals yesterday."

"I did, didn't I?" Jill said. "I think I have a talent for it. Well, I'd better go and dress. Perhaps Tony will be up by the time we're back." She went to the door and stood with her hand on the knob. "I'll give him a shout, but if he doesn't get up, you're to drive him out with a broomstick. He's a dreadful sluggard."

"I'll have him up by the time you're back," Ben said. "And the lunch made. We'll go over to the sound and make a day of it."

"Super," Jill said. "I'm having a marvelous time, you know."

When she had gone Ben opened the briefcase again, took out the Sure-Set folder and read, twice, a page of copy without being able to make sense of it, his eyes roving along the words mindlessly. After a few minutes Priscilla looked in through the open door and said, "Jill says we're going sailing."

"She said she'd like to. Is that OK with you?"

"Whatever you like. We're going to run in to the village. She's waking Tony up."

"I'll get the lunch made while you're gone," Ben said. "Will you pick up a bag of ice?"

"All right. Anything else?"

"You might get some of that clam dip, if we're out."

"OK. We'll be back in half an hour."

While they were gone Ben went into the kitchen and prepared the lunch, mixing a spread of Boursin cream cheese with garlic and parsley and sandwiches of sliced, apple-wood-smoked duck. He packed them into the cooler with water biscuits, a can of Beluga caviar, a box of *gaufrettes* and pâté, and then shelled eight hard-boiled eggs and began to mix the yolks with powdered mustard in a bowl. While he was deviling the eggs, Tony came into the kitchen looking polished, damp, and rosy from his shower.

"My word, that looks good," he said. "You're quite a chef, aren't you?"

"I'm a devout picnicker," Ben said.

"I should think you were. Can I have an egg?"

"If you don't mind having them again for lunch."

"I don't mind having them all day." He picked a deviled egg out of the bowl and took the top off the teapot. "Is there tea? Ah, yes, good." He poured himself a cup of tea and sat down at the table. "We're going sailing, Jill says."

"Yes. Over in the sound. You like sailing?"

"Never been, at all. It sounds exciting." He sipped his tea and bit into his deviled egg. "My word, these are good. I don't suppose I'll drown?"

"I don't think so," Ben said. "It's very quiet water. And very shallow, if you capsize."

"Good. I shouldn't like drowning." He looked out at the sunlight through the window. "Another fine day."

"Perfect," Ben said. "Good brisk breeze. Westerly. Just right for sailing."

"Doesn't look as if we're going to have that storm."

"No. It's standing out there off Bermuda. It'll drift off to sea, I think. They usually do." He wrapped an egg in foil, studying Tony's face surreptitiously.

It was difficult to decide whether Jill had told him about the incident in the shower stall. He didn't think so. There was certainly no evidence of any such knowledge in his placid manner. On the other hand, he made such a creed of his urbanity that it was almost impossible to say. Ben hoped to God she hadn't. The thought of the man sitting there imperviously munching eggs in possession of that knowledge was indecent. He was sure she hadn't. It would have been a senseless and ruinous thing to do, no matter how intimate they were. She was a very sagacious woman, Ben thought, and it was possible she was playing for something in which Tony was part of the stakes. If that was the case, it was not likely that she would advise him of the fact. The more he considered this, the more possible it seemed. There was no doubt that he still had a very strong attraction for her. He hadn't been sure of that before the incident of the shower stall. The thought gave him, for the first time, a sense of advantage over Tony, and with it a feeling of security and power that amounted to exultation. There was nothing quite as categorical as the act of sex to define situations, recognize the true nature of relationships, dictate the course of one's behavior. An act of sex stood up like a lighthouse above the treacherous shoals of human intercourse, guiding, reassuring, casting light upon the waters. He liked the image. Perhaps, for advertising purposes, it could be modified to a kiss. "A kiss is like a lighthouse in the uncertain seas of life. Do you want her to see the light? Give her a bottle of Baiser for Christmas." Long kiss between couple; misty, Nykvist-style lighting; fadeout to a bottle of Baiser perfume standing on pile of rocks beside the sea; foam beats at base of them; ray of light cast out across the water from the flask. The sound of a horn honking in the driveway below the house disrupted his little fantasy.

"Ah, they're back," Tony said.

"Good," Ben said. "We'll get away early." He went out onto the deck and looked down while Priscilla and Jill got out of the car. He liked to watch women getting out of cars; their long slender legs thrust out, bare and brown, and then a flare of bright colored cotton skirt like the opening of a blossom.

They stood exquisitely in the sunlight, bareheaded, with shining hair. He felt a pleasant proprietary tenderness toward them both, all his unease of the night before quieted by his new sense of security. "Anything heavy?" he called down.

"No, we can manage," Priscilla said, looking up. "Just odds and ends, and the ice."

"Did you get the dip?"

"Yes."

"Good. The lunch is all ready. Tony and I'll get the car packed while you put your suits on."

They came up the stairs to the deck, their sandals pattering on the steps. He took the bag of ice from Priscilla and followed them into the kitchen.

"It's a heavenly day," Jill said. "And I got some super cards."

She set the grocery bag she was carrying on the table and took a sheaf of bright-colored postcards out of it. "Look, Tony." She spread the cards on the table in front of him, photographs of dunes, swampland, flaming sunsets, and the marina at Ocracoke. "This one's the cafe where we had lunch yesterday. That's where we sat, right there, you see?"

"So it is. Might even be me at the table."

"Oh, yes. I think I'll send it to Thelma and tell her it is. I'll say you've lost twenty pounds and grown a red beard."

"Might do that, you know. Would you like that?" He looked up at her and grinned.

"No fear. I like you just as you are." She put her arms around his neck and leaned down, pressing her cheek to his. It was the first show of affection Ben had seen between them, and it struck him as being flagrant. He ripped open the plastic ice bag with his fingernails and poured the cubes into the cooler.

"OK, you two, go and get your suits on," he said. "Tony and I will get loaded up."

"Here's the dip," Priscilla said, taking it out of the grocery bag. "It's got chives in it. Will that be good?"

"Fine," Ben said. "Go get ready. Shoo, shoo."

"Hey, just a minute," Priscilla said. "Don't be so damned masterly. I've got something to show you." She took a small blue velvet jewel case out of the pocket of her skirt and snapped back the lid. "Look what Jill bought me." She held out the open case for Ben and Tony to see. Inside was a silver pendant in the shape of a seagull in flight across a scarlet sun. The sun was a cluster of garnets the size of a fifty cent piece and the gull was very delicately carved of white coral. "Isn't that exquisite?"

"Oh, absolutely," Tony said. "My word. Let's have a look." He took the case from her and examined the pendant for a moment, then handed it to Ben.

"Beautiful," Ben said.

"I couldn't stop her. We went into the Belle Sauvage to look around and I made the mistake of admiring it, so she insisted on buying it for me. She was absolutely intractable."

"It's a trifle compared to what you've done for us," Jill said. "I hope some day I'll be able to give you something of real value. Something you'll truly cherish."

"What on earth do you mean?" Priscilla said. "There's nothing I could cherish more." She held the pendant to the breast of her blouse and smiled down at it. "You really are a prodigal creature, Jill."

"Her prodigality is famous," Tony said, with what seemed to Ben a willful banality.

Ben frowned, and then said quickly, "Well, who's for a sail?"

"I for one," Jill cried.

"Good. You'd better get your swimsuits on. It's wet sailing, in a dinghy."

While the women changed into their swimsuits and robes, Ben and Tony went down and loaded the station wagon with the cooler, the beach umbrellas, the folding chairs and table, and the dinghy and sailing gear. The dinghy was very light, a twelve-foot, sixty-five-pound Styrofoam shell covered with plastic hide, which they lifted easily and strapped to the roof rack with tension cords.

It was a perfect day for sailing: high, gliding wisps of cumulus, a flax-blue sky, and a fresh cool westerly breeze which meant that they could sail on a reach along the coast and back again without tacking. They drove in along a sand road from the highway to their favorite spot on the eastern shore of the sound where there was a stand of mangrove whose roots made firm ground for the tires, and a beach wide enough for sunbathing. The water of the sound was very shallow, warm, and gentle. It lapped at their ankles like a lake, and far out in the center it was stippled slightly in the wind and lay fuming in the sun like a blue pane of cobbled glass between the brown sand of the shores. They set up the beach umbrellas and the folding chairs and table and Ben and Tony carried the dinghy down to the shore and fitted it with the daggerboard, rudder, and mast, and rigged the sail.

"Looks a very trim little boat," Tony said.

"She'll sail, too. Skips over the water like a leaf. I think you'll enjoy it."

"I'm sure I will."

Ben tugged the boat down to the shoreline by its painter and waded out into the warm, tea-colored water, pulling the dinghy behind him until the hull was afloat up to the centerboard. "OK, shall we have a go?"

"Why don't you take Jill out first?" Tony said. "I think I'll sit down for a bit. Catch my breath."

"You're a humbug," Jill said. "You don't wriggle out of it, you know."

"No, no. Just want a bit of rest. I'll see how you make out."

"I'll take him out after you get back," Priscilla said.

"All right," Jill said. "I don't know if I could wait, anyway. Shall I take off my robe?"

"I think you'd better," Ben said. "It'll get soaked, otherwise."

She took off her robe and tossed it into a beach chair and then clambered into the boat with the lovely, awkward eagerness of a newborn colt, staggering slim-legged in the dinghy as the hull rocked with her weight. Ben tugged it off the sand until it was fully afloat and tossed her the line. He climbed over the gunwale and took the rudder as the dinghy came

around with the sail full and suddenly sped out into the sound like a
horse with a loosened rein.

"Oh, crikey," Jill said. "This is lovely."

There was a weightless, lubricious sense of swiftness, almost of bird-flight,
as the dinghy heeled to the wind, her sail full and tight, the rudder biting, the bow lifted above the riplets that broke in a quick, light tapping
against the hull. Ben turned the bow up the coast toward Roanoke Island, the breeze from the mainland full abeam, feeling the cool wind of
their passage begin to stream across his face and shoulders as they gained
hull speed.

"God, it's like flying!" Jill said.

She sat with her legs crossed, clutching both gunwales, leaning to windward against the rake of the heel.

"It gets the dust out of your brains, all right," Ben said. He loved sailing almost as much as he loved swimming. There was the same feeling
of cleanliness, freedom, and exaltation. When he swam or sailed he thought
of a poem of Yeats's he had once learned for a diction exercise:

What if I bade you leave
The cavern of the mind?
There's better exercise
In the sunlight and wind.

Seek those images
That constitute the wild,
The lion and the virgin,
The harlot and the child.

Staring at Jill's slender back and arms and shoulders and her blowing
hair, he thought that there was something of all those elements in her:
lion, virgin, harlot, and child. The odd thing was, she had a first-rate
mind, too, which made the wildness all the more appealing. Of course

it wasn't simply wildness; raw wildness, the drunken violence of a Saturday night in a juke joint in Groveland, Florida, he detested. It was wildness plus imagination, vision, conviction, tenderness, a kind of inspired audacity. Passion: that was a much better word for it. Passion, intrepidity, maybe even valor; whatever it was, it was pretty damned exciting—once every twelve years, anyway, and as long as it didn't jeopardize anything of value. It was also very different from the expensive, ritual license of a convention in New Orleans or a Christmas office party. Those kinds of events were only travesties of the glorious inebriety that seemed to rage in Jill constantly, unquenchably. He turned and looked back toward the shore and Priscilla. She was standing beside her chair watching them. He waved to her and she waved back, raising her hands above her head and clapping in applause.

"They look very far away," Jill said.

"We've come a couple of hundred yards already," Ben said. "We're making five or six knots."

"It's glorious. Do you know, I've never been sailing before in my life."

"Do you like it?"

"I feel as if I'd been born to it. I never want to go back. How far can we go?"

"How far do you want to go?"

"Well, that depends on you. I could go on forever."

"I think they might miss us," Ben said "You see that little island up there, to starboard? We'll go up that far and back. That'll take us an hour."

The dinghy skipped over the water very smoothly in the steady offshore breeze, the light rigging quivering with tension and the riplets making a swift, liquid chuckling sound against the hull, as clean and merry as the feeling in Ben's breast. He tucked the helm under his arm and kept the mainsheet in his fingertips, bringing it in tightly enough to keep the sail hard and the boat heeled sharply. It was blue-water sailing, sweet and fast, with an almost dreamlike sensation of bodilessness and levity. He felt the steady tug of the tiller against the inside of his arm and the shivering of the mainsheet in his fingers as he watched the coast slide by, wheeling slowly to stern with a look of fantasy in the morning light. Up ahead of them the low spit in the center of the sound grew in clarity and detail as they bore down on it, and he could see the ash-gray branches of the clump of mangrove in the middle of it and the rim of yellow sand that encircled it like a collar, and a kingfisher perched on the tip of a driftwood stump like a finial on a flagpole.

"You want to take the tiller?" Ben asked.

"I jolly well do, you know." She turned and smiled at him broadly.

"OK, we'll pull in there and change positions. You can bring her back."

"Can I? Oh, super!"

Ben turned into the wind a little and let out the mainsheet, coasting in to the shore of the islet until the hull grated on the sand.

"Hop out and pull her ashore," he said.

Jill stood up and stepped over the gunwale into the clear shallow water. She took hold of the painter and waded ashore, holding the line tight while Ben raised the daggerboard and turned up the blade of the rudder.

"OK," he said, "I'm going to get up front. Then you can shove her back in and take the tiller."

"Right."

She bent to take hold of the bow and shoved the boat back into the water, grunting mightily. Ben took an oar and pushed the tip of it down into the sand to hold the dinghy steady while she climbed back over the transom into the stern. When she was aboard he pushed off with the oar into open water and the sail flopped out to leeward as the boat drifted in irons.

"Now push down the daggerboard and let down the rudder."

"Like this?"

"That's it. Now take hold of the mainsheet. You pull it in until she starts to sail, then put the tiller a little bit to windward until she's sailing a

straight course. If she starts to shoot up into the wind, put it back to leeward. You'll get the feel of it in a minute. You have to balance the sheet
against the rudder. If she starts to capsize, let out the sheet. That'll slow you
down."

"Jeepers, it sounds complicated," Jill said.

"It's not. It's very simple. It's all rhythm and feel, like riding a horse.
Just don't panic. If you get scared, let out the mainsheet, then everything
stops."

She took the tiller and tugged in the sheet until the boat began to
heel. As it gained speed, the bow began to turn up into the wind. She pulled
the tiller inboard until the bow turned back toward the shore, and then
worked it nicely back and forth to keep the bow pointing steadily toward
the far-off beach umbrellas that stood out like red and yellow mushrooms
on the distant strip of brown sand. They settled down to a steady reach,
the waves splashing lightly along the windward hull.

"I'm starting to get it, I think," she said exuberantly.

"You're doing great. Bring in the sheet a little and you'll go faster."

"Like this? You sure we won't go over?"

"No. You can bring it in tight in this light a wind. There are two ways
you can stop a capsize: let out the sheet, or turn up into the wind. But if
you've got your sheet cleated, you can't let it out. That's why I like to
hold it in my hand, in a small boat. If you get a gust you can let go instantly
without changing course or losing speed. You couldn't do that in a large
boat. You wouldn't have the strength to hold it."

"No, I can see that."

She sat handling the boat with a look of concentration and delight
that made him feel a great respect and affection for her. She sailed very differently from Priscilla. Priscilla enjoyed it and was a competent skipper,
but you could not say there was anything resembling rapture in the way
she handled a tiller or brought a boat into the wind. He smiled, watching her.

They sailed for another half hour, reaching south along the coast through the bright blue water until they were opposite the picnic site where Priscilla and Tony stood flapping towels at them from the beach.

"Now swing around to starboard," Ben said, "and we'll run before the wind to shore. Take this very easy. It's a tricky point of sailing. You ready?"

"OK," Jill said. "What do I do?"

"Put your tiller amidships until you're headed for the beach and let your sheet out while you turn. Let the sail full out, at right angles, but don't let the wind get back of it, or you'll jibe. The boom will go right across the cockpit and slam up on the other side. It's apt to crack you on the head and capsize you."

"Whillikers. Is this right?"

"That's it. Slow and easy. Steady now. No further. Hold her right there."

"Oh, wizard. It's jolly exciting, isn't it? My word, we're really moving, aren't we?"

They could feel the hull lunge forward, the bow rising, with the wind behind them. They sped toward the beach weightlessly with the sail out full to starboard.

"This is the fastest point of sailing," Ben said. "Running downhill. It's the most exciting and the most dangerous. You've got to keep awake."

"Very difficult to nod off, when you're moving like this," Jill said. "What do I do next?"

"Get your board and rudder up," Ben said. "Then all you've got to do is slide in. Not too soon, though, or you'll lose steerage."

"You tell me when. I don't want to muck it up."

"OK. Board up, now!"

"What about the sheet? I've only got two hands."

"Let it go."

She let go of the sheet and tugged up the daggerboard with her free hand, the sail flopping in loosely to landward.

"Now get up the rudder."

She turned and raised the rudder, pulling the blade up between the jaws of the post, and they coasted into the beach until there was a rasping sound

of sand beneath the keel. Tony and Priscilla stood cheering, holding up
plastic glasses of wine in salutation.

"That was wonderful!" Priscilla said. "You sailed like a swan!"

"It was jolly impressive," Tony said. "When did you learn to do that?"

"Just now."

"You're not serious."

"I am. Ben just taught me."

"Well, you must be a very good student. Looked as if you'd been doing it all your life."

"She's a natural," Ben said. "She's got salt water in her veins."

"I should think she does."

Jill stepped out of the boat and splashed up through the warm shallow water to the beach where Tony stood with his plastic goblet. She
took it from him and raised it to her lips, tilting her head back until the cup
was empty.

"Drinks like a salt, too," Tony said. "I suppose you're hungry, as well."

"Ravenous," Jill said. "Nothing like a sea voyage to get the juices flowing. What about you chaps?"

"We're ready," Priscilla said. "It's all set out."

Ben tugged the dinghy up onto the sand and they went up into the shade
of the umbrellas where Priscilla had set out the luncheon on the metal
table, the sandwiches of sliced duck and deviled eggs and a bowl of fruit
salad and a basket of croissants and a wheel of Brie and bottles of white
wine, cool and dripping from the freezer. They sat in the shade of the
umbrellas in the breeze from the sound and washed down the food with
the cold chardonnay and looked out at the blue water sparkling in the sun.
There were whitecaps building up on the open water where the wind
was freshening and sometimes the brief, blown shadow of a cloud. Ben
thought he had never seen the water so blue or the light so pure, with an
absolute, luminous transparency that stupefied him sweetly, like the
wine. Where it lay on his naked ankles and feet outside the circle of shadow
it made his skin cringe tenderly in its motionless, radiant caress and
sent a stream of glittering, voluptuous shivers through him, like a school

of minnows. There had never been a more beautiful summer, he thought. Never one of such ravishing luxury and peace. He wanted it never to end, and he felt suddenly the chilly, inconsolable sadness that he felt sometimes in moments of great happiness that were accompanied by the almost simultaneous awareness of their impermanence and brevity. In the midst of the utter contentment that bathed him on the little beach where he sat with his wife and friends in the summer light, he felt a throe of the anguished nostalgia with which he would one day remember it, a bleak foretaste of the bereavement he would feel when this beautiful day was lost irrecoverably. The sorrow in the heart of his happiness numbed him for a moment, like a drop of venom in the sunlight that kissed his skin.

"A penny for them," Priscilla said, reaching across the table and laying her hand on his. Ben smiled at her.

"I was just thinking how happy we were," he said. He turned his hand to close his fingers over hers. "Are you happy?"

"I couldn't be happier."

"I hope not, love."

"Anyone not happy in this lot deserves to be certified," Tony said. He raised his eyebrows at Jill. "You feeling any pain, poppet?" She smiled at him slyly, her mouth full of caviar and croissant. "No, I thought not. More like base, animal delight, from the look of you."

"It's nothing of the sort," Jill said. "I'm feeling very spiritual, as a matter of fact. It washes you all clean and pristine, sailing. You've got to have a go at it, Tony."

"Yes, come on," Priscilla said. "It'll make a new man of you."

"I'm not sure I want to be a new man," Tony said. "I'm quite happy with myself as I am." He scowled at Priscilla. "Are you a good sailor?"

"She's a great sailor," Ben said. "You'll be as safe as in church."

"Well, I suppose I'd better get it over with," Tony said. He finished his wine, wiped his lips with his napkin and stood up. "I don't normally like these baptismal experiences, you know. Nothing comes of them but trouble."

"I guarantee you there won't be any trouble," Priscilla said. "You'll love it." She tossed her robe onto the back of her chair and went down to the dinghy, taking the painter out of the bow and tugging the boat into the water. Tony followed her and stood looking down at it unhappily, ankle-deep in the water. "Come on, get aboard."

"Are you sure it won't sink? I weigh a good fifteen stone, you know."

"It'll carry three your size."

He stepped uncertainly aboard, clutching the gunwales and collapsing wobbly onto the life preserver in front of the mast. Priscilla tugged the hull clear of the sand and leapt aboard as it drifted past her, settling onto the stern seat and taking the tiller as they came about in the wind. Ben and Jill sat at the table and watched them, grinning. Priscilla put down the daggerboard, unfastened the mainsheet and pulled it in until they began to make way, heeling suddenly as the sail filled and hardened in the wind. Jill waved and cheered, "Bon voyage! You're not to shave until you get back!"

"No bloody fear," Tony said. "I say, this thing goes jolly fast, doesn't it? Is it meant to tip over like this?"

"If it didn't tip, the mast would break," Priscilla said.

"I see. They've got you either way."

They settled into a steady reach along the shore, their voices fading as the boat grew small in the distance, the bright yellow sail slanted against the blue sky like a candle flame.

"She handles it very well, doesn't she?" Jill said.

"She's a good skipper," Ben said. "Very methodical. He'll feel very safe with her."

"Will he? Well, we've none of us to worry about safety, then." Ben suppressed his impulse to glance at her. "Can I have a bit more wine?"

He lifted the bottle and filled her glass to the brim, too full to raise without spilling. She lowered her head and sipped at it, raising her eyes to peer up at him while she sucked noisily from the rim.

"Makes me think of those Black Velvets you used to make at my place in Hammersmith. Always slopped them over and got my bottom wet."

Ben thought about this, gazing without expression at her face. "What I could never understand," he said after a moment, "was why you always sat on the table."

"Dunno," Jill said. "Just a quirk, I suppose. Something to do with the genes."

"You liked to dance on the table, too. You did that at our wedding."

"Did I? Oh, yes, I remember that. At the American Embassy, in Grosvenor Square. I remember your father-in-law was very upset. I think you scolded me about it. Yes, I remember that."

Ben lowered his eyes. "I was a very thick-witted young man," he said.

"I didn't think so. I thought you were quite bright. You've certainly got on well."

He reached for the pack of cigarettes that lay on the table, drew one out and began to turn it in his fingers, gazing at it thoughtfully. "I want to apologize about yesterday afternoon," he said at last.

"Apologize?"

"Yes. That was a stupid thing to do. I don't know what got into me."

"Oh? I know what got into *me*," Jill said. She smiled wryly. "Well, no harm done. Just one of those . . . lyrical moments . . . I suppose, that people fall prey to once in a while. They're quite harmless, as long as they're not taken seriously."

"It was stupid. I behaved like an idiot. I wouldn't have blamed you if you'd slung a brick at me."

"Well, I don't remember there being one about. Anyway, I didn't raise a lot of fuss, if you remember. I thought it might be rather a lark, I suppose."

"A lark?"

"Yes. 'One more time, for the old times,' as the song says. Isn't that how you thought of it?"

"I wasn't doing much thinking at the time," Ben said.

"No. I suppose it was one of those 'depraved impulses' of yours, as you used to call them. I always thought they were your most impressive moments. You still get them, do you?"

"Not very often," Ben said.

"Oh. I suppose I should feel flattered, then." He looked into her eyes for a moment. She smiled, then leaned forward in her chair and patted his hand reassuringly. "You're not to worry, love. I'm not upset, at all. It's just the apology that put me off a bit. If I have anything like a creed at all, it's that one should never apologize for anything but insincerity." He went on turning the cigarette between his fingers. "Perhaps it's Priss you should apologize to." He didn't reply to this. "I think I'll have that thing, if you're through fiddling with it." She nodded toward the cigarette. He grinned and handed it to her. She put it between her lips, felt in the pocket of her robe, took out a lighter, lit it, and inhaled deeply. "This is your lighter, I think. I forgot to give it back to you." She held it between her fingers and peered at it. "Curious sort of thing. What's it meant to be?"

"It's one of the company lighters," Ben said. "Advertising gimmicks. We hand them out to clients. Keep it, if you like. I've got hundreds of them."

"What's this figure on it? Looks like Razullo or someone."

"It is. That's the name of my company."

"Is it really? How very whimsical. Yes, I'll keep this." She smiled at him and put the lighter back into her pocket.

"Can we call our score settled now?" Ben said. He grinned at her faintly.

"Score? Did you think you owed me something? It isn't as if there was anything for sale."

He blinked and then nodded, chastened. "You're a pretty remarkable woman, Jill."

"Rubbish. I'm just a girl from Shewsbury who's had a bit of luck, and who likes a lark. So there's no need for a lot of humbug about remorse and guilt on your part, or outraged virtue on mine. We've had a bit of fun to celebrate the old days, and that's all there is to it. If there's one thing worse than fraudulent piety, it's fraudulent remorse." She picked up her wineglass and settled back in her chair, staring out languorously at the blue water of the sound. "I like this place, you know. It's just my sort of place. Very elemental, and not too stylish. I should like to come back here one day."

"Come back next summer," Ben said. She turned her head and raised an eyebrow at him. "We'd love to have you, any time. Or you can rent a cottage very inexpensively, if you'd rather be private."

She dropped her head to one side, smiling into her wine. "Would you like that? Having me about all summer?"

"I think it would be great. You'd get a lot of work done here. It's a great place for writing."

"Well, that's very kind of you, love, but I'm going to Yugoslavia next summer. Place called Dubrovnik, on the Adriatic." She smiled at him. "I appreciate the offer, however."

"Dubrovnik," he said. "That's supposed to be a beautiful place."

"Yes. There's a little hotel there I've been told about that's supposed to be ideal for writing."

"Are you working on another play?"

"I've got one or two ideas I'm sorting out. It's a matter of them falling into place." She raised her head and looked up at the sky which had darkened suddenly. The sunlight had faded around them and the shadow of the umbrella that had lain on the bright sand was absorbed by the gray penumbra of a huge, fat-bellied cloud that had appeared above them. The breeze freshened in the cloud shadow and rippled the scalloped edges of the umbrella. Across the water there were other clouds looming in a great bruise-colored mass that had drifted across the sound in the mysteriously unnoticed way in which a herd of cattle will occupy a meadow while one is picnicking.

"I say, it's got jolly dark all of a sudden," Jill said.

"There's a squall coming," Ben said. He stood up and looked down the shore to where Priscilla and Tony were beating toward the islet where he and Jill had put aground. They looked very tiny in the distance. "These things move in awfully damned fast."

"Are we going to have a storm?"

"I don't know. It could blow over, if we're lucky." The edges of the umbrellas began to flap in the wind and the air was suddenly chilly on their skin. Out on the sound there were waves building up and whitecaps blowing from their crests. "I hope she brings that damned thing back."

While he watched he saw the boat come about, swinging 180 degrees through the wind, and begin to reach back toward the beach, the mast slanted very steeply in the stiff breeze. Priscilla had the sheet in tight and the boat was moving very fast, leaving a white wake in the steel-gray water. There were sheets of foam flying up from the bow. "Well," he said. "Tony's going to get a very lively maiden voyage."

"They're not in any danger, are they?" Jill said. She stood up, looking out across the water.

"No. Priss is very good in weather. I'll tell you, I think we'd better get those umbrellas down, and the stuff in the car."

"You don't think we ought to do something about Tony and Priss?"

"Not much we can do. If it gets bad, she'll just put in to shore and wait it out. Nothing to worry about." The umbrellas were straining against their staffs now, threatening to go over in the wind. He let down the ribs, tugged the poles out of the sand and carried them to the station wagon, shoving them in onto the floor. By the time he went back to the beach and had folded the chairs and table and carried them to the wagon there was thunder rumbling in the east like the sound of barrels tumbling in a hold and lightning spraying through the purple of the sky in quick distant flickers. Jill had packed the luncheon things into the cooler and folded the towels and blankets into the duffel bag. They carried them to the car, closed the tailgate and stood watching the sailboat beat across the sound toward them, heeled very steeply to leeward with the weather hull bared to the centerboard. Big single drops of rain began to splatter on their skulls like berries and their beach robes fluttered in the wind.

"It's very exciting, isn't it?" Jill said. She smiled into the wind. "Poor old Tony. I expect he's terrified."

The boat was close enough now for Ben to see Tony's and Priscilla's figures clearly in the hull. Tony was struggling to put on his life vest, swinging his right arm wildly as he tried to put it through the loop of the cushion that was flapping in the wind. The boat was heeled so sharply that he could not sit upright; he had to clutch the port gunwale with his left hand while he snatched at the loop of the flying cushion with his right. He looked in danger of spilling out of the steeply raked boat and he was floundering about so violently that the hull skewed in the rough water. Ben could see that Priscilla was having trouble managing it, with the wind coming in heavy gusts now under the low clouds. There was foam blowing off the crests of the waves and the boat was thumping through them, shattering the water into spray that blew up over the bow like tossing plumes. The thunder was closer now, breaking in sharp cracks and rolling toward them like artillery fire. He saw Priscilla come about, letting the sail out full to starboard and running hard before the wind to shore. The boat began to yaw in the following sea, and she had to struggle to keep steerage, working the tiller frantically with the sail snapping and thumping at the end of the sheet and the stern sprawling. They're going to jibe, Ben thought. A very clear and terrible fantasy took place in his mind, so vividly that he saw every stage of it with the precision and momentary stasis of a set of single-frame exposures taken from a motion picture film. He saw the boom swing across the cockpit hitting Priscilla in the head and knocking her over the port gunwale. He saw her snatch at the tiller as she went over, and the boat capsize on top of her, mast-down in a swatch of foam, as Tony tumbled out of it, flailing at the water frantically and clutching at the upturned keel while he went down, his fingernails scrabbling along the slippery wet plastic of the hull. The life vest drifted toward the shore, rising and falling on the sharp-edged crests of the choppy waves with a look of total indifference to what was going on behind it. The vision was so exact and meticulous in its details that Ben was certain it was an experience of clairvoyance. He knew it would happen in exactly the way he was foreseeing it, and that there was nothing he could do to stop it. He saw himself plunging into the water, swimming out desperately to where the upturned hull wallowed in the waves, diving down, again and again, his lungs bursting, coming up to gasp them full and dive again, searching in the murky water with his fingers along the sand of the bottom for Priscilla's body, feeling himself inflated by a ringing nothingness, as if he were in a metal tank into which a bodiless ether were being pumped. Several years before, he had had his gall bladder removed, and while he was breathing the anesthesia he had had the same curious ringing sensation and the same sense of being divested of feeling and identity.

"God's teeth, they're having quite a time of it," Jill said. "I think it's a bit more than he bargained for."

"I think we'd better get down there," he said. "I'll tow the boat back."

He starting loping along the sand to where the dinghy would come aground, restraining his desire to run, taking long bounding strides while he raised his arm and waved Priscilla toward the shore. Jill ran beside him, her footfalls thumping on the hard sand. When they were abreast of the dinghy Ben splashed out knee-deep into the waves and cupped his hands to his mouth, yelling across the water, "Let the sheet go. Run in on your pole."

Priscilla let the sheet go and the sail whipped forward, flopping noisily and loosely across the bow. Tony cowered under it, clutching his life vest to his chest. With the sail luffing empty, the boat slowed and they ran in quite gently to where Ben stood, waist-deep now, in the water. He took hold of the bow.

"Well, you had quite a trip," he said, grinning at Priscilla.

"We sure did. It was pretty exciting for a minute there." She pulled up the daggerboard and dropped it into the boat. "Tony thought so too. He enjoyed it very much, didn't you, Tony?"

"Oh, very much," Tony said. "Like riding a rabid buffalo. I can't wait to go again."

"You're all the better for it," Jill said. "You've got a steely-eyed look that's quite impressive."

"I shouldn't wonder," Tony said. "The iron has entered into my soul. I shall never so much as drink a glass of water again."

"How about a dry martini?" Ben said. "Come and have a hot shower and a drink and tell us sea stories."

He felt suddenly very gay and full of a sweet hilarity for the restored sanity and normality of things. He towed the dinghy back along the shore toward the car, splashing knee-deep through the water while the others went running along the sand in the sheets of cold rain that suddenly lashed at them almost horizontally as the gale broke. The sound was misted with white streamers of driven spindrift and the rain pelted the sand like shot. He took a delight in the storm and in the happily frantic job of lashing the dinghy to the roof rack in the wet wind and in driving along the sand road to the highway peering through the rain-sluiced windshield to follow the wheel-ruts between the tossing pines, and in running up the steps of the beach house in the rain and in the benison of hot water as he stood under it in the shower stall and afterwards a sense of benediction in the comfort of sitting in clean dry clothes with a martini in his hand listening to the storm outside the house while he waited for the women to dress.

"Is it the hurricane?" Jill asked, coming out of the bedroom and pausing to turn her head to the sound of the rain drumming on the windows. "Are we going to be inundated?"

"No, it's just a line squall. You get them after a hot day, along the coast."

She was wearing a pair of silk turquoise slacks and a turtle-necked sweater of coral colored angora with a necklace of heavy bone-white beads hanging between her breasts and her red hair blow-dried and swept up in a lustrous chignon. Ben had never seen her dressed so elaborately or femininely, and it gave him a feeling of rather tender awe, like seeing a young girl dressed up for her first ball. Now that the danger had passed, her desirability was reborn doubly, in the way that everything in the world seemed to have become more precious, fragile, winsome, and innocent. While he looked at her he realized that in some curious, very complicated way this was related to the fact that Priscilla had escaped disaster.

"How about a martini?" he said.

"Oh, yes, please. A very strong one." She sat down on the blond leather sofa and raised her head as a burst of hail rattled on the dome. "Lord, listen to that."

"Sometimes they can be just as fierce as a hurricane, for a while. But they don't last. Nothing to worry about."

"I'm not worried at all. I love it. It's so marvelously elemental."

He went to the bar and made the drink for her and brought it to the coffee table, smiling into her eyes as he set it on the onyx top in front of her.

"You look very pretty."

"Thank you."

He sat down facing her in one of the matching leather chairs and looked across the room at the water sweeping in sheets across the panes of the glass sliding doors.

"I love the sound of rain."

"Yes, I do too."

"When I was a boy we had a house with a tin roof on it, and the two things I loved most in the world were the sound of rain on that tin roof and the light after a thunderstorm."

"Oh?"

"It's like no other light in the world. Everything sparkles in it. You see things you've never seen before."

She plucked a pill of wool from her sweater, rolled it between her fingertips and said, "Why did you never tell me that?"

"I don't know. Why didn't I?"

"Didn't tell you what?" Priscilla said. She was standing in the arch, fastening a silver bracelet around her wrist. "What didn't you tell her, Ben?" She was wearing a white sheath dress with the seagull pendant that Jill had given her lying across her breast on its silver chain. Ben smiled at her and said, "That we have this sort of weather down here."

There was a terrifying crack of thunder like a boulder being split apart and a noon-bright flash of light above the dome and outside the glass door of the room, and then a long, diminishing rumble like boulders rolling down a mountain.

"God's teeth," Jill said. "That was close."

"If you can hear it you know you're safe," Priscilla said. "You never hear the one that kills you."

"No, I suppose you wouldn't."

Priscilla came across to the sofa and switched on the pedestal lamp that stood beside it. "It's getting very dark." She sat down beside Jill and leaned toward her, holding out the pendant with her fingertips. "You see what I've got on?"

"Oh, it's lovely on you," Jill said. "It goes marvelously with that dress."

"Doesn't it? I'll think of you every time I put it on."

The rain began to lash with renewed intensity at the dome and the glass panels of the doors. It came in gusts, with a sound of fury that seemed to be directed toward the house itself. Priscilla looked at Ben and frowned.

"It's getting pretty wild out there," she said. "I hope they can get here all right. You think we ought to give them a call?"

"I'd hate to call it off," Ben said. "We've got all those tons of food out there."

"I'm just wondering if they can get here, in this deluge."

"Well, let's wait half an hour and see what happens. It may settle down by then."

Tony came out of his bedroom door and shut it behind him, standing for a moment to stare up at the flashes of light above the dome. He was wearing a navy blue blazer with the arms of Trinity College embroidered in gold thread on the left breast and a white silk ascot looped over at his throat. "Sounds like the bloody blitz," he said. He came into the room, fumbling with the cuffs of his shirt. "How long is this apt to go on?"

"Oh, not long," Ben said. "These squalls usually blow themselves out pretty quickly. But they settle down into a steady, all-night rain sometimes. It doesn't look too good for tomorrow."

"Well, sufficient unto the day," Tony said. He came and stood in front of Jill, thrusting out his arm to her across the coffee table. "Jill, do my cufflinks, will you? You know I can never do the bloody things."

"Hold still then."

"Are you ready for that martini?" Ben asked.

"Am I not. With an olive, if you've got one."

"What about you, Priss?"

"I'll have a Cinzano."

Ben went to the bar and made the drinks slowly and fastidiously, peeling a long strip of rind from a lemon, twisting it between his fingertips until the oil broke out in tiny droplets on the skin, rubbing it around the inside of the glass, draping it across the rim, adding a cube of ice, then pouring the glass full of the heavy, sweet vermouth. While he did this he tried to recall exactly what he and Jill had been saying when Priscilla came into the room: Why did you never tell me that? I don't know. Why didn't I? Something like that. Nothing very incriminating. But a little odd-sounding, nevertheless. At least to someone less innocent and trusting than Priscilla. Those were qualities he could always count on to preserve him from suspicion. He wasn't really concerned, but his feeling of euphoria had dwindled, like the flame dying on an ember.

"There now," Jill said. "That should keep you together for a while." The words rang in his memory like a gunshot echoing through a wood. He suddenly remembered her saying them in just that housewifely way when she had finished sewing a button onto his shirtfront, the last time he had ever been to her flat in Hammersmith. He measured out the gin and vermouth for the martini with a shot glass, five to one, pouring it carefully into a glass beaker.

"Were you in the blitz, then, Tony?"

"Well, I missed the worst of it, of course, because I was off in Italy with Alexander. But they saved a bit for me, when I was home on leave in '45." He adjusted his sleeves and sat down in an armchair across from the women.

"That was thoughtful," Ben said.

"Yes, wasn't it."

While he stirred the martini in the beaker he made a rapid calculation of Tony's age. If he had been home on leave in 1945, he might have been twenty or twenty-one at the time. That was forty-one years ago. He would now be sixty-one or sixty-two at the youngest. The man was almost thirty years older than Jill. He dropped an onion into the glass, took a pair of coasters from the bar and carried the drinks to the coffee table, setting them down in front of Priscilla and Tony with a pair of cocktail napkins.

"Ta," Tony said. He picked up his glass. "Cheers."

"Cheers."

"Cheers."

They sipped, and when Ben set down his glass, the lights went off and the steady soft purr of the air-conditioning stopped. He had scarcely been conscious of the sound, but in the sudden dim silence of the room there was an air of unexpected, ruthless finality, as if the patient one had been visiting in a hospital room had died in the middle of a sentence.

"Well!" Priscilla said.

"What's happened?" Tony asked.

"The power's gone," Ben said. "It happens sometimes in thunderstorms."

"Oh, yes. Will it come back on again?"

"I hope so," Priscilla said. "Or we're going to have very rare roast beef." She set her drink down and stood up just as Esther came to the archway from the kitchen. "Has it gone off in the kitchen, Esther?" she asked.

"Yes, ma'am. The stove and everything. And I've got the roast in there."

"I don't suppose it's anywhere near done."

"No, ma'am. It'll need another half hour, anyway."

"Well, we'll just have to pray it comes back on. It won't matter if we're a little late. Do you know where the hurricane lamps are?"

"No, ma'am, I can't seem to find them."

"I think I put them in the utility closet with the vacuum cleaner last fall. I'll come and see."

"Yes, ma'am, thank you."

"You want me to bring them?" Ben said.

"No, stay here with Tony and Jill. I won't be a minute."

She went around the coffee table to the arch and followed Esther into the kitchen.

Tony said, "It looks to me as if these people of yours may have a bit of trouble getting here."

"I'll call up and cancel if it doesn't get any better," Ben said. He picked up his glass and sipped from it. "You were telling us about the blitz."

"Was I? Well, I was with the Eighth Army in northern Italy when we took Imola in the spring of '45, and I stopped a bit of shrapnel. So they gave me a furlough when I got out of hospital, and I went home to London." He paused as a flash of lightning lit the room raggedly from the dome. "We had a house just off Holland Park in Kensington. It was a lovely Sunday afternoon in May, and my mother made tea for us in the parlor. There were just the two of us; my father was killed in Tobruk in '41. I remember I had a sweet bun in my hand and there was this sudden absolutely shattering explosion, as if the Albert Hall had fallen down or something. A V-2 had come over and taken out the church in Kensington Church Street, not three turnings down. All the windows went in the drawing room and the picture she kept of my father on the piano fell off and smashed to bits on the floor. Glass everywhere. That's what I remember mostly about the whole thing, broken glass. You never realize how much glass there is in a house til it all gets smashed."

Priscilla came through the archway with a glass hurricane lamp burning in each hand. She carried them to the piano, set one of them down, and brought the other to the coffee table where she stooped to adjust the wick. The lamps cast a soft yellow glow in the room that reminded Ben of his childhood.

"What a lovely light," Jill said. "We might be in the eighteenth century."

"I think maybe I'd better call the Bishops," Ben said. "This doesn't sound as if it's going to get much better."

"Maybe you'd better," Priscilla said. "I don't think we're going to have roast beef tonight."

"Quite all right with me," Tony said. "I could go for a week without eating again."

Ben took the lamp from the coffee table, carried it into the den and set it on the desk. He picked up the phone, dialed the Bishops's number and stood holding the receiver to his ear until it had rung five times. "They don't answer," he called out through the door. "I guess they've left already."

"Oh, Lord," Priscilla said. "What shall we do?"

Ben put the phone down on the cradle and came to the study door. "Listen, why don't we call up Luigi's and have them send over some ribs and slaw? It's the simplest thing, and we won't have to worry about the power."

"I suppose it is, really," Priscilla said. "I guess they'll forgive us, on a night like this. But what about Luigi's? Won't they be out too?"

"Doesn't matter," Ben said. "They're charcoal broiled. I'm sure they're open."

"Oh, that's right." She turned to Jill. "Do you like ribs?"

"I don't know that I've had them," Jill said. "What are they like?"

"Barbequed pork ribs. They're delicious."

"Sounds lovely."

Ben went back to the desk, flipped open his directory, and dialed Luigi's. "Listen, how are you making out with this storm?" he asked. "Can you send us an order of ribs?"

"Yes, sir," the order clerk said. "We're always ready. These are our best days."

"Good." He ordered barbequed spareribs, coleslaw, baked potatoes, and cherry cobbler for six. "We'd like it around eight," he said. "Can you make it?"

"It'll be there," the clerk said. "If we have to bring it by boat."

When he came back into the living room Priscilla was coming out of the kitchen with another pair of lighted oil lamps. She set one on a teak desk at the western arch of the room and another on the piano, and then sat down again beside Jill on the sofa. In the golden light their faces had the glamorous and tragic look of women in a Caravaggio painting.

"I've often wondered what it must have been like to see a performance of Shakespeare in the eighteenth century," Priscilla said. "*Hamlet*, by lantern light. Can you imagine that?"

"Must have been very dangerous," Tony said. "I should have thought they'd always be having fires."

"They were," Ben said. "The old Covent Garden burned down in 1808, and Drury Lane the year after. Right to the ground."

"Did many of them burn during the blitz?" Priscilla asked.

"No," Tony said. "The West End got off very lightly. It was The City that got the worst of it. Of course one fell through the middle of RADA, didn't it?"

"Didn't it just," Jill said. "There was a great hole where the new theatre is. Students used to have to walk on a plank from the Gower Street side to the Malet Street rooms, for years. They say Shaw came round, the morning after it was bombed, and had a look, and said, 'Well, we'll have to rebuild it.' And gave them most of the money to do it with."

"Do you know what was one of the most impressive things in London, to me?" Priscilla said. "Not the Tower, or Buckingham Palace, or the Victoria and Albert, but that tea garden on the roof of Derry and Tom's, in Kensington, with the bomb sticking up in the middle of it. Do you know where I mean?"

"Oh, yes," Tony said. "Been there many times. Curious sight, that."

"Do you know where I mean, Ben?" Priscilla turned to him. "I don't think we ever went there together." Ben shook his head. "There's a tea pavilion and a roof garden right on top of it, that department store in Kensington. And right in the middle of it there's a bomb that failed to explode, sticking halfway through the roof. They left it there, right where it fell, and made a flower bed around it, with petunias and marigolds and things. I used to sit there while I had a cup of tea, and shiver. Not from fear or anything, but just because it was so moving. It's the most eloquent monument in England, I think." They sat in silence for a moment listening to the thunder, more distant now, like an artillery barrage in the mountains. "Do you know what I've been trying to think of, for years? A song I heard once, from that musical of Ivor Novello's about the war. Something about lilacs."

"'We'll Gather Lilacs,'" Jill said.

"Yes, that's it. It made me feel the same way, when I heard it, like that bomb on the roof. It's certainly not very great music, but it certainly is moving. It makes me think about that line of Coward's in *Private Lives*. 'It's astonishing how potent cheap music can be.' Do you know how it goes?"

Jill raised her head and hummed, groping for the melody. "How does it go, Tony?"

He hummed a couple of bars, tapping his finger against his glass.

"Oh, that's it," Jill said. "Why don't you play it for us?"

"Oh, please do!" Priscilla said. "I haven't heard it in years."

"I will if you'll sing it," he said to Jill. "Do you know the words?"

"I think so, most of them."

Tony got up and carried his drink to the piano, setting it down carefully on his cocktail napkin. He sat down on the bench, opened the keyboard, and began an elaborate introduction full of wilting arpeggios. Jill followed him to the piano and leaned against it, closing her eyes and swaying voluptuously, like a cocktail bar chanteuse. When she began to sing her frail, sweet voice welled with the tender, sentimental pathos of the wartime ballad:

We'll gather lilacs in the spring again,
And walk together down an English lane.
We'll share the sweetness of the English rain,
When you are home again.

We'll sit together in the firelight's glow.
Your eyes will tell me all I need to know.
I'll hold you close and never let you go,
When you are home again.

"Oh, that was glorious!" Priscilla said. "It destroyed me." She dabbled at her eyes with her cocktail napkin. Jill bowed gravely, and without a pause Tony swept elegantly into another melody of the same romantic vintage. Jill closed her eyes and sang it softly and poignantly, her face lit fitfully by lightning flashes from the dome, almost as if by the flare of falling bombs:

> That certain night,
> The night we met,
> There was music abroad in the air,
> And as we kissed and said good night,
> A nightingale sang in Berkeley Square.

They went on to "The White Cliffs of Dover," and "Maybe It's Because I'm a Londoner," and "I Left My Heart in an English Garden." Ben listened ruefully, seduced by the nostalgic glamor of the music. It was the music of a world heroically and picturesquely at war, united in a fraternity of fortitude and virtue in a struggle against a known, identifiable, and absolute evil, one which obligingly spoke the German language and which, unquestionably, after the expenditure of much glorious blood, sweat, and tears, after many anguished partings and dauntless vigils and ecstatic reunions, would be driven down into the dust whence it arose, and there would be bluebirds over the White Cliffs of Dover, and the lights would go on again all over the world, and the *Normandie* would sail again. It was a different war than the one I was in, he thought. One that you could look back on with nostalgia and pride. One that you could take part in and remain a gentleman. There wasn't any glamor about the one I was in. In Nam, you were never sure who your enemy was, and every time you killed somebody you wondered if you had killed a friend. Nobody wrote songs about it and you didn't come out of it a gentleman. Everything in his history, he thought, conspired to deny him gentility.

Jill was singing:

There'll be bluebirds over
The White Cliffs of Dover
Tomorrow, just you wait and see.
There'll be love and laughter,
And peace ever after,
Tomorrow, when the world is free.

He plucked a scarlet peony out of the vase on the coffee table and tossed it to her. She caught it and held it to her breast, bowing like a diva.

There was a thudding of footsteps on the stairs that led up to the deck and the rapping of knuckles on the pane. Chuck and Linda Bishop were standing under the canopy outside the glass door letting down their umbrellas and waving frantically through the pane. Ben went across quickly to the door and slid it open.

"Hey, you made it! You guys are pretty brave. Come in and get dry. Just drop your umbrellas on the deck."

"My God!" Linda cried, stepping in onto the carpet. "What a night! We didn't know what it was like until we got out of the house." She undid the straps of a plastic rain scarf from her chin and flapped it behind her on the deck.

"Didn't know whether to come or not," Chuck said. "But we thought we'd give it a try, since we were on the road. Pretty stupid, I guess. Looks like you've lost the current."

"No problem," Ben said. "We've sent out to Luigi's for spareribs. Come on in. Have a drink."

"Spareribs, great. You sure you can manage?"

"Absolutely. We're going to have a hurricane party."

"Oh, how glamorous," Linda said. "It looks so *cozy* in here. Hi, Priss."

"Hi," Priscilla said. "It's certainly good to see you. We were afraid you might be floating out to sea." She came and kissed Linda on the cheek and took their coats. "Come and meet everybody."

The Bishops were in their late thirties, handsome and immaculate people dressed in expensive, pastel-colored summer clothes and smelling discreetly of cologne. Chuck was an area representative for IBM, a large man with a plump, pink face and very mild, pale blue eyes who smiled constantly in a shy, abstracted, anxious way, as if he had something on his mind. Linda was tall, very thin, vividly dark, wore lipstick the color of aluminum, and had an air of intense interest in everything anyone said to her except her husband. They brought into the room a faint air of unresolved conflict, of animosity toward each other and of waning discretion that suggested they had been drinking before they came and that they had brought a quarrel with them. They gave the indefinable impression of people who have driven through the rain to a party in total silence, both of them staring straight ahead through the windshield. Tony and Jill rose to meet them. Chuck took Jill's hand and then let go of it with feverish diffidence, like a man caught in an act of heresy. Linda held onto it a good deal longer—a full ten seconds—looking intently into Jill's eyes.

"You don't know how I've looked forward to this moment," she said. "To think you're the woman who wrote that wonderful play, and who *acted* in it. It's the best new comedy I've seen in ten years. Easily. Since *Joe Egg*, I think."

"Well, it's very sweet of you to say that," Jill said. "You wouldn't like to call up my producer and tell him that, would you? He's been going on at me about the second act."

"Don't change a word of it," Linda said. "I'll haunt you if you do."

"Oh, I don't think I'd like that," Jill said. "Perhaps I'll leave it, then."

"You'd better," Linda said. "Or you'll have posterity to deal with. Not just me."

"Oh, well, I will, then."

"You remember Tony," Ben said.

"How are you?" Chuck said. He shook Tony's hand briefly and heartily.

"Hello," Linda said. "You're not in the company."

"No, no," Tony said. "Nothing to do with it. I'm not an actor, at all."

"You're the director."

"No, nothing to do with the theatre. I'm a journalist, I'm afraid. An ink-stained wretch."

"In England?"

"Yes. I do a weekly bit for the *Observer*."

"On the theatre?"

"Well, a bit of it, yes. This and that."

"A *Renaissance* wretch."

"Well, I suppose you could say that, yes. What a quaint way of putting it. Something of the sort."

"Come and sit down," Priscilla said. "Ben will make you a drink."

"Indeed I will," Ben said. "What'll you have?"

"A martini for me," Linda said. "A very stiff one, please."

"Stiff martini. What about you, Chuck?"

"That'll be fine," Chuck said. They sat down on the sofa and Linda bent to feel her shoes.

"God, my shoes are soaked," she said.

"Take them off," Priscilla said. "I'll get you some slippers."

"Can I?" She took off her shoes and tucked them under the sofa. "I don't usually do this til much later."

"Well, we're reverting to the primitive here tonight," Priscilla said. "Hurricane lamps and finger food. No one stands on dignity."

"Good. I've got very little of it to stand on."

"You can have pink ones with pom-poms, or blue ones with bows."

"I think I'll just sit on them for a while, til they get warm. Is that all right?"

"OK, let me know if you want some."

"You just missed a great concert," Ben said, mixing drinks. "Jill was singing war songs. World War II, I mean. All those great old numbers."

"Oh, God!" Linda said. "Don't tell me we missed that! Will you do some more, Jill?"

"I'm afraid I've had it," Jill said. "Run right out of petrol. After I've had some ribs, perhaps."

"Oh, please! I *love* the way you sing. That lullaby you did in the play was absolutely devastating. What's it called?"

"'Can Ye Sew Cushions?'"

"It was just the most enchanting thing I ever heard. And so surprising. For *her*, I mean. It was the last thing in the world you'd have expected her to sing, and yet it seemed so absolutely right, when she did it. You could see the girl suddenly, so perfectly. We were just shattered."

Chuck smiled, nodding gravely.

"You must have been there the night I was on key," Jill said.

"You certainly were," Linda said. She gave Jill a quick, confidential smile.

Ben brought their drinks to the coffee table. "Now this is something very special," he said. "It's called *martini mit dunder und blitzen.* You have to hold your nose when you swallow."

"Like this?" Linda said. She held her nose, sipped from her glass, closed her eyes, breathed deeply, and let out her breath in a long, shuddering gasp. "Oh, my," she said. "You're a very sinister man, Ben, you know that?"

"Just merciful," Ben said. "To all who come to my door in need."

Chuck sipped at his glass, raised his eyebrows, puffed out his cheeks and said, "Hey, I don't know about mercy, buddy."

"Do you good," Ben said. "You've had a hard trip."

Linda sat back on the sofa, took hold of her ankles and tugged them tight against her flanks. She looked at Jill for a moment in a mock-reproachful way, opened her mouth to speak, closed it, then opened it again and said, "What you've done, young woman, is to confront me with the greatest dilemma of my life."

"Have I?" Jill said. "Good Lord. How?"

"Well, of course I hope your play will run forever, as it deserves to, but at the same *time* I'm praying that it will close and become available for stock, so I can do it at the Hilltop. That's the theatre where I play. I don't think I'm going to sleep at night until I play that part."

"What, you want to play Nona, do you?"

"*Do* I? My God. That woman speaks for me like my own *heart*beat. I would *kill* to play that part."

"Oh, well, I hope you don't have to do that."

"She speaks for all of us," Linda said. "Every woman alive. All that buried talent, burning inside her. All that terrible desire to be heard, and to be loved! That's the wonderful, tragic paradox of it. The need to be heard, and to be loved. That's our dilemma, exactly. No man could ever write it that way. Not even Ibsen." She smiled at the glass in her fingers. "You know, I'll tell you something. I've always thought there was something a little bit fraudulent about *A Doll's House,* don't you? It's from the *out*side. I can't help feeling there's something condescending about it. It's a sociologist's play, not a poet's. I've often wondered what Sappho would think if she sat through it. Haven't you?"

"Well, no, I haven't, actually," Jill said. "It never occurred to me. Sappho."

"*If* she sat *through* it," Linda said, with another confidential smile. "Yes."

"Of course it's a very well-made play. The structure is there, and it's full of good intentions, but not the poetry. Not the pain. Give that plot to Sappho and see what she would do with it." She raised her eyebrows. "Or to you."

"Oh, don't give it to me," Jill said. "I've problems enough, as it is."

"It's sort of an acid test I have for literature," Linda said. "If I'm reading a poem or a novel, or watching a play, I try to imagine what Sappho would think of it. I try to imagine her face while she's reading, or watching."

"Why not Shakespeare?" Chuck said. "Why not try to imagine what Shakespeare would think of it? I mean, that's the test."

Linda closed her eyes.

"Will you do something for me?" she said to Jill. "The next time you play that part, will you try to imagine Sappho sitting out front listening to every word you say? Just as an experiment. I'll bet you'll be surprised."

"Yes, why don't you do that?" Tony said. "Think about Sappho out there in the front row. Be jolly interesting."

"Jolly nerve-wracking, I should think," Jill said.

"Or Shaw," Chuck said. "Shakespeare or Shaw. That would be the real test."

"Shakespeare and Shaw," Linda said, turning her head to him and speaking very gently and distinctly as if to a child, "as you may recall, were men." She blinked several times while she said this.

"So?" Chuck said. "They were pretty good writers, too, weren't they? I mean, Shakespeare knew something about women, didn't he?"

"Shakespeare's women are shrews, strumpets, and puffballs," Linda said. "Not women as we know them. And Shaw's simply do not exist. They're the fantasies of a eunuch."

"Yeah, well why Sappho?" Chuck said. "I mean, how much better off are you with a dyke?"

"He might just have a point, you know," Tony said. "She'd bring a rather special point of view, wouldn't she?"

Linda sighed. "Well, all right, fellows," she said. "If you're offended by her sexual preference, let's say George Eliot. Does anyone feel threatened by George Eliot?"

"Why do you have to feel you're being judged by anyone at all?" Priscilla said. "Why not just write?"

"I think you must," Linda said. "I think it's necessary and natural to compare your work to someone's you admire. For example, Hemingway said that when he wrote he was always hearing the voice of Mark Twain, or Stendhal." She paused and smiled ironically. "He *certainly* didn't hear Sappho's, or he'd have burnt his entire oeuvre." She pronounced *oeuvre* perfectly and lingeringly. She picked up her glass, sipped from it, and said, "*Anyway.* I am *dying* to play that part you've written, Miss Davenport. And you know whose voice I'll be hearing when I do it, don't you?" She gazed at Jill and shook her head sadly. "To my eternal confusion."

"Not mine, I hope," Jill said.

"Who else's? Who else's, in this world? Not that I want to imitate you;

that would be mimicry. I don't want to do any nightclub tricks. But I want to use what I've learned from you about that woman. And about life. Which, let me tell you, is quite a lot." She gazed into her drink, her eyelids sinking slowly. "Chuck, what did I tell you?"

"When?" Chuck said.

"When we came out of the theatre? You remember, I didn't say a word until we were driving home. When you asked me what I thought about it."

"Oh, yeah," Chuck said. He frowned. "Well, you said you liked it. You said you thought the dialogue was real good."

Linda's eyelids sank lower. "No, that's not what I said. I said she was a woman who 'shrieked silently.'"

"I don't remember that," Chuck said. "Maybe so."

"And who bled champagne." She looked across the table at Jill, smiled, squared her shoulders in a resolute way, breathing deeply. "Now. If I can master those two rather difficult feats, I think I'll come somewhere near the part."

"What an interesting idea," Jill said. "I'd love to see you do it. I think you'd do it far better than I."

Linda dropped her mouth open and stared up at the ceiling.

"Now, you'll do it beautifully, you know you will," Priscilla said. "Linda's a very good actress. We saw her in *Streetcar* last summer, and she was wonderful."

Linda moaned, closing her eyes and swinging her head slowly from side to side.

"No, you were, really," Priscilla said. "You gave Blanche such a wonderful . . . fragility."

"*Fragility*," Linda groaned, rolling her eyes. "I was as fragile as a stone griffin. If I'd seen *Thoughts of Love*, I'd have done it very differently, believe me."

"You did it very well," Priscilla said. "I wouldn't have wanted you to change a thing."

"It was her *vulnerability* I was after," Linda said. "The nakedness of spirit. The tenderness. That scene with the newsboy! I didn't begin to touch it." She turned to Ben. "Now, Ben, you know something about the theatre. Tell me the truth."

"I thought you were great," Ben said.

Linda patted him on the wrist. "All right, my sweet. You're a very generous soul." She turned again to Jill and smiled. "They're friends of mine, you see. I can't get the truth out of them."

"You know what I liked about your play?" Chuck said to Jill. "That scene with the bear." He chuckled earnestly. "Where she talks to the bear, you know? And then dances with it? That was a riot."

"Oh, I'm glad you like that bit," Jill said. "It was rather fun, writing that."

"Where did you get that thing, anyway? You must have had a heck of a time finding a property like that."

"No, I had him," Jill said.

"You had him already? Before you wrote the play? You mean like the girl says?"

"Yes, I've had him for years, actually. He's been one of the greatest influences on my life, Humbert. We're inseparable."

"No kidding," Chuck said. "You had a stuffed bear. I guess you kept him around because he had a message for you or something. He meant something special to you, right?"

"Here we go," Linda said. Chuck held up his hand, palm out, as if to deflect a thrown object.

"Now wait a second," he said. "I want to ask her something."

"I think you could say I love the creature," Jill said. "You've no idea of the comfort, and companionship, and loyalty one can get from a stuffed bear. That's something you wouldn't understand unless you'd spent a good deal of time with one. But you can ask any child about it."

"That's it *exactly*," Linda said. "It's as if you'd invested it with life, almost. Like a child with a teddy bear. You feel the compassion she has for it, the communion between them. After all, they're fellow victims, aren't they?

Of masculine savagery?" She shook the ice in her glass and shuddered. "One thing I'll never understand is the male impulse to kill something and then cut its head off and hang it up on the wall. God. Can any of you gentlemen explain it to me?"

"Well, I think I could explain it, if you'd had the benefit of an acquaintance with Mr. Thornburg," Tony said. "The Member from my district. I've often pictured his head hanging in my library, just above the mantel. If you knew the man, I think you'd find it a very sound instinct."

"*That* I can appreciate," Linda said. "In fact, I can think of a couple of U.S. senators I'd be willing to contribute, if you've got the wall space."

"Well, most of it's reserved," Tony said. "We have so many candidates in Parliament."

"Yeah, well, that's different," Chuck said. "That's not because you respect those guys, but because you don't. But suppose you had a pet dog, for example. I read about this woman whose dog died, and she had it stuffed because she couldn't bear to part with it. She'd move it around all over the house, from the living room to the bedroom, and put it in the car with her when she was driving somewhere. I mean, she loved this thing, like Jill says."

"Well, she didn't *kill* it, for God's sake," Linda said. "Do you suppose Jill killed that bear she's so fond of? Did you?"

"Good God, no," Jill said. "I rescued him from bondage. From a Philistine shopkeeper."

"You see?" Linda said.

"Well, what about Audubon? He used to kill birds and have them mounted so he could paint them. And he kept them around. That's a fact. You can't say he didn't love birds."

Linda opened her mouth and sighed. "What this is all *about*," she said, "is the fact that he went hunting last year in Colorado with some friends of his, and killed this moose. And then a couple of months later he came home one day with its *head*, if you can imagine such a thing. He'd brought it back and given it to some taxidermist to have it stuffed. I'm not lying to you. Now that had absolutely nothing to do with liberation, or with mercy, or with a very sound taste in decor, or with *love*, God knows. It was male vanity, pure and simple. And then he was furious because I wouldn't have the awful thing in the house."

"Elk," Chuck said. "Not moose. They don't have moose in Colorado. Great big buck with a ten-point spread. You never saw such a gorgeous thing."

"Gorgeous," Linda said. "If that's your idea of beauty. It was absolutely appalling."

"Well, in a sense, all artists could be called taxidermists," Tony said. "I mean, it's a very similar impulse, isn't it? The desire to preserve things in as lifelike a condition as possible. Places, people, moments of one's life. Things one remembers with love or passion. Works of art are like museum exhibits, in a way: paintings and statues and stories. They're frozen moments of time."

"That's what I mean," Chuck said. He nodded deeply. "That's exactly what I mean. Even a photograph. I mean a snapshot of some guy and his girlfriend standing by the Grand Canyon. Or holding up a bass he's just landed, or with his little girl sitting on his shoulders. It's the same thing. You don't want to lose things like that. You want to save them." He stared into his drink and puffed out his cheeks wearily, as if he had just climbed a flight of stairs. "I'll tell you what's the saddest thing in the world," he said, "is for things to change, to lose things. Boy, I'll tell you." There was a kind of respectful silence for several moments for the intensity with which he had spoken.

Jill said, "I think you're quite right about that. You know that picture Monet painted of his wife standing on a hillside with a parasol on a lovely summer afternoon? It almost breaks your heart, that picture. Did you know that very shortly after he painted it, she died of a complication from pregnancy? Can you imagine the joy it gave him, after she was dead, to know he'd preserved that beautiful moment of their lives? I think it's the most moving thing in art, that. They're not all such lovely moments, of course.

But they need to be saved as well." She looked down at the glass she held between her hands.

"That's exactly what I was talking about," Chuck said. "That's just the way it was up there in the mountains in Colorado. I mean everything was so peaceful. For once in my life, there was nothing to worry about. Everybody I cared about was OK. Linda was going to stay with her mother over in Annapolis and they were going to raid the antique shops. Betsy was home from Mount Holyoke and she'd just got a job she was thrilled about with this congressman from back home. She had a couple of weeks before she started and she was going to take care of the plants and the cat and just have the house to herself. She likes that. And Rick was back at Georgetown Prep. He'd just made the tennis team and he was happy as a clam. So I knew everybody was OK. It was one sweet fall. Just like a long summer, really. There was a soft wind blew, almost every day. This warm, soft summer wind. You'd see the tops of the trees bending over in it, you know? You wanted it never to end. Then one day this guy calls me up, out of the blue. Bill Crenshaw. He and this other guy, Ted Michaels, were going out to Colorado deer hunting, and he wanted to know if I'd like to go along. I'll tell you, it sounded just like a message from heaven. I hadn't been hunting since I used to go out with my dad up in Michigan, when I was a kid. So I went out and bought myself a gun, a beautiful Austrian rifle with a walnut stock, and I went out to Colorado with these guys. It was one of those private lodge deals, where you hunt from drop camp with a guide. On the Strawberry Creek, not far from Meeker. Jesus, what a spot. High and cool and a sky as blue as your mother's eyes. I used to stand by that stream in the morning and just breathe it in. I couldn't stop smiling. I mean, this old earth had been rolling around for a couple of billion years, and then I came along and spent another forty-two, working and worrying my ass off, and all of a sudden I'd been handed one little slice of it, one week, all to myself, one little slice of eternity, like a slice of cake. We went out there on the second morning, up the draws toward Eagle Pass. And then this buck came around the corner of a boulder and just stood there and looked at us." He looked at Linda. "You said, 'Is that your idea of beauty?' or something. Well, honey, I want to tell you it is. That was one beautiful thing. I looked at him and I thought, Jesus." He shook his head, overcome, and fumbled in his pocket for a cigarette.

"There's some on the table," Priscilla said.

"Oh, yeah." He took the glass lid off the box and plucked out a cigarette.

"So then you killed it," Linda said.

"Honey, that's what I came up there to do," Chuck said. "And that's what I did. I wanted that baby. I wanted to have him in the den with me so I could remember that week up there in the mountains for the rest of my life. Every time I looked at him I figured I'd feel just the way I did then. Now I know that doesn't make sense to you, but I don't think that was any more of a desecration than cutting a wildflower and bringing it home from a picnic and pressing it in a book. Or catching a trout out of that stream and eating it. I mean, there are things you have to *feed*, any way you can."

"Including the predilection for blood sports," Linda said.

"OK," Chuck said. He lit his cigarette and set the lighter down carefully on the table. "OK, I'm through trying to explain it. That's my spiel. I'll shut up now, for the rest of the evening."

"Oh, don't do that," Jill said. "I think you tell a wonderful story."

Linda looked down at the floor and made a little ticking noise detaching her tongue from the roof of her mouth.

"Jolly interesting," Tony said. "I've been after stag, myself, up in Scotland."

"No kidding," Chuck said. He seemed heartened by this news.

"Oh, yes. Wonderful experience. Bit difficult to justify, I suppose, but then so is eating pig's ribs. Which I must say I'm looking forward to enormously."

"Well, I don't see any point in pursuing it any further," Linda said. "But there's one thing I just don't understand. I'd just like to have it explained to me, in the name of reason and logic. And after all, you're the big advocate of reason and logic, aren't you? Scientific method, computers, the march of progress? Well, could you tell me what logical connection there is between a beautiful, peaceful autumn and the desire to kill a magnificent, innocent animal?"

"That's what I've been trying to explain," Chuck said. "Maybe you weren't listening. I've been trying to explain this psychological phenomenon, which I don't think is all that uncommon. I thought actors were supposed to have such tremendous insight into psychological phenomena, but I guess not all of them do. You brought this thing up, so I went into it in considerable detail because I don't like people thinking I'm some kind of crazy butcher."

"No one thinks you're a butcher," Priscilla said. She reached across the coffee table and touched his knee.

"I think I am just as civilized as most guys my age," Chuck said. "And I also think I am a pretty good father. I don't say I'm a great father, but I'm not too bad at it. Just ask Betsy or Rick, if you don't think so. I don't think they complain too much."

"You're a very good father," Linda said. "So let's drop it, OK? Jill, there's something I'm dying to ask you about *Streetcar*."

"I just want to say one more thing," Chuck said. "One more little thing I'd like to add here. Who was it that went out and looked for Marmalade that time when he didn't come home? In the rain. How many guys you know would spend a couple of hours looking for a cat in the rain? You forget about those times."

"Oh, you didn't lose Marmalade?" Priscilla said.

"We would of, if I hadn't gone out there and looked for him," Chuck said. He raised his eyes to Jill. "We have this cat," he explained.

"Oh, have you?" Jill said. "I have one too. I love cats."

"I do too," Chuck said. "Beautiful things. They've got a lot more personality than a dog, I think. This one has got this funny little way of biting the tip of your nose if you put your face up close to him. I love that cat. I really do. I tell you, it nearly killed me to think about that cat out there in the rain, maybe run over on the road or something. Maybe all squashed, out there in the rain. The point I'm trying to make is that it's perfectly possible for a guy to go deer hunting and still to love animals. Or people. A guy can kill a deer once in a while—once in a *lifetime*, for God's sake— and still be capable of love. That's all I'm saying."

"I think you're absolutely right," Jill said. "People can kill *people*, as far as that goes, and still be capable of love. I don't know how many times that's been demonstrated."

"Right," Chuck said. "OK. That's all I'm trying to say."

"I don't know what's happened to those ribs," Priscilla said. She looked at her wristwatch. "Would anybody like some crackers and cheese?"

"This cat, Marmalade, that we've got?" Chuck said. "Well, Linda wanted to have him fixed a couple of years back. Fixed. That's a hell of a word, isn't it? Would you think you were fixed if you couldn't get laid any more? Jesus. So, anyhow, I took him down to the vet's in this box. This sort of suitcase thing we got to take him out to California one time. I think he must have known something was up because I could hardly get him in the damn thing. Cats can sense things like that, you know? They're very sensitive animals. So I parked the car outside the vet's office and sat there looking at him for a minute. He was in the box making this funny noise, just like he was pleading with me, honest to God. You never heard anything like it. This kind of desolate wail, like a lost soul. I thought to myself, Christ, old buddy, I can't do this to you. You'd be better off dead. So I brought him back home."

"Sweetheart, do you think maybe we've heard enough about Marmalade?" Linda said. "I mean, cats are fascinating animals, but they really can't compare to people, can they? Don't you think we might talk about people for a change?"

"That's what I'm talking about," Chuck said. "People. People's attitudes towards animals. And that even if they kill one once in a while they can still be capable of love."

"Well, I have to say that's an attitude I find quite a mystery," Linda said. She smiled with a huge private amusement. "My goodness, such an impassioned one. On *your* part. I mean, if it's *there*, you don't really have to insist on it, do you?"

Chuck's face turned slowly into a photograph, like the face of a movie actor in a freeze-frame. He stared at her for a moment, then moved his eyes down to his drink, raised it, and drained his glass.

"I think I'd better get a few snacks together," Priscilla said. "You must be starving. I was going to have some hot ones, but I guess I'll have to give up on that. We've got some caviar, though, from lunch, if that doesn't bore anybody."

"Nothing boring about that caviar," Tony said.

"Lord, no," Jill said. "I could live forever on it."

Chuck rattled the ice in his glass and said, "Ben, old buddy, you think you could build me another one of these giant killers?"

"Absolutely," Ben said. "That's what I've been waiting to hear. Anybody else? Jill, you look like you're ready."

"Oh, yes. Always."

"Linda?"

"A tiny, tiny one," Linda said. "About half strength. *Somebody's* got to get us home."

"I'll go help Esther get some things together," Priscilla said. She got up and went out through the arch.

"And speaking of getting home," Linda said, "do you think I could have the car keys, my pet?"

"I'll get you home," Chuck said. "Did I ever fail to get you home?"

"Not *yet*," Linda said. She held out her hand, palm up, and jiggled her fingers. "Come on, baby boy. I want to show Ben. He doesn't know about MA."

"MA," Chuck said. He twisted in his chair, digging in his trouser pocket. "Cute as a goddamn bug."

"Who's MA?" Ben said.

"*Aimeé*," Linda said. She spelled the word. "She is the love of my life." Chuck tossed the car keys onto the coffee table. They were fastened to a brass plaque that rattled on the glass top. "Chuck brought home a beautiful new playmate for me last week who is *the* most *beautiful* creature you have ever seen." She picked up the car keys and handed them to Ben. "Look at this. Doesn't this kill you?"

"No kidding?" Ben said. "You've got a new baby, huh?" He took the keys from her and read the inscription engraved on the brass plaque: "'The one who dies with the most toys wins.'" He chuckled, nodding. "Not far from the truth," he said.

"It came with the car. Isn't that a riot? A little bonus incentive. You get philosophy with the merchandise."

"What is it, anyway?"

"A 200-XZ. *Pink*, if you please. With pink leather upholstery! It's like sinking into a bubble bath."

"Wow," Ben said. "That's pretty voluptuous. I'd sleep in it."

"I may," Linda said. "It is a *very* erotic automobile."

"I had to get it special-ordered for her," Chuck said. "Looks like a goddamned coffin."

"He keeps saying that," Linda said. "Darling, that is *morbid*. Don't you understand that?" She took the keys, opened her purse, and dropped them into it. "I don't see any reason why a car shouldn't be a little frivolous. I am so *sick* of these battleship gray things he always brings home. That is the most miasmal color in the world."

Priscilla called from the kitchen, "Ben, do you think maybe we ought to give Luigi's a ring?"

"Yeah, I'll do that," Ben said. "I'll just get these drinks first." He gathered up the glasses, took them to the bar, and began to mix a fresh set of drinks.

Linda put her feet down on the floor, stretched out her legs and laid her arms along the back of the sofa, looking about the room in a faintly smiling, rapturous way. "God, this *room*," she said. "I love to come into this house. It's so full of *feeling*. Of sensitivity. It practically *trembles*."

"Been trembling this evening," Tony said. "All that hullaballoo out there."

"If everyone in the world had this environment to live in," Linda said, "think what a different world it would be." She revolved her eyes about the walls. "My God, all these treasures. What they must have cost. You must have a fortune invested in this room, Ben."

"More than I had any right to spend," Ben said.

"That Bonnard, my God. And that Picasso. And that Rudel. It's just divine."

"Well, they weren't very important when I bought them," Ben said. "But they're getting there."

"You better believe it. My God, anything they put their name to. You know what Van Gogh's *Sunflowers* sold for this spring, don't you? Thirty-nine point nine million dollars. Can you imagine it? And Sotheby's sold a Degas bronze this year for ten point twelve million. Ten point twelve *million*. You know those nursing-mother things of Renoir's? Not long ago one of those went for eight point eight million. It's absolutely fantastic. And that Mary Cassatt, that pastel, that brought four point fifty-one million. A Giacometti sculpture, for three point eight five. You can't *believe* these prices! Forget about Krugerrands or real estate. I'll tell you, art is the greatest investment on earth right now."

"That's what I'm told," Ben said.

"That Rudel of yours over there on the piano. That'll be in seven figures this time next year. You wait and see."

"Well, I wouldn't sell it, no matter what I was offered," Ben said.

"Sell it or not, you're making money, every minute. With every breath you draw. You can just sit your little rump down in one of these chairs and have a couple of drinks and by the time you get up you'll be a millionaire ten times over, at the rate things are appreciating."

Ben brought their drinks to the coffee table and set them down. "I'll tell you one thing I regret," he said. "A couple of years ago there was a Degas called Laundresses Carrying Linen in Town, at the Impressionist exhibition at the National Gallery. Lovely little thing, only eighteen inches high, on paper. Maybe you saw it. Boy, I missed my chance on that. It was on sale for one and a half million when the New Painting exhibit opened. Well, that's pretty stiff, but it wouldn't have been impossible. I mean even if I'd had to borrow on my life insurance or sell my gold inlays or something. But while I was still diddling around about it, it was withdrawn from sale. The owners decided to auction it off at Christie's instead. You know what that painting brought? Seven point thirty-five million. I lie awake at night sometimes and think about that."

"My God," Linda said. "You'd have made almost six million dollars! In two years!"

"Two years," Ben said.

"God in heaven. Think where you'd be now. You'd never have to lift your hand again."

"Difficult to believe that," Tony said. "It's rather terrifying."

"Of course, the all-time record is Van Gogh's *Irises*," Linda said. "Do you know what that sold for, last November, at Sotheby's? You won't believe this. *Fifty-three* point nine *million* dollars. For one *canvas*. Doesn't that give you the chills?"

"Yes, it does," Jill said. "How can you possibly remember all those figures?"

"How can you *forget* them?" Linda said, widening her eyes. "And manuscripts. Original manuscripts. It's the same thing with them. Even contemporary ones. I read the other day that Saul Bellow has just sold the manuscript of one of his early books. You wouldn't believe what he got for it." She took her hand from the back of the sofa and pointed her forefinger elegantly at Jill. "You hold onto your manuscripts like gold, young lady. They'll make you a millionaire one day."

"Will they really?" Jill said. "Tony, what have we done with my manuscript?"

"I think I remember you wrapping fish bones in it," Tony said.

"Oh, Lord. There goes my riotous old age."

"Just as well," Tony said. "You'd have drowned in a tubful of laudanum or something."

Esther came in from the kitchen carrying a silver tray on which were canapés made up from the remains of their luncheon: pâté, caviar, Brie, and radishes fashioned into rosebuds.

"Oh, thanks, Esther," Ben said. He made room on the coffee table for her to set it down. "I guess you'll be needing a ride home, with this rain."

"It's OK," she said. "I called Elbert and he's coming to pick me up."

"Oh, good," Ben said. He gave her a glance. "Things going pretty well, are they?"

She nodded, smiling shyly.

"Hello, Esther," Linda said.

"Hello, Mrs. Bishop."

"Did you do these rosebuds, with the radishes?"

"Yes, ma'am."

"Well, they're absolutely lovely. They're too beautiful to eat."

"Thank you, ma'am." She set down the last of the canapé dishes and took the empty tray out of the room.

Linda turned to Ben and raised her eyebrows significantly. "Still having trouble with Elbert?"

Ben nodded.

Linda turned to Jill. "I don't know if Ben's told you, but she's having a little *maladie d'amour*. She worked for us last summer, when Ben and Priss went back to town, and it was—well, quite a melodrama, all month long." She rolled her eyes. "Oh, *les liasons des* Outer Banks!"

Jill smiled faintly.

"I guess Elbert's found fairer pastures," Ben said, sotto voce.

"Well, he won't have to look far," Linda murmured. "I suppose she's suffering, but it's hard to have sympathy for a woman like that. She's such a *rag*. I think she *enjoys* being abused." She turned to Tony. "Do you use the word *wimp*, in England?"

"I don't, no." Tony said.

"Actually, I think she's rather sweet," Jill said. "Rather vulnerable."

"A rag, a bone, and a hank of hair," Chuck said. "You know who said that?"

"Yes, dear, we know," Linda said. She dipped a cracker into the caviar.

Priscilla came into the room with a bowl of onion dip. "I made this with one of those powders," she said. "I don't know what it'll be like." She set the bowl down on the coffee table and sat down beside Jill. The moment she did so the doorbell chimed. Ben looked across to the door and saw the delivery boy from Luigi's standing outside on the deck in a yellow oilskin and sou'wester hat. He held up a large white box and grinned at Ben through the glass pane.

"Rib time," Ben said, getting up.

"Wouldn't you know that?" Priscilla said. "The minute I serve canapés."

"Always the way," Tony said. "Light a cigarette to make the bus come."

Ben went across to the door and slid it open.

"We didn't know if you'd make it," he said to the delivery boy.

"Yes, sir. We always deliver. But, boy, I'll tell you, it's up to the hub caps out there, all the way from Avon. I thought I might stall out there a couple of times."

"I'm mighty glad you didn't," Ben said. "How much is it?"

"Twenty-six fifty, sir."

Ben took his money clip out of his pocket and peeled off two twenty-dollar bills. "Keep the change," he said.

"Thank you very much, sir. You-all enjoy these ribs, now."

Ben slid the door closed and carried the box across the living room, holding it above his head like the victor at Wimbledon displaying his trophy. "It was a tough match," he said, "but I guess it was just my day. I want to thank everybody who believed in me."

"I've never stopped believing," Priscilla said. "Bring it out to the kitchen, champ. I'll put them on a platter."

"OK, it won't be a minute now, folks. You can get up to the table if you want."

He carried the carton out to the kitchen and set it on the counter. There were baked potatoes wrapped in foil, containers of coleslaw and cherry cobbler, and a box of steaming, spicy barbequed ribs. Priscilla and Esther took them out of the containers and set them onto separate platters. When he carried out the tray of ribs the guests were standing at the table with their drinks.

"We don't know quite where to sit," Tony said.

"OK, I'll sit up at this end," Ben said. "Then how about you, Jill, on my right? Guest of honor. Linda, over here. Then you two guys, and then Priss at the other end. OK?"

"Oh, good," Jill said. "I get this chap. Perhaps I'll get to hear another tale of adventure." She reached out and patted Chuck on his thigh as he sat down unsteadily beside her.

"You bet your life," he said. "Way I feel, I'll tell you anything you want to hear."

"I think he means that," Linda said.

Priscilla brought the tray of baked potatoes from the kitchen and a large stack of paper napkins which she set down in the middle of the table. "We're going to need these," she said. "Ribs are meant to be gnawed." Chuck got up and drew out the chair for her very ceremoniously, tottering slightly. Linda closed her eyes and bowed her head. "Thank you," Priscilla said. "Now help yourselves. Don't let them get cold." Ben held the tray of ribs for Jill and said, "Just use your fingers. This is a very elementary kind of meal."

"Oh, good. Then I won't be scolded." She plucked a section of ribs from the platter, set it on her plate and bent her head to sniff at it. "Lord, they smell divine."

Esther brought the tray of coleslaw from the kitchen and a bottle of wine which she set down beside Ben.

"Is that what you wanted, Mr. Oakshaw? The Boordy chablis?"

"That's it," Ben said. "Thanks, Esther."

While he opened the wine and filled their glasses, the platters of ribs, baked potatoes, and coleslaw went around the table. "Now dig in," he said. "And damned be he that first cries, 'Hold, enough!'"

"What's that from?" Chuck said. "That's from something. This guy

Ben has always got a quotation from something. I never saw anything
like it."

"It's the truth," Linda said. "I don't think you can mention a piece of
literature this man can't quote from."

"Hey, Ben, you know the one about the three tarts that came down from
Canada and got drunk on sherry wine?" Chuck said.

"*Eat*," Linda said, looking at him darkly.

Jill nibbled at one of her ribs, holding it between her fingers, and frowned
ecstatically. "Oh, my, they *are* divine!" she said. "Tony, aren't these heavenly?"

"It's just what I would call them," Tony said. "Although I doubt they're
served in heaven."

"Well, it's just as well I've been so wicked, then. I shouldn't want to spend
eternity without another taste of these."

The telephone rang, in the study and kitchen. Priscilla turned her head
toward the arch and called out, "Will you get it, Esther?"

"Yes, ma'am," Esther called back from the kitchen.

"What do they eat in heaven, do you suppose?" Jill said. "I think it's
something one should know, before plunging into a life of reckless piety."

"Manna," Tony said. "Six days a week. Weak tea and toast on Sun-
days."

"Oh, yes, manna. What's it like, do you think?"

"Something very nutritious, I should think. And very bland. Nothing
overstimulating, you can be sure. One of those health-food concoctions,
like tofu. Rather gray and wobbly, I imagine, like blancmange."

"Yes, that's what I'm afraid of," Jill said.

Priscilla sat with her head turned toward the arch, listening. "I guess it
was for Esther," she said.

"Must have been," Ben said.

"And of course, the company," Jill said. "Can you imagine sitting at
the dinner table every night with a group of people like John Calvin,
and Oliver Cromwell, and Cotton Mather, and the rest of the righteous?

Every night, for eternity? It doesn't sound at all like heaven to me. Much more my idea of hell."

"And St. Paul," Linda said. "Don't forget St. Paul."

"Well, at least you could count on a glass of wine with St. Paul, which I suppose would help you get all that manna down. But what you'd do after dinner, I can't imagine."

"Well, he did believe in marriage, didn't he?" Priscilla said. "Sort of? At least he said it was better to marry than to burn. So I suppose you could look forward to a night of marital bliss."

"Oh, *my*," Linda said. "Think of that."

"I should go absolutely potty listening to that lot at the table every night," Jill said. "What on earth do you suppose they talk about?"

"Not what on *earth*," Tony said. "What in *heaven* do they talk about? Virtue, naturally. Self-denial, chastity, sobriety, abstinence. All the things one loves to chat about. Jolly little anecdotes about the witches they've burned, the heretics they've set right, the joys of self-flagellation, the pleasures of the rack."

"I think I'd rather hear about the three tarts who came down from Canada," Jill said.

"Just say the word," Chuck said. "I can give you all ten verses."

Linda gave him a long black stare.

"Of course the trouble with the Christian concept of heaven," Tony said, "is that it's somewhere other than earth. Somewhere distant and rather misty and exalted. The empyrean, the Elysian Fields. Which is a fairy tale. If we're to have any experience of heaven, it will be here on earth, or not at all."

"Do you think anyone does?" Priscilla asked.

"Oh, I think so. A very few, and only at moments, perhaps. A Blake. A Gerard Manley Hopkins, a Beethoven. But everyone, I think, has glimpses of it, now and then. I doubt if there is anyone under this roof who hasn't had intimations of the sacred and the eternal. In thoughts of love, in a good dinner party"—he looked about the table and smiled, his eyes coming to rest on the cluster of garnets that twinkled on Priscilla's breast in the candlelight—"in a jewel seen by candlelight. Such things hint to us that there is a divine harmony of things. But, as Lorenzo says—" He turned to Ben and smiled quixotically, as if inviting him to supply the observation.

"'Whilst this muddy vesture of decay doth grossly close it in, we cannot hear it,'" Ben said. He could not suppress his feeling of elation at having successfully met Tony's challenge.

"Exactly."

There was a distant crystalline tinkle, like the falling of a glass star from a Christmas tree. Priscilla raised her head and listened.

"Esther," she called. "Is everything all right?" She listened for another moment. "Esther?" She laid her napkin on the table and stood up. "I'd better go and see."

There was a clatter of something falling on the floor and then a heavy thumping sound from the kitchen, like a dropped sack of potatoes.

"Oh, my God," Priscilla said. She shoved back her chair and ran across the room to the arch. Ben got up so quickly that he knocked his chair over backwards and then stumbled against one of the upturned legs stepping over it. From the kitchen he heard Priscilla say, "Oh, no, no, no," in a stark whisper. He kicked the chair out of the way and strode quickly across the room, through the arch and across the hall to the kitchen door. In the soft yellow light of the two kerosene lanterns that illuminated the room, the scene had a dire, theatrical quality that made him think again of Caravaggio. Priscilla was crouched on the floor beside Esther who lay facedown beside the counter with one arm twisted underneath her body and the other extended along the side of her face, turned loosely supine from the elbow, the hand palm up in a pool of blood that welled gently from a glittering red slit across her wrist. A carving knife lay in the middle of the floor among splinters of glass and the stem of a crystal goblet, snapped off neatly at both ends. There was blood splashed on the countertop and smeared down the length of the cabinet doors where she had fallen, and a festoon of glittering scarlet drops across the wall where she had apparently swung her sliced wrist in falling. The pool in which her hand lay had spread slowly as the blood pulsed from her wrist, welling into the shape of a bright blossom, like a Venus's-flytrap that was slowly devouring her fingertips. Priscilla knelt beside her, clutching her own face between her hands as if she had a toothache, her eyes closed tightly.

"Oh, Jesus," Ben said. He knelt down beside the girl and reached out toward her vaguely, laying his hand on her shoulder. He could not think of what to do first. He had seen a great deal of blood and death and had helped to bind the wounds of men who had been blown apart in battle, but confronted with this bloody debacle in the kitchen of his house of light, he felt confusion, shame, and indignation. His chief emotion was an angry resentment that this idiotic girl should have interrupted his dinner party so grotesquely and thoughtlessly. He had a bizarre impulse to throw a blanket over her body, turn cheerfully to his guests and say, "Nothing's happened. Everything's all right here. Let's get back to those ribs." He looked up at them with a weird, apologetic smile.

"Oh, God," Linda whispered. "Is she dead?" She stood with one hand pressed to her face, her mouth wide open.

"No, she won't be dead yet," Jill said briskly. "She's only fainted. But she will be, if we don't stop that bleeding." She looked quickly about the kitchen, plucked a tea towel from the rack at the counter-end, and knelt down beside Esther. "Can you turn her over?" she said to Ben.

Ben took the girl by the shoulders and tugged at them. She was very limp and very heavy. "Chuck, give me a hand," he said. Priscilla stood up and moved aside and Chuck knelt down and took the girl's ankles. Together they turned her body gently so that she lay on her back. Jill was folding the tea towel into a narrow bandage. She lifted the bloody hand and said to Ben, "Hold it up, like this, so I can get it bandaged." Ben held the hand while she wrapped it tightly in the folded towel. "Priss, have you got a safety pin?"

"I'll get one," Priscilla said. She went quickly to the door. "And a pebble or something, if you've got such a thing. Perhaps a small seashell."

"I'll see what I can find."

"What we want now is a bit of cold water, to bring her round. Will you get it, Tony?"

"Yes, right," Tony said. He went to the sink and filled a tumbler with water.

"I don't suppose there's a hospital down here?" Jill said.

"Not between here and Nags Head," Ben said. "There's a clinic in the village, but I think it's closed now." He looked at his watch. "There may be a doctor on call. I'll call them."

He went to the wall phone at the end of the counter, took it off the hook and stood holding it for a moment while he tried to remember the number.

"I'll have to call from the den," he said. "I can't remember the damned number." He hung up the phone, went quickly across the hall through the living room and into the study, where he opened the phone book on his desk, ran his fingertip down the C's and found the number. When he dialed it a recorded voice announced, "The Hatteras Village Clinic is closed at present. Our hours are nine to eight daily. In case of an emergency, call the following number." Ben muttered the number, hung up, and dialed it. In a moment a middle-aged, masculine voice said, "Dr. Whittaker."

"God, I'm glad to get you," Ben said. "My name is Oakshaw, doctor. I'm just up beyond Buxton. Are you in the village?"

"Yes. What's the trouble?"

"We've got a young woman here who's cut her wrist. She's unconscious. I don't know whether she's fainted or what."

"She bleeding badly?"

"She was. I think we've stopped it, for the moment."

"She lost a lot of blood?"

"Well, we got to her pretty quickly. I don't think she's had time to lose an awful lot. But I tell you, it's one holy mess in that kitchen."

"You know where the clinic is?"

"Yes."

"I think you'd better bring her down there. I'll have to stitch that up, and she may need a transfusion. How long ago did this happen?"

"Oh, five minutes."

"You got a tourniquet on it?"

"We're putting one on now, yes."

"Put it on the upper arm, above the elbow. Not too tight, and loosen it occasionally. Have you got ammonia in the house?"

"I don't know."

"If you have, give her a whiff of that, to bring her around. Or an ice pack on the head. Don't give her alcohol."

"OK," Ben said.

"How soon can you be down there?"

"Twenty minutes."

"I'll meet you there. Who is she, a local?"

"Yes. Esther Padgett. She works for us."

"Esther," the doctor said. "Have you called her parents?"

"No, I haven't."

"Might be a good idea. Drive carefully."

"I will," Ben said. "Thanks very much, doctor."

He hung up and dialed Esther's number, which he knew by heart. Her father answered in the strange, liquid, Devonshire-like accent of the older inhabitants of the Banks: "Gregory Padgett here."

"Mr. Padgett," Ben said. "This is Ben Oakshaw. Your daughter works for us?"

"Yes. Well?"

"First I want to say there's nothing to be unduly alarmed about. Your daughter's had a minor accident. She cut herself with a knife while she was working in the kitchen. It's not serious, but it does need medical attention. So we're taking her down to the clinic. I phoned Dr. Whittaker and he's meeting us down there in about twenty minutes."

"Not serious, you say."

"No. But it probably needs a few stitches. I thought you might want to come down and pick her up there."

"I'll come right down."

"Good," Ben said. "I'll see you then."

He hung up and went back to the kitchen. Esther was still unconscious, her eyes closed and her face very pale. Jill had put some kind of an object under the bandage and fastened it with a safety pin. She was crouched in front of Esther washing her face with a wet tea towel. A basin of water with ice cubes floating in it sat on the floor beside her.

"What did you use for the tourniquet?" Ben asked.

"Brooch I gave Priss. Just the thing. Did you get the doctor?"

"Yes. He wants us to bring her down to the clinic. He'll meet us there."

"Good. I think she's coming round now."

Esther opened her eyes and blinked at them.

"Hello, love," Jill said. "How d'you feel?"

Esther stared at her for several moments, then moved her eyes to Priscilla, then to Ben, and blinked again. "I'm still here," she said. "I thought I'd be dead."

"Lord, no," Jill said. "There's to be no dying around here. We're not keen on dead people, at all."

"Not at all," Tony said. "It's quite out of the question. I thought we were to have some more of that beach plum pie?"

"I've got to sit down," Linda said. "I've got to go and sit down." She was clinging unsteadily to the counter, her face bowed into her open hand.

"Yes, come and sit down," Priscilla said. She took Linda by the shoulders and steered her out of the door into the living room. Chuck followed them to the door and turned back to Ben with a small, writhing movement of apology. "I'll be back in a minute," he said. Ben nodded.

Tony had lifted Esther to a sitting position, crouching behind her with his hands under her armpits. "There we are," he said. "That's much better. Take some good deep breaths, now, and you'll be right as rain."

"Esther, we're going to take you down to the clinic," Ben said. "Dr. Whittaker wants to stitch up that cut. You think you can stand up?"

"I don't know," Esther said.

"Well, let's give it a try, shall we?" Tony said. He clasped her ribs firmly underneath her armpits. "Now, when I say *up!*" Ben took her by the elbows to help lift her. "Ready? Up!" They tugged her to her feet and she stood limply, her eyelids fluttering.

"I'm going to carry you down to the car, Esther, so you won't have to walk down the steps," Ben said. "You just relax, OK?"

Priscilla came back into the kitchen with Chuck behind her. "Oh, you're on your feet again!" she said. "That's wonderful. Are you feeling better, Esther?" Esther nodded weakly.

"Jill, there's an umbrella in the closet there, by the door," Ben said. "Will you get it, and try to keep her dry while I bring her down?"

"I'll get it," Priscilla said. "I want to come."

"Why don't you stay with Linda?" Ben said. "Tony and I will manage. I might need him at the other end."

"All right." She glanced around the kitchen. "Maybe I can straighten up a little."

"I'll go along too," Jill said. "Just for company." She laid her hand on Esther's back. "Would you like that?"

"Yes, ma'am," Esther murmured. "I'm sorry to cause you folks so much trouble."

"Don't be silly," Priscilla said. "You're the one who's had the trouble. Now you let people take care of you for a while."

"Quite right," Jill said. She went to the door, opened it, and stepped out onto the stoop, opening the umbrella over her head.

"Chuck, are you blocking me down there?" Ben asked.

"No, you can get out," Chuck said. "I parked right beside you. You sure I can't help?"

"No, we're fine," Ben said. "You stay here and finish those ribs." He stooped and picked up Esther, lifting her with one arm behind her knees and the other cradling her shoulders.

"I'll pop down and get the car open," Tony said. "Is it unlocked?"

"Yes," Ben said. Tony went out and down the steps to the driveway. Ben carried Esther to the kitchen door and out onto the stoop. Jill held the umbrella over them, backing down the steps in front of them to the paved areaway in front of the house. Tony stood by the open door of the parked car, his hair dripping in the rain.

"You're getting soaked," Ben said.

"Feels jolly good," Tony said. "Freshens one up. Let me give you a hand." He got into the car and took Esther's body as Ben eased her in onto the backseat, guiding her head through the doorway and adjusting her carefully upright. Jill stood holding the umbrella over them. When they had Esther inside, she lowered it and got into the car beside her. Ben got into the front seat, fished the keys out of his pocket, started the ignition, and pulled slowly out into the highway. It was flooded from shoulder to shoulder and the water splashed up inside the wheel-wells with a constant drumming sound as he drove. He drove very slowly, craning forward to peer through the pelting rain that struck the windshield like volleys of arrows through the headlights. Occasionally he glanced into the rearview mirror to see what was going on in the backseat. Esther had begun to cry with a hopeless, keening sound, like a child put to bed for misbehavior. Jill took her hand and stroked her arm. "Now then, what's it all about, love?" she said. "Got a beastly phone call, did you?" Esther went on whimpering softly. "Who was it from, then? Your young man?"

"He said he was coming to pick me up," Esther said, gasping out the words between wails. "But he didn't mean to, ever. He was in *Raleigh*. That's where he called me up from. Raleigh!" She dissolved into another fit of wailing.

"That's right," Jill said. "Get it all over with. You've got a good cry coming to you."

"He didn't have any idea of picking me up," Esther said. "He was up there with this girl, all the time. This girl he's been fooling around with all summer."

"Well, if he's that kind of a chap, you're much better off without him, aren't you? Think what you'd be letting yourself in for if you'd married him. Much better to get rid of him."

"How'm I going to do that? How can you just forget about somebody if you think they're going to marry you?"

"Oh, I didn't say forget about him, no. What you want to do is just get rid of him. Get him out of your system, like a bad tooth." Ben glanced into the mirror and saw that Esther was staring straight ahead, her face a rubbery-looking ruin. "You don't want to forget about him, no. Anyone who forgets a thing like that is letting herself in for a great deal of trouble in the future. But if he's the kind of chap you say, it's nothing terribly serious. Honestly. You think it is, right now, I know, but it really isn't, love. It's jolly painful, of course, just as a bad tooth is, but it's quite as easy to put right. Have it out, roots and all, it's the only thing to do. Are you listening to me?"

"Yes, ma'am," Esther said.

"Jill, that's my name. Can you say Jill?"

"Yes, ma'am, Jill."

"You think he loves you, do you?"

"He said he did," Esther said. "He said he was going to marry me. We was counting on it." Her voice shot up suddenly into a desperate wail that was racked by a set of anguished sobs. Jill held her hand and separated her fingers, stroking them methodically, like a masseuse.

"Well, I shouldn't put too much stock in that," Jill said. "Not if he's been carrying on with some girl all summer, as you say. You must just think of the man as if he were dead. It's going to hurt for a while, just as it does when you have a bad tooth pulled, but it will heal over very soon." Esther went on sobbing, her body jerking convulsively. "In any case," Jill said, "what you've got to do now is stop this wailing and start to sort things out properly. You deserve a good cry, and you've had it, and I suspect that's all it's worth. Shall I tell you what I think? I think perhaps you're being a very foolish girl indeed. Very foolish and very selfish. I suspect you have much more important things to think about just now than this wretched man and how badly you've been treated by him. Very much more important indeed. Are you listening?"

"Yes, ma'am, Jill."

"Good. Because you don't want to do anything foolish, you know. Anything you'll regret for the rest of your life. Tony, have you got a handkerchief?"

"Yes, right," Tony said. He plucked the handkerchief from the breast pocket of his blazer and handed it to her.

"Here you are," Jill said. "Now sit up properly and blow your nose. Is that better?"

"Yes, ma'am."

"Now then, what about your dad and mum? What sort of people are they? Do you get along with them?"

"Yes, ma'am."

"Truly? You think they love you?"

"Yes, ma'am. They take real good care of me."

"Do they? Well, that's a comfort, isn't it? Nice to have a dad and mum like that. How do you think they'd feel if you were to have a baby?"

Ben switched his eyes up quickly to the mirror and saw that Esther's face had convulsed into a mass of agonized wrinkles and creases, like a withered balloon. She hung her head weakly and began to sob again.

"Now then, we weren't going to have any more of that," Jill said. "I thought you were going to be sensible and sort things out properly. Are you pregnant, Esther?"

Esther nodded hopelessly.

"Well, you needn't look so wretched about it. It's not the end of the world, you know. It's only just the beginning, really. Nine women out of ten would give their eyeteeth to be in your position."

"Not if they wasn't married, they wouldn't," Esther said gaspingly. "Not if they lived here."

"Oh, rubbish. Times are changing, you know. No one gives a fig about that sort of thing anymore. Even if they did, what do you care what a lot of spiteful, envious people think? You'll have a bonny new baby to love. There's nothing in this world can equal that." Esther went on sobbing soundlessly, her shoulders quaking. "After all, the important thing is how your parents feel about it. If you're able to live at home with them you'll find things will work out very well."

"I don't know," Esther said. "I just don't know how they're going to take it."

"Well, if they love you as you say they do, I should think they'd be delighted. Nothing like the pride of becoming grandparents for people who are getting on. I shouldn't worry about that if I were you. Would you like to use this handkerchief again? That's better. Now, I'll tell you what I'll do. I'll give you a call when I get up to New York, and we'll have a good long talk about it. You'll be a bit calmer then, and you'll have had a chance to think about things. Shall I do that?"

"Yes, ma'am, I'd like that, Jill."

"Good. Let me have your number, and I'll ring you up as soon as I get up there. Tony, take it down, will you?"

"Yes, right," Tony said. He took an appointment book and a fountain pen out of the breast pocket of his jacket. "Now then."

"It's 555-986-4211," Esther said.

Tony wrote down the number and repeated it. "That right?"

"Yes, sir."

"Good," Jill said. "I'll give you a ring after I get up there. What about Tuesday evening?"

"That's OK, Miss Davenport. You'll be real busy. You won't have time to do that."

"Oh, yes, I will. I'll be very anxious to know how you're feeling. Now, I'll be rehearsing in the daytime, so it'll have to be in the evening. Some time around eight or nine. Is that all right?"

"Yes, ma'am."

"Good. That's just what I'll do, then. You mustn't call me ma'am. Have you ever been to New York?"

"No," Esther said. "I haven't never been outside of North Carolina."

"Haven't you? Oh, you'd like New York. I say that, although I've never been there myself. But I think it's jolly exciting. Tony's been there and he says it is. Don't you, Tony?"

"Oh, very," Tony said. "All sorts of things to see and do there."

"You know what I think," Jill said. "I think it'd make a jolly nice change for you to come up there and have a look round. You might even come and see my show. If you haven't been to a Broadway show, you might find it quite interesting. There'd be no trouble about the tickets."

"Oh, I couldn't do that," Esther said. "That would cost a lot of money. I couldn't spend money like that, just on a trip."

"Well, perhaps something could be worked out," Jill said. "It's worth thinking about, anyway. The thing to do right now is to get this arm patched up and get a good night's sleep. And remember, there are people in this world who care about you. You never know where you'll find a friend. It's a funny old world."

Ben was unaccountably perturbed by this conversation and very glad to see the lights of the Harbor Inn and the Red and White Grocery store sparkling through the rainy windshield as they approached the village.

"Lights have come on," he said.

"Jolly good," Tony said. "We've had the all clear."

Beyond the grocery store there was a Texaco station, and across the street from it, the clinic, a low, modern building made of imitation stone with a flagstaff rising from the middle of a flower bed in the front yard, its halyard slapping noisily against the metal pole in the wind. The lights were on in the windows of the waiting room. Ben pulled in to the curb at the end of the concrete walk and got out. Jill got out of the off-side passenger door and came around to the curb with the umbrella. She opened it and held it over them while Ben and Tony got Esther out of the car and stood her up on the front walk.

"You think you can walk, Esther?" Ben said.

"Yes, sir," Esther said. "I'm all right now, Mr. Oakshaw."

"Good. Take it easy. We'll give you a hand."

He and Tony steadied her while she went slowly up the front walk and a flight of three stone steps to the clinic. Dr. Whittaker opened the door for them and stood with his hand on the knob while they got her through the vestibule into the waiting room. He was a gray-haired man with a bronzed face who smiled at them cheerfully revealing a set of the whitest, most perfect teeth Ben had ever seen.

"Well, Esther, what in the world have you done to yourself?" he said. "My goodness me."

"I'm sorry to cause you so much trouble," Esther said. "I bet you had to get up from dinner."

"Well, I tell you, we were having Brussels sprouts, so I figure you done me a favor," he said. "You better come on back here in the examination room, let me have a look at that. You gentlemen want to bring her in here?" He went across the waiting room in front of them and opened the frosted door to the examination room. "Just set her down in that armchair there." Ben helped her across the room and eased her down into a leather chair beside the examination table.

"That's fine," Dr. Whittaker said. "I reckon you're Mr. Oakshaw."

"Yes," Ben said. "This is Miss Davenport and this is Mr. Griswold."

"How do you do?" the doctor said. "I'm glad to meet you folks. You gentlemen can wait out there in the parlor, if you don't mind. Maybe the young lady would like to stay in here with us."

"I would, yes," Jill said.

"Thank you. You'll find some interesting magazines out there if you like fishing. I guess Esther's dad will be here before long. Would you let him in, if you don't mind? I got that door locked because we're closed officially."

"Yes, we will," Ben said.

He and Tony sat in the waiting room smoking cigarettes and listening to the rain against the windows. On the wall above a leather sofa there was a huge stuffed purple marlin with a brass plate underneath giving the date and details of its capture. Ben picked up a *Smithsonian* magazine and read an article about man-eating tigers in India, the statistics of which were startling. In 1882, five hundred human beings and two thousand cattle had been killed by tigers in a single district of the Bombay Presidency. Between 1902 and 1910, an average of 851 people had been killed and eaten every year in India. Even in recent years, the annual number of killings in the Sundarbans district was between 55 and 60. The notorious Champawat tigress alone had killed 436 people before being slain by Col. Jim Corbett. Ben found himself automatically memorizing the figures and considering possible opportunities to introduce them into a conversation. In a discussion of ecology, for example, they might furnish a very dramatic illustration of the perils of sentimentality in deciding issues of conservation. Did reverence for life take realistic account of the fact that, in preserving it, one theoretically increased the peril to oneself?

"Chap pulling up outside," Tony said. "Looks like he might be her father."

Ben looked out of the window and saw a battered Plymouth pickup pulling in to the curb in front of the clinic. Esther's father got out, slammed the door, and strode up the front walk to the building wearing a yellow foul-weather suit and a sou'wester hat.

"Yes, it is," Ben said. He got up and went out to the vestibule.

"Hello, Mr. Padgett," he said, opening the door for him.

"Evening," Mr. Padgett said. "She OK?"

"Yes," Ben said. "Dr. Whittaker's stitching her up in there. I guess you can go in, if you like."

Mr. Padgett nodded and went across to the waiting room to the frosted door, opened it and went in. Ben sat down, picked up his magazine and resumed reading. Since 1975, in which time the Indian government had increased the number of national parks from five to fifty-four, wild tigers had increased in number from two thousand to four thousand. They had also mysteriously increased in ferocity in many districts.

"Just look at the size of that thing," Tony said. "Absolutely phenomenal. Did you ever see a fish like that?"

"Not alive," Ben said.

"Terrifying thing. I should hate to come across one, swimming."

"I don't think they attack humans," Ben said.

"Well, of course I'd just run into the one that did."

Jill came out of the examination room and sat down beside Tony, laying her hand on his knee.

"Everything all right?" he asked.

"I think so. He's got her stitched up. He says she doesn't need a transfusion."

"Oh, good. She calmed down a bit?"

"Yes. I think she'll be all right. What do you think about having her up to New York?"

"Might be just the thing," Tony said. "I could show her round a bit, if you're tied up at the theatre."

"Would you mind that?"

"Not at all. Might be rather a lark."

Ben felt an odd sense of resentment at their concern for the girl. After all, she was *his* cook. What cause did they have to go to such lengths to console her? It was an intrusion, and an ostentation. One that seemed to imply that he was somehow responsible for the girl's plight, and for not showing the proper amount of compassion.

Dr. Whittaker came out of the examination room and drew the door closed behind him.

"I think she's going to be just fine," he said. "Lost a little blood, which will make her weak for a day or two, but I don't think she needs a transfusion. I don't know just when she'll be back at work. Can you get along for a day or two without her?"

"Oh, sure," Ben said. "You tell her to take off as long as she likes."

"Well, I'll have another look at her on Monday and see how she's doing." He stroked his hair and frowned. "It's pretty obviously self-inflicted. You have any idea what made her do this?"

"I think she's been having some trouble with her boyfriend," Ben said. "He was supposed to pick her up tonight, but he called and said he wasn't coming, and she went all to pieces."

"That wouldn't be the Humphries boy, would it?"

"Yes," Ben said. "I guess they've been having trouble for some time."

"Yeah, that's how it goes." He looked at his shoes and frowned again. "Elbert is a good boy, but he's kind of hard to nail down. Well, I don't guess there's anything we can do about *that*. I gave her a little sedative to calm her down so she can get some sleep. I guess you folks can get along back home."

"All right," Ben said. "I'm glad to hear she's all right."

"Yeah, she's going to be just fine."

Driving back to the house, no one spoke for some time. Finally Ben said, "Did he examine her?"

"Do you mean for pregnancy?" Jill said.

"Yes."

"No. She didn't tell him."

"*Why*, for God's sake?"

"I don't suppose she wanted her dad knowing just yet."

"Jesus," Ben said. "What a mess. I wonder why she didn't tell *us*." Jill didn't answer. "Are you really thinking of asking her up to New York?"

"I thought we might, for a day or two. Take her round to the show, show her a few sights. I think she'd enjoy that."

"My God, that'll be an awful load on your shoulders, won't it? With everything you've got to do."

"Oh, I don't think so. I think, actually, I'd rather enjoy it too."

"Well, it's a very kind gesture. But I don't see any need to put yourself out like that. I mean it's not your responsibility, after all."

"Oh, I don't know. When things are thrown your way, you can't just pretend they didn't happen, can you?"

Ben looked at her in the rearview mirror and saw that she was staring serenely at the back of his head. "It's a damn shame," he said. "Something like this happening in the midst of your vacation. Wonderful way to spend a holiday. God. I'm sorry. I really am."

"You've nothing to apologize for," Jill said. "Most interesting thing that's happened to me in years."

"Interesting?"

"Yes, very."

"Well, I hope it hasn't wrecked your holiday," he said. He felt a vague sense of chagrin at the whole course of the evening: the power failure, the nasty situation with Chuck and Linda, the girl's messy, melodramatic attempt at suicide, Jill's enigmatic equanimity about it, the fact that he was sitting in a very wet, very crumpled, blood-stained Dior silk shirt that would probably have to be thrown out. Everything, the whole mess. "It's wrecked your meal, I'm sure of that. Those ribs will be stone cold."

"Oh, well, one can always heat them up again. Bit different from a love affair."

As they approached the house they could see that the lights were on. The Bishops had gone, and Priscilla was down on her knees scrubbing the kitchen floor with a sponge and bucket of water. She had changed into blue jeans and a T-shirt and her hair was tied up in a silk scarf. The water in the bucket had turned scarlet.

"God, why didn't you wait?" Ben said. "I'd have helped you. That's an awful job."

"Oh, I couldn't leave it like this. Is she all right?"

"Yes, she's fine. He's sewed up her wrist and given her some Nembutal or something to calm her down. Did you know she was pregnant?"

"Pregnant!" Priscilla put down her sponge and stared up at them from her knees. "Oh, my God, no. Is she?"

"Yes."

"How do you know? Did the doctor find out?"

"No. She told Jill."

"Did she really? You don't think she could be mistaken?"

"No, I don't think so," Jill said. "She's taken one of those urine tests they sell at the chemist's. They're very good. Ninety-nine percent, or something like that."

"Oh, my lord," Priscilla said. "The poor girl. What she must have been going through. I had no idea. Isn't that stupid of me? My God. What will she do?"

"Have a jolly fine baby, from the look of her," Jill said. "Sturdy as an ox. Look, let me just pop into my shorts, and I'll give you a hand with that floor."

"No, I'm almost through," Priscilla said. "I've got the ribs in the oven, so I think they'll be warm. Go and get changed. You're all soaking wet. I'll be right in."

"What's happened to the Bishops?" Ben asked.

"Well, I made them eat, or tried to. But Linda wasn't up to it. She was feeling pretty woozy, so I told Chuck to take her home. I said I'd call them."

"Just as well," Ben said. "Christ, I could use a drink. Shall I make you one?"

"When you've changed. We can settle down then. You're sure she's all right?"

"Yes, fine. Jill was great. She talked to her and got her calmed down. You'd have thought she was a therapist or something. You know what she's thinking of doing? Having her up to New York."

"Oh, she's *not*! Really, Jill?"

"I thought it might do her a bit of good," Jill said. "Wouldn't be any trouble. I'd rather enjoy it."

"What a wonderful idea. You're an angel, honestly." She got up from the floor and laid the sponge in the sink, smiling wonderingly at Jill. "Honestly, what a sweet thing to do. But listen, you're certainly not going to pay for it."

"Oh, it wouldn't come to much," Jill said. "Couple of hundred dollars. I can't think of a better way to blow it. Just go for booze, otherwise."

"No, now *listen*! We wouldn't hear of it. Ben and I would be delighted, if she wants to go."

"Well, we'll talk it over," Jill said.

"Yes, we will. Let's get into some clean clothes and have that drink. Ben, go and have your shower. I'll be through by then."

While he was putting on dry clothes after his shower, Priscilla came in and took over the bathroom. He listened to her humming in the shower in a sweet but very unsteady soprano that clung desperately to the pitch between each note like a child swinging uncertainly from hand to hand along a pair of horizontal bars. She sang in the same way she played the piano and as once, disastrously, she had tried to paint—with a brave, shy, reverent ineptitude that generally disintegrated into mutters of futility. It made him smile, not condescendingly, exactly, but with a kind of philosophical bemusement at the fact that anyone with such a passionate appreciation of music should sing so badly. There was something not only unfair but somehow sinister in the fact that fine and generous people with a genuine devotion to the arts should so often be totally devoid of talent for performing in them, while greatly gifted artists should so often be such utter scoundrels. The painter whose work most genuinely moved him to wonder was Caravaggio, and evidently a greater rogue had seldom trod the earth: a brawler, drunkard, braggart, bully, thief and murderer. He scowled with the darkness of this thought while he laced his shoes, then went out into the living room and made a pitcher of very dry martinis.

When the others came in he served them gravely and ritually and they sat and talked about the evening with a growing comfort and tranquillity that progressed into the almost festive feeling of relief and restored serenity that comes after a storm. Ben sat and looked at his wife and guests appreciatively, elegant and easy in their clean, dry clothes, the women fresh and fragrant, holding icy martinis in their slim, sunburned fingers, all of them rendered splendidly invulnerable by wealth and talent to the carnivorous flower that had broken into scarlet, startling blossom in the kitchen. Behind and above Jill's head was a Pollock painting, and he noted for the first time how suggestively and skillfully the artist had splashed the canvas with scarlet drops of paint from a slung brush, almost like the garland of blood drops on the kitchen wall where Esther had slung her sliced wrist. A wonderful piece of work, a marvelous metaphor. And a very expensive one, which fortunately did not have to be washed off the wall. He began to feel expansive, philosophical, in his relief. After all, the evening had come out very well. It could almost be considered

an esthetic event, an embellishment of their lives, as were the paintings on
the walls that surrounded them. Jill was truly an artist, or a sorceress. She
had performed something like a miracle in evoking this fresh appreciation
of life in him, in them all, as she had in her play. It was something that
Esther would profit by as much as anyone. She would be wiser, happier,
better fit for life, a greater connoisseur of it. It had been, really, quite a remarkable evening.

They ate by candlelight, lingering at the table when the ribs were finished to drink a bottle of Benedictine, growing blither and more voluble
with the sweet golden liqueur, enclosed in a kind of charmed circle of qua-
vering light surrounded by the soft, ravening shadows in the corners of
the room and the sound of rain outside the house.

.   .   .

It rained all night, a steady, comforting rain that drummed on the roof
and on the planks of the deck outside the glass doors of the bedroom.
Ben woke several times in the night and lay listening to the ceaseless, soothing murmur that bathed the world like a benediction. He felt like a fetus
in the womb. In the instant after he woke, before he remembered who
he was and before he had any memory or history, it was like the sound of
blood pulsing secretly and sweetly all around him, the endless utterance
of a long, dark syllable that stood for safety, peace, rest, warmth, cleanliness, innocence, a serene anticipation of the certain, eventual delight of
light. He felt no impatience, anxiety, haste, discomfort, or unease. The
morning would come when it came, and it would bring the unknown,
unimaginable splendors of the day, action and renown and love, and meanwhile you lay and listened to the long, sweet serenade that preceded it,
the grave, oracular blessing before birth.

Then he remembered who he was and he reached out and clutched
Priscilla's hair, which lay beside his face on the pillow, his fingers closing
around a strand of it in panic. He lay in the dark breathing quickly, clenching her hair as if it were a rope by which he dangled from a precipice. Christ

Almighty, he thought, what is the matter with me? Where the hell am I? I feel as if I'd never been born. The sound of the rain, which had been like a caress, seemed to have become relentless and malign, an acid down-pour beating mercilessly on the earth. It was wearing the world away, erod-ing the dunes, leaching the timbers of the house as if they were flesh macerating in lime, reducing everything to a shapeless, sodden insolvency. The roof would soften and dissolve and sag inward like a Dali watch and then he would feel the rain fall on him in the bed, as sharp as lye. It would eat away his hair and face and flesh and then the ligaments that held his bones together and then the bones themselves, reducing them to a seething pulp that melted into pools of liquid and then into a pale vapor that drifted up and dissipated into nothingness.

He lay feeling himself being gradually unmade, fading to bodilessness and soullessness and anonymity, shorn of memory and finally of all sen-sation except the incessant, dire sibilance of the rain. The sound was slowly transformed into the hissing of steam from the cylinders of a huge, old-fashioned locomotive like the black iron monsters that had stood hissing in the rail yards beside the warehouses of the Central Florida Citrus Grow-ers Association when he was a boy. It was standing in the middle of a meadow with a string of coaches behind it beside a water tank and he could hear the hissing of the steam a hundred yards behind him where he sat under a single oak tree among the scattered boulders that lined the bank of a stream that flowed through the cornfield in a meandering diagonal from left to right. The roadbed ran straight as a long plank through the cornfield to the horizon, the rails gleaming in the bright noonday light. It was late summer and the corn was ripe but had not yet been picked, the plump green ears tufted at their tips with yellow corn tassels that shone in the sun like clumps of moist amber thread. He had taken off his jacket and laid it across a boulder folded neatly lengthwise so that the embroidered es-cutcheon that decorated the left breast was turned upward, the gold threads glinting softly in the shadow. The escutcheon was the coat of arms of his family, a shield emblazoned with an oak tree like the one under which

he sat and inscribed with the name Oakshaw. It was cool in the shade of
the oak among the boulders, and the shadow of the tree fell straight
downward in the noon light where he sat with his back against the trunk
and looked out at the water of the creek that flowed swiftly through the sunlight and then through the shadow of the tree and then out into sunlight
again. In the sunlight the water sparkled like mica and there were little gray
minnows swimming upstream through the clear water over the stones of
the creekbed, their bodies rising in the bulge of swiftly flowing water over
the larger stones. As they bulged up into the light with the current their
bodies became transparent so that you could see the faint tiny lattice-
work of their bones. Sometimes a breath of breeze blew in under the
tree from the cornfield, hot and dry and smelling of green corn husks
and dry earth, and off above the field the sky was a depthless burning
blue with five very small clouds, as delicate as cottonwood blossom, drifting motionless against the blue. He had a sense of peace that was almost
as profound as sorrow because everyone he had ever known he had loved
deeply and beautifully, and he knew that when they thought of him they
smiled with the memory of his kindness and devotion and generosity, as
they were smiling now, thinking of him on his way to the special command
performance where, with an audience of chosen guests, he was to attend
the production of a play by an unknown author that would reveal the meaning of life to those who had been invited to witness it. But the beauty
and serenity of the scene before him contended with the pride he felt at
the privilege he was to share with his fellow guests, and it seemed to him
that no spectacle or revelation could compare with the sweetness of sitting under the oak tree in the quiet summer field beside the clear bright
ripple of the creek on this endless afternoon. He became conscious suddenly that the hissing of the steam from the locomotive had changed
into the regular, chuffing, concussive thump of the pistons as they were
driven in and out of the cylinders of the great engine, and he turned suddenly, feeling a thrill of dark alarm run through him, and saw that the train
had begun to move away leaving a long, tubular billow of black smoke

above the field. The last of the passenger coaches was now fifty yards beyond the water tower and gaining in speed as it receded, the click of its
wheels on the track joints gaining in tempo, and then there was a long,
shrill, departing shriek from the whistle like a shrill, scornful laugh. He
leapt up and began running across the field toward the roadbed, the
cornstalks breaking and scattering before his legs as he ran. He reached the
gravelled rise of the right-of-way and ran along it desperately, his feet
scattering stones between the ties, seeing the observation car recede into
the distance and the passengers who stood behind the railing of the platform waving to him as he ran, shouting to him soundlessly down the track.
He gathered all his strength and took an enormous leap, sailing weightlessly through the air toward the speeding train like Superman, reaching
out for the railing of the observation deck as he plunged toward it, then
clutching the rail with his crooked fingers as the passengers took hold of
his arms and the back of his jacket and tugged him up across the railing,
laughing and cheering as he tumbled over it and fell safely onto the
deck, aboard the train. One of them was Priscilla; she knelt beside him and
wiped the sweat and soot from his face with a lace handkerchief and
said, "I didn't call you because I wasn't sure whether you wanted to stay.
Would you rather have stayed?"

He clenched her wrist very tightly with his fingers and said, "No, I
can't miss the performance. Jesus, I almost stayed too long."

She helped him to his feet and they went back inside the coach and
took their seats, looking out of the window as the train sped clicking over
the rails through the countryside and then ran through the scattered
houses and shopfronts of the suburbs and then slowed down and rolled
to a steaming stop beside the platform of a railway station. Then they
were hurrying through the booming, high-ceilinged vestibule, running
with their luggage out through the portals to a taxi rank in front of the
station portico. They got into a taxi and because he was afraid they
would be late he kept glancing at his watch while they drove through
the wide boulevards and across the marble plazas and past the arcades

of a great city whose stone facades and towering domes and cenotaphs
rose up in black silhouette against the crimson glow from the sunset that
suffused the sky. Eventually they stopped in front of the pillared portico of a Palladian theatre and got out of the taxi and hurried in through
a pair of bronze doors that were closed behind them by uniformed at-
tendants. They were ushered up a flight of marble stairs and along a marble corridor to the door of a private box whose panels were embossed
with a carved duplicate of his coat of arms. Then they were seated high
inside the domed theatre in the fragrant dusk that smelled of velvet and
rosewater and ancient damask in a bay-fronted loge decorated with
gilded cupids with stubby wings and tousled plaster ringlets, some of
them holding long-stemmed herald's horns to their lips, under a crystal chandelier as vast as the Milky Way that lit the enormous vault above
them. All around them were elegant, beautifully dressed spectators who
smiled and nodded to them in their private box, and then the chandelier dimmed slowly like a dying galaxy and a hush fell over the rapt as-
sembly of the chosen as the great crimson curtain rose. It rose on the
moonlit garden of an Italianate palace whose gilded dome towered
above the garden walls which were draped in garlands of purple
bougainvillea. In the center of the garden there was a fountain with the
statue of a nymph holding on her shoulder a tilted urn from which a
stream of water poured over her white body and splashed into the marble basin in which she stood. The fountain was encircled by a stone
bench on which sat a lady wearing a jeweled diadem and a gossamer
white gown girded with golden cords whose tassels touched the ground.
She gazed sadly into the mist from the fountain and sang the words of
an Elizabethan ballad:

> Sleep, wayward thoughts, and rest you with my love;
> Let not my love be with my love displeased.
> Touch not, proud hands, lest you his anger move,
> But pine you with my longings long diseased.

A man appeared in the shadows beyond the garden wall and after listening for a moment to the lady's song, he took hold of the gnarled vines of the bougainvillea and scaled the wall, dropping onto the slate squares of the walk below. The lady rose and held her fingertips to her face in fright, but the man held out his hands to her in supplication, and when she did not flee, he moved toward her and knelt at her feet. He was dressed in the tattered hose and doublet of Razullo, with a feathered cap on his head and a lute strapped to his back, and wearing the grotesque beaked mask of a mummer. As he knelt before the lady, she reached out slowly to remove his mask and when she took it from his face Ben was astonished to see that the minstrel's features were his own. He leaned forward in his seat, laying his hand on the velvet rail of the loge, and saw his ghostly minstrel self lift the embroidered strap of the lute from his breast and lay the instrument across his thigh and begin to strum it softly as he replied to her song with his own. But as he began to sing, a mist rose from the footlights and enveloped the stage, obscuring the actors and the moonlit garden in a dense billowing cloud, and he could not hear his song because rain had begun to drum on the great vaulted dome of the theatre. It beat down in wind-driven sheets that sluiced down the sides of the crystal dome, a corrosive acid rain that slowly ate away the glass so that there were ragged gaps in the arch through which you could see the depthless black of the void above the dome, and then the rain began to fall onto their hair and shoulders, a fine, bitter mist that dissolved the programs in their laps to sodden rags and seeped through their disintegrating clothing and burned their flesh like lye. It fell onto the backs of his hands, biting into them like vitriol, and he raised one of them in horror and saw that the flesh was eaten away and that his fingers were only a set of bony spokes that seethed softly as they melted into pulp. Slowly the great vaulted theatre began to crumple and collapse like a sand castle in the tide, the walls slumping inward and pouring down like wet mortar to bury the skeletal spectators who sat sliding forward on their seats on the collapsing tiers of the balconies

until there was only a mass of bubbling flesh and molten bones and ravaged cupids with blistered golden skin and dripping faces buried under a mound of streaming rubble that hissed and smoked as it dissolved
into an acrid vapor that drifted up and was absorbed into the blackness
of the void.

He opened his eyes hoping to see the light once more before he was
blinded by the scalding rain, and saw Priscilla standing at the open door
with the curtains blowing in the wind and the sound of water drumming
steadily on the planks of the deck. She was wearing a negligee of pale
gray chiffon that rippled around her body in the wet breeze and her dark
hair shifted along her throat. He said, *"Priss?"* in a startled, anguished
way that made her turn quickly to look at him.

"What?"

"You OK?"

"Yes. Why?"

"Jesus Christ. I was having one hell of a dream."

"You were? What happened?"

"I don't know. Everything just collapsed." He shook his head and
shuddered.

"You look pretty shook up."

"I was. Jesus." He sat up and stared beyond her into the falling rain.
"What time is it? How long you been up?"

"I just got up. It's ten after eight."

"After *eight*? Good God, I was out like a light."

"You had quite a bit of liqueur last night."

"I guess so. I don't suppose you've put any water on yet, for the tea."

"No. I was just going to do it. You want a Danish?"

"No, thanks. I'll do it."

"No, you take your shower." She came across to the bed and looked
down at him gravely. "What was it about?"

"Oh, it was that railroad thing."

"You haven't had that in quite a while, have you?"

"Oh, I get it once in a while, but not like this. This was a real production number."

She laid her hand against his face. "Well, take your shower. Wash it away."

"OK. Anybody up yet?"

"No. They'll probably sleep til noon."

He got up and went across to the bathroom door where he turned back to say, "Listen, Priss—" but she had gone out of the room. He took a long shower, first very hot, then so cold that it made him shudder and clutch himself with his arms. He opened the bathroom door to let the steam out and wiped off the mirror with a towel and shaved carefully, observing that his face was plump and flushed from the steam and that the line of his lower jaw was softening into the suggestion of jowls. Maybe it was time to grow a beard. In his acting days he had looked very striking in an Elizabethan beard, which lengthened the chin and framed the lips dramatically, giving the face a sensuous, faintly piratical look suggestive of swordplay, poetry, and elemental passions. Staring at his face in the mirror he made the sudden impulsive resolution that next summer he would grow a beard and in the fall they would travel to the Dalmatian coast. He had not seen Eastern Europe at all, and it was time for him to make an acquaintance with it. It was one thing to quote trade figures or political or social lore from the editorial pages, but another thing entirely to say, at the dinner table, "That wasn't the impression I got, at all, in Belgrade, a lovely city—" Nothing gave one such a sense of engagement, vitality, prosperity, and accomplishment as travel. The studious, disciplined bustle and exhilarating activity of buying airplane tickets, making out itineraries, hotel reservations, arrangements for rental cars to be picked up in Trieste, Dubrovnik, Prague, getting on and off of airplanes, sampling exotic foods in expensive restaurants beside the Danube. The world was a place of infinite variety, animation, industry, something which travel confirmed and celebrated. A man with an appointment book and a Baedeker did not need a Bible.

When he went out to the kitchen Priscilla was drinking tea and reading the *Charlotte Journal* which she had brought in from the deck. There was a buttered croissant on the plate in front of her which she picked up and nibbled occasionally while she turned the pages.

"I called Esther," she said, looking up when he came into the kitchen.

"Oh, good. How was she?"

"She wasn't up yet, but her mother said she seemed much better last night when she went to bed. I told her not to wake her."

"I don't suppose she's told her about being pregnant."

"It didn't sound like it. How do you think they'll take it, Ben? Do you think Jill's right?"

"I don't know. I don't know them well enough to even guess. Let's hope so. Can I have some of your tea?"

"Yes, but it's a bit cold. Why don't you make some fresh? There's another croissant in the oven. I thought you might change your mind."

"No, thanks. I'm going to stay away from the butter for a while. I'll just have some tea."

"The world news section is on the lower rack getting cooked. It got wet."

Ben poured himself a cup of tea from the pot on the table and took the newspaper out of the oven. It was warm and dry and faintly brown along the edges, threatening the features of the president, which occupied two columns on the top right side of the page.

"You just about cooked Ronnie," he said.

"He needed it. He was only half-baked."

He glanced briefly at the headlines, then turned to the financial section.

"Well, there's *some* good news," he said after a minute. "Consolidated Edison has gone up five points, and Giant Food five point four."

"How much extra can I spend this week?"

"You can spend an extra week in Belgrade next fall."

"We're going to Belgrade next fall?"

"I think we ought to go somewhere," he said. "We haven't been to Europe for two years. We've got to shake the dust off. We're getting very provincial."

"I don't feel provincial at all. I feel very happily ensconced here."

"Well, I do. My pulse rate is going down disastrously."

Priscilla lowered her paper and looked at him. "Why Belgrade?"

"I don't know. We haven't seen Eastern Europe, and I think we ought to, before they get a McDonald's on every corner."

She went on looking at him with a long somber gaze which Ben read as reproach; for years he had advertised a chain of fried chicken parlors constructed in the shape of a rooster in a top hat smoking a cigar. "You don't want to go to Belgrade?"

"I don't know, it just seems so damned selfish, when people like Esther are worried about having enough money to raise a child. Life isn't fair, at all."

"No, it isn't," Ben said. "That's what Kennedy lived to tell us." He folded the newspaper to the editorial page and read an article about gun control by a columnist named Richard Cohen. Halfway through the piece the urgency of its tone began to oppress him like the banging of a hammer on an anvil. What was the man so damned worked up about? What did it matter if people bought guns and killed each other? Did he really care? He dropped the paper on the floor and stared out of the window at the rain.

"What's the matter?" Priscilla said.

"I don't know. Every now and then things seem so goddamned . . . pointless."

Priscilla folded her section of the paper, laid it on the table, picked up her teacup and sipped at it thoughtfully.

"How long do you suppose this damned rain is going to keep up?" Ben said.

"It's supposed to stop by noon."

"Noon." He looked at his watch. "That's three hours from now. What will we do til then?"

"Why don't we talk?" she said.

"OK, let's talk," Ben said. "Who goes first?"

"You go first."

"All right." He stared out of the window at the rain falling on the rail of the sundeck sending up an effervescent spray like the mist from a freshly opened bottle of Asti. "When I was a boy I almost killed a panther. Did I ever tell you that?"

"No."

"Well, I did. Almost did. I was twelve years old. It may have been the last panther in Florida. It was certainly one of the last. It started killing the chickens one fall. It would jump right over the fence at night and go into the henhouse and grab one in its mouth and then come out and jump back over the fence and carry it off into the fields outside our farm. This must have gone on for a month or more. We didn't notice it until the flock was beginning to visibly thin out. This cat was so silent and stealthy that he never woke them up. I guess the one he grabbed he killed instantly. I suppose he crunched it between his jaws before it started to squawk. Anyway, there was never any racket or anything. But then we began to notice that there weren't as many chickens around as there should have been, so my old man went out and studied the ground around the henhouse. It was all soft white sand—that's the way the ground is in Florida underneath the surface scrub—and he found some bloody feathers by the fence and paw prints in the sand. They were as big as the bottom of a coffee mug. This was a big cat. I tell you, when I saw him he scared the hell out of me. He must have stood four feet tall at the shoulders and weighed two hundred pounds. You see a cat like that in the moonlight, the way I did, and it does something to you you don't forget.

"This was the first time a panther had showed up in our area in twenty years and my old man couldn't figure out where he'd come from. There had been brush fires in the Everglades that summer, and he said maybe he'd been driven out by the fires and come north. That was a long trip through a lot of built-up land, but panthers were smart animals, my dad said. He said they were the smartest, wildest things left alive in North America. The only gun my old man had was a beat-up old twenty-twenty single-shot rifle that you couldn't hit a barn with, so he decided the best way to get the panther was with poison. He went in to Orlando to the

Fish and Wildlife people and got some cyanide pills. This was way back in the late fifties before there was all this fuss about endangered species and everything. He cut up some raw beef into chunks and slit them open and tucked the cyanide pills inside them and dropped them beside the chicken-yard fence. The next morning there were paw prints leading up to the fence from the front gate of our farm and the chunks of meat had been pushed around and nuzzled on the ground, but they weren't eaten. One of them was lying ten or twelve feet away from where my old man had dropped them, as if the panther had tossed it away in contempt. But he had taken another chicken, because you could see his paw prints on the sand inside the yard leading up to the chicken house, and then away from it, and there was a patch of bloody feathers in the sand outside the wire where he'd vaulted the fence.

"The next night my old man took a rocking chair outside the house and sat there all night in the shadow of the front porch with a bottle of wine and the rifle across his knees. When I went out in the morning he was sitting there sound asleep with the empty bottle lying in the sand beside his chair. I don't know what time he passed out but it wouldn't have made any difference if he'd stayed awake all night because there weren't any paw prints in the sand around the fence or inside the chicken yard, where he'd raked it smooth before he went on watch. He sat there for five nights in a row, and there wasn't a sign of that cat. Sometimes he took a six-pack of beer instead of a bottle of wine, and the last two nights he didn't take anything but the rifle, and he managed to stay awake all night—at least he was awake when I went out in the morning—but that panther never showed a hair. My dad said, 'Well, I guess he's gone. I guess he foxed us, that son of a bitch. He'll be back in the 'Glades by now.' He came back in the house that night and went to sleep in his bed. He thought it was all over. But the next morning there were paw prints inside the chicken yard and a trail of bloody feathers through the sand. I thought my old man would turn blue. He looked like the veins were going to explode in his neck.

"I said, 'Daddy, why don't we just make doors for the coop and bolt it shut at night? He won't get any more of them that way.' But he said, 'No, I'm not building any goddamned doors. I'm going to kill that son of a bitch. All I need is a couple of good nights' sleep. Ben, you go out there tonight. You sit up there in the chinaberry tree where he won't catch no scent of you, and keep your eyes open.' I said, 'Daddy, I can't sit up in no tree all night,' and he said, 'You sit up there and watch for that cat or I'll kick the shit out of you.' So I went out and sat up in the chinaberry tree all night with the rifle. I fell asleep after a couple of hours, I guess; I didn't even try to stay awake. I didn't want to kill that panther. I felt like I was more kin to that panther than I was to my old man. I wanted him to get back to the 'Glades without a scratch on him, sleek and fat and full of chicken meat and licking his chops. I wanted him to die of old age out there in the swamps thinking about the times he'd raided chicken coops right under our noses and made it back a hundred and fifty miles through towns and housing developments and across highways, back to the big cypress. My old man sure as hell didn't feel that way about him, though. He wanted to kill that cat.

"The next night he went out with a ladder and climbed up on the roof and sat there with the rifle and a bottle of wine. It started to rain around midnight. I could hear it beating on the tin roof and it woke me up. I don't know what made the most noise—the rain on that tin roof or my old man up there swearing like a wet hen. He sat there all night, soaked like a sponge and drunk as a skunk. It's a wonder he didn't fall off the roof and kill himself. He was sick for a week, and he made me sit up in the chinaberry tree and keep watch. I didn't see the panther 'til my third night. I stayed awake later than usual that night because it was so beautiful. It's one of the most beautiful nights I can ever remember. There was a half moon that rose early, before sunset, and it was riding high in a clear, luminous sky with three pale stars beside it, and there was a smell of orange blossom everywhere. I wasn't even thinking about the panther. I used to go kind of nutty in the moonlight, anyway—I'd get sort of drunk on it. The sand was very pale and there were sharp shadows on it from the fence posts and the house. I was looking at that luminous sand like a sea of mist down there, and all of a sudden I saw the panther come loping across it from the gate. He was moving warily but steadily across the yard, his shoulders rising and falling as he set his front feet down, and he was glowing in a spooky way, so stealthy and graceful that he nearly made my heart stop. Honest to God, I think it missed a couple of beats when I saw that cat come loping through that moonlight like a ghost. He stopped at the fence of the chicken yard and lowered his head and sniffed the ground, and then raised his head and turned toward the house and stood absolutely still. He stood there looking up toward the front porch and I could see the cream of his face-fur and his eyes glowing like yellow jelly in the moonlight.

"I was sitting up there in the branches with my back resting against the trunk of the tree and the rifle laid across the crotch of a branch beside my elbow. I moved my hand very slowly and lifted the rifle out of the crotch and set the stock against my shoulder and then lowered my head and sighted along the barrel. I moved the tip of it until I had the bead right on the middle of his breast in the hollow between the front edges of his shoulder blades, and held it there for a minute. I said to myself, 'I got you now, buddy. You're gone.' Then I raised the tip of the barrel until it was pointing at the moon and fired straight up into the sky.

"That panther was gone so fast I didn't even see him leave. He just all of a sudden wasn't there any more. I looked out across the yard and saw him sailing through the moonlight like a comet. He was moving in these tremendous leaps that carried him five feet or so into the air, so fast you couldn't see the motion of his legs, just this soft, gold-colored blur through the moonlight. I'll tell you, I was shaking like a leaf. I was too weak to climb down out of that tree. I sat there until my dad came running out of the house, down the porch steps and across the yard like a wild man, staring out toward the fence, up toward the front gate, everywhere, then finally up at the tree where I was sitting.

"'You see him?' he yelled at me. 'You get that bastard? What happened?' 'I saw him,' I said. 'He was right over yonder at the fence, Daddy. I got a bead on him, and I shot, but I missed him. You can't hit anything with this old gun.'

"Well, I got the hell beat out of me that night. When I jumped down out of that tree my old man took off his belt and chased me around that yard for ten minutes. He caught me by the front gate and beat me til his arm was tired, all the time yelling, 'You shit-headed, shiftless little fool! You're not no more count than one of them chickens.' Then he threw his belt across the yard and went back in the house. I slept in the feed-house that night on a sack of cracked corn. It was hard as gravel, but I never slept better in my life."

Priscilla wrapped her fingers around her coffee cup and sat staring at it for a minute. "Did he come back?" she asked.

"No, we never saw him again. We never heard anything about him from anybody that lived around there, either. My old man went through the county *Sentinel* that week but there wasn't anything in it about any panther. I guess he made it back to the 'Glades. I hope so."

"I hope so too," Priscilla said. "What made you think of that?"

"I don't know," Ben said. "I guess listening to Chuck tell that story last night about that elk he shot up in Colorado."

"I liked your story better," Priscilla said. She reached across the table and laid her hand on his. "I'm so glad you didn't kill him."

"I didn't," Ben said. "Honest to God, Priss." She sat with her hand resting on his, smiling into his eyes. "So now it's your turn," Ben said.

"I don't know what to tell you." She lowered her eyes to the table and frowned, then looked up at him again. "I never did anything important until I married you."

"Well, you let me be the judge of that. For example, what were you doing on the fifteenth of June in 1969?"

"In 1969? Well, let's see. I would have been—what? Thirteen years old. Oh, *I* know what I was doing. I went to Europe with my parents that summer, instead of going to camp. And we sailed from New York on the twelfth. I remember because that's my mother's birthday and that was my father's present to her—a cruise to Europe. So on the fifteenth I must have been just about in the middle of the Atlantic ocean on the *Isle de France*."

"The *Isle de France*," Ben said.

"It was a glorious trip, because that was the first time they let me stay up late and go to the *galas* with them. I'd been to Europe before, but I'd never been allowed to go to the *galas* at night. God, I thought I was so glamorous! My mother bought me my first real evening gown—this gorgeous pink chiffon thing we got at Bergdorf's, and I got my ears pierced because she said all the young girls in Europe were wearing gold beads in their ears. The night before we landed at Calais there was a farewell *gala* and I had on my pink gown and my gold earrings and I danced with an oil man from Texas who was a friend of my father's. He was very courtly and grave and called me *mademoiselle*." She chuckled. "I dreamed of him all summer. I was sure he was going to write me an impassioned letter, but it never came. What were you doing?"

"I was sitting up in that tree," Ben said.

"Oh, I wish I'd known." She clasped his hand more tightly. "I would have climbed right up there with you."

"That would have been nice," Ben said. "I could have used some company."

"The next time you get treed by a panther, you let me know."

Ben lifted his teacup and drank and set it down. He looked beyond her out of the window at the rain pelting on the deck rails.

"Christ, it's a grim sort of day, isn't it?"

"You want to play Trivia?" Priscilla asked.

"OK. Why not."

She opened the table drawer in front of her and took out a stack of cards. They often played Trivia in the mornings.

"What category do you want? Popular Music, Sports, Fads, Disasters, Awards—"

"Disasters," Ben said. "What the hell."

"OK, here you go. In 1871, the second largest city in the United States went up in flames. What city burned, and how was the fire reportedly started?"

"Chicago. Mrs. O'Leary's cow."

"Right. In 1889, a dam broke and one of the worst floods in American history engulfed a Pennsylvania town. What was its name?"

"Johnstown," Ben said. "These are simple."

"They get harder. The worst natural disaster in the United States, occurring in the Gulf of Mexico in 1900, was a hurricane that claimed more than six thousand lives. Which city was practically destroyed by this monstrous storm?"

"Galveston, Texas," Ben said.

"Right."

"What's this about hurricanes?" Jill said. She came in from the hall in her red silk Hopi coat, barefooted, shoving her uncombed hair around with her fingertips. "Are we going to have a hurricane?"

"No, we're playing Trivia," Priscilla said.

"Oh. What's that?"

"It's a quiz game. How do you feel?"

"Awful. Can I have some tea?"

"Yes. Sit down and I'll make some fresh. Do you want a Danish?"

"No, thanks. Don't get up, Priss. I'll get it. Go on with your game." She went to the stove and turned the flame up under the kettle, turning to stare out of the window. "Raining cats and dogs. Did it go on all night?"

"All night," Ben said. "Doesn't look as if we'll get much swimming in today."

"Bother. Still, we've had our share, haven't we? What do you do when it rains here? Ben reads to you, you said."

"Sometimes," Priscilla said. "Or we watch television, or play records, or old movies on the VCR, or Trivia. We usually have a bout of Trivia on rainy mornings. Ben's a whiz at it."

"Is he really?" She brought the kettle to the table and filled the teapot.

"How did you learn so much, anyway, Ben? You never used to know all these things."

"I'm an incurable polymath," Ben said.

"Good Lord. I hope you're taking something for it."

"You'll need more tea in that."

"No, I'm going to have it very weak. I'm going to go very easy on the stimulants this morning." She sat down at the table and poured herself a cup of tea. "Tony's sleeping like a bloody log. I think he overdid it a bit last night."

"Didn't we all," Priscilla said. "I got up with an awful headache, but it's better now, since I've had tea."

"*I* shall be better when I've had this. I don't suppose you've had time to give Esther a ring?"

"Yes, I called as soon as I got up," Priscilla said. "I didn't talk to her because she was still sleeping, but her mother said she was much better."

"Oh, good," Jill said. "She'll be right. I'm sure of it." She put cream and sugar into her tea and stirred it, blinking sleepily. "Get on with your game," she said. "Just pretend I don't exist. I barely do, actually."

"No, you have to play too," Priscilla said.

"Me? I don't know my own name this morning."

"We'll play Trivia poker," Priscilla said. "You bet a dollar on every question. If you win, everybody pays you. If you don't, you pay whoever does."

"Good God, it's all so complicated."

"I'll keep score. Now, here's your first question: In 1915 the British liner *Lusitania* sank in the north Atlantic off Ireland causing one thousand one hundred ninety-eight deaths. What caused the ship to sink?"

"Struck an iceberg," Jill said.

"No, that's wrong. Do you know, Ben?"

"It was torpedoed by a German submarine," Ben said. "It was the *Titanic* that struck an iceberg."

"I shall lose my soul at this game," Jill said.

"OK, Ben, here's one for you: In 1556 more than eight hundred thousand people died as the result of an earthquake in China. What was unique about that disaster?"

"Greatest death toll of any earthquake in history," Ben said.

"Right. Now you, Jill. The worst epidemic in American history, in 1918, claimed a half million lives—ten times as many Americans as were killed in World War I. What was the name of the epidemic, and how many people died in it, worldwide?"

"I haven't a clue," Jill said. "What? How many?"

"Do you know, Ben?"

"It was the Spanish flu," Ben said. "But I'm not sure of the death toll. Over ten million, I would think."

"Twenty-one thousand six hundred fifty," Priscilla said.

"God's teeth," Jill said. "Quite a cheerful game this, isn't it? Just the thing for a rainy day, with a hangover."

"All right, here's another. What was the worst disaster of all times, in terms of human life?"

"You mean there are worse? Good God. I don't know. I don't think I want to know."

"It was the Black Death," Ben said. "Or that's what it was called. It was the bubonic plague, actually. It killed approximately seventy-five million people, half the people living at the time in Europe, Asia, Africa, and Iceland."

"Right. You ready, Jill?"

"I think perhaps I've had enough, you know," Jill said. "I shall shoot myself if we play this any longer. I wasn't too well to begin with."

"Here's Tony," Priscilla said. He stood in the doorway with a wan look, his shoulders bowed and his hands shoved deep into the pockets of his dressing gown. "Good morning," he said. "Figuratively speaking, of course."

"How do you feel?" Ben asked.

"How do I feel?" He looked out of the window mournfully. "I feel as if I'd had a very bad job of embalming done on me by an apprentice mortician."

"Oh, well, you must join in this jolly little game we're playing," Jill said. "It'll put you right in no time."

"What sort of game?"

"It's called Apocalypse. It's all about bubonic plague, and earthquakes, and hurricanes. Wonderfully exhilarating."

He looked at her bitterly. "I shall have tea and toast which I intend to sit here and consume very quietly, and if there's any unpleasantness of any kind I shall go back to bed immediately. Is that understood?"

"Perfectly," Priscilla said. "Sit down here and I'll get it for you. Do you like cinnamon?"

"Cinnamon?"

"On your toast."

"I don't know. It sounds a bit frivolous. I don't know that I'm up to frivolity this morning."

"All right, you can have it plain," Priscilla said. She got up and went to the counter and put two slices of bread into the toaster. Tony sat down with a groan and stared bleakly at Jill. "You're up very early," he said. "What accounts for this unseemly zeal?"

"I've been getting educated," Jill said.

"Oh? What have you learned?"

"All sorts of fascinating things. Do you know how many people died in the Black Death? Half the people in the world."

"Oh, yes? And the rest of us, I suppose, will be done in by the ruthless hospitality of North America."

"Don't be ungrateful," Jill said. "It's your own fault, if you don't know your own limitations."

"I know them very well," Tony said. "But I frequently get drunk before I reach them. Something a really thoughtful host would understand." He glanced reproachfully at Priscilla. She set a saucer in front of him with buttered toast on it and poured him a cup of tea.

"There," she said. "Will that atone?"

"It goes a long way toward it," he said. He sipped and murmured, "Aah. Have you heard how Esther's getting on?"

"Her mother says she was much better last night," Priscilla said. "She was still sleeping when I called."

"Very sensible," Tony said. "She feels a good deal better than I do, I'm sure of it. I would have done well to follow her example."

"I say, do you know what we ought to do this morning?" Jill said. "We ought to go and see her. After all, it's raining, so we can't go to the beach. Why don't we buy a basket of goodies and take them round? She'd like that."

"Oh, that would be fun!" Priscilla said. "That's a wonderful idea. We can go shopping in the village."

"Yes, right. Get her some cards, and fruits, and sweets. It would mean the world to her. Don't you think so, Tony?"

"Well, of course, it would mean putting clothes on," Tony said. "Brushing one's teeth, all that sort of thing. Still, I suppose you're right. It would mean a lot to her. Might just turn the scale at this point."

"Yes, we'll do that this morning," Priscilla said. "And it may have cleared up by noon; it's supposed to. So we'll have the afternoon to swim."

"I mean to say, it's a great deal better than sitting here playing this wretched game," Jill said. "We shall *all* be slitting our wrists if we keep that up."

"Ben?" Priscilla said. "You want to? Hey. Are you listening?"

"Sure. Fine," Ben said. "I think it's a great idea." The scent of last night's perfume had drifted out of Jill's hair and he had fallen into a reverie in which he saw her sitting cross-legged on the table of her flat in Hammersmith in an almost identical silk jacket with a gold dragon embroidered down her spine, her head tilted ceiling-wards, her eyes closed, drinking Watney's ale from a paper cup while the foam ran down her throat. He looked quickly and furtively at the twin papillae of her nipples against the smooth red silk and at her brown thighs and legs, bare below its hem. Did she bring that jacket on purpose? he wondered. The image in his mind changed to one of her standing in the shower stall, the water streaming down her naked belly.

"OK," Priscilla said. "That's what we'll do."

By eleven o'clock they were dressed, and when they stepped out of the car to walk up the village street, the rain had stopped and the gray of the overcast was breaking up. There were rags of clear, soft, cerulean blue among the clouds above the housetops and momentary patches of vivid sunlight on the street. The flag in front of the clinic snapped and snarled in the fresh cool breeze that smelled of salt and there were gulls sailing like kites above the harbor. Jill raised her head to look at them as they walked up the street.

"God, it's good to be alive," she said. "I feel a different person." She was walking with Ben behind Tony and Priscilla. Ben put his arm around her and clutched her hipbone, clenching the edge of it almost savagely with his fingertips. "*Oh,*" she said convulsively, and added instantly, "Oh, my, what a lovely day."

"Isn't it?" Priscilla said, turning back to look at her. "It makes you want to sing."

They came to a gift shop called The Pirate's Nest and stopped to look in through the window.

"I don't know if it's done here or not," Jill said, "but in England, if you're a houseguest it's customary to leave a little present of some sort for the servants. Do you think Esther would be offended if I did that?"

"Oh, no," Priscilla said. "She'd be delighted, I'm sure of it."

"Oh, good. I'll go in then, and have a look round, if you don't mind. I'd like to leave her a little gift of some kind."

They went into the shop and wandered along the aisles looking at trays of holiday mementos and seaside curios. The place was full of people with sunburned faces, banished from the beach by the rain, large restless men in plaid shorts and women with bare, scarlet shoulders idly fingering ash trays made of seashells, coral necklaces, mother-of-pearl photograph frames, and lamps with driftwood bases. Ben was ordinarily impatient in such places but it was a beguiling and unexpectedly poignant experience, he found, to shop with Jill. He watched her holding a huge pink conch shell to her ear and closing her eyes to listen rapturously;

trying on a pair of sunglasses with rhinestone-studded frames while she peered into a mirror with her teeth bared in a glaring, vapid smile; kissing a stuffed bear and turning to grin at him; lifting the lid of a cheap plastic music box and falling into a still-eyed reverie while it tinkled out a dwindling rendition of "I Believe in Yesterday." She dabbled among the shopworn wares with a kind of avid, unabated buoyancy, like a butterfly dancing over an autumn garden. A gloomy, salmon-colored gentleman in a Hawaiian shirt seemed to find the day redeemed when she opened a frayed paper fan, spread it across her face and fluttered her eyelashes at him over the edge of it. Ben rejoiced with him when, a few minutes later, she plucked a stick of cinnamon striped-candy from a jar, licked it surreptitiously, shuddered, and slipped it back into the jar. After twenty minutes or so, in the clothing section at the back of the shop, she discovered a pale pink cashmere cardigan with red coral buttons, which Priscilla agreed was practical and yet so nearly frivolous that Esther would never have bought it for herself. Jill asked to have it gift wrapped and said they would pick it up in an hour or so when they had finished marketing.

They went across the street to the Red and White market, a general store of an astonishing range of wares that catered to almost every possible need or whim of the vacationer, from camping gear and hardware to table delicacies. While Ben pushed a shopping cart along the aisles they filled it enthusiastically and recklessly with apples, navel oranges, bananas, kiwi fruit, a pineapple, a gigantic scarlet mango, a jar of crystallized ginger, a box of Liederkrantz, smoked oysters, anchovies, marmalade, chocolate-covered orange peel, and a jar of maraschino cherries, which Jill said were indispensable to anyone suffering from depression. "I lived on them for weeks when Olivier got married," she said. "It's all that got me through."

When their cart was full they went back across the street to the gift shop, bought a gigantic wicker picnic hamper and packed it with the groceries, the gift-wrapped cardigan, and a box of chocolates.

The Padgett house was a square cottage set on cinder blocks and covered with faded asbestos shingles which halfway from the ground had been painted a brilliant peacock blue. There was a screened porch at the front and a bed of petunias in the front yard enclosed by a white-painted automobile tire. Mrs. Padgett met them at the front door in a "good" dress, a cotton print from Woolworth's or Sears, Roebuck—the kind of dress Ben's mother had worn to town on Saturdays—with the collar fastened at the throat with a Victorian cameo brooch that was obviously a family treasure. She was gaunt and pale, with cloudy, wary eyes and a solemn, measured courtesy that seemed to mask immeasurable misgivings.

They sat in the parlor and drank coffee at a round oak table that smelled of furniture polish while Esther unwrapped her sweater and unpacked the hamper with a delight so genuine and huge and humble that it was wracking to see. Her injured arm was suspended in a sling fastened across the shoulder of a blue terry cloth bathrobe that was worn thin at the elbows, and her hair was teased out fluffily in a style weirdly reminiscent of film stars of the twenties. She could not hold the sweater to her breast to judge its size and appearance, so Jill did this for her, spreading the pink wool across Esther's chest to the tips of her shoulders while Esther peered down at it and murmured, "Oh, my goodness. That's the prettiest thing I ever did see. Oh, my goodness, I didn't expect anything like *this*. Look, Momma." She unpacked the hamper with shy solemnity, laying each article on the table as she removed it from the basket and making little birdlike titters of wonderment over it. "Look, Momma," she said, lifting a tin of anchovies or smoked oysters from the basket, "We'll be able to use *these*." Ben became increasingly depressed and filled with a vague sense of shame at the imposition of their visit and its condescension of these people. Did he really care how Esther was feeling? And if he didn't, what was the purpose of this visit, with its frivolous gifts, its disruption of their lives and privacy, its pretense of concern? It was a long time since he had been in the home of humble people and he did not like the experience. He did not like poverty or pain, and he did not like the way Mrs. Padgett reminded him of his mother or the thoughtful way in which she studied his clothing,

his Rolex wristwatch and his signet ring, as if she suspected his possession of them was as spurious as his charity. He felt a profound disposition
toward penitence in her presence and in her tiny house with the damp
smell of its shabby sofa and worn carpet.

No one else seemed to share his unease. Priscilla chattered animat-
edly with Mrs. Padgett about a recipe for crab soup that Esther had made
for them, Tony was amiably attentive, and Jill had entered into a murmuring
intimacy with Esther that wound up with the two of them retiring together
to the bedroom to re-style Esther's hair. There was a lot of chuckling and
muttering from the bedroom, and when they returned, with a flourish from
Jill as she swung open the door ("Ta-Taa!"), Ben was astonished at the transformation she had wrought in Esther's appearance. A kind of ragged,
harrowed Zazu Pitts had been converted into a delicate, elfin Mia Far-
row, her face framed by two soft sheaves of honey-colored hair, her lips
glowing with pale lavender lipstick like a pair of bougainvillea petals,
and Jill's silver-and-turquoise bracelet encircling a wrist whose delicacy Ben
had never before suspected.

"Oh, my goodness, it's *lovely*, Esther!" Priscilla said. "You should never
wear it any other way."

"You see, you didn't know how beautiful this girl *was*," Jill said. "There
are lots of chaps around here who don't, either."

"Absolutely smashing," Tony said. "You've got a whole new career as
a model, Esther."

Esther was enchanted with herself. She smiled shyly, patted her hair and
fondled the bracelet with her fingertips. "Look, Momma, isn't this pretty?"
she said.

"Yes, indeed it is," Mrs. Padgett said. "You look like one of them people on TV."

"You're to keep that bracelet," Jill said. "It's absolutely perfect with
your eyes. It was made for you."

"Oh, I couldn't," Esther said. "My goodness, you've given me enough
already."

"Don't be silly," Jill said. "No one else in the world has any right to wear it. It was a stroke of providence, my wearing it today."

When they left, Esther waved good-bye to them from the porch steps while her mother watched inscrutably through the screen door. The girl's face was glowing.

"Now, don't forget—I shall call you from New York on Tuesday," Jill called to her through the car window as they drove away. Esther nodded happily.

"My God, you've transformed her," Priscilla said. "Like Cinderella. I think you must be a fairy godmother."

"Never been called that," Jill said. "Been called all sorts of things."

"Circe, more often," Tony said.

"Only by very stupid people. I say, I'm beginning to feel as if I could use a hair of the dog. Anyone for a Bloody Mary?"

"That's not a bad idea," Ben said. "Why don't we go back to the house and have one while I put a lunch together? Then go down to the beach. Looks like it's going to be a very good afternoon."

"Well, I never thought I'd agree to it a couple of hours ago," Priscilla said. "But I must say it makes a certain amount of sense. What do you think, Tony?"

"Well, perhaps a glass of white wine and a bit of pâté," Tony said. "Might just make the difference."

They sat in the kitchen drinking Bloody Marys and white wine while Ben prepared a lunch of Smithfield ham and salmon sandwiches. He sliced the ham very thin, meticulously as a surgeon, laying the almost transparent slabs on very thin rye bread spread with Dijon mustard. He felt very happy making and wrapping his sandwiches in plastic film, listening to the pleasant, idle badinage of his wife and friends, engaged in his ritual of the picnic. Outside, the sand fumed tranquilly, the sea sparkled, the sky stood open and infinite, the endless summer had resumed. They took their luncheon hamper to the beach with their blankets and umbrellas and folding chairs and a cooler full of icy bottles of white wine, and sipped and nibbled and chuckled and let themselves be folded into the fathomless luxury of the white, still afternoon. The tide was out and the beach lay wide and pure in front of them, washed clean even of footsteps, with a gentle surf lapping at its lower edge bringing a ceaseless rumor of distant, fern-clothed jungle islands, cool streams, smiling, bare-breasted girls, the songs of green and scarlet birds among the vines. Ben basked in this fantasy for a while, and when the others appeared to have fallen asleep he got up and went down to the center of the beach to build a sand castle. He found a large clam shell and just above the low, foot-high bluff that marked the upper line of the last high tide he began to excavate the cellar. He tossed up the soft dry sand until he had reached the damp, close-packed level beneath, and then dug down another foot until water had begun to seep into the hole. Jill got up from her chair underneath the umbrella and came down to watch.

"What are you doing?" she said.

"Building a castle," Ben said.

"Can I help?"

"I don't know. Have you had any experience?"

"Oh, yes, I've built a lot of castles," she said. "Mostly in the air, of course. Not like yours. Are you sure you need another?"

"Those are just rough models," Ben said. "Not really my dream castle. This is going to be the real thing."

"Oh, something really grand. A sort of Xanadu, I suppose." Ben smiled at her. "Or Camelot, perhaps. Do you fancy yourself as Kubla Khan, or King Arthur?"

"You never know," Ben said. "You grow to fit your accomplishments. That's what makes it interesting."

"Aren't you doing it all wrong? What's that great hole you're digging?"

"This is the dungeon," Ben said. "It's where I'm going to keep prisoners, and torture people. You can't have a castle without a dungeon. Haven't you been in the Tower of London?"

"You're digging it jolly deep. Are you expecting a lot of them?"

"I have a lot of enemies," Ben said.

"Have you? I wouldn't have thought that. It seems to me you're infinitely admired."

"Are you going to work, or criticize?" He scowled at her. "I ought to warn you, the first people who go into the dungeon will be the critics."

"Well, I won't risk that. What shall I do?"

"We need some sticks, for beams and floorboards. You can go find some sticks."

"Right." She went off along the beach, stooping to gather up small pieces of driftwood. When she came back with a handful of them Ben had finished excavating the dungeon. There was now an inch of water in the bottom. "Looks as if you had a moisture problem in the basement," Jill said.

"That's OK. They're not supposed to be comfortable down there. Let's have the sticks."

She handed her bundle of sticks to him. He laid several of them across the hole to form a floor and then sprinkled sand on them and patted it down firmly with a piece of flat lath. He left a small hole in the floor and laid a clam shell on top of it for a trapdoor.

"I suppose that's where you toss them down food," she said. "Mouldy bread and muffins."

"That's right," Ben said. "You're beginning to understand the basic principles of castle building."

"I know a good deal about castles. I was a great castle-goer once. There was one I used to haunt when I was a girl. I suppose you don't remember that."

"No. How should I remember? I didn't know you when you were a girl." She smiled an odd, crooked smile at him.

"You can help with the walls if you like," Ben said. "Make them good and thick at the bottom, or they'll collapse. We want them about two feet high."

They poured the damp sand that Ben had excavated around the

circumference of the hole and patted it flat and firm with their sticks. They worked seriously and silently, pausing occasionally to study their progress.

"You're doing very well," Ben said. "I think you have an instinct for it."

"Perhaps I have. It's the very best way of doing anything, by instinct. Did you know that the great cathedrals of Europe were built by men who were almost entirely illiterate? They knew nothing whatever about mathematics or engineering, in the modern sense. They couldn't have added up the grocery bill, and yet they built these great stone temples flawlessly, with flying buttresses and cross-vaulted domes and transepts, knowing exactly how much weight of stone they'd bear and how well they'd stand up under snow and rain and wind, every sort of weather. And out of all the hundreds of them built, only two collapsed, I think, in all of Europe. I call that marvelous. I suppose you knew that. You seem to know almost everything."

"I knew they did it," Ben said. "But I don't know how."

"Oh, I think you do. How did you know how to play Richard, or Cyrano?"

"I can't remember."

"Rubbish. You don't forget that sort of thing, and you don't learn it. Understanding stone is very much like understanding language, I suppose. Of course, some people who understand it never build cathedrals."

"This isn't a cathedral," Ben said. "It's a castle."

"I know that very well, but the principles of masonry still apply. Even if you're building a privy. Of course you wouldn't get a master builder to do that sort of thing."

She poured and patted the sand vigorously. Ben stretched out and propped himself on his elbow for a moment to watch her working. She rubbed her nose with the heel of her sandy palm and then blew sand from the tip of her nose, sticking out her lower lip.

"What are you looking at?" she said after a moment.

"You. I like to watch you make things. You look very pretty. I'd like to just sit quietly in a chair and watch you write, sometime."

"Oh, would you. Well, you'd have to be pretty nimble to do that. I generally tramp about the place with a cup of coffee in one hand and a cigarette in the other, muttering like a madwoman. It's an awful business, writing. Far worse than acting."

"But you enjoy it." She didn't answer this. "Don't you?"

"You wouldn't say so if you saw me." She picked up her stick and rapped at the wall. "Come on, now. You're loafing. We've got another foot to go, at least."

They went on pouring sandy mortar and patting it flat with their makeshift trowels until the walls reached almost to the level of their eyes as they were sitting.

"I think that's high enough," Ben said. "We've got to do the ramparts now. This is very tricky. We've got make a walkway all the way around the inside of the wall, where the knights stand to defend the place, and then build up a parapet in front of it and cut slots in it. Crenelations, they're called."

"Yes, I know that," Jill said. "What they shoot their arrows through. I can do them very well."

She began to construct a battlement around her side of the castle, slicing away half the thickness of the top edge of the wall and patting flat the inner side to form a circular rampart. She very carefully cut slots into the parapet and patted them square with her wooden trowel to form arrow ports. She worked with a look of total absorption, pausing occasionally to rake back her hanging hair with her fingertips. Ben began to work on his side of the well, bending forward with the sun on his back and the wash of the surf below them. He felt very happy.

"How's it coming?" Priscilla called from the shadow of the umbrella.

"Jolly well," Jill said. "You're not to see it, though, til it's finished."

A boy and girl who had been wandering along the edge of the water with a bucket caught sight of them and ran up the beach to watch. The girl was six or seven and her brother a year or two older. He wore a T-shirt with a drawing of a baseball player lithographed on it. Under the drawing was printed:

JIM PALMER, BALTIMORE ORIOLES

Cy Young Award Winner
1973–75–76

A King of the Diamond

The two children stood silently, yellow-haired and solemn-eyed, their slender arms hanging.

"You making a castle?" the boy said.

"Yes. How's it look?" Jill said.

"OK. It really looks like a real one. What's down there in the hole?"

"That's the dungeon," Jill said. "That's where we put our enemies."

"Who are your enemies?"

"Oh, all sorts of people. One never lacks for enemies. The Porfendooflers, mainly."

"The what?"

"The Porfendooflers. These dreadful great brutes who come across the border and try to steal our muffins and ginger beer and sweet buns. They want to make us serve them and do all their work and learn to speak their language and worship Zog."

"Who's Zog?"

"He's this great hairy beast who looks just like them, only worse. And of course we don't want to have anything to do with them."

"I never heard of the Porfendooflers," the boy said.

"Haven't you? Well, perhaps you know them by some other name. They're apt to call themselves all sorts of things. What have you got in that pail?"

"Sand fleas," the boy said.

"Sand fleas? Let's have a look at them." He held the pail toward her and she leaned forward, peering into it. "Good Lord, they're not sand fleas at all, they're Porfendooflers. Where did you get them?"

"Down there." He pointed to the wet sand at the water's edge. "They go down in the sand."

"Yes, they do that," Jill said. "Try to bury themselves, so you won't find them. How many legs have they got?"

The boy held the bucket up close to his face and poked inside of it with a fingertip, counting. "Fourteen," he said.

"Fourteen? Well, there you are. They're Porfendooflers, no question about it. The very worst sort."

"You want to put them in the dungeon?"

"Oh, yes, we'll have to. Jolly good thing you caught them. Pop them right down there in that hole."

She lifted the clamshell trapdoor. The boy squatted down beside the castle and plucked the sand fleas one at a time out of the bucket in his curled fingers, dropping them through the hole in the castle floor.

"That's it," Jill said. "They'll make no trouble down there."

"He put the porfendooflers in the dungeon," the little girl said.

"Yes. Jolly good thing, too. That many less of them to worry about." She began to sprinkle sand in the center of the circle enclosed by the castle wall and tamp it down firm with her palm. "Do you know what I'm making now?"

"No, what?" the boy said.

"This is called the keep. It's where the people live inside the castle. They keep all their supplies here, food and weapons and so on, and they have their bedrooms here, and the kitchen, and the sitting room, where they have tea every afternoon. Every castle has a keep in the middle of it. Did you know that?"

"No," the boy said. "How come you know so much about castles?"

"Because I come from England, where we have lots of castles. Hundreds of them."

"Have you ever been in one? A real one?"

"Oh, yes, lots of times. Shall I tell you about my favorite one?"

"What?"

"It's called Stokesay, and it's very near a town called Shrewsbury, where I used to live. A lovely little castle, just like the ones in my picture book when I was a little girl. Very much like this one, actually. I used to go out

there every Sunday afternoon when the weather was fine and stand on
the ramparts—these are the ramparts, this part here—and look out across
the marches into Wales. And do you know what? If you stand very still
and listen very carefully, you can hear the knights riding in across the fields
from battle with their armor clinking and the leather squeaking on their
saddles. I used to pretend sometimes that I was a lady who lived in the
castle and I was waiting for my knight to come riding back from battle.
Let me show you." She reached out and took the hand of the little girl,
spreading out the two forefingers like legs and setting their tips on the sandy
parapet. "There now, that's just the way I'd look. I'd stand there looking out
across the marches for the glint of sunlight on his shield and the tossing
of plumes on his helmet."

"Did you see him?" the little girl asked.

"No, he never came back. He was killed in battle. I waited and waited,
until I could wait no more. And then I made a song about it, because that's
what you do when your knight is killed in battle. Would you like to hear
it?"

"Yeah, sing it," the boy said. He crouched down on the sand with his
mouth open. Jill clasped her knees and hung her head mournfully, her
hair shining in the afternoon light:

Ye highlands and ye lowlands,
O, where hae ye been?
They hae slain the Earl o' Moray,
And laid him on the green.

He was a braw gallant,
And he rade at the ring;
And the bonny Earl o' Moray,
He might hae been a king.

'O lang will his lady look
Frae the castle doon,

Ere she see the Earl o' Moray
Come ridin' through the toon.

The children sat silently for a moment, their eyes wandering.

"Maybe you'll see him *some* day," the little girl said. "Maybe if you go back there and watch, he'll come back some day."

"Oh, I don't think so," Jill said. "But I like to think he died fighting bravely and well."

"That's a neat song," the boy said.

"Did you like it? It's very sad, isn't it?"

"Yeah, but it's neat. Did you really write it?"

"No, I fibbed about that. It's a very old song, really."

"I thought so. It sounds like it was written way back in those old ancient times. It sounds like it really happened." He looked at the castle. "It's a neat castle, too. What are you going to do next?"

"Well, we've got to finish the keep, and put a flag up, and then we've got to dig the moat."

"That's the river, like, that goes around it, right?"

"That's right. You know about castles, do you?"

"I used to have a knight suit," he said. "It was just plastic, but it was cool. It had a helmet and shield and armor and a sword and everything. We used to have these battles."

"I hope you didn't get killed," Jill said.

"Sometimes I would. Sometimes I'd get killed and sometimes the other guys would."

"Oh, dear. And did your lady mourn for you?"

He dropped his head and grinned bashfully. "Nah."

The little girl put the tips of her fingers on the sand rampart again and turned the back of her hand toward the sea. "I'm watching for my knight," she said. "There he is! I can see him! I'm waving to him. Look." She wiggled her thumb.

"So you are," Jill said. "Oh, I'm so glad he's come back. What will you do now? Will you marry him?"

"Yes, we're going to get married and have seventeen children."

"Seventeen? Good Lord. You'll need a larger castle. You'll have to build another wing."

"She's always saying that kind of dumb stuff," the boy said. "She wants to get married all the time."

"Well, so she should," Jill said. "Don't you?"

"Nah, I'm never going to get married." He looked at her furtively. "Are you guys married?"

"No, we're not," Jill said. "We're just friends."

"But you like to *play* together," the little girl said.

"Yes, we do. We like playing together. Come along, now. If you're going to help with this moat we've got to get cracking."

"I've got a shell here you can dig with," Ben said. "It's easier when you've got a shell."

"OK," the boy said. "Where should I dig it?"

"Oh, a couple of feet away from the wall, at least. We have to have room to work."

"OK. About here?"

"Yes, that's right. Dig it good and deep, mind."

He took the shell and began to dig furiously, crouching like a dog on all fours and throwing the excavated dirt back between his legs.

"My, you're a very fast digger," Jill said.

"I'm going to dig a moat too," the little girl said. She took the empty pail, sat down and began scooping up dry sand and tossing it recklessly in all directions.

"Hey, you've got to dig it over here, Aggie," the boy said. "That's no good, way over there."

"I'm going to dig mine over here," Aggie said. "This is a better place."

"It's supposed to be around the *castle*, for gosh sakes," the boy said. "Come on, dig it around the *castle*."

"Yours can be around the castle," she said. "Mine's going to be over here." She dug happily, chanting to herself, "Bubble bees, bubble bees, bubble bees."

The boy grinned apologetically at Jill. "She means bumble bees. She always says bubble bees."

"Well, perhaps there are bubble bees," Jill said. "I've seen bees that looked *very* bubbly. Come along, now. Get on with the moat. Don't worry about Aggie."

"She never puts stuff in the right place," the boy said. "Look where she's putting it."

"Well, that's all right. We'll have two moats. All the better, to keep the porfendooflers out."

They worked silently for a while, the boy digging, Ben cutting crenelations into the ramparts, Jill pouring moist sand into the yard to build up a minaret for the keep. Below them the wash of the surf grew louder as the tide came in, and the lacy edge of each flat pane of water that raced up the beach left an arch of delicate foam higher on the sand.

"I think, you know, it might have been a good idea to build it a bit higher up," Jill said. "I have an idea we're going to get inundated."

"No, we won't," Ben said. "It won't come this high. This is the high tide mark."

"I almost finished," the boy said. "Hey, look, there's water coming in the bottom."

"Good," Jill said. "It's got to have water in it, you know, so they can't get across."

"We could put alligators in it," the boy said. "Then they'd get all eated up when they fell in."

"Now there's a very good idea," Jill said. "We'll have to find some alligators."

"Mine's going to have *fishes* in it," Aggie said. "You know what kind of fishes mine's going to have in it?"

"No, what kind, love?"

"*Pickle* fishes!" Aggie said. She burst into a spasm of giggles and thrust her face into Jill's, mashing their noses together. "*Pickle* fishes!"

"Oh, pickle fishes," Jill said. "Yes, I've heard of them. They're sort of green and lumpy, aren't they?"

"No. They're *purple*, and *prickly*!"

"Come on, don't be so dumb," her brother said. "Why do you have to be so dumb all the time?"

"She's not dumb at all," Jill said. "She knows all about bubble bees and pickle fishes, which is more than many people know."

The boy sat back and gazed at Jill for a moment, his eyes roving from her face to the sand and back again. "Are you guys going to get married?" he said.

"No, we can't very well do that," Jill said. "Because we're married already, you see. To other people."

"Who?"

"Those people just over there, under the umbrella."

The boy turned and looked up the beach to where Priscilla and Tony sat in the shade of the umbrella.

"Those guys right there?"

"Yes. What do you think of them?"

"They're OK." He poked the sand with his toe several times. "Hey, why don't you tell us another story about what you used to do?" he said. "Like when you used to go to that castle and all."

"Sing us another song!" Aggie said.

"Yeah, sing us another song."

"All right, I'll sing you another song. A very old one, that was written by William Shakespeare. Do you know who he was?"

"He wrote plays," the boy said.

"That's right. Plays and poems and songs, all sorts of things. Well, this is a song he wrote over four hundred years ago." She put down her stick and clasped her knees with her elbows, staring off across the water.

Sigh no more, ladies, sigh no more.
Men were deceivers ever.
One foot in sea and one on shore,
To one thing constant never.

Then sigh not so, but let them go,
And be you blithe and bonny,
Converting all your sounds of woe
Into, Hey, nonny, nonny.

"They're all real sad," Aggie said.

"They are rather sad, yes. But then, life has some rather sad moments, doesn't it? Especially when you're in love."

"I'm never going to be in love," the boy said.

"Oh, aren't you? Why?"

"I think it's dumb. All people do is sit around and cry." He picked up a handful of sand and flung it into the air. "My other sister, Mary, all she does it sit around and mope all the time about her dumb boyfriend. She looks like a tomato most of the time. Yuk."

"Like a tomato?"

"Yeah, her nose is red all the time. Boy, I'd rather be dead. I'm never going to fall in love with *anybody,* even if I live to be a hundred and fifty million years old."

"Oh, I don't believe that for a moment," Jill said. She reached out and clenched his hair gently. "Now you just look me in the eye and tell me that."

He blushed furiously and sat with his head hanging.

"I shan't let you put the flag on top of my castle if you talk like that. Not if you don't believe in love."

"You want to put a flag on it?" he murmured, his eyes downcast.

"Yes, I do, very much. I don't know what we're going to use, though."

"You could use a piece of my T-shirt," he said.

"Oh, we don't want to tear your T-shirt. That would never do."

"It's got this tag thing on it," he said. "You could use that." He bowed his head forward, plucking up the back of his T-shirt and pushing out the tag with his thumb. "This thing here. Look."

"What does it say?" Jill said. She held the tag between her thumb and fingertip and peered at it. "'Diamond King Specialties. Made in USA.' Oh, that's very nice. You don't mind?"

"Nah. It doesn't do any good."

"Well, we'll use that, then." She ripped off the tag with her fingernails and he sat up, grinning. "Now we'll have to have a little stick, for a flag-pole."

"Here's one," the boy said. He picked up one of the sticks from the pile she had gathered.

"Oh, good. Will you just make a little slit in it, at the top? So we can stick the flag in?"

"OK. Neat." He sliced the twig at the top with his thumbnail and handed it to her. Jill slipped the edge of the cotton tag into the slit and stuck the twig into the top of the keep.

"There, that's perfect," she said. "It's the castle of the Diamond King. That sounds very grand, doesn't it?"

"We got a flag!" Aggie said.

"Yes. It's lovely, isn't it?"

"The Castle of the Diamond King," the little girl murmured. "That's where he lives, the Diamond King."

"Yes, that's where he lives."

A young woman in a blue bathing suit stood up on the beach a hundred yards away and shouted to the children, "Larry! Aggie! Come on back now. We're going up to the house!" She waved her arm above her head as she called to them. The boy got up and picked up the red pail from the sand. "We've got to go," he said. "Come on, Aggie." She leapt up and ran along the beach toward her mother. "So long, you guys."

"So long," Ben said. "Thanks for helping."

"Yes," Jill said. "You were a very great help indeed."

He turned and ran after his sister through the soft sand. Jill watched him for a moment and then lowered her eyes to the castle. "Well," she said. "There's your castle. Will it do?"

"It's not bad," Ben said. "A little gloomy maybe. But the furniture will liven it up."

"Yes, one or two Renoirs, and a grand piano."

He leaned back on his elbows and looked at her. "You like kids, don't you?"

"Yes, I do, rather."

"I never knew that."

"Oh, didn't you?" She gazed at him for a moment and then shifted her eyes to the castle with a faint, wry smile.

"No. I never knew all that stuff about Stokesay Castle, either. Were you making that up?"

"No, it's quite true."

"You never told me that."

"Oh, yes, I did. Something else you've forgotten. You've forgotten quite a bit, evidently. Or perhaps you were asleep. You had a way of dropping off to sleep when we'd had a bit of fun. I'm not sure you heard half the things I told you. Just as well, perhaps."

He looked off at the sea. Priscilla got up from her chair and came down the beach to where they were sitting.

"Is it done?" she asked.

"All finished," Jill said. "We've got the flag up, you see."

"I see you have." She knelt down and examined the castle, touching the little flag with her fingertip. "It's a wonderful castle. It has a dungeon and everything."

"It is rather splendid, isn't it?" Jill said. She stared at the sandy white walls that were already whitening and eroding in the sun, and quoted in a singsong voice, like a child reciting:

Safe upon the solid rocks
The ugly houses stand.
Come and see my shining palace,
Built upon the sand.

"Whose is that?" Priscilla asked.

"Your New England lady. What's her name? Edna Millay."

"Oh, that's right. 'Figs from Thistles.'"

"Yes, I think that's it. Jolly clever, that woman was."

Tony came plodding through the sand toward them. "Well, let's have a look at this architectural wonder," he said. "Oh, yes, very impressive. I hope you've built it far enough up the strand. All for naught, if you haven't."

"Oh, it'll be safe here," Ben said. "Nothing to worry about."

"Well, you must be worn out from all this construction work," Priscilla said. "I think you'd better come have a shower and a martini." She looked at her watch. "It's five already."

"Is it really?" Jill said. "Good Lord, where does the time go, when you're busy having fun?"

When they got back to the house the phone was ringing. Ben dropped the wet towels he was carrying on the kitchen floor and took it from the cradle on the wall.

"Hello?"

A man with a British accent said, "Is this the Oakshaw residence?"

"Yes."

"Is Miss Davenport there?"

"Yes, hold on." He held the phone out to Jill. "It's for you."

"Oh, Lord," she said. "I suppose there's a hassle about something." She draped the towel across her arm and took the phone from him. "Hallo. Jill here. Oh, hello, Nathan." She listened for a moment, scowling. "Well, I re-did those before I left. Do you mean to say you haven't been rehearsing them? Too academic? What a bloody lot of rubbish! I've never written anything academic in my life. Well, he's a ruddy idiot, and he's got a tin ear, anyway." She raised her eyes to Ben and lifted her brows lugubriously. "Oh, he wants to cut, as well, does he? Rot, there was no fidgeting in London. Well, look here, Nathan, I'm having a perfectly heavenly time down here, and I think it's a beastly lot of bother about nothing. What difference is six minutes going to make? Well, let them *get* bloody well fidgety, they've nothing all that important to do, anyway. Oh, it's Buchholtz who's going on about it, is it? I ought to have known we'd have trouble with him. We shouldn't have brought him over, at all." She sighed heavily and held out her hand to Tony, scrabbling desperately with her fingers in the air. Tony poured a Bloody Mary into a kitchen tumbler from the thermos and handed it to her. She gulped at it, holding the phone to her ear and frowning, first at Ben, then at Priscilla. "Tomorrow? No, that's absurd, I couldn't possibly get back tomorrow. Well, it'd be an awful bind, if I could do it at all. I've no idea what the plane schedules are or where the nearest airport is. We're miles from anywhere down here. Well, I'll have to see. I'll do my best, yes. I'll ring you back this evening, where will you be? Yes, I've got it somewhere. Right. Well, try not to have a hemorrhage. I'll do the best I can. Ta, love." She hung up the phone and made a wry face. "Well, I've got to get back tomorrow, it seems. Buchholtz doesn't like the new lines I've given Ian. They're too academic, he says."

"Oh, no," Priscilla said. "That's awful!"

"Yes, it is. What the devil does he know about academics? He dropped out of school when he was six."

"Can't you phone them in?" Tony said.

"Oh, well, they want to cut six minutes out of the last act, anyway. Buchholtz says it's running over. They won't stand for it in New York, he says."

"Bloody fool," Tony said.

"Yes, he is. And we're having such a marvelous time here. Still, that's the theatre for you, isn't it?"

"I wouldn't let them cut a *minute* out of your play," Priscilla said. "I think it's sacrilege."

"Oh, well, I don't know about sacrilege, but it does seem a bit idiotic. What are they so bloody fidgety about in New York, anyway?"

"Very short attention span," Tony said. "I noticed that, when I was there last."

"Do you think we can get a plane out of here tomorrow?" Jill asked.

"Well, there's no problem about that," Ben said. "If you absolutely have to go, I can have the plane sent down. I often use it myself if I'm coming down for a weekend. But it's a terrible disappointment."

"Do you mean to say you've got your own plane?"

"It's the company's, theoretically. We get a tax write-off, that way, as a business expense. But it's at my disposal."

"Crikey. Can you fly it yourself?"

"I can, yes; I have a license. But we have a company pilot to get people to conferences and things. He could have it down here tomorrow, if you like. I don't think there's anything scheduled this week."

"Where would he land it? Is there an airport here?"

"Yes, there's a strip just up at Frisco, only fifteen minutes away. It's long enough for a Learjet, which is what we've got. You don't think you could put them off?"

"Lord, I don't think so. Buchholtz has come over. He's one of the producers, and he's evidently having a baby about it. Awful man."

"OK. I'll give him a call. What time do you want him?"

"Well, I suppose I should leave by ten. Buchholtz wants to have a meeting at one. You sure it won't be a lot of trouble?"

"Not a bit," Ben said. "Go have your shower and I'll give him a call."

While they showered and dressed, he went into the study and called his office. "Margo," he said to his secretary, "I'm going to need the plane down here by ten o'clock tomorrow morning. Is there anything scheduled?"

"I don't think so," she said. "Mark was going to New York, but he's put it off til Monday. Are you coming back?"

"No, but my guests have to leave a couple of days early. Jill's got some doctoring to do on the play."

"I'll call Max. You want him by ten?"

"Yes. Tell him we'll meet him up at Frisco. He should be fueled and cleared to Dulles. Give me a call, will you?"

"Yes, sir. Are you at the house?"

"Yes."

"I'll get back to you within the hour."

"Thanks, Margo."

He hung up the phone and went out to the bar to mix drinks. A feeling of sorrow came over him while he mixed the martinis. Outside, the sun had fallen low into the sky above the sound and the shadows of the house and the dunes lay seaward on the sand, long and soft in the late light. The sea was calm and gray and an evening breeze had begun to send sand sprinkling along the beach, blunting the footprints and gathering into drifts behind the shells and flotsam. The quality of everything had changed; the blazing, fervent world had become abandoned, enervated, a place of drifting sand and smothered footprints and lengthening shadows. He realized suddenly that the delight he had felt burning in him all week was fading like the sunlight, and something close to desolation suffused him like a cold draft seeping through a blanket. Priscilla came out to the bar and stood with her back to him, elbows out, her hands holding the two ends of a necklace behind her neck.

"I can't get this," she said. "Will you do it for me?"

"OK."

He took the two parts of the clasp from her fingertips and fastened them together.

"It's pretty."

"Isn't it? It was so sweet of Jill to give it to me. Did you get fixed up about the plane?"

"Yes. Max is bringing it down tomorrow at ten o'clock."

"It's a pity they have to leave. I wanted to take them over to see the play tomorrow night."

"Maybe they'd like to go tonight."

"I don't know if there's time." She looked at her wristwatch. "It's nearly six already."

"Are you ready for drinks?"

"Yes. Shall we sit in front?"

"I think so. It'll be hot in back."

He followed her onto the deck with the tray of drinks and set it down on the tile table. Jill and Tony had not come out yet. He sat beside Priscilla in a sling chair and watched the light fading on the sea. Far out, there were lanes of smooth dark gray on the silver water. A gull went over in a slow, plodding flight, beating the still air. The tide was coming in, the long swells bulging shoreward, smooth and gilded in the evening light. It seemed to him like autumn.

"Did you hear that woman in the gift shop this morning?" Priscilla said. "The one in the red dress? She had a Jersey accent."

"No, I didn't notice her."

"There are more people from up north down here every year. I suppose it's because the beaches are getting so polluted up there."

"Terrible," Ben said. "They find syringes, and lab vials, and raw sewage, even blood bags from laboratories. Some of them contaminated with AIDS. God, it's awful."

"Even Ocean City is getting it," Priscilla said. "There were syringes on the beach there this spring. I suppose this is one of the last clean places left in America. God, I hope it stays that way. At least as long as we live."

Tony slid open the glass door and he and Jill came out onto the deck.

"Sorry we've been so long," Jill said. "I had a tub bath, and I fell asleep. In the tub, mind you. Haven't you started? Oh, you should have."

"No hurry," Ben said. He stood up and handed them drinks from the tray, holding his own at eye level. "Here's to England," he said, "and all that she's given us. Wisdom, language, law, and *Thoughts of Love*."

"Hear, hear," Priscilla said.

"And here's to America," Jill said. "Our lost paradise."

"It isn't lost entirely," Priscilla said. "You're always welcome to reclaim this little corner of it."

"How very kind of you," Tony said. "You must come and see us, in London, you know, when you're there next."

"Yes, we will," Priscilla said. "We won't lose touch again."

"How did you make out, about the plane?" Jill asked.

"All set," Ben said. "Our man will be here at ten. You'll be back in your hotel room by noon."

"Oh, thanks, Ben. That's good of you. I *suppose* I should thank you, although it's awful to think we've only a day left. Less than a day. Still, we've had a jolly good innings, haven't we?"

"What would you like to do this evening?" Priscilla asked. "There's a play about the Croatan settlement called *The Lost Colony* that's done every evening at Manteo. They do it outdoors, and it's really quite good."

"Sounds jolly interesting. Would there be time?"

"We might just make it. It starts at eight thirty."

"Oh, well, let's not rush. It's our last evening, and I don't feel like dashing about. Do you, Tony?"

"All for loafing, myself," Tony said. "We shall have enough of the theatre, next week."

"Yes, that's what I say. Let's just loaf and invite our souls. Would you mind that?"

"There's nothing I'd like better," Priscilla said. She laughed. "We've seen it half a dozen times, anyway. I just thought I'd give you the choice between culture and decadence."

"Oh, well, you never want to give me a choice like that. It's decadence every time, with me. How's the castle holding up?" She got up and went to the railing, carrying her glass. "Can you still see it? Yes, there it is." She pointed out across the sand to where the castle stood, casting a long shadow in the evening light. "It seems to be holding up."

"So it is," Tony said. "Tide's getting jolly close to it, though. I don't think it'll last through the night."

"You want to bet?" Ben said. "Ten dollars says it will." He felt an absurd resentment of Tony's languid, supercilious air. It seemed to him pointedly derogatory, an aspersion on his own competence or judgment. He was suddenly far less sure than he had been a day ago that the man was unaware of what had happened in the shower room. There was something coolly, amusedly provocative in his manner, as if he were secretly enjoying the knowledge of Ben's reckless impropriety. Could Jill possibly have told him of it? Was there an intimacy between them that included sharing the knowledge of each other's sexual exploits? Had they possibly laughed together about Ben's frenzied assault upon her? It was a monstrous and humiliating idea, but Tony's faint, sardonic smile seemed to suggest its possibility.

"I don't know, old chap," Tony said. "Looks a bit dicey to me. Don't want to take your money too. Not on top of everything else. I'll tell you what: let's have a couple of drinks, and if it's still up by that time, you must take us out to dinner tonight."

"But then you lose, even if you're right," Priscilla said. "You're betting against yourself. That's not fair."

"Oh, well, prophets always lose, don't they? No profit in being a prophet. But at least it's only the price of a meal. Not my head, like Cassandra."

"I don't think you have to worry about it," Ben said.

"Still, we'd like to," Tony said. "Owe you something in return for your really extraordinary hospitality. Don't we, Jill?"

"Absolutely," Jill said. "I've never had such affection lavished on me by a host. Got to show our gratitude in some way. Now you're not to fuss."

"OK," Ben said. "But only if the castle falls."

"Right," Tony said. "I give it another twenty minutes. Not more. That last wave was very close."

Ben sat and watched in a kind of dogged, surly suspense. It had become very important to him that the castle should survive, that Tony's skepticism should be exposed as idle, perhaps malicious irony. He recognized this as being ridiculous, but the frivolous dissent had hardened, it seemed to him, into a subtle, unspoken conflict between them. He didn't know about what, exactly. Principle, pride, authority perhaps; maybe nothing more than an expression of his disappointment and Tony's triumph in the fact that Jill was leaving. After all, the man was bearing her away tomorrow, to New York, to London, to Yugoslavia, to some sunny, Edenic, uninterrupted future that Ben would never know. It seemed insufferable to him that he could not purchase that prerogative as he purchased a Renoir or a Pollock. Reclaim it, as a matter of fact, not purchase it. This plump, condescending pedant had won it by default, as it were, certainly not by grace or wit or passion. He felt the need to make this clear in some way.

"Oh, goodness!" Priscilla said. "That was close." She got up and went to the railing to stand beside Jill.

"Doesn't look too good, old chap," Tony said. He sipped at his martini nonchalantly. Ben stared silently.

"This castle in Shropshire where I used to go as a girl, Stokesay," Jill said, "it had what was called a Priest's Room in it, in the keep. It was a sealed room where a priest was kept in hiding for the purpose of saying clandestine masses. It was a common practice in the Reformation. They were nominally Protestants, of course, because they didn't want to risk their necks by offending Henry; but they didn't want to risk their souls, either. So they kept a priest around, just as insurance. It was the prudent thing to do, I suppose: cover all their bets. But it always troubled me, even as a child: to think that in all those castles, all over England, there was always that secret little cell hidden away in the heart of them. I was never quite sure what they kept walled up in there—apostasy, or faith."

"It's a very common custom," Tony said. "Still practised widely, I believe." He got up and went to the railing, standing beside Jill. "How's it going, down there?"

"Oh, there goes the bluff!" Jill said. "That last wave just washed up against it. It's starting to crumble."

"Oh, no!" Priscilla said. "This is very tragic. Ben, look."

Ben carried his drink to the railing and stood looking down across the sand. The bluff on which the castle stood had begun to crumble, as Jill said, and the moat was caving in.

"I'm afraid you're for it, old man," Tony said.

"We'll see," Ben said.

"I think I need another drink," Priscilla said. "I want to be prepared for this."

"Jill?"

"Yes, I'll have a drop."

Ben took their glasses to the table and refilled them from the martini pitcher. When he brought them back to the railing and put the glass in Jill's hand his fingers touched hers as they encircled the stem. He held them for a moment, pressed to the stem.

"Thank you," she said.

"You're welcome." He turned to Tony. "Tony, how are you doing?"

"I'm doing very well indeed," Tony said.

A breaker crashed onto the shore with a massive, concussive sound, like the collapsing of a mountain.

"Oh, my, that was a big one," Priscilla said.

Ben looked across the beach and saw the shallow pane of water run swiftly up the sand, sweeping over the crumbled edge of the bluff in a frothing torrent, flooding the moat and washing around the castle wall.

"Oh, there it goes!" Priscilla cried. The castle slumped seaward, its walls dissolving into mud, the tiny white flag falling slowly atop the sinking spire of the keep. "What a pity! Oh, I'm sorry, Ben."

"Bad luck," Tony said. "Still, you put up a jolly good show." He raised his glass. "'Sic transit gloria mundi.'"

Ben took his money clip out of his pocket, detached a ten dollar bill from it and laid the bill on the top railing.

"No, no," Tony said. "We're to take you to dinner. Those were the terms." He plucked the bill from the railing with his thumb and fingertip and held it out to Ben. "I won't profit by any man's loss."

"Or I by any man's charity," Ben said.

"Ah," Tony said. He raised his eyebrows whimsically. "Then we'll give it to the wind." He opened his fingers and let the bill flutter away from the deck, watching while it blew away across the sand.

Jill smiled, licked a fingertip, and smoothed her eyebrows with it. "I think we should decide where to eat," she said. "Have you a favorite place?"

"I think *you* should decide," Priscilla said. "After all, you only have one more night with us. What sort of food would you like?"

"Something thoroughly American," Jill said. "What's the most typically American thing you can think of?"

"A cookout, I suppose," Priscilla said. "Hamburgers on a grill."

"That sounds jolly good. Ben, what's your idea?"

"If you want to be really aboriginal, a weenie roast. Hot dogs cooked on a stick over a bonfire. And corn ears roasted in the coals. And burnt marshmallows."

"A bonfire!" Jill cried. "Oh, that's absolutely wizard! Can we build one on the beach?"

"If you like," Priscilla said. "We do, sometimes, when we have a swim at night."

"It sounds divine. What do we have to do?"

"Gather driftwood," Ben said. "I don't know if we'd find enough of it. There's not much on the beach right now. Of course we could take down some fireplace logs."

"Oh, let's do that. It's a marvelous idea. Far more exciting than sitting in some stuffy restaurant. Don't you think, Tony?"

"Sounds quite a lark," Tony said. "Something we shan't be able to do in New York."

"No, I should think not. A weenie roast. Is that what you call them? Weenies?"

"That's right," Ben said. "I think we'll have to go and get them, though. I don't think we have any."

"Tell us what we need and we'll pop in to the village and get it. Will you let us have the car?"

"Maybe we'd better go with you and help pick things out," Ben said.

"All right, but we're to pay for it, mind. What a glorious idea!"

They made their second expedition of the day to the Red and White market, one even merrier and more animated than the first. Amid the chatter and laughter, the gloom that had settled in Ben's mind like a miasma was gradually dispelled, and he began to share the feeling of frolic and gaiety with which they foraged along the aisles plucking bottles and boxes from the shelves, thumping watermelons with their knuckles to test their ripeness, tugging down the tips of corn husks to see if there were worms inside, making happy improvisations to their menu. He had drunk four

martinis, and a vaguely saturnalian festivity began to take possession of him
as he bumped the shopping cart along the aisles. Delectable wanton images flickered through his mind of bodies bathed by firelight, caresses in
the shadows, frolicking in the warm, velvet water, clandestine kisses in
the foam. It was perhaps the way to end it: a midsummer night's dream
of revelry under the stars. He was entitled to it, he thought with something like bravado; he had earned the license for it. They all had. They
were a company of peers, the chosen of the earth. They would perform the
rites of privilege, the jubilee that had been promised at their birth by
their endowments of talent, intelligence, ambition, perseverance. It was
fitting and just that they should celebrate their blessings. It was an incumbency of the fortunate to display to the admiring heavens the pageant of earthly prosperity, the brilliance with which the brightest and
best creatures of this dusty cinder shone in the dark wastes of the universe.

   This feeling of festive grandeur grew greater in him when they had
got back to the house and drunk a bottle of Cinzano while he supervised
the preparations for the weenie roast. He slit the hot dogs lengthwise, in-
serted strips of cheddar, wrapped them in slices of bacon and bathed them
in barbeque sauce, then wrapped the baking potatoes and the ears of
corn in aluminum foil, and concocted a relish of chopped watermelon
pickle, chutney, and dried mustard.

   "I thought you said it was to be an aboriginal affair," Jill said. "Looks jolly
sophisticated to me."

   "It's going to be a picnic worthy of a Manet," Ben said. "We should have
an artist of his genius here to depict it."

   "I'm not sure I'd like that," Priscilla said. "Being exhibited on the walls
of a museum for centuries. Especially at fun and games."

   They changed into their swimsuits and lugged their provisions down
the basement steps and across the soft sand to the beach: a watermelon
nested in a bucket of cracked ice, a cooler filled with pony bottles of Rolling
Rock and cabernet sauvignon, a hamper full of rolls and baking potatoes,

a box of marshmallows, ears of Silver Queen corn, paper plates and napkins, plastic cups, bottles of relish, mustard, pickles and catsup. There
was a driftwood expedition in the twilight from which they came back with
armloads of twigs, gnarled gray branches and chunks of bleached timber. Ben brought newspaper, a bag of charcoal, a can of starter fluid, and
an armload of firewood from the basement. He laid a base of charcoal
and built a crosshatched tower of twigs and fireplace logs on top of it that
burst into a great muttering sheet of scarlet flame when he tossed a match
into it. Everyone cheered.

He put de Falla's *Nights in the Gardens of Spain* on the portable tape
player and then opened a bottle of wine and poured it into paper cups
and handed them around and they sat in the sand around the fire drinking wine as the sky grew black above them and the stars came out and a
high milky moon shone through pale shoals of cloud. The sound of the
guitars came throbbing out of the darkness and their shadows billowed
on the sand like a pack of cavorting monsters. Far below them the breakers thundered with an endless peaceful booming and sometimes at the
far rim of the circle of firelight a little pale gray crab would go racing like
a ghost across the sand.

When the fire had fallen into steadily flickering low flames they roasted
the hot dogs, impaling them on long forked twigs that Ben cut with a
carving knife, turning them slowly over the scarlet coals until they had burst
their skins and bubbled with melted cheese inside their wrappings of
barbequed bacon. He dug the ears of corn and baking potatoes out of
the coals, buttered them, and passed them around on paper plates with
pickles and beach plum jelly. They ate ravenously, muttering like jackals
and pausing sometimes to groan with bliss.

"Lord, it's a sin to eat like this," Jill said. "I shall put on a stone at this rate.
I'm bursting my costume as it is."

"Everyone's entitled to a bacchanal once in a while," Ben said. "When
in Rome, do as the Romans do."

When they had finished the hot dogs and roasted corn and baked potatoes they ate slices of cold watermelon and toasted marshmallows which they plucked charred and melting from the tips of their toasting forks.

"I don't know about Roman," Tony said. "I think I've slipped back to the Neanderthal age, myself."

"Yes, so have I," Jill said. She raised her hands which were covered with catsup and watermelon juice. "Look at me. Absolutely dripping with gore. I look like Lady Macbeth."

"'A little water cleans of us this deed,'" Ben said.

"I don't know. I think I shall rather the multitudinous seas incardine."

He looked at her across the fire, her face glamorously shadowed and rouged by the firelight, the dark mass of her hair glinting with copper-colored threads as if it were bound in a gold snood. She lifted her hand to brush it away from her brow with the back of her wrist, her fingers twinkling through the firelight like minnows. He felt reduced to a reckless, feverish turmoil by her beauty. While he stared at her she raised her eyes to his and stared back at him with a look of steady, baffling candor that blew his heart aglow like an ember blown by a gust of breeze. He remembered with odd and piercing precision a line of MacHeath's from *The Beggar's Opera* that had stuck in his mind like a splinter of glass from his acting days: "A man who loves money had as well be content with one guinea as I with one woman." It was true, by God, and let those who loved money for itself go count their guineas and judge him if they dared. He had never loved money except as a means of making people admire him, of making them acknowledge his presence in their world, and he would be damned if he understood why he should be troubled by the cynical pieties of that world, whose killing he had done, whose indifference and contempt he had survived, and which was willing to forgive every kind of depredation and excess imaginable in the name of success. Jill's gaze had not wavered.

"Shall we go and wash off the blood?" she said.

Ben nodded. He scrubbed his hands with a paper napkin, stood up and untied the belt of his robe with his fingertips. "What do you say, Priss? You ready?"

"I guess so," Priscilla said. "It's going to be very, very cold." She stood up and began to shrug her robe off over her shoulders, shivering in the cool air.

"Come along, Tony," Jill said. "You're not going to get off, you know." She was out of her robe by now, glittering like a sardine in the firelight. She took him by the wrist and tugged him to his feet.

"You don't think it's a bit too soon after eating?" he said. "I shall sink like a bloody log."

"Rubbish. Keep you from nodding off. You look like you're going into a coma. Let's have the sweatshirt." He drew his arms out of it very reluctantly and she snatched it impatiently over his head and tossed it onto the sand. "Right. Now in you go." She shoved him ahead of her down the slope of the beach to the flat wet sand at the water's edge where he stood grappling with her frantically.

"Now look here, this is a bloody indecency," he cried. "Just let me take my time about it."

"No, no! I know all about your machinations. In you go!" She gave him a violent shove that sent him toppling backwards into the shallow surf, his arms flailing wildly, collapsing with a huge watery explosion into the crest of an oncoming wave. They stood laughing as he thrashed and sputtered in the foam.

"You're a bloody lot of sadists!" he bellowed, his hair streaming over his face as he staggered to his feet. "As sure as there's a god in heaven, you're to be punished for this." He came splashing to the shore raking the wet hair from his face.

"It's what you've been needing for years," Jill said. "Good dip in the briny every evening after dinner."

He advanced upon her, raising his hand and pointing his finger at her dramatically. "You're a savage, bloody-minded witch," he said. "My mother was quite right about you."

"Oh, was she! Well, did she warn you about this?" She reached out and snatched the waist of his trunks, yanking them down to his knees. He bent down and tried desperately to pull them up again, clinging to the wet cloth while she tugged it lower, down to the calves of his legs.

"Now this is a bit much," he muttered hoarsely. "Honestly, it's not funny at all, Jill. That's quite enough."

"Come along," she said. "There's to be no false modesty. Off they go."

He tried to flee, turning and hobbling bent-over through the shallow water while he tugged furiously at his trunks. Jill ran after him and gave him another shove that toppled him into the surf in a wild splash of foam where he lay wallowing and gasping, flailing futilely with his arms while he tried to get to his feet. Jill reached down and seized the fallen trunks, tugging at them like a terrier until she had managed to yank them off over his feet. She waved them triumphantly aloft.

"There now. You have reentered the elemental flow of things. The rivers of raw being. Don't you feel a good deal better?"

"I feel a bloody fool," he said. He sat up to his waist in the ebbing water, glowering at her. "You shall pay for this, you know."

"Don't make such a fuss," she said. "We're all going to join you." She flung his trunks up the beach and reached behind her neck to untie the strings of her bra, whisking it away by a strap and flinging it up the sand after his trunks. "We've got to be revealed as God made us, in the glory of our nakedness, as Michelangelo said." She peeled off her bikini pants and bent down to step out of them, kicking them away and then standing naked, her arms upstretched rapturously, clawing at the stars. "It's a divine feeling."

"Divine for some," Tony said. "Others of us are not so ornamental."

"Rubbish, you're quite beautiful. A great majestic sea lion, like that statue of Balzac." She turned to Ben and Priscilla. "Come on, you two. No malingering."

"Is it awfully cold?" Priscilla asked. She plucked timidly at the straps of her swimsuit.

"Actually, it feels quite pleasant now," Tony said. He had lowered himself to his neck in the surf and was paddling gently, puffing through his nose like a large comfortable amphibian. "Bit of a shock when you first hit the water, but it's the first moment that's the worst."

"I know. I suppose I've got to get it over with."

"*Au naturel,*" Jill said.

"Well, I don't suppose it's any colder that way." She pulled down her shoulder straps and then peeled off her suit, leaning down to lift it over her feet, her bent back making a pure, white, nebulous parabola, like a feeding heron, in the faint light. Ben watched her with startled admiration. They had often swum nude together, but never with their guests. It occurred to him that he had never suggested it, assuming that she would have been dismayed by the idea. He wondered why he had made that assumption, for when she had stepped out of her suit she stood up and looked down at her slim, narrow-hipped body with an endearing insouciance, hugged herself, and shivered, crushing her breasts carelessly with her arms.

"That's right," Jill said. She moved toward Priscilla and took her hand to lead her to the water. Ben looked at the two naked women with delight. It was a superb moment, one of the finest of his life, he thought. It seemed to take place in a region of clarity and simplicity under a protective arch that sheltered it from time or trespass. He felt gentled suddenly, touched by chivalry and privilege, as he watched them wade out hand in hand, their bodies beautiful and fragile as if carved in frost, into the welling water that broke against their thighs in a wash of moonlit foam. So tranquil and tender was the scene and so chaste and formal, that it was like a passage from a ballet. He could almost have predicted that they would pause, as they did, where Tony was stretched out in the surf, and each extend a hand to him, and that he would rise dripping from the sea and stand between them, almost majestic—as Jill had said—in his big-chested, big-bellied masculine bulk, and that the three of them would stand for a moment hand in hand in the swollen, lambent water before Jill turned to Ben and said, "Are you coming, love?" It seemed to him an invitation so benevolent, profound, and tender that it was the culmination of the whole history of human intercourse.

"Come in, sweetheart," Priscilla said. She smiled and held out her hand to him.

"All right, I'm coming," Ben said, and then realized that his words were so soft with awe that they could not be heard. "I'm coming," he repeated, but he stood without moving for a moment, chastened by their beauty. He did not feel entitled to join them. They were different from him, almost tragically so. They were splendid in their nakedness, which was immaculate. It was untainted by prurience, prudery, or pride, and revealed no blemishes or disfigurements. They had nothing to be ashamed of, standing naked in the great dark sea that murmured at their loins. He felt like an imposter among them.

"Come in, Ben," Priscilla said. "You'll get used to it in a minute."

"All right. I'm coming." He stripped off his bathing trunks and waded out to where they stood and took Priscilla's hand.

"There, you see?" She tightened her fingers about his and led him forward as she waded out into the lustrous dark water toward the line of breakers where the waves collapsed in front of them in a long, luminous scroll of foam. The water laved their thighs and bellies as they advanced into it, cool as glycerin and astringent on their skin and yet voluptuously warm after they had lowered their bodies into it, surging over them in a great dark diastolic flood as suave and sumptuous as blood. When they reached the line of breakers they held their breath and plunged beneath them, coming up with streaming hair and salty lips into the flat, foam-streaked troughs beyond, where for a moment they could look out across the endless, deep-breasted, moon-silvered sea. They swam out into it slowly in a languorous breaststroke, their bodies breaking the polished obsidian of the surface as they glided through it as silently as otters, their faces lifted to the stars.

"This is truly heavenly," Priscilla said.

"Far lovelier than heaven," Jill said. "Anyone who prefers heaven to this is off his rocker."

Ben turned onto his back and paddled gently with his hands, rising and falling in the huge soft undulations of the swells, staring up into the black, star-splattered sky. Boötes and the Dippers lay in glittering patterns across the sable dark like the shards of a great shattered jewel, ceaselessly, steadfastly scintillating. They were so infinitely distant, and numberless, and arcane in their configurations that his feeling of beatitude was daunted by them. He felt a slowly growing dread of the black immensity above him, and of the black immensity below on which he floated like a tiny, feeble fly borne out on the breast of darkness into the endless gulfs of darkness, away from the green meadows and golden shores of earth. The vast silent constellations seemed like the ruins of some awful primordial catastrophe, splinters of a sundered unity that was endlessly disintegrating. He looked back toward the land and saw the faint glow of the bonfire on the beach and the lighted windows of his house twinkling in the dark. They seemed far and lost to him and he felt a sudden appalling throe of loneliness and peril. Suppose he were to drown out here, in this awful blackness? To get a sudden cramp that curled his toes and stiffened his legs like stone? To go down, thrashing wildly, his lungs flooded with the strangling black liquor as he sank into its depths? Suppose an offshore current were to seize him with its huge irresistible strength and sweep him out into the measureless, eternally heaving wastes?

He felt his heart wither with dread like a blighted plum. He looked across the water to where Jill and Tony swam, a few yards to his right, their heads small and black against the glimmer of the surface, like drifting coconuts. A sudden deep affection for his frail, naked companions wracked him in the way that a strain of music could suddenly plunge him into a bewildering tenderness. He felt a kind of castigating pity for them, for their weak, white bodies, their naiveté, their touching, dignified insouciance, their childlike pleasure in this dire adventure. He wanted to embrace them, to express his gratitude for their comradeship, to ask forgiveness of them for his malice and deceit and pride, for all the ugly, arrogant disorder of his life.

He rolled over onto his belly and swam toward Priscilla, reaching out to touch her shoulder with his hand.

"You OK?" he asked.

"Yes, wonderful."

"I don't think we ought to go out any further. It's a long way back."

"I feel fine."

"I know, but you don't want to get too tired. There are currents out here."

"All right. If you want to go back."

He called to Tony and Jill across the water, "Hey, people. I think we'd better start back."

"Start back?" Jill said. "I could go on for hours."

"I know, but there are some pretty strong currents out here. You don't want to tempt fate."

"I think it's just as well," Tony said. "I'm getting a bit winded, you know. Not used to this."

"All right," Jill said. "But I think you're great bores, both of you."

They turned and began to swim back to the beach, the soft heave of the swells thrusting them gently landward. Ben felt a gradual resurgence of vitality and confidence as he approached the shore, and he slowed the pace of his stroke, realizing suddenly that he was swimming with a desperate, unbecoming haste. He watched the tiny glow of the bonfire grow in size and clarity until he could see the individual scarlet tongues of flame dancing above the coals, and the bucket and cooler, rosy-sided in the light, and the white patches of their towels and robes on the sand. Beyond the fire the panes of the sliding sundeck doors shone tranquilly with the lamplight behind them, and the illuminated dome of the salon hung like a huge Chinese lantern in the night sky. The scene warmed the cold that had settled in his entrails, and the bonfire and the scattered paraphernalia of pleasure on the sand comforted him like the trivia of his study — his books and etchings, his pen-holder and his marble ashtray, his framed certificates, a glass of bourbon on the desk. These were his possessions, his creations, his testimonials, the works and wages of his sojourn on the earth, and they warmed him and gave him refuge and exonerated him. He felt a returning pride in them and in the fact that in the acquiring and fashioning of them he had fashioned his own salvation. No one needed to be ashamed of that, or to disparage it. What he felt ashamed of as he swam back to his estate was his moment of panic out on the water, the senseless dread that he had succumbed to, and the craven humility that had made him so abjectly tenderhearted for a moment. His help was in himself, not in his companions, and to have forgotten that, even for a moment, was a dishonor to himself, a repudiation of his life that he would feel the sting of for a long time.

When his feet touched the bottom he stood up and waited until Priscilla had come abreast of him, and then reached out and took her hand as she scrambled to her feet, to steady her through the surf. Jill and Tony came after them, plunging through the foam. They snatched up their swimsuits from the sand where they had left them and ran up the beach to the bonfire and toweled themselves off, their bodies brazed by the heat of the scarlet coals. They shook the sand out of their robes and struggled into them and stood close to the fire while the women dried their hair with their fingertips spread out in their towels. Ben stirred the fire with a stick and put fresh logs onto it that crackled and blazed up quickly, sending up leaping, avid sheets of flame that washed their bodies with a wave of balm-like heat. He felt anxious to reassert himself, perform essential actions, resume the authority that had been extinguished for a moment in the dark sea.

"Oh, that feels good!" Priscilla said. "I don't know which is best, fire or water."

"Or earth or air," Tony said. "We've got them all tonight, in plenty. Very elemental sort of evening, altogether."

"Isn't it?" Priscilla said. "So many unexpected delights. I haven't had such fun for ages."

"Well, it's all here for the asking," Jill said. "The wonder of it is so few people ask."

"We're trained not to," Tony said. "Forbidden to."

"It's true," Priscilla said. "We must have broken half a dozen laws tonight."

"What sort of laws?" Jill asked.

"Well, building fires on the beach, nude swimming, drinking alcohol in public. God knows how many. They're busy making them up all day long, the guardians of our virtue."

"Who are these guardians of virtue?" Jill asked.

"One of the most impassioned of them is the senior senator from this state, Mr. Jesse Helms. He never stops huffing and puffing about corruption and obscenity. He's the most indefatigable champion of virtue in America."

"I suppose he's a pillar of it himself," Jill said.

"Oh, yes," Priscilla said, and laughed. "Do you know how he got into the senate? And how he maintains his power and influence? By stoutly defending the interests of people who make cigarettes."

"Not really," Tony said.

"Oh, yes. North Carolina grows more tobacco than any other state in the union, and without him to help them sell it, their whole economy would collapse. They'd have to find something less lethal to found their prosperity on."

"But he gets upset about a bit of nudity, does he?"

"Oh, my! You should hear him go on about indecency and depravity. Especially in the arts. Artists are a gang of slavering degenerates, as far as he's concerned. Unless, of course, they have a good, wholesome message for us, like Norman Rockwell or Walt Disney. Meanwhile, he's blithely destroying the health of millions of kids in this country, who can't smoke enough cigarettes to make him happy. I don't suppose I have any right to fuss about it, as many of them as I smoke." She bent over and began digging in the beach bag. "Where are the damn things? I need one right now."

"Well, you're one of his victims, of course," Jill said. "As we all are. What is one to do?"

"I suppose we could ask him to lead the prayers for our souls when we're dying of cancer," Priscilla said. "He's very big on prayer."

She had found the cigarettes, and sat down and lit one, inhaling deeply as she leaned back on her elbows and looked up at the sky. "What a lovely night. Look at all those stars. Ben, what's that very bright one up there, just beyond the handle of the Big Dipper?"

"Arcturus," Ben said, looking up to where she had pointed. "It's the brightest star in the northern sky. It's part of the constellation of Boötes. *Arcturus* means bear guard, because it's supposed to be defending Ursa Major, or the Great Bear, which is what the ancients called the Big Dipper. They believed that the Great Bear was Callisto, a nymph who was turned into a bear by Hera, the wife of Zeus. After she'd become a bear she was hunted by her own son, Arcas, who failed to recognize her. He was on the point of slaying her when Zeus swept them both into the sky in order to prevent the crime of matricide." He felt a good deal better, having been able to relate this piece of lore. Nothing gave him such a sense of confidence as the display of his learning. It compensated somewhat for his chagrin at Priscilla's diatribe about cigarettes. Ben did not advertise cigarettes, but he had tried to, strenuously, for several years, and had spent thousand of dollars entertaining some of Senator Helms's own constituents, executives of the major tobacco companies, none of whom had been sufficiently impressed to give him their business. Priscilla did not know this, but she was aware of his sensitivity on the subject of morality in his profession, and in giving him the opportunity to exhibit his knowledge about the constellations she seemed to have been trying to redeem her tactlessness in having raised it. His relationship with her called for such a constant, vigilant exercise of discretion, magnanimity and clemency on her part, and of dissimulation on his, that he sometimes felt exhausted by its complexity. What made him cling to it and cultivate it dauntlessly was the knowledge that she loved him and would dismiss her own misgivings about his motives sooner than renounce her faith in him, and because without her faith in him he would be unknown and anonymous. He knew that no one in the world understood the meaning of his performance on the stage of life except Priscilla; and yet strangely enough she did not understand its virtuosity as a fellow-artist would, as Jill did. She loved art, but she did not know how it was made. He sat down in the sand between the two women and looked from one to the other of them.

"I have another question for you," Jill said.

"Fire away," Ben said.

"Did it occur to you that we might drown, out there?"

"It crossed my mind."

"And would you have tried to save us if we had?"

He looked into her eyes and read the question there that she had art-fully evoked with another: Which of us would you have saved? He smiled and replied to both, with her own facetiousness:

"Oh, yes. All those who were worthy of salvation."

"Oh? And how would you have decided?"

"I'd have relied on Senator Helms's standards of judgment, naturally."

"Oh, dear," Priscilla said. "We'd all have perished, in that case."

"Perhaps we all deserve to," Tony said. "Perhaps, with the exception of tobacco, every form of pleasure is sacrilege. Perhaps we were born to smoke, and nothing more."

Jill lay back on the blanket and laced her fingers behind her head, staring up into the sky. "Why did Hera turn Callisto into a bear?" she asked.

"Because she was jealous of her," Ben said. "Zeus fell in love with Callisto and they had a child. Arcas was his son."

"My goodness, it's a regular soap opera," Priscilla said.

"Or a play by O'Neill," Tony said.

"Perhaps that's why I love bears," Jill said. "I'm sure someone turned Humbert into one. He has such anguished, nostalgic eyes, as if he were re-membering the days of wine and roses." She closed her eyes. "Awful to be hunted by your own son. Not to have him recognize you, if he found you."

"I think the sky is haunted," Priscilla said. "All those people frozen up there, like statues, full of their awful passions and crimes and agonies. It's like an attic full of old jewels and daggers and bloodstained lace and por-traits of beautiful, ruined ladies."

"Fascinating thought, that," Tony said. "I never saw it that way, but it's quite true. Attic full of ghosts."

"You know what we ought to do?" Priscilla said, clapping her hands sud-denly. "We ought to tell ghost stories. We used to do that at camp when I was a little girl: tell ghost stories around the campfire at night."

"So did we, when I was in the Girl Guides," Jill said. "Used to make my hair stand on end."

"Well, let's do. Who wants to go first? Tony?"

"Don't know that I remember any," Tony said. "Ghost stories. Well, let me see. I do know one, that's a sort of ghost story, I suppose, although there aren't any bits of ectoplasm floating about. Happened to a friend of mine, actually; so it's true, as well as eerie. Chap who was my roommate when I was up at Cambridge. He wasn't at all a pleasant chap, although he was very good-looking and bright enough and came from a good family. Too good-looking for his own good, as a matter of fact; he was a perfect devil with the women. Made a sort of career of it, and he wasn't at all shy about letting you know the details. Never stopped talking about them. It got to be an embarrassment after a while. I had to say to him once, 'Look here, Colin, I'm not really all that keen about hearing you go on about all these amorous conquests of yours. It gets to be rather a bore, hearing who you've had a tumble in the hay with, every week.' Well, it didn't faze him at all, you know. The man had a vanity that nothing could penetrate. And on top of this, he was a weak, selfish sort of chap who was much too used to having his own way, not only with the girls but with his family, the masters, everyone, because of his looks, his money, and the fact that he stood to inherit a baronetcy.

"Well, eventually, as was bound to happen, I suppose, he got one of the local girls pregnant. She was a barmaid who worked in one of the taverns in the town, The Spotted Hound. He'd no intention of marrying her, of course, or even of admitting paternity, because she wasn't of his own class, although she was a lovely little thing and obviously adored him. I happened to know this girl because the pub she worked in was a favorite haunt of the students and there wasn't a week went by that we didn't stop in once or twice to have a pint or two of ale. I was fond of her myself; we all were; she was a sweet-natured, very gentle girl, and I wasn't at all pleased when he told me what had happened. I asked him what he intended to do about it, and he said, 'Well, naturally, I'm going to have her get rid of it.' 'Naturally?' I said. 'I don't see what's so ruddy natural about it. What makes you think she'll agree to it? That girl adores you. You're a fool if you don't see that. I think she'll want to have your child.' 'Oh, no, she'll agree to it,' he said. 'I know how to make her do that. I'll just tell her that I'll break it off with her if she doesn't. Never see her again. That'll bring her round.' Well, I didn't know quite what to do, of course. It was a bloody uncomfortable position to be in. I couldn't force him to do the right thing by her, and he wasn't the sort of chap who'd take advice from anyone—if there was nothing in it for him. I felt quite certain the girl would have the child, but I was wrong about it. Dreadfully wrong, as it turned out. Evidently, the thought of never seeing Colin again was more than she could bear, even though she must have known that it would come to nothing in the end. Or perhaps she felt that he would come to care for her eventually because she loved him so much. Who knows what a woman thinks, in a situation of that kind. At any rate, she agreed to have it done. He gave her the money for it and sent her round to some wretched old quack he'd got the name of somewhere. Some old scoundrel who'd been on the bottle for years and had lost his license long ago—and so of course he made a mess of it. The girl died in agony a couple of days later. Of course she never mentioned Colin's name, and so he got off scot-free. Very pleased about it he was, too. Thought he'd got rid of her forever, no more trouble at all from that quarter. Suited his plans perfectly. I don't think he ever intended to see the girl again, no matter how it turned out. It seems a perfectly dreadful thing to say, but perhaps what happened was for the best, really. I don't know what the girl would have done if she'd lived, only to be abandoned by him. Bloody strange, how a woman can love such a perfect cad as that.

"Well, as I say, he thought he'd got off scot-free. Free to carry on with the next girl he took a fancy to, stand for Parliament from his district, marry some pretty young heiress eventually, get on very nicely with his life. But then a curious thing happened: he found he couldn't forget the girl. Couldn't get her out of his mind, at all. Found himself wandering out along the Cam where she used to wait for him on summer afternoons. He spent hours sitting out there in the water meadows where they used to meet, thinking about the way her hair would blow in the wind, the way she'd laugh and pluck flowers and toss them at him, the little songs she used to sing—she'd had a lovely voice, this girl. It was as if he was haunted by her, quite literally, he told me later. He'd come back to chambers expecting to find her waiting there for him, he'd hear her voice in the wind; there was hardly a moment when he wasn't thinking of her, imagining her agony when she died. It didn't give him a moment's peace. It got to the point where he was living a life of utter torment, waking or sleeping. Even when he was asleep he'd have these awful dreams about her and wake up trembling and terrified. There was no escape at all, finally, not even with another woman, because he found that he was incapable of pleasure with any other woman, even of taking any genuine interest in anything.

"I didn't realize the full extent of what he was going through until I met the chap again, a couple of years later, after I'd come down from Cambridge. I was down at Brighton one summer where I'd gone to see an exhibition of paintings by a young artist that was supposed to be very interesting. I got down early in the day and I was strolling along the seaside in the afternoon for a bit of air when I saw this chap sitting on a bench staring out at the sea. I wasn't fond of him at all, as I've said, and after what had happened I had nothing but contempt for the man. I wouldn't have spoken to him if he hadn't seen me first. But he happened to catch my eye, and then he stood up and hailed me very eagerly—abjectly, as a matter of fact. So I stopped to say a word to him—seemed the only thing to do—and he asked me if I had anything lined up for dinner. If I wasn't busy, he said, he'd like to take me round to one of the pubs and have a bit of a chat about old times, catch up on each other, one thing and another. Well, he had such a harrowed look about him that I suppose I was curious, more than sympathetic, because this chap had always been the very picture of assurance when we were at school. Couldn't have been more satisfied with himself, and with the world. And here he was reaching out and clutching my sleeve as if he were begging for half a crown or something. So I took

him up on it. We went round to a pub close by and had a bit of shep-
herd's pie and a glass of ale, and he started telling me this story about the
girl, and about the dreadful state he'd been in ever since she'd died.

"'You know what it is, Tony?' he said to me. 'I think perhaps she loved
me, more than I ever realized. And she loves me still, even beyond death.
I don't think I'll ever have a moment's peace again while I'm alive.'

"I was moved, in spite of myself. I could see the man had had all the
punishment he needed, so I tried to cheer him up a bit. Told him to get
himself another girl, get himself a business of some sort, stand for Parliament, do a bit of traveling. It would all work out, one way or another. Things
always did, I said.

"But he wasn't having it; he was too far gone in this obsession of his. I
saw, finally, that it wasn't getting anywhere, and I'd had about as much of
it as I could take, so I said I had to be getting on, had an appointment
with this artist chap, or something. So we left. Brighton's a rather tatty place,
as you know, parts of it at least—shabby sort of carnival town. We went along
through a sort of penny arcade and there happened to be one of those
fortune-telling machines there, all lit up with bright bulbs, with this gypsy
painted on it. Madame Pelletier, it said. 'She reads your future in the
stars. Learn the answers to your crucial questions. Sixpence.' There was
this dial with a pointer on it that you could turn to any of twenty-five or
thirty questions that were printed on a panel. Things of this kind: Will
my love last forever? Shall I take the job that's being offered me? Should
I marry him? The sort of things that come up in everyone's life at one
time or another. Well, as we passed this contraption he put his hand out
to stop me and said, 'Wait a minute, Tony. Look at this.' And he pointed
to one of the questions that were printed on the panel. Number Seven, I
think it was. At any rate, it said: How can I forget her? 'Isn't that extraordinary?' he said. 'That's the question I've been asking myself for a year or
more.' And he started fishing in his pocket for a sixpence. 'Oh, rubbish,'
I said. 'Come along. You can't believe in that sort of nonsense.' 'I don't
know,' he said. 'I have an idea it was put there for me to see. It's worth
trying, anyway. God knows I've tried everything else.'

"So he dug a sixpence out of his pocket and popped it into the slot and turned the dial to this question and pulled the plunger. Well, out came this card, about the size of a calling card, with something printed on it. He picked it up and stared at it, and went quite pale. 'Good God, Tony. Look at this,' he said, and handed it to me. Do you know what it said?"

"No," Priscilla said. "Tell us!"

"It said, 'You cannot. I will be with you always.'"

"Oh, my," Priscilla said. "Isn't that weird! You mean to say that really happened?"

"As truly as I'm telling it to you," Tony said. "I read it with my own eyes. Not the sort of thing one can forget."

"Oh, my goodness," Priscilla said. "The poor man. Whatever happened to him? Do you know?"

"Yes, I do," Tony said. "He shot himself, about a month later. He wandered out along the Cam one day and sat down by the bank and put a bullet through his head. He had the card in his hand when they found his body."

"Oh, that's weird," Priscilla said. "What a very strange story." She sipped her wine and shivered. "Well, that will be very hard to top. I certainly can't. What about you, Jill?"

"I don't think I can equal that one," Jill said. "But I know one that you might find interesting, because it's about the theatre."

"Oh, good. Ben, put another log on the fire."

Ben got up and put a couple of logs onto the fire and poured more wine into their cups. Jill sipped at her wine and set the cup down on the sand between her feet.

"This one's about an actor," she said. "Quite a gifted but rather weak and envious chap whose lifelong ambition was to play the part of Lear. He hadn't the physical equipment for the part at all; he was quite small in stature and had a sort of reedy voice; he didn't have an imposing presence on the stage at all, but he was very talented, as I say. And very vain. He felt it was his right, as well as his destiny, to achieve fame and success, and he resented everyone and everything that stood in his way.

"Well, he found work with a repertory company that did mostly Shakespeare and the classics. It was run by an actor-manager of the old school, a man something like Donald Wolfit only a good deal less benevolent, who had his share of vanity as well. He did most of the leading roles himself, paid his actors very badly, and kept them from leaving the company by offering them occasional respectable supporting roles and promising them great futures if they stuck with him. Well, this chap I'm speaking of— Tom was his name—had been working for the old boy for years, and he wasn't getting any younger. He was quite a good actor, as I say, but like Tony's student, he was a vain and willful man and felt things weren't going his way at all and that he'd never gotten the kind of recognition that his talent deserved. He knew that time was running out and that he'd soon be too old for leading roles, and he was getting pretty desperate about things generally. His passion to play Lear at least once before he packed it in had become an absolute obsession with him.

"Well, as it happened, he got the chance at last—not to play it, but to understudy it, at least, which was the closest he'd come to it in his entire career. The company manager, Sir George, who was a very shrewd judge of talent, realized that Tom was a very versatile and useful actor and was anxious to keep him in his company. *Lear* was the last production of the season, and Sir George was going to play the lead himself, as he generally did, but he offered to let Tom understudy the role, along with playing a very small role, Curan, one of those thankless courtiers who's always standing about looking statuesque in the big ensemble scenes. 'There are no small parts, only small actors.' That was the kind of platitude he was always serving up to keep his people in line. Tom felt he was being bribed into accepting this insignificant role by being offered the understudy of Lear, but even the remotest possibility of playing the mad king was enough to make him agree to almost any terms, no matter how humble or humiliating.

"Well, the show opened, and it was a great success. Sir George performed with his usual brilliance, and got rave notices, as did all the principal players—Cordelia, Regan, Goneril, Gloucester—all of them but Tom, of course, who went practically unnoticed, as one does in that sort of bit part in a big Shakespearean company. Still, he came trotting out on cue every evening, delivered his one or two paltry lines, and then retired to the dressing room to brood for the balance of the evening. He began to get very bitter and resentful, but he stuck to it because his one great hope was that Sir George would become indisposed for a day or two—have a bout of indigestion or gout one evening, or sprain an ankle, or suffer an attack of laryngitis and lose his voice for a few days—anything that would give Tom the opportunity to play the role, if only for a night. And then one day the thought occurred to him: Why should I wait for the man to get sick, or to have an accident of some kind? Why not make sure of it? If I leave it to chance, I'll wait another twenty years, and be too old to play the part, or dead, more likely. I can't die without playing Lear, at least once, in London, in a great theatre, before people who will see at last what I can do.

"Well, the more he thought about it, the more obsessed he got by the idea. He started to think up ways to lay the actor-manager low, some sort of temporary affliction that would seem quite natural and put him out of action for a time. He'd lie awake all night inventing all sorts of mishaps and illnesses of the most unlikely kind—smearing a bit of oil on the stage so that he'd slip and fall, dose of laxative in his tea, tacks on the dressing room floor that he'd be apt to tread on. They all seemed very impractical and uncertain, however, if not downright ridiculous, and as the run went on and his chances of ever playing the part got slimmer, he got more desperate and started dreaming up more drastic measures—pipe bombs, belladonna, automobiles wired to explode when the ignition was switched on, no end of absurdities. Finally he came up with something that seemed very simple and sure: a mugging. It was something that he could do himself, without accomplices or witnesses, that required no expert skill or knowledge or materials that would be difficult to obtain—gunpowder or exotic poisons or the like. It seemed the perfect method.

"This actor-manager, Sir George, lived in a small town house in Hampstead on one of those narrow, winding lanes that wander off High Street at the top of the Heath. It was a quiet, dark street with lots of turns and twists to it, corners to stand in, recessed doorways, things of that sort. So this chap Tom left the theatre very early one evening after the performance and took the tube to Hampstead carrying a hammer in his pocket with a length of tape wound round the head of it. He went up the street where Sir George lived, found his house, and stood in a doorway nearby waiting until the old actor showed up. He had to wait quite a while actually, because Sir George had stopped at a pub to have a pint or two with friends. When he finally showed up he was a bit squiffed, and had trouble getting out of the taxi and even more trouble getting his key into the lock. While he was fumbling with it Tom stepped out of the doorway he was standing in, went up quietly behind him and bashed him on the head. Sir George went down in a heap without a sound, and Tom stood looking at him for a moment in astonishment. He could scarcely believe that he'd done this thing, and for a moment he was horrified at his own brutality. I'm such a gentle sort of chap, he thought, I don't do this sort of thing. He very nearly came apart for a moment; but then he thought of playing Lear at last, and he pulled himself together and knelt down beside Sir George and went quickly through his clothes. He took his wallet, his wristwatch, his cufflinks and a silver money clip and stuffed them into his own pockets, then picked up the bloody hammer and went down the lane into the high street. He dropped the hammer into a dustbin, turned into the high street and took the tube back to his lodgings in Swiss Cottage.

"He slept hardly at all that night—he lay awake tormented by fantasies of audiences booing his performance of Lear and hurling stones and bloody hammers at him from the orchestra—but towards dawn he fell into a restless sleep and slept until late in the day. He dressed quickly in a kind of feverish excitement and went outside to buy a copy of a newspaper at a neighborhood kiosk. On the front page of the paper he found a story about the assault on Sir George under the headline: Noted Actor

Attacked on Street, in Serious Condition at Hampstead Hospital. He called the hospital to ask if he could speak to Sir George and was told the actor was still sleeping but in a stable condition. He then called the director to express the appropriate dismay and disbelief at the outrage. He gave a marvelous impression of a man shocked to the depths of his being by the news. 'I suppose we'll have to cancel for tonight,' he said unhappily. 'Oh, I think we must go on, Tom,' the director said. 'It's what Sir George would want, I'm sure. He was asleep when I went round to see him this afternoon, but I'm sure he'd want you to take over until he's on his feet again. You know how keen he is on tradition.' 'You want me to go on as Lear?' Tom said, apparently astonished by the thought. You'd have thought it had only just occurred to him. 'Yes, of course,' the director said. 'After all, that's why Sir George made you his understudy. We owe it to him, and to the public, and to the tradition of the theatre. He'd expect you to rise to the occasion.' 'Yes, of course he would,' Tom said. 'You're quite right. I'll carry on as best I can.'

"And carry on he did. He got to the theatre very early that evening because of course it takes an hour or two to make up for the part of Lear, and it was something he wasn't used to doing. There was a great white wig, and a flowing beard, and false eyebrows, and a putty nose, and all the rest of it, and he wanted to do it to perfection. The director was on hand when he arrived and tried to steady him down, giving him all sorts of reassurance and advice, and offering to have Sir George's personal dresser come down and help out if Tom felt he needed assistance. Tom said no, it was quite all right, he'd make out quite well. He'd rather manage by himself, as a matter of fact, so he could commune with the part, get himself into the spirit of the role. It was something he felt he needed. He wanted his performance to be a credit to Sir George.

"And a credit to Sir George it was. It was quite magnificent. From the moment he stepped onto the stage he held the audience and his fellow actors as well spellbound with the power of his voice, the strength and subtlety of his reading, the passion and command of his performance. Everyone in the company agreed that they'd never seen it played better.

"When it was over there was a standing ovation from the audience who were aware, of course, of the situation because the director had announced at the beginning of the performance that the part of Lear was being played that evening by the understudy because Sir George was indisposed owing to the vicious attack he'd suffered the night before. Knowing the circumstances, the audience was doubly appreciative of Tom's accomplishment, and their applause went on for five minutes or more. When it was over and Tom had taken his last curtain call, the director, who had been watching from out front, went round to the dressing room to congratulate him. But before he could do so he was stopped backstage by the stage manager who announced very gravely that he'd just received a call from the hospital. Sir George, he said, had died that evening, not long before the performance had begun.

"Shocked and grieved by this news, the director went on to Tom's dressing room and knocked gently at the door. 'Tom,' he said. 'It's Derek. I want to tell you first how splendid you were. Absolutely magnificent. But I'm afraid I've some very bad news for you.' There was no answer, so he knocked again and said, 'Tom? Can I come in for a moment? I say, Tom.' There was still no reply, so he opened the door and looked into the room, and what he saw made him go rigid with astonishment.

"The understudy was sitting at the dressing table staring into the mirror with a look of horror, and what was wholly incomprehensible was that he was still dressed in his street clothes as if he'd never got out of them, and there wasn't so much as a dab of makeup on his face, although the performance had not been over for five minutes. He was stiff as a poker, his eyes wide open, motionless and glazed, like those of a dead fish. Lear's costume was hung up neatly on the clothes stand and the white wig had been replaced on its wooden form. The director could make nothing of it for a moment; then a sense of dread crept over him. He felt an awful chill inside him as if his blood were freezing. He whispered, 'Tom?' and went slowly across the room to where the understudy sat, and touched his hand. It was cold and rigid as marble.

"He'd died of a heart attack, the doctor said when he arrived a few minutes later. Been dead for hours."

"Oh Lord, that's even eerier than Tony's!" Priscilla said. "What a marvelous story."

"A pretty chilling tale," Ben said. "Where did you hear it?"

"I can't remember," Jill said, and smiled at him. She picked up the cup of wine from between her feet and drank. "Well, now it's your turn, Priss."

"I'm not really very good at ghost stories," Priscilla said. "I don't know why I suggested it. I certainly can't equal either of those. But there's one I remember that I always loved. It's something like Tony's story, because it's about immortality and love, but it has a very different ending. It's about a young man named Peter who went to England for a vacation one year in order to forget an unhappy love affair. He'd been betrayed by a girl whom he loved very much and who, he discovered, was carrying on an affair with another man, although she and Peter were engaged to marry. He was so devastated by the girl's treachery that he became totally disillusioned with life. Although he was quite a successful young man, a stockbroker in a large investment firm, he lost all interest in his work and all faith in his future. His boss became concerned with Peter's constant distraction, and he suggested that the young man should take a vacation in some very different environment where he would be exposed to new and stimulating experiences, gain a fresh perspective, develop a wider vision of life and a reawakened appetite for it.

"So Peter went to England, rented an automobile, and took a random, wandering tour of the country, from London through Kent and Devon and along the Cornish coast from Polperro to a tiny village called Gwithian where he found a lovely old stone inn on a headland above the sea. The place was so beautiful and peaceful that Peter decided to spend his entire vacation there.

"The inn was run by a merry, congenial Cornish couple who felt an immediate affection for Peter and did all they could to make his stay a

pleasant one. Every morning they served him a hearty breakfast and
made up a picnic lunch of Cornish pasty and a jug of cider which he packed
into his rucksack and took on his daylong rambles over the downs and
on the cliffs above the sea.

"One day he climbed a great tawny headland that looked down onto
a small sandy cove enclosed by cliffs over which gulls and gannets soared
in the sunlight. The place was so remote and inaccessible that as he ate his
lunch of Cornish pasty and drank his Devon cider he was astonished to see
a beautiful young girl wandering on the sand of the little beach below him.
She had hair the color of amber that blew lightly in the breeze from the
sea and a face as white and fine as an ivory cameo. She was wearing a faded
blue dress and carrying a pair of sandals that dangled by the straps from her
hand. She wandered up the sand toward a huge boulder that stood in
the center of the beach and when she had reached it she leaned against
the gray stone and stared out at the sea. For an hour she did not move.

"Peter watched her all that time. He was afraid that he would frighten
her if he called out or stood up on the cliff to wave to her, and he felt somehow that it would be an invasion of her privacy. It seemed to him that
the cove belonged to her, that he was an intruder there. So eventually
he gathered up his things and went back down the headland and along the
lane to the inn.

"He could not forget her. That night when he had gone to bed he lay
and listened to the muttering of doves under the eaves and thought about
the slender, golden-haired girl walking barefoot in the sand and leaning
against the boulder to gaze out at the sea.

"The next day after breakfast he took the lunch they had prepared for
him and went back down the white lane from the inn and climbed through
the gorse and heather to the top of the headland and sat down in the
sunlight above the cove. This young man loved poetry, and he had brought
with him a copy of the poems of Yeats in which he had found consolation since his unhappy love affair. He opened the book and read for an
hour or so, and then he laid the book down in the grass and fell asleep in
the sunlight. When he woke up he was filled with delight to see the girl

again, walking in the sand of the cove below him. She was wearing the same blue dress and her hair blew in the wind. This time she stopped before she had reached the boulder in the center of the beach and sat down in the firm sand at the water's edge where she began to inscribe letters in the sand with her fingertip, her eyes downcast sorrowfully.

At last Peter summoned up the courage to speak to her, and so he stood up and called out, waving from the clifftop. She looked up, startled, at the sound of his voice and then stood up swiftly and stared at him, clutching her face between her hands. She pressed one hand to her breast and tottered weakly, falling facedown in the sand. Peter was horrified. He snatched up the jar of cider from his rucksack and went plunging down the slope of the headland, stumbling on the stones and ripping his trousers on the gorse thorns, until he had reached the beach below the cliffs. He ran up the sand to where she lay and knelt beside her, taking her by the shoulders and turning her body gently until she lay faceup in the sunlight. He had never seen a face so beautiful. After a moment she stirred and opened her eyes and stared at him fearfully.

"'Who are you?' she asked in an astonished whisper.

"'My name is Peter,' he said. 'Peter Kindred. I'm afraid I frightened you. I think you fainted.'

"He asked if she would like something to drink, and she nodded. He unscrewed the cap from his jar of cider and handed it to her. She took the jar, her hand trembling, and sipped from it, then handed it back to him.

"'Thank you,' she said. She gazed into his eyes with a look of perplexity and pain. 'You're American,' she murmured.

"'Yes,' Peter said. 'I'm just here on holiday. I'm staying at a little inn near Gwithian. The Traveler's Rest.'

She gazed at him silently for a moment. 'Will you help me to get up?' she asked.

"'Yes,' Peter said. He stood up and held out his hands to her and pulled her to her feet. She brushed the sand from her dress and tossed her hair to shake the sand out of it and raked it briefly with her fingers.

"'I'll have to go now,' she said.

"'I'm sorry I disturbed you,' Peter said. 'I won't come here again, I promise you. I feel as if I've intruded on your privacy.'

"'That's kind of you,' she said. 'But of course you're just as entitled to come here as I am.'

"'I don't think so,' Peter said. 'I think you want to be alone here. I feel like a trespasser.' He frowned, not knowing how to express himself. 'I think you're very sad,' he said at last. 'I think your sorrow has to be respected.'

"'Do you respect sorrow so much?' she asked.

"Peter nodded. The shadow of a gull raced across the sand and she raised her head and followed the flight of the bird across the headland, her eyes roving thoughtfully. Then she returned her gaze to Peter and said, 'If I come tomorrow, will you be here?'

"'If it doesn't trouble you,' Peter said.

"'No,' the girl said. She gazed into his eyes for a moment. 'You must come at noon,' she said. 'I'll bring you some wine and an apple. And you must tell me about America.'

"'I will,' Peter said.

"'I'll have to go now,' she said. 'But I want you to go first. Go back up to your hilltop, and when you look down I'll be gone.'

"And so every day for the two weeks of his vacation that were left he came to the cove at the foot of the headland, and every day she was there to meet him. And as they talked and ate the apples and drank the wine that she brought, her sorrow seemed to fade away and she grew more serene and contented in his company. He told her about the city of Washington where he lived, its monuments and museums and parks, and she listened with an air of wonder. Sometimes they would exchange pretty little things they had found—he brought her a little seashell shaped like a heart with scalloped edges and a scarlet pebble from the creek that flowed through the glen beside the headland, and she brought him a tiny hollow egg that she had found under a tree and a bunch of azalea blossoms that she had picked in the lane as she came to meet him. He took the scarlet blossoms back to the inn and pressed them between the pages of his book of

Yeats's poetry, and set the finch's egg on his bureau and would hold it sometimes in the palm of his hand and touch it with his fingertip and smile.
One day when it was very warm and he had chased her splashing through
the water she lay down to rest in the shadow of the boulder and fell asleep.
On this day Peter had brought his camera, and he took it from his rucksack
and took three photographs of her sleeping in the sand. I've captured
your beautiful face, he thought, as I will capture your beautiful spirit.

"The days fled by one after another as swiftly as minutes, and Peter realized one day that his sorrow was forgotten and that he'd never been
happier in his life. It seemed to him like an endless idyll that would go
on forever, but one morning when he woke up he realized that it was
the last day of his holiday. He had promised his employer that he would
be back in Washington on the fifteenth of that month to arrange a very important stock transfer, and this was the fourteenth. The days had passed
in such a trance of happiness that he had almost forgotten the life he
must return to. It seemed to him that he had known this girl from the
moment of his birth, and yet he knew nothing about her, not even her
name. It astonished him that it had not seemed to matter to him.

"That day he met her in the cove with a sad heart, determined to ask
her name and where he could write to her when he returned to Washington. He asked if she was Cornish.

"She said no, that she came from Warwickshire.

"'Then you're on holiday, too,' he said. She nodded. 'Do you come here
every year?' he asked.

"'I've come every summer for the last three years,' she said.

"He asked her where she stayed and she told him that she stayed at
an inn called The Red Hart on the road to St. Agnes and that every morning she walked down the lane to the cove.

"'Will you come again next year?' he asked.

"'I don't know,' she murmured, so softly that he could barely hear her.

"'I hope you will,' he said. 'If you come again next year, I'll come too.
I couldn't bear to think that I'd never see you again.'

"She looked out at the sea and after a moment or two she said, 'I promise that I'll see you again.'

"'I'll remember that promise,' Peter said. 'But tell me your name, at least, and where you live. I want to write to you when I go back to the States.'

"'My name is Claire,' she said. 'And I live in Warwickshire, but you mustn't write to me. Wait until we meet again, and if you feel as you do now you can tell me everything that's in your heart.'

"He took her hands and kissed them. She closed her eyes and bowed her head.

"'When must you leave?' she murmured.

"'This is the last day that I can spend with you,' Peter said. 'I have to leave tomorrow. I have work to do.'

"'Is it very important work?' she asked.

"'Yes,' Peter said. 'It's the way I earn my livelihood. And I've promised to be back tomorrow.'

"'What would you lose if you didn't go back tomorrow?' she asked in a moment.

"'A great deal of money, I suppose,' Peter said. 'And very likely my job. But nothing compared to what I'd lose if I lost you.'

"She searched his eyes with hers, her face grown very still with a solemnity he'd never seen in her before. 'If you could see me only once more,' she asked at last, 'would you come tomorrow?'

"'Yes,' Peter said. 'For an hour with you I'd give up everything I ever hoped to have. All the money I'd ever earn in this world. All the comfort I'd ever know. Nothing could be worth an hour of your company.'

"'Then you must believe this,' she said. 'If you come tomorrow it will mean salvation for both of us.' She raised her hand and laid her finger on his lips. 'Don't answer too quickly,' she said.

"But Peter did not hesitate, although he didn't understand her words. 'I'll be here tomorrow,' he said.

"She stared at him with a strange, terrible intensity. 'If you don't come,' she said, 'it will be a black day for both of us.'

"'I will be here,' Peter said.

"'Oh, my love,' she said. She clutched his hand to her throat and kissed his fingers passionately. 'Oh, my dearest love. Would you sacrifice so much for me?'

"'I'd give my life for you,' Peter said.

"'You won't need to, ever,' she said. 'I'll never leave you, Peter. Believe me. I know we must part soon, but I'll be with you every hour we're apart, and when we meet again it will be forever.' She took his face in her hands and drew his lips to hers, sealing her vow with a kiss of such tenderness that a golden ingot of serenity formed in his heart like a nugget of amber.

"That night he sat at the window of his room in the inn and looked out at the great sea glimmering in the moonlight, smiling with happiness as he remembered the words of her vow, and in the morning he strode up the lane toward the cove with his heart caroling like a wild bird in his breast at the thought of seeing her again. But it was to be the worst day of his life, because she did not come.

"He stood watching from the cliff above the cove until the sun had sunk almost into the sea, his heart grown cold and heavy as a stone with grief. At last he turned and went plunging down the headland in despair, the gorse tearing at his trousers and the daws scattering before him with cries of mockery. He had plodded along the white lane almost to the inn before he remembered that she had told him she was staying at The Red Hart on the road to St. Agnes. He ran to where he had parked his rented car in the meadow behind the inn and leapt into it, and in a moment he was racing up the road with white dust billowing in the lane behind him.

"It took him less than ten minutes to find the Red Hart Inn, a cob-and-thatch cottage with a red deer painted on a sign that hung from an iron shaft above the door. He leapt out of his car and ran up the stone path to the door and went into the parlor where an old man with white hair and bright blue eyes sat behind an ancient mahogany desk.

"'Good day to you, sir,' the old man said. 'Will you be wanting lodging?'

"'No,' Peter said. 'There's a guest of yours that I'd like to speak with, or to leave a message for, if she's out.'

"'A guest of ours,' the old man said. 'A lady, is it?'

"'Yes,' Peter said. 'Her name is Claire, but I'm afraid I don't know her surname. It's very important that I get in touch with her.'

"'Claire,' the old man said. 'I wonder if you could just give me an idea of her appearance, sir? A young lady, is it?'

"'Yes, very young,' Peter said. 'She has hair the color of amber, and pale blue eyes, and she very often wears a blue dress. She's from War-wickshire. She comes here every summer, I believe.'

"'Ah. Claire Coverack,' the old man said. 'That's her to a T.' He nodded gravely. 'She came every year indeed, but she's not here this fine spring. Nor will she be again.'

"'She's not here?' Peter said incredulously. 'But I've seen her. I talked to her only yesterday.'

"'Nay, young man,' the innkeeper said. 'You've not seen Claire Cov-erack, for she's been dead these three years.' Peter stared at him speech-lessly. 'Didn't you know, then?' the old man asked.

"'No,' Peter whispered, almost inaudibly. 'I don't believe you. You must be mistaken.'

"'There's no mistake about it,' the old man said. 'For I was called to iden-tify her body. Poor little lass, like a rag doll cast up by the sea. A terrible sad thing it was.'

"'What was?' Peter whispered hoarsely. 'What happened?'

"'She came here every year, just as you say. She and her young man. She came out from Warwickshire and he all the way from America to meet her, every year of the past three. He'd arrive a day or two later, and they'd take separate rooms, of course, because they were not wed, and she was a lass of quality. They were to be married that summer, and he was to take her back to America. You've never seen a woman so happy, sir. It would have made your heart dance to see her.' He shook his head and lowered his eyes sorrowfully.

"'And what happened?' Peter asked in his harrowed whisper.

"'Why, he never came, sir. She waited for him every day in a little cove just south of here, near Gwithian, where they used to meet. Every livelong day she'd pace the strand, and she'd come back here in the evening and ask if I'd heard anything from him. "Did he not call?" she'd say. "Is there no letter from him?" It would have broken your heart to hear her, sir. I think she was half mad with the grief of it. She'd lie sobbing in her room all hours of the night and she'd eat nothing, although I'd take her up a glass of wine and an apple in the evening. It was something she was fond of; she always took a basket with a bottle of wine and an apple in it when she went to meet him. A proper rogue he was, to leave a lovely lass like that in the lurch. There are men who don't deserve to bear the name.'

'"You were called to identify her body?' Peter asked hoarsely. 'Was she drowned?'

'"Aye,' the old man said. 'Her body was found by someone roaming on the downs, and I was called by the constabulary, for it was known she stayed here. But there was no foul play about it, and it was no accident, either, for she was a fine swimmer. And I'll tell you the way of it, for I said to her on the last morning she left here, "He's not coming, lass, and you must not grieve for him any longer, for he's not worth your tears." And she said to me, "If he won't come to me, I'll go to him." I didn't know what she meant by that until they found her body, but I knew then.'

'"You knew what?' Peter asked in his hoarse whisper.

'"Why sir, it's plain enough. I can almost see it in my mind. What she did was to swim out towards America as far as her strength would take her, and then she sank beneath the waves. On the last day they were to spend together, and he'd still not come.'

'"This was three years ago?' Peter asked. His voice had sunk to a bewildered murmur.

'"Aye. And it's sore missed she is,' the old man said. 'It's not been the same since the day she died.' He frowned at Peter. 'Did you say you'd seen her, sir?'

'"Perhaps I was mistaken,' Peter said. 'Perhaps it was someone who resembled her.'

'"Aye, that's far more like,' the old man said. 'Though there's mysteries

enough in Cornwall. There are piskies on the moors—mischievous creatures that delight in plaguing men. They've driven many a poor soul
mad with their tricks. It may be you've run afoul of them, sir.'

"'It may be,' Peter said. 'Thank you. I appreciate the time you've given
me.'

"'You're very welcome, young sir,' the innkeeper said. 'I hope I haven't
upset you with my tale.'

"'No,' Peter said. 'There's an ounce of awful comfort in it, I suppose.
Though God knows it's the last kind I ever hoped to hear.'

"He spent a sleepless night staring out of the window of his room at
the vast, moonlit, silent sea, and in the morning he drove back to London staring sightlessly through the window of his car, his mind numbed by
the mystery of the old innkeeper's words. It was not until he got to London and presented his ticket to the clerk at the BOAC airline desk that
another mystery—one as faint and merciful as the sunlight breaking through
the mist on the moors—helped to lessen his bereavement and bewilder-
ment. He explained to the clerk that he had missed his flight of the day
before. He had been unavoidably detained, he said, and would be willing to pay whatever penalty was required to change his flight.

"The clerk took his ticket and read it with a look of growing astonishment.

"'Lord save us,' he said. He looked up at Peter and shook his head in
wonder. 'It's a stroke of providence that held you up, sir, wasn't it?'

"'What do you mean?' Peter said.

"'You mean you haven't heard?' the clerk asked.

"'Heard what?' Peter said. 'I've been on the Cornish coast. I haven't read
a newspaper or listened to the radio for weeks.'

"'Why, your flight went down, sir,' the clerk said. 'It lost an engine
and went down into the sea, not ten miles off Bristol. There was no one
saved.' Peter stared at him in wonder. 'It's been on the wireless for hours,'
the clerk said. 'It's a miracle you missed that flight, sir. It would have
been a black day for you if you hadn't.'

"But when Peter got back to Washington there were greater, agonizing mysteries to greet him. When he opened the volume of Yeats to the place where he had pressed the azalea blossoms she had given him, there was nothing between the pages, not even a pinch of dust. And when he unfolded the handkerchief in which he had wrapped the finch's egg she had given him, there was nothing enclosed in the clean white linen, not even a tiny scrap of eggshell. He drove frantically to the camera shop where he had left the photographs he had taken of her to be developed, but when he tore open the envelope and shuffled swiftly through the pack of glossy prints, he was horrified to find that her image did not appear on any of the pictures he had taken of her sleeping on the sand. There was the sunny beach, there was the granite boulder, but where she had lain in its shadow there was only bare sand, unmarked by even the imprint of her body."

Priscilla paused in her story, lifted her paper cup of wine from the sand and drank the last of it. She handed the cup to Ben and said, "Will you give me a little more, Ben? My mouth has gone all dry."

"That's not the end of it, surely," Jill cried.

"No, there's a little more," Priscilla said. "But I'm afraid I'm boring you. It's a very long story. Maybe I'll finish it tomorrow."

"There won't be time tomorrow," Jill said. "And you're certainly not boring me. You can't leave it like that. It isn't fair, at all."

"Yes, I think you're bound to tell us the rest of it," Tony said. "I've a feeling the most mysterious part of it is yet to come. You're a jolly good storyteller, Priss."

"Indeed you are," Jill said. "You should have been a novelist, I think. But you can't leave us up in the air like this. What happened to the poor chap?"

"Well, there was an even greater mystery in his life," Priscilla said. "The most profound that he would ever know." Ben filled her cup from the wine bottle and handed it back to her.

"The last of the wine," he said.

Priscilla drank from the cup, crumpled it in her hand and tossed it into the fire. She watched it flare up and then sink into a mound of ash.

"He used to think about the girl's name," she said after a moment. "And it used to comfort him. It seemed to him the most beautiful and mysterious of all names. Claire: light. The light that God called into the world even before he made the sun or moon or stars. The light that existed before there was any matter, and that cannot be extinguished.

"He tried to believe in this, even after he knew that she was only a ghost, a phantom that perhaps he had created out of his longing. When he realized that it was no more than a ghost he had tried to photograph, he was almost totally demoralized. He couldn't work or sleep or bathe or shave himself. He didn't even go out to eat. He lived on the sandwiches and an occasional piece of fruit from the baskets his friends brought him. He would lie staring up at the ceiling for an entire day, remembering every moment they had spent together, every word she had said to him, her every smile and gesture. Nothing in the present, or in the world around him, had the reality or significance of the beautiful ghost who had loved him as no woman ever had.

"His employer, who had a great respect and affection for Peter, saw that something had to be done or he would drift so far from the world that he would never find his way back. He took Peter to see a psychiatrist, who decided that he was schizophrenic, and had him admitted to a sanitarium in the Adirondack Mountains. There he was treated with Prozac and a regimen of vegetable casseroles and basket weaving and psychiatric analysis, which had little effect, probably because these measures were administered by people who did not believe in miracles, or resurrection, or the need to find something that transcends the reality they urged him so earnestly to accept. The only real therapy he found was in the poetry of Yeats and in listening to birdsong in the pines when he was sitting in a deck chair on the lawn.

"There was a nurse who came out every morning while he was sitting there and brought him oatmeal and a carton of milk and the morning paper. He didn't like her at all. She was prim and fastidious and would identify everything she set down in a cheerfully idiotic way. 'Milk,' she would say. 'Sugar. Oatmeal. Morning paper.' He used to take the paper apart, sheet by sheet, and make paper hats out of it, or airplanes that he would sail across the lawn.

"But one day another nurse came in her place, one whom Peter liked the moment he saw her coming across the lawn with quick, eager steps, as if she were hurrying to keep an appointment she had been looking forward to for days, for weeks or months perhaps. She stopped and bent down to pick a dandelion from the grass as she came toward him and set it on her tray. Then she came to the table and smiled down at him and said, 'Hello. I'm Beth.'

"'Hello,' he said. 'I'm Peter.'

"'Yes, I know,' she said. She set the tray down on the table and took the dandelion from it and held it out to him. He took it without speaking and stuck the stem into the buttonhole of his lapel. He watched the sunlight glistening on her oak-colored hair as she took things from the tray and set them on the table—without naming them, he was very glad to see. When she set down his bowl of oatmeal she grimaced and said, 'Do you like this stuff?'

"'No, I despise it,' Peter said. 'It tastes like sawdust.'

"She laughed silently, lifting her chin to arch her white throat, which Peter thought was like a lily frond tossed upward by a breeze.

"'Then I'll bring you something much nicer tomorrow,' she said. 'I'll steal something out of the refrigerator for you.'

"'I don't want you to get punished for my sake,' Peter said.

"'Oh, I'll be very careful,' she said. 'But you mustn't tell, or Dr. Threlkeld will be very upset. Can I sit down?'

"'I wish you would,' Peter said.

"She sat down across the table from him in one of the wicker chairs and propped her elbow on the table and rested her chin in the palm of her hand, watching him drink the orange juice she had brought. She had eyes of a deep lustrous gray, like dark pearls, and her face was cut as clean and fine as if from abalone shell.

"'I didn't bring the paper,' she said. 'Do you mind?'

"'Thank God,' Peter said. 'There's nothing in it but horror. I expected to find my obituary in it any day.'

"'Don't talk like that,' she said, and smiled at him sweetly. She turned her head to read the title of the volume of Yeats that lay on the table. 'Would you like me to bring you some poetry instead?'

"'Yes,' Peter said.

"'Do you like Dylan Thomas?' she asked.

"'I don't know him very well,' Peter said. 'I haven't read him in years. But there's a line of his that I remembered just now, when you gave me this dandelion.' He looked down at it and touched the stem. "'The force that through the green fuse drives the flower/Drives my red blood.'" He turned the stem of the dandelion between his fingers. 'It is like a green fuse, isn't it?'

"'Yes,' she said. 'And the flower at the end of it is like a little bright explosion. It's a lovely image.'

"'I think I'd like to read some more of him,' Peter said.

"'I'll bring you a book of his tomorrow,' the young nurse said.

"He finished his orange juice and looked at her gray eyes with shameless admiration.

"'Why are you here today?' he asked. 'What happened to the other nurse?'

"'She left the Lodge,' she said. 'I've taken her place.'

"'I thought I'd never seen you before,' Peter said.

"'No, I only came yesterday. I thought I'd rather work here than in a hospital, which is where I've been working. And so just on an impulse I called up to ask if there was a position open here, and they said there was. So I came.'

"'Why would you rather work here?' he asked.

"'Because I'd rather help people whose suffering is in their minds than those whose suffering is in their bodies. I think it's a greater kind of suffering.'

"'You must have known that kind of suffering,' he said.

"She reached out to touch the table with her fingertip, drawing an invisible dandelion there. 'I think everyone does, who ever loses anything they love,' she said. She raised her eyes to Peter and smiled. 'I have to go now,' she said. 'But I'll come back tomorrow, and I'll bring you Dylan Thomas.'

"She came just before noon the next day when the morning dew was still on the grass and there were siskins stirring in the pines and little yellow butterflies dipping over the clover on the lawn. She brought the tray to the table and set it down with a defiant ducking of her chin as if taking pride in the fact that it held no oatmeal. On the tray there was a slim volume of poetry and a bowl of fresh fruit and a pair of glasses and a bottle of unlabeled white wine. Peter gazed in wonder at these offerings.

"'Now this is a much more suitable breakfast for a man in your condition,' she said.

"'It answers every need a man could possibly have,' Peter said. 'In sickness or in health. Where did you get the wine?'

"'I made it,' she said. "It's dandelion wine. I make it every spring. My grandfather taught me how. Would you like some?'

"'Yes, very much,' Peter said.

"She took a corkscrew from the tray and tugged out the cork, then filled the two glasses, which she set onto the table. She raised her glass and said, 'To your quick and complete recovery, and your future happiness, Peter.'

"'And to you,' Peter said. 'And to your mercy.' He lifted his glass and drank. The wine was shrill and dry. 'It's wonderful,' he said. 'It tastes like sunlight.'

"'I'm glad you like it,' she said. 'Would you like a piece of fruit?'

"'Yes. Can I have an apple?' Peter said.

"'Yes,' she said. 'I brought you some Granny Smiths. They're the best apples in the world.' She handed the bowl to him and he took a glistening green apple from it.

"'Will you share it with me?' he asked.

"'Yes,' she said. She took a knife from the tray and sliced the apple in half and handed one of the halves to him. They sat and munched the tart, juicy flesh, smiling at each other. 'Mmm,' she murmured. 'Aren't they good? I love Granny Smiths.' She held the apple in her hand and looked at it, smiling. 'When I was a little girl we used to go out to my grandfather's farm and pick apples every fall. He grew Granny Smiths and Winesaps. I loved to climb up the ladder and stand there in the leaves with the sweet smell of apples in the air and up above me the sky as blue as my grandfather's eyes. In the fall I'd help him make apple butter in big copper pots. I had a lovely childhood. I was a very lucky little girl.'

"'I wish I'd known you then,' Peter said.

"'I wish I'd known you, too,' she said. 'What sort of things did you do when you were a little boy?'

"'I liked to camp a lot,' Peter said. 'And swim, and wander on the beach. In the summers we used to go to Assateague. That's a great long stretch of unspoiled shore on the Maryland coast where wild ponies roam. I used to gather beach plums on the dunes and my grandmother would make them into beach plum jelly. I love beaches more than any other places in the world. They're so clean, and perpetual. I used to sit there for hours and stare out at the sea. I'd dream about beautiful women who were waiting for me somewhere in the world.'

"'Did you find any of them?' she asked.

"'I found one of them,' Peter said. 'I don't know where she is now, but I feel as if she's very close to me sometimes.'

"She looked at him silently for a moment and then took the book of poetry from the tray.

"'I think we should have some poetry now,' she said. 'Would you like that?'

"'Yes, very much,' Peter said.

"She opened the book to where a rose was pressed between the pages.

"'I'm going to read you my favorite poem,' she said. 'It's called "And Death Shall Have No Dominion." Do you remember that one?'

"'No,' Peter said. 'I'd like to hear it.'

"But when she began to read he was so enchanted by the depths of her gray eyes and the delicacy of her coral-colored lips that he scarcely heard the first words of the poem. But as she went on reading her voice took on a soft, oracular eloquence that made the words flame up like blown embers, and as he listened the glow of them dispelled the lingering shadows in his brain in the way that raked coals will flame up and bring light to a darkened room:

They shall have stars at elbow and foot;
Though they go mad they shall be sane,
Though they sink through the sea they shall rise again;
Though lovers be lost love shall not;
And death shall have no dominion.

"It seemed to Peter as if her voice came to him through fathoms of cool green water. When she set down the book he sat looking into her gray eyes that were washed clean of all sorrow, as rich and strange as pearls."

When Priscilla had finished speaking they sat silently for a time listening to the waves pound on the shore.

"Well, that's my ghost story," she said. "I don't remember whether I read it or heard it. I seem to have known it forever."

"I think perhaps you have," Jill said. She stared into the fire. "I think perhaps it's a story every woman knows." She turned to Ben and gazed at him for a moment. "It's your turn now," she said.

"I don't know any ghost stories," Ben said.

"Oh, come along. You don't get off that easy."

"No, it's true," Ben said. "I never seem to remember ghost stories. I can't think of a single one."

"Do you remember playing Prospero in *The Tempest*?" she said. "I do. Gave me the chills, the way you did that speech of his at the end."

"Yes, let's hear that," Tony said. "I've not heard you do Shakespeare, and from what Jill says, you're jolly good at it."

"I don't know if I remember," Ben said. He stared into the fire and seemed to see in the flickering scarlet flames all the rose-fleshed, lambent muses that had beckoned to him from the stove-fires of his youth. He had not read the speech in twenty years but when he began to speak the words welled up to his tongue like water from a spring:

Our revels now are ended. These our actors,
As I foretold you, were all spirits and
Are melted into air, into thin air:
And, like the baseless fabric of this vision,
The cloud-capp'd towers, the gorgeous palaces,
The solemn temples, the great globe itself,
Yea, all which it inherit, shall dissolve
And, like this insubstantial pageant faded,
Leave not a wrack behind. We are such stuff
As dreams are made on, and our little life
Is rounded with a sleep.

"Oh, that's the ghostliest one of all!" Priscilla said. She hugged herself and shivered.

"It is indeed," Tony said. "Ghosts of ourselves. Those are the scariest sort of specters there are."

"I'm afraid I didn't do it justice," Ben said. "I've lost my touch."

"You don't do badly at all," Jill murmured.

The tape had run out. He got up and put another tape on the player and stirred the fire with a stick. They sat until the embers had faded, sipping the last of the wine and listening to the thunder of the surf while they watched the slow descent of the moon through the reefs of cloud and the low stars waning in the mist above the sea. When she had finished her wine Jill tossed her cup into the fire and watched it flare up for a moment in the coals.

"Well, I suppose I'd better pack it up," she said. "It's off to Washington in the morning."

"Oh, let's not go yet," Priscilla said. "It's such a lovely night, and it's your last."

"I know, but I think perhaps I'd better," Jill said. "I'm going to get up very early tomorrow and have that sunrise walk I've been promising myself. I've been too sluggardly to do that yet."

They tossed sand onto the coals and gathered up their empty basket and ice chest and their wet towels and plodded back across the cold sand to the house. When they had gone to bed, with the deck door open and the sound of waves booming in the summer night, Priscilla reached out to take his hand in the darkness and said, "Ben, I didn't know you had played Prospero."

"Yes," he said. "Some people said it was the best thing I ever did."

.　　.　　.

He woke very early, at five thirty, put on a pair of slacks and a sweat-shirt and went out to the kitchen. He made a cup of tea and carried it out to the deck and sat in one of the sling chairs in the moist warm air. The moon had set and it was black above the sea, the air so dense that the sound of the surf carried loudly from the shore, the clap of the breakers coming ceaselessly and rhythmlessly, each report as sudden and startling as a rifle shot. He felt a nervous excitement of the kind he had felt after a night of sentry duty in a jungle foxhole, when you were not yet quite sure whether you would make it back from the mission or whether the next round of sniper fire would be the one that got you, half an hour before your relief showed up. When the sky began to pale above the sea, he carried his teacup into the kitchen and went down the stairs and through the dressing room to the sand and began to walk along the beach.

The sand was moist and cool and the slack tide had bared shell-beds that bubbled with a silvery stipple in the starlight, like field-frost. The glow in the east grew brighter as he walked toward it, until he could see the line of the horizon defined in the darkness, a roseate welling of light be-hind the sharp edge of the purple water, and then the scarlet rim of the sun's disc slipped up above the long dark line of the sea, as sharp and stark as a blood-colored paper lantern as it rose, and the sky was flushed with a soft, peachskin pink that sprinkled across the sea in glittering shards of light like a trail of sequins. He walked toward the rising sun until he could see the frail, sticklike, charcoal skeleton of the Frisco pier against the dawn sky and then he sat down on a stranded timber to watch the great scarlet globe climb up through the sea-mist into the middle sky.

He felt full of a surly, festering, confused excitement. He knew that by this time Jill was almost certainly abroad somewhere on the beach, and he knew that she had deliberately let him know that she would be before they had left the fire the night before; and he sat confounded by this knowledge and by his abject desire to profit by it and by the feeling of ignominy that the desire produced in him, and by his certainty that she was aware of his confusion. He felt a kind of craven victimization, like a dog that is being lured by a man with a piece of meat in one hand and a stick in the other. Still, it might be a genuine proposition, he thought; she might have been honestly and candidly inviting him to a last, illicit interlude before she went her way forever. Something to seal their odd, quixotic passion. She was certainly capable of such impetuous, gypsy-like gestures. She was after all a woman of the flesh far more than of the intellect, as sensual as she was intelligent, sensitive, and subtle. Subtle, above everything. Maybe she just wants to have a final, quiet conversation with me, he thought, to explain the nature of her feelings, to speak of the mystery of human relationships. Or of metaphysics. Oh, metaphysics, almost certainly. She wants to sit and talk about metaphysics, with her legs spread. He smiled bitterly.

The thing to do, he decided, was to finish his walk in his customary way, with a determined unconcern—to stroll back to the house at his usual pace, with his usual enjoyment of the solitude of the fresh morning world, as if the woman didn't exist. If she appeared, he would greet her affably, with a show of mild, teasing surprise that she had managed to get up so early, and invite her, not to tarry with him on the beach—no, no!—but to accompany him back to the house. He would talk lightly about trivial, impersonal things—the details of her flight to Washington, the changes in the city over recent years, the fine weather. He would point out phenomena of interest—the freshly excavated sand-crab lairs, the various species of gulls and sandpipers, the curious behavior of turnstones. He would trump her invitation to intrigue with a composed, good-natured imperviousness to it. It would be hugely satisfying to see her fume inwardly at his indifference to the opportunity with which she had so deviously presented him. The impression he would give would be of a man who has outgrown his enthusiasm for any such opportunities, who has transcended what is base and ignoble in his nature. He would finesse the damned witch as she deserved.

He got up and began to wander back toward the house in his usual meandering path across the beach, pausing sometimes to look back at the sunrise or to study a flight of pelicans across the water or to bend down and dig up a seashell from the sand. If she happened to be watching, he thought, it would demonstrate his complete absorption in the pure and guileless beauty of the world, which was what he truly loved, whose charms would outlast all the ephemeral glamor of the little Circes of the stage. Nevertheless, he occasionally cast a quick furtive glance along the beach in tribute to any such Circes who might be abroad. Anyone he saw, even if too distant to be identified, he could reasonably assume to be her, since there was seldom anyone abroad so early. But he walked for a quarter of an hour without seeing anyone, which began to erode his self-possession considerably. Of course she might have walked the other way—south, toward Hatteras rather than north, toward the lighthouse, as he had done. In that case he would miss her, even if she had come out. Unless, of course, he walked past the house and on down the beach toward Hatteras. And the house was now no more than fifty yards away, the dome rising above the dunes in the low morning light like a great gray pearl. He glanced at his watch and saw that it was six fifteen. There was not a lot of time left for anything—a conversation, a dalliance, or even a decently extended overture to one—before the others began to stir in the house. Priscilla was seldom

up before seven thirty or eight, but he wasn't sure about Tony, especially
if Jill had awakened him when she got up. If she had got up. And especially
if he were aware of their tryst, and indecently imagining its details at the
very moment. If it could be called a tryst, of course. Probably not. Probably her remark had been innocent and offhand, not extended as an invitation, a provocation, or a promise of any kind. After all, she was nowhere
in sight.

He had reached the house; he stood uncertainly abreast of it for a minute
or two before he went on, past it, down the beach toward Hatteras. He
walked more quickly, abandoning his pretense of being occupied with
the beauty of the morning, his eyes candidly scanning the dunes.

After fifteen minutes more of walking he saw her in the distance sitting on the crest of a sandhill at the edge of a brake of sea oats whose golden
stalks and tassels had begun to glimmer faintly in the early light. He had
no doubt whatever that it was she; even sitting, and motionless, there
was a kind of lissome, feral grace about her attitude—one leg outstretched,
one hand resting on the sand, one upraised knee gathered into the crook
of a slender arm—that was unmistakable. Even the tumble of her copper-
colored hair across her shoulders had a gorgeous, deep, burnished disorder that was like the hair of no other woman he had ever seen.

She was a hundred yards away. He walked along the beach until he was
abreast of her and then without hesitation plodded up through the soft sand
and climbed the dune to where she sat. She was wearing a hip-length
dark blue sweater beneath which her bare white legs and the pink V of
the crotch of her bikini pants were mesmerizingly revealed.

"Well, good morning," he said. "You made it. I didn't think you would."

"Oh, yes. If there's something worth losing a bit of sleep over, I don't
mind the sacrifice."

"Was it worth it?"

"Oh, my word." She smiled gently and shook her head in wonder.
"Do you know, I've been trying to think when I last saw a sunrise. I don't
mean just watching the sky go sort of sickly gray over the chimney pots

in Hammersmith, but actually seeing the sun come up like that, over the edge of the world, like a great red ball of fire—and I can't remember a single blessed time. I don't think I ever really saw a proper sunrise before. I don't think there's one person in ten who has."

"It's very beautiful," Ben said.

"Well, I don't know about beautiful. One speaks of a painting of a sunrise, or even a photograph of one, as being beautiful. Seems a bit ridiculous to use the same word for the real thing."

"I know," Ben said. "Like love, in books."

"Exactly." She smiled at him quaintly, let go of her knee, stretched out both legs and leaned back on her elbows. "You do put things well sometimes. Still."

"Still?"

"Yes. As you still do Shakespeare. And picnics. Do you come out every morning and watch that sight?"

"If the weather's good," Ben said.

"Odd. One would think it bred no end of humility in a man. Of course it may be what keeps you sane."

"I've never felt my sanity particularly threatened," Ben said. He sat down beside her on the dune.

"Haven't you? Good Lord, I feel mine threatened every day."

"Perhaps you live in more perilous circumstances," he said.

"Do you think so? Not much genuine peril in South Kensington. No more than here, I shouldn't think."

"No, that's true." He looked at her for a moment and then out at the beach. "You've got a good view up here."

"Yes. I saw you coming, quite a way away."

"Did you? See anyone else?"

"Only a dog that was here earlier, scrounging about. Looked a very pleasant creature. I whistled to him, but he wasn't having it. Just went on nosing down the beach."

"Wise dog," Ben said.

"Oh, really? What a beastly thing to say."

"Idle remark." He grinned at her repentantly. "Meant to be witty."

"Honestly! And I just complimented you for putting things well. I take it back."

"Sorry," he said. "We shouldn't quarrel. This might be the last conversation we ever have."

"The last we ever have? I thought you were coming over to London next year."

"Well, that was just a kind of social nicety," Ben said. "It's the sort of thing people say, isn't it? 'We'll have to do lunch one day.' I wasn't sure you'd want to hear from us if we did come over."

"I see. So you didn't intend to call."

"Not unless I thought you really wanted us to. It can be an awful bore when people thrust their company on you."

"As we've done, you mean?"

"No, I didn't mean that at all. I haven't been less bored for the last twenty years."

"And how would you have determined whether we really wanted to see you?"

"Well, that's one of the reasons I came out here this morning," he said. "I was hoping I might run into you."

"Thought you might get it cleared up, did you?"

"I had that in mind. If you remember, I asked you to come and see us again next summer, and you said you were going to Dubrovnik."

"So I am."

"Well, I thought that might just be a nicety on your part. A graceful way of declining the invitation."

"You have that much confidence in my social graces, have you? After the way I behaved at your wedding reception?"

Ben looked down at the sand for a moment. "Well, that was forgivable, in the circumstances," he said.

"Oh, you've forgiven me. I'm very glad to hear that. It's troubled me for years."

"That's very hard to believe," Ben said.

"No, truly. I was afraid you might be thinking of me as a dreadful little Cockney churl of some kind. I suppose I misjudged the depths of your magnanimity." Ben didn't reply to this. She broke a stem of the dune grass, clipped it off with her fingernail and sat fondling the golden tassel in her palm.

"Lovely grass, this," she said. "What's it called?"

"Sea oats."

"Oats? Can you eat it, then?"

"I don't know," Ben said. "I suppose so."

She plucked one of the flat seeds from the tassel, put it between her teeth and nibbled it tentatively. "'Tisn't bad," she said. "Bit bland, but I suppose it could be seasoned up. Do they make porridge of it or something?"

"No," Ben said. "It's what keeps the dunes together. You're not supposed to pick it. It's against the law."

"Another law we've broken," she said. "I think I shall take this stalk back with me as a souvenir. Bit of forbidden fruit."

Ben smiled. "I wonder if Eve took the core of the apple with her, out of Paradise?" he said.

"I suppose she must have. We've got plenty of them about."

"Well, you'll have to plant some of those seeds in Hyde Park. Give them a taste of native American bane."

She laughed. "Oh, yes. As if there wasn't enough confusion in Hyde Park as it is." She lay back flat in the sand and jiggled the tassel of grass above her face. "Lovely. Like plumes." Ben looked down at her white legs in the sand.

"You going swimming?" he asked.

"I thought I might take a last dip. What about you?"

"I didn't put my suit on," he said.

"That didn't bother you last night."

"It's light now. And people start walking on the beach about this time."

"And they'd run and get the constable, I suppose."

"Probably. Virtue never sleeps."

"I suppose you'd tell him about my plucking the grass."

"I might, yet, if you try to get away for good." He gazed down at her face and after a moment of hesitation he took a strand of her hair and ran it between his fingertips. "It might be a way to get you back here. I could start extradition proceedings."

"Well, you'd have no trouble from Maggie Thatcher, I'm sure. She'd be only too glad to get rid of me." He replaced the strand of hair and separated another. Her hair was still cool in the morning air. "You'd go that far, would you, to get me back here?" she said.

"To serve justice," he said, "I would stop at nothing."

"Oh, really? I didn't know you were all that keen on justice. That's something you want to be very sure about." She brushed her lips with the tassel of sea oats and smiled. "Bring me to justice, would you? You think you have the spunk for it?"

"I don't know. I doubt it," Ben said. "I can be too easily swayed." He replaced the strand of hair and laid his hand on her thigh, stroking the cool skin with his fingertips.

"I don't think I should do that if I were you," she said. "You won't be proud of it, later. I won't."

"Does that mean you don't want to?" Ben said.

"No, it doesn't mean anything of the kind."

"Well, what does it mean?"

"It means I've grown quite fond of your wife, for one thing. And that I'd like to get away from here with as much dignity as possible."

Ben withdrew his hand. "Tell me something," he said. "Why did you come out here this morning?"

"Because I wanted to see the sunrise."

"It wouldn't have been to get even, would it? Give me a taste of my own medicine?"

"No, it wouldn't." She sat up and clasped her knees, looking at him earnestly. "Look, we've been all over that, Ben. I've told you how I feel, quite honestly. I think you've done jolly well for yourself, and I'm very pleased about it. You've got a very good job and a lovely wife and a perfectly marvelous existence, and you deserve to be congratulated. I've not done too badly, either, and I'm quite contented. I've got a bit of a career going, and a man who respects me, who's a marvelous companion, and who gives me every sort of support I need. I don't know what more either of us could ask. I think we'd both be a good deal more comfortable if we let it go at that. I enjoy you and Priss—you're jolly good company, both of you— and I should hate to feel that I'd never see you again." She looked out at the sea. "We're getting to the age, you know, where it's very hard to come by anything as valuable as an old friend—someone who shares memories with us, some of our old ideals, a little of the fire of our youth, someone who was part of the foolishness and fun we had once. That isn't something you let go down the drain without a second thought. Or that you muck up for good, for the sake of a little something on the side— something you could get just as well from a handsome young juvenile, or a girl out of the typing pool."

"I don't know much about the current crop of juveniles," he said, "but I couldn't find anything like you in the typing pool."

"Well, perhaps not. But maybe in the board room." She smiled and laid her hand on his knee. "I hope you come to London next year. Truly. I know a marvelous restaurant that you'd love."

Ben leaned down and kissed her fingers on his knee. "OK," he said. He turned his head and smiled at her. "Will you pick up the check?"

"I always seem to," she said, and smiled back at him. "I did the last time."

Ben looked toward the house, then at his wristwatch. "You going for your dip?"

"I think so, yes. I won't be long."

"I'd better wait and keep an eye on you, then," he said. "It's dangerous to swim alone."

"Do you mean to say you'd plunge in after me, if I started to drown? Trousers and all?"

"To keep a great artist alive. Oh, I think so." He smiled at her. "It would be a way of paying some of my debts, I suppose."

"You said last night you'd only bother with those of us who deserved salvation."

"Well, I guess you deserve it."

"Perhaps if you knew me better, you wouldn't think so." She stood up and stripped off her sweater and stood staring out for a moment at the sea. "Perhaps I won't, after all," she said. "It looks a bit cold out there." She sat back down on her towel. "Perhaps I'll just sit here for a bit. You go along."

"You sure?" he said.

"Yes. I'd like to have a last look round before I go. I may just wade along the edge a bit. I won't be long."

"OK. Remember your plane will be here at ten." He stood up. "I'll have some tea ready for you. Brewed properly, in the pot."

"Yes, and not too long, mind. Not for more than three minutes. D'you remember?"

He nodded. "'Not till I hear you on the stairs.' Wasn't that what you used to say?"

She reached up and took his hand. "Just a moment," she said. She drew him down and kissed him lightly and lingeringly on the mouth.

"Don't go in that water, now," he said, straightening up. "I don't want you drowning."

"No, no. I've a thing or two to do, before that."

He loped down the deep sand of the dune and at the bottom turned and raised his hand to her. After he had walked fifty yards along the beach toward the house he heard her call, "Good-bye, love." He turned and waved to her again. She was standing on top of the dune looking after him.

.   .   .

Priscilla was sitting at the table with the paper and her toast and tea when he came into the kitchen. "Hello," she said. "Did you have a good walk?"

"Very pleasant. It's a great morning. You're up early."

"Jill said she wanted to take a walk, so I thought I'd make sure she got up. I guess I ought to wake her. She wants to press a blouse, too."

"She's up," Ben said. "She's out on the beach. I was just talking to her."

"Really? She didn't come back with you?"

"No. She wants to poke around by herself for a while. She said she wouldn't be long."

"I hope she's not going in the water," Priscilla said.

"No, I warned her about it. She said she might just wade a little."

"I worry about people going in that ocean alone. It's so dangerous."

"Well, don't worry about Jill. She can take care of herself if anyone can."

"I don't know. She's so reckless sometimes. I have a feeling she's very prone to disaster. That she almost courts it."

Ben went to the stove and lifted the lid on the kettle. "Is this hot?"

"I think I used it all. You'd better heat some more." He filled the kettle at the faucet, replaced it on the stove, and turned the fire up under it. "Ben, just step out on the deck, will you, and make sure she's all right?"

"OK, OK. You're becoming a mother hen." He tugged her hair affectionately as he went past her to the salon. He crossed the room to the glass door, slid it open and went out onto the deck. Leaning against the rail he looked down the shore toward Hatteras and saw Jill coming up the beach toward the house, her hands plunged into the breast pockets of her sweatshirt. He waved to her and she waved back.

The kettle was whistling on the stove when he came back into the kitchen. "She's on her way," he said. "Be here in ten minutes. I promised to get her tea ready."

"Oh, good," Priscilla said. "I had a funny little feeling there for a minute. I don't know why."

Ben turned the kettle down to simmer, took the teapot from the table, lifted the silver ball out by its chain, emptied the wet leaves out of it into the sink and refilled the ball with a spoonful of dry leaves from the canister. He put a clean cup and saucer on the table from the cupboard and then sat down across from Priscilla, separated the financial section from the newspaper, folded it lengthwise, and scanned the business news. Officials of Union Carbide, he read, were insisting that a 47 million dollar settlement for victims of the 1984 gas leak in Bhopal, India, remained binding even though the country's new government had disavowed the settlement. AT&T had risen by five-eighths of a point. Beech-Nut had suffered a decline in stock values after pleading guilty to 215 felony counts of intentionally distributing millions of jars of bogus apple juice for babies. He frowned.

"Listen to this!" Priscilla cried. "Do you know what that man Iacocca said?"

"No," Ben said. "About what?"

"About the fact that he earned twenty-three point six million dollars in 1986. 'That's the American way,' he said. 'If little kids don't aspire to make money like I did, what the hell good is this country?'" She flung the paper across the kitchen, drew an enormous breath and expelled it in a great hoarse croak of indignation. "Grroff!"

"You'd better have a glass of orange juice," Ben said.

"I'd better have a strait jacket. I'm never going to read a newspaper again. I mean it. It just gets you upset for the rest of the entire day. You know what I'm going to do? I'm going to watch old movies for the rest of my life. I'm going to sit in there with the VCR and watch *Casablanca*, and *Miracle on Thirty-Fourth Street*, and *It's a Wonderful Life*, forever and ever."

"They're colorizing them all now," Ben said.

"Oh, God, wouldn't you know!" she cried in a kind of hopeless wail, dropping her face into her hands.

Ben heard the sound of water splashing in the shower stall below the kitchen. "Here's Jill," he said. "I'd better get her tea on." He went to the stove and filled the teapot with hot water from the kettle. As he set it on the table he heard Jill's footsteps on the stairs and a moment later she opened the basement door and stood at the top of the steps holding a tangled mass of brown seaweed that dripped down her arm. She raised it above her head and chanted:

What would the world be, once bereft
Of wet and of wilderness?

"Be dry and tame," Ben said.

"'Long live the wet and the wilderness yet.'" She tossed the clump of seaweed to him across the kitchen and came to the table where she dropped into a chair beside Priscilla with a huge puff of fatigue. "God, I'm done in! I've been galloping for miles. Is there tea?"

"Ben just fixed you some," Priscilla said.

"What a lamb he is. Is this it?" She lifted the lid from the teapot and peeked inside. "Hasn't brewed too long, I hope."

"Only just put in," Ben said. "When I heard you on the stairs."

"Quite right. What is that stuff I found?"

"Common sargassum," Ben said. "Grows in the open sea, but it often washes in. There are hundreds of square miles of it offshore. It's called the Sargasso Sea." He dropped the clump of seaweed into the wastebasket.

"Really? I didn't know that. Of course I know next to nothing about the natural world. Except that it's very beautiful. God, what a glorious morning. You should have come along, Priss."

"I'm a slugabed," Priscilla said. "Did you see the sunrise?"

"Did I not. It was spellbinding. I shall never forget it. I said to Ben, I don't think I've ever truly seen a sunrise before. Is this my cup?"

"Yes," Ben said. He took the tea ball out of the pot and poured the cup full for her.

"Ta. 've you seen Tony?"

"Not a hair of him," Ben said.

"What time is it?"

"Ten after seven."

"Perhaps I'd better give him a shout."

"I'll do it," Ben said. "Have your tea."

"Thanks, love."

He went out into the hall and tapped at Tony's door. There was only a muffled murmur of protest from inside the room. "Come on, hit the deck!" Ben called through the door. "*Vita brevis, ars longae!*" Tony grumbled distantly and incomprehensibly.

"Did he respond, at all?" Jill asked when he came back into the kitchen.

"He speaks in tongues," Ben said.

"Yes, he does that, of a morning. Nothing that a hot muffin won't put right."

"Why don't you have one too? And some strawberry jam," Priscilla said. "It will settle your stomach for the flight. You won't get anything to eat until noon."

"I think perhaps I will, for a change," Jill said. "I feel just a bit queasy this morning. I don't know why."

"It's because you're leaving too soon," Priscilla said. "Call them up and say you've broken your leg."

"Shall I? It wouldn't take much, you know. I hate this all to end." She looked out of the window. "I haven't had such a holiday since I was a girl and we went to Liverpool one summer. It was the first time I ever saw the sea. So huge and clean it was. I'd no idea. Felt I'd been shriven." She blinked into the sunlight. "Precious little I had to be shriven of, then. Only a kid with pimples who gave me free rides on the whirligig."

"Stay another day and get shriven again," Priscilla said.

"Oh, Lord, it'd take more than a day. More like a fortnight."

Priscilla got up and went to the refrigerator. "Well then, I'm going to fix you a genuine blueberry waffle, with Vermont maple syrup," she said. "A last tribute from the New World to the Old."

"Oh, Priss, don't go to a lot of trouble."

"It's no trouble at all; it's just a mix. It won't take ten minutes."

"I'll go have a shower," Ben said. He went into the bedroom, showered and changed into clean slacks and a sports shirt. When he came back into the kitchen Tony had joined the others and sat at the table in his dressing gown eating waffles and maple syrup.

"Jolly good, these," he said, nodding to Ben.

"Glad you like them," Ben said. "Sorry about having to rout you out."

"I should hope you were," Tony said. "Shouting Latin mottoes at one, at the crack of dawn. It's a bit much."

"Do you good," Jill said. "Stiffens the moral fibre. A person ought to start every day with something from Horace."

"Oh, yes?" Tony said. "Here's one for you, then: '*Procul hinc, procul este.*'"

"What does that mean?" Jill asked.

"Roughly, 'Get lost.'"

There was a strange, slightly feverish air of merriment among them like that which takes possession of a household on some crucial, valedictory occasion—the departure of a son for his first year at college or at summer camp, or the morning of a daughter's wedding. They chattered with an unnatural gayety and there was a kind of nervous animation in the way they buttered their waffles and poured their tea. There was a sense of both bereavement and relief, like the breaking of a trance. Priscilla didn't even wash or stack the dishes; she left everything on the table—plates sticky with syrup, bitten halves of muffins, blobs of butter—in a spasm of delinquency that showed the depths of her discomposure. When she went to dress, Ben cleaned up the kitchen and then sat at his desk in the study and made out a list of New York restaurants for Jill and Tony. When he had finished he went into the living room and straightened all the pictures on the walls and then sat staring at the sunlight on the deck until Priscilla came into the room and asked him to zip up the back of her dress.

"You cleaned up," she said. "Thanks, Ben. I feel all out of joint. As if we ought to be planning a picnic or something."

"It's OK. I didn't have anything to do."

They sat smoking cigarettes until Jill and Tony came out of the bedroom with their bags. Jill set her suitcase down beside the piano and stood looking around the room, at the pictures, the furniture, and the bright blue sky above the dome.

"I shall miss this place," she said. She turned toward the piano and put out her hand to touch the metal figurine of the child in the swing.

"Will you take it with you?" Priscilla said. "Please. It would make me very happy. I remember you said it would console a person for everything he'd ever lost."

Jill caressed the child's hair with her fingertips. "No," she said after a moment. "It's very sweet of you. But I won't be consoled."

The drive to Frisco took only twenty minutes. They did not pass another car on the narrow asphalt road and the world seemed deserted in the clear bright morning. The beach cottages stood silent on their tall, frail legs and the surf boomed distantly behind the dunes.

"I hate leaving places," Jill said. "Gives me the willies."

"Where will you stay in New York?" Priscilla asked.

"I don't know. It all gets arranged by the producer. Some place near the theatre, I should think."

"Will you send us a postcard after you open, and let us know how it went?"

"If you like. We probably shan't last through the week."

"You'll run forever. We may come up and see you again, in the fall. I'd love to see the play again."

"Would you? That would be lovely."

"I've made you out a list of restaurants that we like," Ben said. He took it out of his breast pocket and handed it to Tony. "Most of them are in the Village. You'll have to go there when you get a day off. You'll like the Village."

"So I understand. It's a bit like Chelsea, isn't it?"

"More like Notting Hill Gate, in the old days. If you like Edna Millay, you'll have to go and see her house. It's on Seventh Avenue there. I've written the directions."

"Oh, jolly good. How very nice of you. I must say you've been marvelous hosts. You really must come over to us, you know."

"We will," Priscilla said. "After all, it isn't as if we were saying good-bye forever."

"No, it isn't," Jill said. "Now that we've got in touch with you, we shall make the most of it." She suddenly opened the small straw bag she was carrying and scrabbled through it with her fingertips. "Bloody hell," she said. "I've forgotten my postcard. The one to Jennifer. I meant to post it on the way."

"I'll mail it for you," Priscilla said. "I'm going in to the village later."

"Will you, love? I think I've left it on the dressing table."

"I'll find it," Priscilla said.

Ben turned off the highway and took the side road to the airstrip. It was a very small installation for private planes. There was no tower or hangar, nothing but a waiting pavilion and a single runway, paved north and south, with a yellow wind sock flapping gently at either end in the morning breeze. Two small private planes, a Cessna and a Piper, stood in their berths on a parking ramp beyond the pavilion, moored by wire cables to iron rings in the blacktop. Ben's company plane had already arrived and was parked on the tarmac at the edge of the runway, its passenger door latched open and the boarding ladder let down from the fuselage. Max, the pilot, sat on a bench in the pavilion with his hands in his pockets and his legs stretched out into the sun. He was a lean young man with bright red hair and the look of a long distance runner. He got up and, smiling, walked out across the parking lot to meet them.

"Hello, Max," Ben said.

"Good morning, Mr. Oakshaw." They shook hands.

"You got here early."

"Yes, sir. Ten minutes ago. It was smooth as silk, all the way down."

"Good. This is Miss Davenport and Mr. Griswold. Max Fischer."

"How do you do," Max said. He shook hands with them. "We've got a great day for flying."

"Haven't we, though?" Tony said. "It's very nice of you to come down for us."

"It's a pleasure," Max said. "Nothing I enjoy more."

"You cleared for National, Max?" Ben asked.

"Yes, sir. Did you say Dulles?"

"No, National," Ben said. He turned to Jill and took her by the shoulders. "Well, it's been great to see you, Jill."

"Yes, it has," she said. She kissed him quickly on the cheek. "Thanks, Ben." She turned to Priscilla and embraced her, pressing their cheeks together. "Priss, I don't know what to tell you. You've been an absolute angel. I shan't forget it, ever."

"I won't either," Priscilla said. "Thank you for coming."

"We shall expect to see you in London, mind."

"You will," Priscilla said. "Maybe before. In New York." She embraced Tony lightly and kissed him on the cheek. "Tony, I don't know when we've had nicer guests."

"Certainly never had nicer hosts," Tony said. "Absolutely unforgettable. Couldn't begin to thank you." He held out his hand to Ben. "Cheers, old boy. Far more than we deserved."

"It was good to meet you," Ben said. "Have a good trip."

"If you folks are ready, I'll take your bags," Max said.

"Oh, thank you."

He picked up the suitcases and walked ahead of them across the tarmac to the Learjet in the sunlight. Ben and Priscilla stood under the eaves of the pavilion and watched with fading smiles. Tony went up the boarding steps first and Max handed him the bags. At the top of the steps Jill paused and turned back to wave. Ben and Priscilla waved back and stood watching gravely as Max went up the steps, pulled them up behind him and closed and latched the door. After a minute or two the rudder waggled and the wing flaps raised and lowered as he went through his preflight routine and then the engines started with a coughing roar and the plane taxied out onto the runway and faced south into the breeze. The engines revved with a growing roar, the light plane trembling at the end of the strip, and then he let go of the brakes and it started down the runway, gaining speed until it rose into the clear blue sky. When it banked north across the sun a shower of light flashed from its wings like the splash of light from a leaping marlin.

"Well, there they go," Priscilla said. "I'm going to miss those two. It's going to be very dull around here without them."

Ben nodded. Watching the plane disappear into the bright haze above the sea, he felt a profound and weary gratitude come over him, too solemn for celebration, like the dumb, depthless sense of commutation you felt when you ended a tour of duty in the jungle and flew to the hot, beery, idle, aching solitude of a week of R and R at Cam Ranh Bay.

But when they got back to the house, the sense of Jill's and Tony's absence was acute. The place seemed inconsolably silent and empty of their presence. Ben went into their bedroom and felt an almost physical throe of regret at the sight of their unmade beds and their damp towels tossed across the rim of the bathtub. On the dressing table he found the postcard Jill had forgotten. It was a livid color photograph of the sound at sunset, addressed to someone named Jennifer in London. On the back of it Jill had written:

Had dinner here last night. The photo is only a very small exaggeration of the view—a scene from the Apocalypse. It's very hard to sustain ambition, vanity, or malice in the midst of all this splendor, but no doubt they'll all be resumed when I get back to dear, dirty London. As you shall see, if I find you've forgotten to feed my cat!

When Priscilla came into the room he turned quickly, holding out the card to her.

"Jill's card," he said.

"Oh, good. I'll drop it in the box when I go in. What are you doing?"

"Making the bed. I'm going to share the work with you until Esther gets back." He bent and began stripping the sheets from the beds.

"Oh, that's sweet. But just strip them, Ben. I'll make them up when I get back." She peered at the postcard, squinting her eyes, and chuckled.

"Very naughty," Ben said. "Reading the guest's mail. What's she say?"

"Listen to this." She read the card and laughed. "It's metaphysical, I think."

"It's frivolous," Ben said.

"It's both. She's a sweet, frivolous, metaphysician. The only one alive. My goodness, I'm going to miss her."

"I will too," Ben said.

He found that he did so with surprising intensity and for far longer than he had expected, in spite of the profound relief he felt at her absence. Perhaps because of it; free of the threat of her presence and of the further absurdities and indignities it might have inspired in him, he could relish all the more those he had already committed in its spell—and with guaranteed impunity. He relived the dangerous thrill of them with the immunity one feels in reading the reckless exploits of lovers in a novel. In the early mornings when he sat on the sundeck having his solitary cup of tea in the darkness, he would re-create in scalding detail the savage pleasure of the episode in the shower stall, the exquisite, feral look of her bent over a rubble of scarlet crab shell at the cafe table in Ocracoke, the way she had of closing her eyes and lifting her head to the cry of a gull, a jest, a memory, or the feel of sunlight or sea spray on her face. These images were so persistent and poignant that he had to make a conscious effort not to appear unduly abstracted in the days after her departure. He tried to disguise his frequent lapses into silence by reading a novel that someone had left behind a couple of summers before, Camus's *The Stranger*. This proved to be a mistake because it was a book that Priscilla admired, and she was eager to discuss it with him every time he put it down, although he couldn't remember a word of what he had read from one moment to the next. Finally he gave up all pretense of interest in it, tossing it onto the floor of the deck one afternoon and muttering, "This is rubbish. I can't read another word of it."

"Rubbish? It's *Camus*."

"So it's Camus. What did he know?"

"He knew that we define ourselves by what we do, and that what we do helps to define humanity as well. And that what men do is the only thing of any real significance in the universe."

"Why didn't he say so, in so many words? Why does he spin out this dreary fable about it?"

"Oh, for heaven's sake! You're an artist and you ask a question like that."

Ben considered this for a moment in sudden, fulminating, bleak impatience at the fantasy she had invented and nurtured about him for so long, and in which he had complacently, fatuously, encouraged her. It was ignoble in both of them, he suddenly realized. What gave him the courage to recognize the fact after so many years of the mutual self-deception they had practised he didn't know, but it seemed to be born in a wave of nausea, disgust, frustration, loss, or loneliness.

"If we define ourselves by what we do, maybe you'd better think of something else to call me besides an artist," he said.

"What else would I call you?" she said. "It's what you are."

He looked at her and saw that for the first time in her life she was asking mercy of him—expecting it, demanding it, perhaps—in the way that he demanded mercy of Linda and Chuck and the rest of his friends. She deserves that much from me, at the very least, he thought.

"Well, I don't think Tony would agree with you," he said, and grinned at her. "He's pretty fastidious about that sort of thing. If he called me an artist he'd say the word like a man plucking a hair off his tongue."

Priscilla smiled back but said after a moment, "I thought you liked him."

"I like him fine," Ben said. "But he bores me."

"Why does he bore you?"

"I don't know. He's epicene. He reminds me of Henry James or Alexander Woollcott or somebody. All that damn whimsey." He kicked the book across the floor and leaned forward with his elbows on his knees. "Let's have a drink."

"It's a little early to start drinking, isn't it?"

"Not for Jews. The Jewish day begins at sunset. It's getting well along toward midnight, by their clock."

"But you're not Jewish."

"I'm thinking of converting. How about a glass of Manischewitz?"

"Well, a very light chablis, maybe. On ice."

When he came back with the drinks he stood beside her chair, kneading the nape of her neck with his fingertips. She bowed her head and murmured rapturously.

"I suppose Jill bores you too," she said after a moment.

"A lot of the time. When she's being so damned elfin. But most of the time she's very sweet, I have to admit. She's a nice girl to have visit, but I wouldn't want to live with her."

"Would you want to live with me?"

"I'm thinking about it," he said. "I'll let you know."

"I mean I'd like to make plans."

"Now *you're* doing it," he said.

"Doing what?"

"Being elfin. You see? It's catching."

Four days after Jill and Tony had left, Esther came back to work, astonishingly light of foot and bright of eye. She had received a letter from Jill with an airplane ticket to New York, a hundred dollars in cash, and instructions on how to get from Kennedy to the Windsor Hotel in uptown Manhattan where she was to be Jill and Tony's guest for a week. Ben and Priscilla drove her to the airport in Elizabeth City on Thursday, two days before Jill's play was to open at the Helen Hayes. The girl was in a soft, glowing state of conflagration, like a bed of coals with blue flames flickering over them. Ben was moved to kiss her on the cheek and say, "Now you have a great time, little lady. And don't worry about a thing." He saw Priscilla flinch and close her eyes at the phrase "little lady."

On Sunday morning he bought a copy of the *New York Times* at the Red and White and read Frank Rich's review. The play was an amiable, sentimental comedy, Rich wrote, in the style of post-war British realism, such as *A Taste of Honey,* and *Room at the Top,* but burdened with an artificial and somewhat pretentious invention of plot that left one not only groping for its meaning, but its outcome. The chief distinction of the production was the appearance of the author in the leading role, a winsome and spirited performance that gave the play dimensions one might search in vain for in the text. It would be interesting to see more of her, in something less obviously tailor-made for her picturesque charm.

"What a vile man!" Priscilla said. "Did you ever hear such condescension!"

Ben pretended to share her indignation, but he was secretly gratified by the tone of the review, and surprised to find that he felt a sense of relief something like that he had experienced when Jill had boarded the plane for New York. He did not understand this, and felt guilty enough about it to give it a good deal of thought. Perhaps, he decided, he had subconsciously wanted her to fail, to disappear, to flee back into the obscurity out of which she had so unexpectedly appeared, and to trouble him no more with the dilemma of his ambivalent feelings toward her. It was not difficult to forget friends or lovers who had failed or who had fallen into the abyss of obscurity; it was very hard to dismiss the successful and celebrated from one's thoughts and feelings. This was a melancholy truth that he preferred to any further poetic longueurs on the subject. What he felt for Jill was no doubt mere idolatry, less discriminate than genuine affection or love, but very difficult to discourage. Cruelty, vanity, selfishness, calculated charm, every kind of vice, venality or flaw could be forgiven in an idol except nonentity. When her celebrity had dimmed, she would dissolve into thin air, like an incubus or—he thought, with a pleasant little flush of virtuosity—like an actor.

What she had inspired in Esther was of a different order, apparently. Two days after their housekeeper went to New York she wrote Ben and Priscilla a letter that embarrassed Ben for many reasons: its innocence, its ecstasy, its utter lack of equivocation, and the fact, as well, that he could be embarrassed by such virtues:

Dear Mr and Mrs Oakshaw:

Well, I don't know how to tell you what all I have been doing! I went to Jill's play last night and my goodness it was wonderful! The only play I have ever seen before was the tangled web which we put on at school but it was nothing compared to the thoughts of love! I did not know a play could be so real! You just believed everything she said and did! I almost felt like I was her up there on the stage and there was places where I wanted to shout at the man don't you talk to her like that or don't you dare to treat her like that or something of that sort.

On thursday after I got here we had diner in the windsor hotel which is the most beautiful place I have ever been in. I certainly never dreamed I would sleep in such a place and have people to wait on me like I was a queen. You would not believe what a wonderful diner we had! I thought I could cook some but I am going to have to improve, I can see that! Jill and Mr Griswold have a sweet here too and after the play there was a party in their sweet and there was more good things to eat as if we hadn't had enough allready! I met so many famous people who was real nice, actors and writers and all that sort of thing and I could not discribe to you such a time as I had! I did not know everybody in this city was so nice. I don't know how long it went on but I had to go to bed about midnight because I could not keep my eyes open any longer. I had seen so many sights that day I guess they were wore out! Tomorrow Mr Griswold is going to take me to the radio city music hall and then up in the empire state bldg. I don't know if I can stand any more excitement but I tell you if I was to die tomorrow it would be ok with me because I have allready found out there is so much more to life than I ever did know and more than most people know I guess. I don't mean because they have not been to N.Y. city but because they did not ever know a lady like miss Jill.

I surely hope you are enjoying yourselves at the beach. I will come back to work on Saturday instead of on monday because I know there will be a lot to do there, I have been away so long.

Your friend Esther

"She felt differently about the play than Mr. Rich, evidently," Priscilla said.

"Yes," Ben said. "I think she missed her calling. She should have been a drama critic."

"Well, if Esther loved it like that, I don't know why everyone won't. It's just bound to be a success."

It was not a great success, although it was not what could be called a failure. It ran for three months, long enough to earn respectful attention from a discerning group of theatregoers, if not to equal the éclat of its London run. For this, too, Ben was darkly grateful.

He was very busy for the rest of the summer, and since the play closed in the first week of October, he was relieved of the obligation of going to New York and seeing it, and Jill, again. When it closed they called to offer consolation and say good-bye and to reaffirm their intention to visit her in London.

"It's a damn shame," Ben told her. "We wanted to come up around Christmas and see it again. I was absolutely certain you'd run through the winter, at least."

"Oh, well, you're not absolutely certain of anything in this trade," Jill said. "Still, we had a jolly good run for the money. Some of them liked us quite well, I think."

"Why don't you drop down to Washington for another visit with us before you go back?"

"Oh, I wish I could, love, but Tony's fussing about having to feed the cat."

"Oh, he's gone back, has he?"

"Oh, yes, a month or more ago. He's getting a bit fed up with bachelorhood."

"Well, maybe it's just as well," Ben said. "You'll have a chance to work on the next one. You want to strike while the iron's hot."

"Yes, I'm putting it together, slowly. Don't know what'll become of it, but we'll see."

"We're really looking forward to it, you know."

"You're sweet to say so. Is Priss there?"

"Yes, I'm on," Priscilla said. "I'm in the kitchen."

"It was a marvelous summer down there with you chaps. It was well worth coming over, just for that."

"Come back next year."

"No, you're to come to London, next. And don't make it too long, mind."

"We won't. Next fall, perhaps."

"Right. Till London, then."

"Good-bye, dear. Give our best to Tony."

"I will, yes. Cheerio."

They did not go to London in the fall. In September the Sta-Put commercials made their debut, and Ben stayed close to the scene to nurse them through their initial production problems and monitor their impact on the market. It was very good—an 8 percent rise in sales, which produced elation on the part of the manufacturers and an additional contract for their entire line of men's toilet products. In November the opportunity arose for a takeover of the agency of Ben's old partner, Ted Oglesby, who was riddled with ulcers, had had a large portion of his stomach removed, and was anxious to sell off his major share of his company. The acquisition increased Ben's business by a third, gave him virtual control of the Washington TV market, and kept him hectically occupied through February. It also effectively banished any disorderly and poignant thoughts that might have lingered in his mind about Jill. When he thought of her at all— occasionally while sipping a before-dinner martini or falling into a daydream on the massage table after a game of squash racquets at his club—the poignancy was gone, along with the faint sense of apprehension, like that of a man freshly escaped from a nightmare, that had accompanied them previously. His memory of her visit to Hatteras had softened into an idyllic reverie, rendered more remote, innocuous, and roseate as the weeks and months fell over it like veils. Eventually it seemed like something more imagined than remembered, and the fact that they did not hear from her again made it more immaterial and fabulous. She had disappeared, as he had hoped and anticipated, vanished back into the obscurity of London winter nights, the smoky pubs of Bloomsbury, the mist among the gorse on Hampstead Heath, the legends of his youth. He was left touched but unscathed, in possession of a delicate souvenir which he could take out and smile over at will in idle moments, as if he were putting a Barbra Streisand record on the phonograph. He was sure that he would never see her again.

The next summer when they went down to Hatteras for two weeks he discovered that he had not yet entirely eluded her. They would have to find a new housekeeper. Esther had had her baby in December and was living with her parents. She had given up domestic work and was taking a course in stenography and office management in Nags Head where her father drove her daily. She came to see them on the first Sunday of their stay and brought her baby daughter, whom she had named Jill.

"Oh, she's *beautiful!*" Priscilla said. "And do you know, she looks like Jill, she actually does! She's even got red hair."

"Yes, ma'am, that was the first thing I noticed," Esther said. "I think Jill left her mark on this baby somehow."

"You must be so proud of such a beautiful little girl."

"I am. My momma and poppa are too. They just fuss over her like a queen."

"And now you're going to school in Nags Head."

"Yes'm. I'm getting along real good. I get through in September, and I'm going up to Raleigh or Richmond. This school I'm going to, they guarantee you a job. There's a lot of work up there with these new computer companies and all."

"I think that's wonderful. I know you'll be a great success."

"I think it's going to work out. You can do anything you want. I never knew that before. I didn't think I could do anything but cook and clean house."

"Of course you can. Oh, it's so good to hear you talk like that. You sound like a different person. And you look like one. You look wonderful, Esther."

"Thank you, Mrs. Oakshaw. I feel a lot better. Jill showed me how to fix myself up right when I was in New York, my hair and makeup and all. She bought me some clothes, too, you know that? Prettiest little dress and shoes. I just couldn't stop her."

"What a sweet person she is. Have you heard from her since she went back to England?"

"Yes, I have. I got a letter from her that said she was going to the country of Yugoslavia. A place called Dubrovnik. I looked it up on a map.

She said she was fine, and she would write me again when she got back
to London, but not to hold my breath. I don't think she writes a whole
lot of letters, but that doesn't make any difference. I wouldn't forget that
lady if I never heard from her again. Have you heard from her, ma'am?"

"No, we haven't," Priscilla said. "We were going over in the fall, but Ben
was too busy. I wrote, apologizing, but we didn't hear from her. And I
sent her cards at Christmas. I think she's so busy working that she forgets
the time."

"Yes, ma'am. But I don't think she forgets much else."

"No, I don't either."

At Hatteras, it was more difficult to dismiss her memory than in the world
of activity and commerce of Washington. The aura of her still haunted the
place, sometimes nymphlike and numinous, like a tender wraith that wandered among the rooms, sometimes like a Lorelei singing from the dunes.
There were days when the whole island seemed pervaded by her presence.
He could not go into the Red and White store or past the Bayside restaurant without an unsettling throe of memory. Even the sight of the ferry
setting out across the still blue sound to Ocracoke cast a pall of troubling
nostalgia over him. Eventually he resolved to indulge himself in these sentiments instead of resisting or allowing himself to be demoralized by them.
After all, he had done very little to reproach himself for. What man, faced
with such temptation, would have behaved with very much more self-
control than he? It wasn't as if anything gross, brutal, or unwelcome had
occurred. She had been very willing, certainly not indignant or repelled.
"No harm done," she had said, or something of the sort. "I'm a girl who
likes a lark." It had been a mutually agreeable and romantic interlude which
she would probably cherish the memory of as much as he. He had a
right to indulge himself in it, as a mark of sensibility, even of spirituality.
A man capable of such delicate and enduring feelings had a claim to
fineness of nature that somehow redeemed or transfigured the event itself, however unfortunate it may have been. God in heaven, Jack Kennedy,
Roosevelt—even Eisenhower!—had been guilty of far more flagrant in-
discretions. Such gallantries were common among men of feeling, energy,

and fire. He found this a reassuring attitude—worldly, realistic, and seasoned—one that allowed him to forgive himself the faint flare of recollected desire that assailed him every time he stepped into the shower stall, even to welcome it. By the end of the second summer he came to regret the fact that that sensation, too, had faded to a wry, momentary flicker in his memory, like the flash of a minnow in a stream.

In Washington he had few such accommodations to make although, habitually, when he had finished reading the business sections of the *Times*, the *London Observer*, the *Wall Street Journal*, and the news magazines, he would search the film and theatre columns for news of current and forthcoming productions. When, after almost three years, her name failed to appear in any of them, he decided that her brief hour of eminence was over. She had had her day in the sun and had evidently slipped back into the shadows of provincial repertory, B movies, or low-budget TV. The world of theatre changed with the same relentless constancy as that of life itself. Every year there was a parade of new stars and personalities stepping into the limelight with the same ferocious eagerness and energy that their now forgotten elders had exhibited twenty years before. For anyone of Jill's age who was not already a star, it was a bit late in life to make a claim on immortality, even on regular employment. She had said what she had to say, cleverly and with a momentary blaze of passion that for a season had captured the attention of the rabid, restless world. What surprised him most was that her name did not appear even in Tony's column, which for a while he read faithfully in the conviction that if she had done anything at all of note in the theatre Tony could have been counted on to celebrate it. Maybe they've separated, Ben thought. Maybe they had an inevitable fight and decided to go their own ways. No relationship with Jill could be expected to survive forever, however platonic its foundations. After a year, the column itself disappeared from the pages of the *Observer*. Maybe he's dead, Ben thought; he looked the type who might drop over some afternoon at a cocktail party after one too many martinis. Maybe they're both dead.

This was a weird and startling thought which, after being momentarily

shocked by its audacity, he found increasingly easy to consider. Over the
weeks it grew into an oddly comforting conviction which he nourished
secretly. Even when he and Priscilla visited the Kennedy Center, the
performance of Jill's play they had seen there three years before seemed
as remote and mythical as the events it had commemorated, the dialogue he had heard spoken in that shabby facsimile of her flat in Hammersmith as curious, quaint, and implausible as the characters who had
spoken it. It was not truly himself he had seen portrayed there on that stage,
those were not truly his thoughts and feelings he had heard expressed, or
his deeds he had seen enacted. They were fantasies, forgeries of forgeries. The specious evocation of an hour in a man's life was no more
truly an evocation of that man than a badly out-of-focus snapshot taken
in his adolescence. The truth of a man could not be photographed or
dramatized. A man was truly only what he might become, what he intended
to become, what he dreamt of being. That alone was inviolable, invulnerable to any incongruous origins or interludes, any ephemeral vows made
in the turmoil of a moment, any unseemly deeds done in the heat of
battle or in an hour of weakness, error, or infatuation, any picturesque
impostures assumed out of innocent ambition or insecurity. And certainly immune to any promiscuous portraits of his nature by any frivolous, presumptuous, or invidious playwrights. Drama was an absurdity and
a pretension, he began to realize. No play he had ever seen on any stage
was true, only the ideal, unwritten play that was performed on the misty
stages of a man's dreams.

I've outgrown the theatre, he thought. I'm not really interested any longer
in all this shabby make-believe. What he longed for, he began to believe,
was that nobility of spirit that could not be impersonated. At a certain stage
in their development, people outgrew art entirely. The only thing that could
delight them any longer was that sovereign truth of things that art blighted
and disfigured in its clumsy attempt to reveal it. Whether or not he had
reached that lonely, lofty height, he was certain of one thing, at least: he
had outgrown Jill, and all her mischievous inventions.

Nevertheless he felt a swift, tingling spasm of pleasure along with his astonishment when, almost three years after she had left Hatteras, he received a letter from her from the village of Much Hadham in Hertfordshire. It was written in an untidy hand on three sheets of tea-stained notebook paper and was, for a letter from the dead, surprisingly cheerful and voluble:

Dearest Priss and Ben:

What an unforgivable long time since we watched the sun set over Pamlico Sound! Did I dream that, or does that lovely, lonely place truly exist? I'm sure it must, because I have a sand dollar on a silver chain that I got *somewhere*! I know you're both well and happy because anything else would be a monstrous travesty of fate, and I rejoice in the fact when I think of you two, which I do far more frequently and fervently than you'd believe. I am quite well too, considering the amount of gin I drink and the number of cigarettes I smoke, and the fact that Humbert has further succumbed to mortality—to the extent of losing three claws on his left hind paw. Still, his dignity is intact, as is Tony's. Dignity and carcass as well, in his case. The man is utterly immune to time. He eats twice what I do without gaining a pound, although he seems to gain daily in intelligence, while I drift further every day into senility.

Why haven't we heard from you? *I* don't write letters, of course, but the fact that I'm constitutionally incapable of normal civilities is no excuse for you. Or perhaps you *have* written, and the fact that we've moved up here to Herts without leaving a forwarding address has something to do with not getting your letters. I wanted to leave everything behind—bills, pubs, speaking engagements, my rapidly mouldering friends, parties, the lot—and find some place with a garden, lots of bees, birds' nests, and thatchery where I could finish this wretched play. I knew I should never get it done otherwise. We live in an old rectory called Bishop's Folly (for reasons on which it's become my chief diversion to speculate) and I sit on the terrace every morning for three hours and get my few frayed thoughts onto paper before they dissipate into shameless, atavistic longings which I don't believe I need name. It's our Lake Isle of Innisfree, although there's no lake water lapping and no beanpoles. But there are linnet's wings and glorious dewy mornings and primroses and more hours in the day than I would ever have believed. Tony has taken a leave of absence from his column and is heroically embarked on a history of English drama that I'm sure will have the ghost of Allardyce Nicholl howling from its grave. He drives in to London twice a week to the B.M. library, as he irreverently calls it, and brings me back gossip from the Rialto and brioches from my favorite bakery. Altogether we're quite contented and very busy, and have little to complain of except the fact that human nature seems to be impervious to change, braggarts and bullies continue to rule the world, the poor and patient suffer on, humbug and horror are endlessly celebrated, and everywhere the ceremony of innocence is drowned. Somehow, in Bishop's Folly, none of that seems to matter quite so much, and anyway, I've no real right to complain since this letter, I'm afraid, is written in something of the same disreputable spirit.

When we were down at Cape Hatteras with you, Ben, you made the sweet and rather foolish suggestion to me one day that you'd be pleased to help back a play of mine if ever the occasion or need arose. Well, I have to confess that, woefully, they have, and I'd like you to know that if you feel even the tiniest twinge of regret about that gallant and quite unnecessary offer, or if anything has arisen in your circumstances to make it awkward or impossible to carry out, you don't need feel any qualms whatever about saying so. I mean that, truly. In fact I feel guilty about imposing on your benevolence to the extent of taking it literally, and I wouldn't—*honestly*—if you hadn't expressed it in such a heartfelt way. However, I've finished this play which I've been working on for so long, and now the odious task has arisen of finding people prepared to risk good money by putting the ruddy thing on the boards. Whether or not it's any good I don't know, and of course no one can guarantee. Tony insists staunchly that it is, but my old backers, Mssrs. Buchholtz, MacDonald and Killinger, don't seem to share his enthusiasm entirely, although we've gotten together about half the amount necessary to get it put on at the Haymarket in the fall. That leaves us a good 25,000 pounds short, however, and although Tony seems to think we could raise it by September, it would save a great deal of work and anguish if we could count on a substantial investment from a guaranteed source. As I say, I don't know whether you're able or willing to put all or any part of such a sum into a play, and God knows I wouldn't blame you if you weren't (*I* wouldn't be!), but the memory of your suggestion lingered in my mind and so I thought I'd just see. Of course no one should be expected to buy a pig in a poke, so I thought I'd let you know that my little pink beast is now born and can be inspected by anyone interested at all in pigs, God save their souls. I've re-done the last act (which they were least fond of) since I sent it to Buchholtz and Killinger, and it's in a shape now that I wouldn't be ashamed to have you see. I'm having it duped and bound, and if you're at all interested I can send you a copy of it by the 1st, so you can decide for yourself whether or not it's fit for serving up in rashers. It's a sort of comedy, I suppose, although a bit gloomier than the last, which may be what makes the angels frown and bite their lips. Of course, being the cunning creature that I am, I've written a part for myself (I'm incorrigible, I'm afraid), which may put them off a bit as well.

Whether or not you feel like putting a few quid into it, I'd love to have your opinion, Ben—but *only* if you have the time, mind!—because it's one I truly respect. I think you know by now that I hate humbug, so if you find it bloody awful, I trust you to say so. And for God's sake, don't feel any obligation, please, to come in on the backing. You must promise me that.

I hope you've sold a million cans of that hair spray you were peddling, and I can promise you that if it comes on the market over here

before he's in a condition to consider it a cruel jest, I'll buy another
hundred for Tony. Will that help at all?

I don't know how much longer we'll be here, but through the
summer at least, or until we get this bloody play on the boards. *Do*
come to see us. We've got a spare bedroom upstairs with a robin's
nest by the window and a view of the downs that's pure heart's ease.
Will you try? We'd truly love to have you, and it would be a *very*
small repayment for the lovely time we had at Hatteras.

Tony sends his very best and promises to make Scotch eggs if
you'll come to see us. I send my love and a primrose from the
garden.

Jill

The primrose was pressed flat between the sheets of notebook paper like
a small yellow sunburst. Ben laid it on the breakfast table in front of Priscilla.
She picked it up and smoothed the petals with her fingertips.

"What do you think?" he asked.

"About what? Visiting them?"

"No, I mean the play."

"Well, I think you should invest in it, of course. There isn't any question
about it, is there? I call it an opportunity."

"I suppose not," Ben said. "It *would* be a pretty handsome gesture."

"Well, I don't know about that, but I think it's the only thing to do.
My heavens, we've talked for years about helping to keep the theatre
alive, investing in young playwrights. And we know she deserves it. How
could we possibly refuse?"

"You're right," Ben said. "Anyway, it would be pretty hard to say I'd
changed my mind about it. Especially after I'd read the play. It might be
better if I didn't even ask to see it. Might sound as if I was too concerned
about making a profit or something."

"I'm so glad you said that," Priscilla said. She leaned across the table and
kissed him on the forehead.

He sent a bank draft for twenty-five thousand pounds to Jill's credit to

Barclays Bank in London the next day and wrote a letter to her at the address in Hertfordshire:

Dear Jill:

I can't tell you how delighted we were to get your letter and know that you've finished your play. Best news of the year! We never got to London last fall—I had too much to do, unfortunately. Priss wrote expressing our regrets, but we never heard from you. I guess you were up there in Herts. We also wrote at Christmas, but I guess the cards are mouldering in the dead letter office. Now that the breach is healed, we mustn't let the perilous narrow ocean part us asunder any longer. We'll certainly see you *next* fall, when your show opens, and it gives me a real sense of privilege to know that I'll be a part of that event. Your money is on the way—it's probably there by now, as a matter of fact. I sent a draft for the twenty-five thousand pounds you need to Barclay's Bank this morning. It's to your credit, since I didn't know the name of your production company. You can disburse it in whatever way is most convenient, and I hope it solves your problems. You can let me know the contract details in due time and I'll pass them on to my lawyers.

All thought of profit and loss aside, it's the best investment I'll ever make. If I never get back a dime, the world will be a richer and better place, and what better bargain can anyone get for his money?

Don't bother sending me the script. I'd rather share the experience of the rest of the first-nighters. You can be sure that my investing in the play doesn't depend on my having read it. Priss and I have absolute faith in your talent, and as far as we're concerned, anything you write *has* to be good, not only worthy to be staged, but a cultural priority of the age. You might tell me the title, however, if you've decided on one yet. We'd like to know what it's going to be called. Keep us informed about how it's going, and let us know when you're going to open so we can make plans. It's a date we'll be looking forward to like greyhounds in the slips.

We're both as well and happy as any mortals have a right to be—much happier, in my case. We had a note from Esther last winter, and she's getting on very well too. She finished her course in office management and has a job in Raleigh with a business consultant. She's really transformed—full of energy and self-confidence and happy as a lark, and her little girl is beautiful. As I'm sure you know by now, her name is Jill. She has red hair and resembles you not a little. Esther is sure there's necromancy involved, and she may be right. What you've done for that girl is little short of miraculous.

Give Tony our best and tell him we've taken notice of his promise to make Scotch eggs, and intend to hold him to it one fine day. I wondered why his column had stopped appearing in the *Observer*. We read and enjoyed it regularly until last March, when it stopped appearing. We were afraid he might be sick or something, and we're both relieved to hear that he's not, and that he's at work on a book. It promises to be a very good year for everyone.

Love from both of us.

She wrote back within the week:

Dearest Ben:

You are an angel, in *every* sense! God, what a blessing to know we can go on in the fall. Of all your beaux gestes, this is surely the most eloquent, and I can promise you that when I die your name will be the last word on my lips. I wish I could promise you also that you'll get your money back and something to boot, but you know what a dicey business the theatre is, as well as I. Still, it isn't entirely inconceivable. No one lost money on the last, you know, and I pray that that's the case with this one. I'll have our business manager, Nick Adams, send a contract with details by the end of the week. I think it's a pretty usual arrangement—something like 5%–10% of box office receipts as production costs are recovered—but if your man is unhappy about anything, have him send it back with his objections, and I'm sure we'll work it out.

We're going to get cracking right away on casting. I've got a girl in mind that I think will be smashing for the ingenue, and Jason Mc-Naughton, who was absolutely marvelous last year in *Home for the Holidays*, is reading the script now. If I can get him for the male lead I'm sure we'll have a smash. He's a wonderful young actor who reminds me a good deal of you in your salad days, although none of them can send the kind of chills through me that you used to do. Still, if we can't actually be on a stage together again, it's wonderful to be united—one way or another—in another piece of mummery! I used to dream of that when we were at RADA. I think the most bountiful part of it was your saying that you didn't need to see the script. That was truly handsome, Ben. I was touched by it.

You asked about the title. I haven't actually decided on one yet, although I've two or three in mind that I've jotted down as they occurred to me—I don't quite know why: *Such Is Youth, We Can Be Happy*, or *That Summer's Trance*. Perhaps you'd like to pick one out for me. I think it's the very least you deserve for the part you've played in bringing this dream child of mine into the world. This dream child of *ours*, I should say, because without you it would not have been born. Let's pray it will survive.

Now, this is for Priss. Hello, Priss. You have the most prodigal husband in the world and I envy you, although I shouldn't, of course, since we both share in his prodigality. I'm very well aware that you had something to do with his participation in this little comedy of mine and that it's just as much a demonstration of generosity on your part as his. I have qualms about your putting so much money into it, and I'm afraid it may mean a sacrifice for you of things you'll have to do without for a while, but I'm determined that you shall profit by it in the long run, as I hope you'll agree when you see it.

I'm so glad about Esther getting on. I know you are too, although I'm afraid I may have had a hand in depriving you of your cook, as well

as 25 thousand pounds. Still, she was bound to go, wasn't she, when
she found out who she was and what she could do for herself. She only
needed waking up a bit, to help liberate her from that beastly man. I
haven't written her for ages and I feel guilty about that, too, but I've
been really desperately busy, and I hope she understands. Give her my
love, will you?

Do take care, you two. Nothing must happen to prevent you being at my opening night. *Our* opening night, I should say, because your
contribution to it is quite as great as mine, since you're paying a large
part of the bill. You must promise to forgive me if it should turn out
to be a disaster.

Love, Jill

Ben sent her a cable the next day, saying only:

THAT SUMMER'S TRANCE. IT RINGS LIKE A GOLDEN GUINEA. BEN.

In October she wrote again to thank him for choosing the title, which
she agreed was the best of the lot. They had thought of opening out of town,
at Guildford or Nottingham, but in order to cut expenses they had decided
to do a week of preview performances in London before the official opening night. That would give them time to get the show smoothed out before
the critics came, and cost far less. She was ecstatic about the fact that
they had got Lisa Thornburg for the ingenue role and Jason McNaughton
for the male lead. They had been in rehearsal for a week and it was going very well indeed—far better than she had dared to believe. They would
open at the Haymarket on the tenth of November. A woman named Tanya
Blakemore was doing both the sets and costumes, and her designs were
fabulous. They were to keep their fingers crossed, pray regularly, light a
candle or two, and perform acts of obsecration. There was to be a first-night
party at their flat which would probably go on until the dawn, and for which
they wanted to be well rested, so they had better come over a day in ad-
vance to get over the jet lag. Why didn't they call her on the ninth, the

day before the opening, and they'd all have lunch together? She and Tony were staying at a flat in Cheyney Walk which they'd taken temporarily, as they'd let his old one when they went to Herts. She gave them the address and her phone number. There would be two tickets in their name at the box office on opening night. If she didn't write again, they were to forgive her. She was frantically busy, vertiginously happy, and full of awful anxieties, like a woman in the last weeks of pregnancy. She asked for their blessing.

They flew to London on the eighth of November, a Thursday, arriving at nine o'clock in the evening, had dinner at their hotel, a small and elegant one in Sloane Square where they often stayed, and went to bed immediately after. In the morning Ben called Jill. He waited until almost eleven because she had had a performance the night before and he knew that theatre people slept very late when they were playing. She was awake, however, and evidently awaiting their call, judging by the fact that she snatched up the phone at the first ring, and the somewhat breathless sound of her "Hullo?"

"Hi," Ben said. "Did I get you up?"

"Ben!" she cried. "You're here!"

"You bet your life," he said. "Where else would we be, on a day like this?"

"Oh, how wonderful! I had an awful premonition that you wouldn't make it."

"Rabid wolves couldn't have kept us away. How's it been going?"

"Oh, God, I don't know. Preview audiences are always such a mystery. Still, they seem to like it, on the whole. I must say we've got a wonderful company. Lisa and Jason are absolutely marvelous. I couldn't have got better people if I'd cast it in heaven." She exhaled heavily, a sound like a gasp. "I'm just so bloody nervous, you know."

"Well, that's perfectly normal," Ben said. "Wouldn't be natural if you weren't."

"I suppose not, no. When did you get in?"

"Just last night. We took your advice and turned in early, so we'd be ready for the party."

"Oh, good. There'll be tickets waiting for you at the box office. Did I write you that? I've got you in the second row."

"Great. Will Tony be out front?"

"No. I'm going to keep him backstage, for support."

"How does he feel about the show?"

"Well, he hasn't actually seen it yet. He's read it, of course. A draft of it, at any rate."

"He hasn't seen it?"

"No. I wanted it to be a sort of present for him. All wrapped up, with a bow on it."

"You haven't had any critics yet?"

"No, not till tonight. God knows what they'll have to say."

"Don't worry about it."

"Oddly enough, I don't. For myself, I mean. Of course I don't want it to flop—that would be awful for everyone, including you. But in the long run, I don't really mind what they think about it. I don't know if that makes sense, at all."

"Sure it does," Ben said. "When you've finished a piece of work you believe in, it doesn't really matter what anyone says."

"That's it exactly. Of course it would be very pleasant if they liked it, but I can't really be concerned about it. I'd be perfectly willing to give them their money back if they wanted it, but not their former state of mind." She exhaled heavily again and laughed a little breathlessly. "Don't know why I'm going on like this. I suppose I'm bloody nervous, in spite of what I'm saying."

"Well," Ben said, "I promise you I won't ask for my money back."

She laughed. "God, you're paying enough to see this bloody show. I do hope you get it back, and more. That's the least I can do for you."

"Don't worry about it. Listen, where do you want to have lunch?"

"Oh, Lord," she said. "Ben, this is awful, but I'm not going to be able to make it. I did a bit of last-minute rewriting last night—there was a bit in the second act that just wasn't right at all, and so I cut a couple of lines and put in a couple of new ones—and we've got to have a line rehearsal this afternoon. I feel absolutely dreadful about it, but it just wouldn't be fair to the cast if we didn't. Can you forgive me?"

"No forgiveness necessary," he said. "The play's the thing. You've got to have it perfect for tonight."

"Well, I don't know about perfect, but I couldn't rest, the way it was. I do apologize."

"Don't apologize for anything except insincerity. A very wise woman told me that."

"Very pompous one, I'm afraid. Is Priss there?"

"Yes, just a moment. I'll put her on. I'll see you later."

"Yes. Good-bye, love."

"Good-bye."

He handed the phone to Priscilla and poured himself a cup of coffee from the urn that had been sent up on the tray from Room Service. He put cream and sugar into it and sat sipping it while he listened to Priscilla chatting on the phone with Jill.

"Yes, of course we will," she said. "Don't be foolish. No. No. Next Tuesday, I think. Will you really? Something you found at Hatteras? I'll be watching for it. It sounds wonderful. I don't think we'll have time, this trip, but maybe next year. That's where Henry Moore used to live, isn't it? I'm going to be saying my special Vedic prayer for you. All right. Break a leg, dear."

Outside the window the slate roofs of the eighteenth-century houses were wet with mist, and lavender-colored in the winter light. A flock of pigeons flew across the window to the rooftops of the square below. A church bell tolled the hour with a hoarse, jangling sound, as if the iron were cracked, from a slate spire that rose above the rooftops. He counted the eleven strokes, tapping his fingertip against his coffee cup.

. . .

When they left for the theatre, Ben asked the taximan to drive up through South Kensington and then along Cromwell Road and Kensington Gardens to the West End so that he could see the part of London where he had lived in his student days. It was a dense, cold November evening so much like those of his youth that he felt not only transported back in time but physically transformed. He sat in the taxicab beside Priscilla and watched the lights of Kensington and Knightsbridge running by the windows twinkling murkily in the winter mist and he was in his twenties again, full of the fresh excitement of going to a play with a pretty girl beside him on a winter night that had opened to him like a page turned freshly in the book of eternity. The great old monolithic buildings along the park loomed up one after another in the gloom — the Albert Hall, the Royal College of Organists, the Victoria and Albert Museum — huge, august, full of glorious ghosts and echoes, the fluting of their carriage entrances and massive, time-worn walls steeped in sumptuous shadow. Their great solemn presences had blessed his youth like grandsires bending above his cradle. This was where he had been truly born, he thought, where he had received the silent benediction of those conservatories of the human spirit like the sacrament of baptism. There was nowhere else he had ever loved as he had loved the stone streets of this old dark city where Marlowe and Shakespeare and Congreve had revelled at the Mermaid and the Inns of Court and Locket's Tavern as he had revelled at The Rising Sun, and where they had ridden in rattling carriages to openings of *Tamerlane,* and *Othello,* and *The Way of the World.* He had felt once as if those men had bequeathed the city to him as the ancient, illustrious stage, worn with their feet, where in his turn he would stride into the light of life, art, and renown.

When they passed the Albert Hall, he said, "We used to go to Prom concerts there, on Sunday afternoons. For two and six. And sit on the floor and eat sausage rolls."

"I did too," Priscilla said. "Malcolm Sergeant and Sir Thomas. That dear man. I was always afraid he was going to tumble out of that pulpit thing he used to stand in."

The dark windows of the Victoria and Albert were running with mist and reflected brokenly the river of traffic that flowed by toward Hyde

Park Corner; and for a moment he saw his own face peering from the taxi window as it sped by in the dark. But inside, he thought, in the musty darkness among the ancient fabrics and parchment documents and the rapiers that had run red at Bosworth Field, there sat the ghost of himself, bent over a desk while he studied for his History of Theatrical Representation exam, copying in his notebook floor plans of the Olympic and the Regency and a proscenium arch designed by Inigo Jones. An aching nostalgia swept over him like rhapsody.

They rounded Hyde Park Corner and crept up Park Lane past the glitter of shop fronts and hotel pavilions to Oxford Street, then between the twinkling shores of Regent Street to St. James Park and along Picadilly to the Circus. The Haymarket was choked with traffic, and the circuitous route had made them late; when the taxi pulled up to the theatre it was almost curtain time. Only a few fervent fans hoping to buy cancellations stood under the marquee shifting their feet anxiously on the cold stone. Ben picked up their tickets at the box office and they went in through the lobby past a gigantic framed photograph of Jill wearing a tunic-like white camisole and a faint, sibylline smile. The house lights were already dimming as the usher led them down the aisle, and by the time they had taken their seats in the middle of the second row the theatre was dark. There was no time to read the program. He settled Priscilla's coat on the back of her chair, and as he turned, the curtain rose with a startling swiftness revealing to his astonishment the living room of his house at Hatteras, bright with sunlight from the dome. It was uncanny in its accuracy. There was the ivory-colored grand piano with the Rudel figurine set on top of it. There was the white sofa with the Pollock on the wall behind it, the Bonnards and the Dufy and the Dehn watercolor of the street at Key West. There was the sliding glass door to the sundeck with the rails behind it casting slanted shadows across the redwood planks, and in the distance, on the cyclorama that enclosed the whole room, was the sea, a slumbrous indigo that stretched to the horizon. And there, coming in through the deck doors with their luggage, were Ben and Priscilla and

Tony and Jill, pausing for a moment to glance about the room until Tony
had said, "This is quite lovely. You must be congratulated."

"Oh, my goodness," Priscilla whispered. "Isn't that amazing."

"Astonishing," Ben murmured.

"I thought you said it was primitive," Jill said from the stage. "My God,
it looks like Hampton Court Palace."

"We didn't say the *house*," the actress who was playing Priscilla said. She
turned her hand up with the fingers held loosely curled in an eerily perfect imitation of Priscilla's gesture. "We meant the Cape itself."

"This is the Rudel," the stage Tony said, advancing toward the piano.
It was the man who had played Tony in *Thoughts of Love*, but older, plumper,
with silver temples, the Tony of Cape Hatteras. He picked up the figurine and clasped it gently between his palms, turning to Jill. "You see what
I was telling you, about this man?"

"Yes," Jill said. She came and stood beside him, reaching out to touch
the figurine with her fingertip. "It's almost enough to console one for everything one's ever lost."

The hypnotic recitation went on, almost as confoundingly exact in its
accuracy as the replica of the room in which it echoed out of the summer three years past. It was not so much like watching a play, Ben thought,
as watching a home movie of a holiday that he had spent with friends;
but there was none of the pleasure of reliving a happy and innocent occasion. It was not happiness and innocence that were being commemorated here, he understood almost immediately; it was too meticulous
and severe in its rendition of reality. Even the first scene, with its apparent gayety and air of anticipation, was ominous in its fidelity, moving inexorably forward to what he knew would follow with the same merciless
precision. The flashes of gayety and wit had a ghostly, hollow sound, like
laughter echoing down the corridors of a museum. He sat petrified, listening to the lines fall tinkling and glittering from their lips like icicles
on a stone floor.

He watched it unfold in the way that his recurrent nightmare unfolded in his mind, knowing it could not be escaped, knowing its awful conclusion, knowing it was his own creation, enthralled and horrified by the ruthless virtuosity with which his own damnation was being contrived.

The scene of their arrival was followed by the first dinner party, and as he watched it he experienced something like the brief, anguished, final moments of the life of a man condemned to death, knowing that for another quarter of an hour, his perfidy would go unrevealed. He glanced out of the corner of his eye at Priscilla and saw that she was smiling in admiration and bemusement. God help her, he thought. God help both of us. God save us from this witch. He could hardly believe the woman's treachery. It seemed to him almost as vile an example of it as the one she was recounting. Maybe I'm wrong about it, he thought. I must be. Nobody could be vicious enough to take money from me to stage this ruinous piece of scandal and then invite me to sit and watch it with my wife. Maybe what she intends to do is to make a comedy of it, a lighthearted sort of thing based roughly on ourselves and on the situation down there, and to improvise on it, so brightly and ingeniously that no one could possibly be offended by it, especially not Priscilla. After all, if she's as fond of Priscilla as she says, she won't tell the whole story. She wouldn't dare. She'd have to expose her own deceit as well as mine if she were going to do that. She won't go that far. No one would, for any conceivable reason. And then he remembered the way he had played Richard once, and he closed his eyes in despair.

The dinner party concluded with his driving Esther home, and was followed by the scene of Ben and Jill's midnight conversation on the deck. They were called Roger and Elaine. They stood before the unlit cyclorama with a few stars glittering through perforations in the backdrop and moonlight shining on the two of them from overhead spots masked with blue gelatins. Ben had come to take a kind of devastated, doomed interest in the stagecraft, like a man noting the technical arrangements for his beheading while mounting the ladder to the guillotine. He took a certain amount of gratification in the performance of the actor who was playing himself; the man was much too tall, too handsome in a vapid way, and attacked his lines with a kind of false energy foreign to Ben's way of speaking, but he had a sensitivity, intelligence, and an air of tortured susceptibility to Jill's charms that gave a degree of dignity to his duplicity which Ben recognized as authentic. He's been well directed, he thought. At least she understood what I was going through.

As he listened, he tried desperately to match the conversation taking place on the moonlit deck in front of him with his own memory of its original. They had spoken of the past; he was sure of that—of their days in London, of people they had known at RADA—but whether what they had said was explicit enough to condemn him he could not remember. It seemed to him that their talk had been diffuse and general, a kind of romantic elegy to their youth rather than a memorial of their affair. As the scene progressed he felt a great tide of relief flow through him to discover that this was the way Jill too had remembered it, or had chosen to depict it. There were only one or two lines of dialogue that could be construed as evidence that *Thoughts of Love* been just as truly a play about the two of them as this one was: her remark that "It must have given you quite a turn, watching it," and his reply: "I have to confess it made me feel pretty strange for a while." Still, these were vague and ambiguous, not certain proof of his betrayal. And yet, he thought: If it be not now, yet it will come. This was only a brief and cunning reprieve, he suspected, one that she had probably granted to prolong his torment.

If that was her intention, it was subtly executed; his innocence was preserved—in this faintly equivocal way—for the whole of the first act, which ended with the scene at the cafe in Ocracoke. There was the sunlight beating down on the tables in front of the harbor, there was the bleached sign hanging above them: BLACKBEARD'S LAIR, and the blue sea in the distance. There was the platter of crabs and the litter of cracked shells, there was Tony vigorously pounding a claw with a wooden mallet, there was Priscilla reaching beneath the table occasionally to excavate the bottle of daiquiri and fill their glasses with faintly tipsy care. There was himself, pedantically reciting history, and there was Jill with her wet blouse and wind-snarled hair sipping her daiquiri and peering over the rim of her glass at him like a sly, seditious child. In spite of the nearness of his doom — because of it, perhaps — he experienced again the timeless tranquility of that sweet, sunlit afternoon as if it were the only, and imperishable, reality in all the senseless furor of the universe. He wanted it never to end. Even though it pulsed with infamy, it seemed precious to him, like the uncouth, beautiful coursing of his blood.

Priscilla was uncharacteristically quiet at the intermission. Usually she was voluble and animated at openings, eager to exchange opinions with him about the performances, the set, the quality of the writing, the probable course of the plot; but when they had made their way up the aisle to the lobby, she stood against the wall and gazed gravely at the crowd of chattering, lively faces that surrounded them. When he brought her a sherry from the bar, she accepted it with a faint, thoughtful smile and gazed at it as if he had put a potion in her hand.

"Here's to its success," he said. "Our first venture as producers."

She nodded and sipped briefly from her glass.

"Well, what do you think?" Ben said. "Kind of a surprise, isn't it?"

"Yes."

"I don't know quite what she's up to. It's not so much a play as a sort of — I don't know what. Memoir, I guess. With a few notable interpolations."

"What sort of interpolations?"

"Well, like the conversation on the deck, for example. It didn't go anything like that. She seems to be setting up a situation of some kind. I guess that's what playwrights do: use reality as a point of departure."

"You did talk to her, out there?"

"Sure, I told you that."

"She didn't say anything like, 'It must have given you quite a turn, watching it'?"

"Nothing like it, that I can remember. That's one of the interpolations. We'll have to wait and see how she develops it."

Priscilla lowered her eyes and gazed into her sherry silently.

"You feeling OK?" Ben asked.

"Yes."

"You seem very quiet. You have a headache or anything?"

"No. I'm just thinking about the play."

"Well, tell me what you think. I'd like to know."

"It reminds me of something I did once," she said. She raised her head and looked at him. "An experience I had that I've never told you about."

"What do you mean? Something that happened before you met me?"

"Oh, no. It was after I met you. It's the only thing I've ever deceived you about."

He stared at her, his mind gone vacant with astonishment. "You deceived me?" he murmured after a moment.

"Yes. Do you remember that day you left me in the pub in Bloomsbury, after we'd quarreled?"

He nodded, his mouth open, and then murmured, "Yes."

"Well, I sneaked into RADA that afternoon, after you left, and watched you rehearsing Richard. I never told you that, but I did. And when I came out, the world was changed for me, forever. I thought: what a strange gift. To be able to make life seem more beautiful, and rich, and mysterious, by depicting the evil of it, the pain of it. I think it's what made me marry you. I never wanted you to know that."

He stared at her silently. The gong sounded for the second act. She handed her glass to him.

"I don't think I'll finish that."

"OK."

He carried their glasses back to the bar and, impulsively, paused to dig his money clip out of his pocket and leave a handsome tip—a one-pound note—on the bar.

"Thank you very much, sir," the barman said.

"That's OK," Ben said, smiling with huge, desolate benevolence.

He walked down the aisle with Priscilla in an eerily disembodied way, as if he were a scientist recording, by means of electrodes attached here and there to his body, its remarkably complex process of perambulation. In the few moments before the house lights dimmed, for no reason he could think of, bits of literary debris floated through his mind—stately, sonorous phrases out of Shakespeare, scraps of remembered rhetoric from diction exercises, wisps of poetry, like the rubble of a cataclysm: "To strive, to seek, to find, and not to yield . . ." "The boast of heraldry, the pomp of power . . ." "It is the star to many a wandering bark . . ." He seemed to have a desperate desire to associate himself with something eloquent and lofty, to hear noble thoughts echoing in his brain and issuing from his lips, like a man quoting scripture before a firing squad.

If he had any hope of clemency from the second act, it was dispelled the moment the curtain rose. In front of him sat he and Jill in their swimsuits on a low mound of sand surrounded by a pale blue Mylar film that billowed gently in the breeze of an electric fan of some kind while clouds projected on the cyclorama behind them drifted slowly above the blue sea. Their dialogue was recorded with a scathing exactitude that Ben knew was beyond any power of his to temporize. As an invention, nothing could have accounted for its cruelty. As truth, nothing could account for it but a resolution that seemed to him inhuman. He heard his own impenitent allusions to their affair in London, his guttural admission of his still unsated passion for the girl who lounged beside him on the sandbar with her white legs stretched out in the water. He heard himself mutter, shockingly, "You're awfully goddamned fucking beautiful. Jesus Christ, I'm wild about you." He watched himself lay his hand on her crotch while, in their bedroom, Priscilla slept, and Tony, invisibly ensconced somewhere above the orchestra, watched from his chaise longue. He sat paralyzed with shame, unable to lower his eyes, or close them, to blind or deafen himself to the indecency taking place before him. Priscilla sat motionless beside him, her hands clasped tightly in her lap.

Neither of them moved or spoke in the moment of darkness after the curtain had fallen on the scene and before it rose pitilessly on the next: a dismayingly perfect reproduction of the dressing room, with the ornate clothes hooks on the wall, the full-length mirror, the lockers, and the shower stall with its sliding glass door and ceramic sea horses. Jill did not spare herself, her fellow actor, or the audience any of the scurrilous details. Ben watched appalled while once again she stepped into the shower stall, untied and dropped off her bra and, at his palsied suggestion, stepped out of her bikini pants and with her head hung backwards and her hair streaming, let the water flow over her nude body. He saw himself strip off his trunks and fling them against the wall in a humiliating imitation of his own fulsome haste. He saw himself step into the stall and seize her in his arms and smother her face and throat with a frenzied shower of kisses, muttering senseless, wanton endearments. The single concession to decency was the fact that the bench to which he carried her from the stall was concealed for half its length by a row of lockers that projected outward from the wings; only their heads and shoulders were visible, shuddering in delirious spasms, their white arms wandering over each other's bodies like white, spellbound serpents as they slaked their desire.

When the scene ended — with the two of them silently putting on their robes and going up the stairs to the kitchen — his feeling of paralysis had spread through every nerve and sinew of his body. He felt as enervated, as incapable of comment, protest, or physical movement as if he were bound in a cataleptic spell. He could only watch in strengthless horror while it ran its course. He thought for a moment of defying it, of protesting to Priscilla that they had no obligation to watch this piece of calumny, that it was the contemptible invention of a mad, morbid woman to which they should refuse to subject themselves, that they should simply leave the theatre and never speak of Jill again; that they should consider her name itself a profanity. But he knew it was in vain. It was his indignation that was the impiety. Some quaint, incorrigible claim to honor made him understand that he must see the shameful spectacle through to its end.

He could not move or speak. He could not even conceive of eventual liberation, of waking, of escape, of the sweet fields of reality that enclosed this terrible playhouse—the rainy streets outside its doors, the traffic and taxi horns and the steeples in the mist and the swans sleeping on the quiet water of the Serpentine. Their gracious substance was unimaginable in the face of the relentless mimicry that reigned in front of him.

The scenes that followed were even more harrowing, although they evoked with a kind of tarnished glamour the enchantment of that summer's trance. All its diversions and adventures—the sailing party, the picnics on the beach, the dinner at the Bayside restaurant, the bonfire, the midnight swim—were blighted by the known hypocrisy and guile they concealed. Only Priscilla remained undefiled by the treachery that fumed around her like the scent of nightshade. In a strange way the play became a eulogy to her innocence. The sweetness of her nature, her gentleness and grace were as scrupulously portrayed by Jill as Jill's own subtlety and stealth. In fact, Ben began to realize, it might almost have been addressed to her as an invocation to recognize her abject idolatry of Ben, to liberate herself from the deluded, ignoble relationship which was being laid bare before her. He didn't understand this truly until the moment in the play when Jill gave her the coral pendant from the gift shop in Hatteras, with the words: "I hope some day I'll be able to give you something of real value. Something you'll cherish more than this pretty trifle." This was her gift to Priscilla, Ben realized, this revelation of his treachery and vanity. She was liberating Priscilla, as she had liberated Esther, as she was liberating herself. He felt suddenly, inconsolably, bereft. He had lost both of them, forever—the women who had fed his desire and his aspiration.

So coldly, formally impassioned was the play that it occurred to Ben that she might truly be insane and that he could escape disgrace on the grounds that it was the product of a diseased mind and not to be taken seriously; but the thought died as quickly as it had been born: no one could doubt the truth of it, however outrageous or unlovely it might seem. There was a terrible, heartbroken intransigence about it, an adamant refusal by Jill to exonerate even herself of her part in the sordid comedy that raised it above any suspicion of mania, subversion, or invective. Toward the end of it, Ben had the weird impression that he was witnessing an act of immolation, that Jill too, along with himself, was being consumed by her own pitiless integrity. There would be nothing left of them but bones and ash, desiccate carcasses littering the beach along with the seashells and the husks of crabs. He raised his eyes to the proscenium arch in a kind of desperate evasion of the shameful scene that it enclosed, staring up at the great overhanging chandelier and into the twinkling gloom of the dark tiers of the balconies where rows of silent jurors sat in silent witness of his infamy. The great dark auditorium had a look of nightmarish familiarity. I have been in this place before, he thought. I see it in my sleep. This is the theatre where Miss Replogle prophecied that I would meet my destiny.

The final scene was the most demoralizing of all: his final encounter with Jill on the beach on the morning of her departure and his attempt to seduce her for a second time, without a jot of remorse or repentance for the first. There was no forgiving it, as the first might have been forgiven as an act of unpremeditated, ungovernable resurgence of old passion. It was too deliberate, too obviously calculated, too flagrant to be forgiven on any grounds, even by someone of Priscilla's matchless charity. Watching it, Ben dug his nails into his palms until they bled. To see such an inglorious moment of his life reenacted before Priscilla and something like a thousand witnesses was a mortification he would not have thought it possible to bear. How Priscilla could bear it he didn't know. He cast a swift, furtive glance at her and felt sickened with guilt at the sight of her face. It looked quite literally like that of a corpse. Her eyes were sightless, motionless, vacantly aghast, like those of a cadaver fixed on the final scene of its existence. Even if I died now, he thought, it wouldn't help her; it would only extinguish the disgrace I feel. She would be left with the knowledge of all those betrayals. Only if I'd never been born would she be exempted from it. I wish to God I'd never been born.

Staring at the stage, he watched himself pluck a strand of Jill's hair and run it through his fingertips. He saw his hand laid on her thigh and his fingertips drawn upward in a delicate caress across the taut, brown skin. He heard her say with awful prophecy, "I shouldn't do that, if I were you. You won't be proud of it, later. *I* won't be."

"Does that mean you don't want to?"

"No, it doesn't mean anything of the kind."

"What does it mean?"

"It means that I've become quite fond of your wife, for one thing. And that I'd like to get away from here with as much dignity as possible."

He bowed his head and listened again to her offer of reconciliation, whose monstrous subterfuge he had never suspected until this moment. He heard himself agree that they would meet again, in London, where he sat now, keeping that dire rendezvous. He heard himself ask if she were going to swim, and his offer to stay and stand watch over her.

"Do you mean to say you'd plunge in after me, if I started to drown?" she asked.

"To keep a great artist alive? Oh, I think so. It would be a way of paying my debts, I suppose. I think you deserve it."

"Perhaps if you knew me better you wouldn't think so."

With his head bowed and his eyes closed tightly now, he visualized the scene. In the pause that followed he saw her rise and tug off her sweater and stand gazing for a moment at the sea.

"Perhaps I won't go in after all. It looks a bit cold out there. Perhaps I'll just sit here for a bit. You go along."

"Are you sure?"

"Yes. I'd like to have a last look round before I go. I may just wade a bit."

"All right." He whispered his own words silently as his phantom self spoke them from the stage. "I'll have some tea ready for you. Brewed properly, in the pot."

"Yes, and not too long, mind. Not for more than two minutes."

"No. Not till I hear you on the stairs. Isn't that what you used to say?"

"Yes. Just a moment."

He opened his eyes and saw her reach up to take his phantom hand and draw him down to her, and he felt again on his lips the light, lingering touch of hers, like the kiss of a ghost.

"Don't go in that water, now. I don't want you drowning."

"No, no. I've a thing or two to do, before that."

He watched himself go loping down the floodlit mound of sand and out of sight into the wings, and he saw Jill rise and stand clutching her throat with both hands as if she were throttling herself. He closed his eyes again and heard her call out to him from the stage in a strangled cry, *"Good-bye, love."*

The two words rang across the auditorium for a moment, fading as they were muffled by the great descending velvet curtain. The moment of silence that followed was shattered by the applause that broke about them like a thunderstorm. All around him people rose and stood in cheering ranks, shouting their tribute to the stage. Ben sat without moving, his eyes fixed on his feet. He did not want to meet Jill's eyes when the curtain parted for the company call. She knew where they were sitting; she could unavoidably challenge him with a look. A look of what? he wondered. Derision? Defiance? Triumph? Pity, perhaps? Whatever it was, he wanted her to know that he repudiated it forever. That he never wanted to see her, or speak to her, or think of her again. That if he were to realize any profits from her loathsome play he would reject them as he would reject the proceeds of an assassination. He waited until a renewed crescendo of applause indicated that the curtain had parted for the author to step forward and acknowledge the accolade. Slowly and deliberately he began to tear to pieces the program he had been clutching throughout the final scene. He ripped it into strips and then laid the strips together and tore them into tiny squares and let them fall fluttering to the floor. When the ovation had momentarily subsided he heard Priscilla say, "Ben, are you listening?"

"Yes."

"If you have any respect left for me at all, I'd like you to do exactly what I ask."

He nodded, not daring to speak.

"I'm going back to the hotel and pack your clothes and have the porter take them to his office. I suppose that will take me a couple of hours. I don't want you to come back until I've finished, and I don't want to hear from you when you do. When you pick your clothes up, please don't come up to the room or call me on the house phone. I won't answer. I'm going back to Washington tomorrow, on the first plane I can get. When you get back, stop at your office before you go home. I'll leave a message for you."

"Priss—"

"Please don't make me say any more. I'd like you to go now. I'm going to sit here for a minute or two."

He sat for a moment with his head bowed and then got up and edged his way out past the row of cheering people. He went quickly up the aisle, struggling into his overcoat. The lobby was still empty; the first-night ovation would go on for some time. He pushed open the street door and stood for a moment breathing the cold damp air of the Haymarket. It had rained during the performance and the wet street glittered. Above the tops of the buildings the fog was tinted with a hellish glow. Across the street he saw a cab pulling up in front of a millinery shop to let out a passenger. He ran across the street through the traffic and leapt onto the curb, vaulting over the river of water that ran down the gutter. He rapped on the window of the cab as it was pulling away, and the driver stopped and ran down the window. It was one of the old, square, box-shaped taxis of his youth with a double scroll decorating the side of the tonneau.

"Which way are you going, sir?" the driver asked.

Ben grasped the door handle and stood vacant-mindedly. "I'd like— I'd like—"

"Is it this side of the river, sir?"

"Yes," Ben said. "Do you know a pub in Gower Street called The Rising Sun?"

"I think so, sir. We'll find it, anyway. It's a very short street, isn't it?"

"Yes," Ben said.

He stood with his hand on the door handle and looked across the top of the cab and the glittering black pavement to the theatre. The ushers had thrown open the doors and were latching them back. He could see the lights from the chandeliers and hear the applause from inside the auditorium: cries of "Brava! Brava! Author! Author!" The pounding of feet and gusts of hand-clapping blew across the windy street and beat against his ears with a ghostly familiarity, as if they were pealing out of a dream.